The Dream-Chosen

Tales of the Kashallans, Book 1
Celu Amberstone

Published by Kashallan Press, 2021

I0661575

The Dream-Chosen

Tales of the Kashallans, Volume 1

Celu Amberstone

Published by Kashallan Press, 2022.

THE DREAM-CHOSEN

First edition. March 22, 2022.

ISBN: 978-1777537937

Written by Celu Amberstone.

Part One: The Call

Chapter One

When they broke through to the ancient's chamber the navigator blocked the opening with its sinewy mass before the excited pod could enter. It trembled, sucking in great mouthfuls of liquid. The inky cavity was cool, silent, unsettling as a drink of the Void.

It eased its bulk carefully into the hollow. Had its parent, the Maker Gladdris, swam so far into its dreams, that it could no longer feel the pulse of the world that gave it birth? Time must pass differently within the long sleep, years going by in a breath, centuries in a single revolution of the world. Out there among the stars was freedom, limitless possibility. Here on the planet Timorna there was only confinement and bitter futility. If the enemy gained their unholy victory all might be destroyed anew.

In the center, the Ancient lay with its head resting atop its massive coils. Even though it had birthed many generations of its own descendants, the Navigator whined, seeking the reassurance of its parent like any child.

Nuzzling the Ancient, it positioned its head beside that well-loved other. Mouth tentacles brushed the ancient's face, penetrated the pitted skin searching for life's essence. The blood was cold, and thick as syrup, but it still pulsed through the inner channels.

The Elder lived.

The navigator withdrew its probe and next bit into its own body, opening a sizable gash in its flesh. Hot blood welled out of the wound, spreading through the chamber's liquid in a pungent ripple.

<<Come back to us my dear one,>> it said in the telepathic speech of its kind, and rubbed the wound against Maker Gladdris's rubbery lips. When it felt the ancient stir, the navigator hastily withdrew from the chamber. <<Quickly now,>> it said to the young hunters. <<Bring your offerings forward and push them through the opening, or some of us will become its first meal.>>

WHEN MAKER GLADDRIS was fully awake and replete, the pod burst into the chamber with squeals of excitement. They coiled about the Ancient in a tangled skein of sleek gray bodies. Mouth tentacles formed "the link," enjoyed the piquant flavor of discovery, and the rapturous sweetness of affection. The communion was delicious.

Finally Maker Gladdris silenced the clamor. <<Your flavor is delightful to me, my descendants, but why have you risked yourselves to come to me? Isn't the surface world doing well?>>

<<The sycophant priests that come to our home pools *say* that all is well above, but I fear they are lying to us, Elder,>> the navigator said.

<<The priests treat us as if we are children, to be soothed with the blood gift,>> a young adult complained.

<<Or, they treat us like slaves, fit only to make the kavay medicines,>> another said.

<<You must help us, dear Maker,>> the navigator said. <<We need you—and all the Ancients. You must rouse them and take council. The kindred choke on the taint of the enemy's plotting.>>

The pod writhed, vomiting their distress into the black water.

Maker Gladdris regurgitated a calming agent while it pondered the pod's news. Finally it said, <<What you have told me is very disturbing. Perhaps we Makers *have* slept too long, and allowed our guidance to falter. But without a host species to free the symbiont children I might make, I fail to savor the answer to this dilemma.>>

The youngest twined itself tighter about the Maker's sinewy neck, and nipped the ancient's lips, like an infant wishing to be fed. <<Then you must use your magics, Elder, and bring a new host species to us. Surely among all the worlds of the Starry River there are people who can host our symbionts. Once the kashallan bond is re-formed, we will know what is truly happening in the world above.>>

<<And the bonded can act as our agents, to restore the harmony,>> another added. <<Please elder, you must use your magics.>>

Maker Gladdris gave the young one an affectionate nuzzle. <<Magics is it? Well, the solution isn't quite that simple, my descendants. But I *will*

come back with you; we will wake the others, and take council with them.>>

<<WE ARE OF ONE MIND,>> the oldest among the Khutani Makers intoned. Within their council chamber the mass of sinewy bodies spun itself into a tightening knot.

<<We are of one mind and one purpose,>> the other Makers chorused, repeating the ancient invocation.

<<And, for those of us who can remember the beauty of Timorna before the Great Destruction, what is that purpose?>> the oldest asked.

<<To re-make the world from the patterns of life we saved.>>

<<That was the task given us by Mother Timorna. What is the charge?>> the Ancient continued.

<<To protect the land and the species we saved and remade to combat Umwira treachery.>>

<<So it has been and so must it always be,>> the oldest concluded the ritual formulation.

A cousin from the blue lake by the Great Swamp opened the council. <<We shouldn't have entered the long sleep, no matter how bitter the taste of our grief after the plague. We should have stayed more connected to our creations in the world above.>>

<<There is no point in moaning over 'should have dones',>> Gladdris said. <<We are aware of the discord now; let us consider what to do about it and pray we aren't too late.>>

The knot of bodies writhed with their collective frustration. They choked on the acrid taste of regret savored anew, and the clawing flavor of fear and uncertainty. Summing up their anxiety, before the communication soured completely, the oldest said, <<The Avairei priesthood, I fear, are proving to be untrustworthy guardians in our absence. We must find a way to reclaim the stewardship of our world.>>

<<How do you expect us to do that?>> someone asked. <<Our host species' life patterns have been lost. Since the plague the Kashallan bond has always killed both host and symbiont.>>

<<If there are no species on Timorna who can now host our symbionts, then we must look beyond Timorna for a new host species,>> Gladdris said. <<There are other worlds that have intelligent life; perhaps on one of those worlds we can find a suitable host.>>

The tangled knot of bodies froze. The sharp tang of surprise combined with the richer flavor of speculation. In all the long years since the plague, no one had ever suggested such a plan. <<We might be able to create a mind-link and make contact,>> the oldest mused.

<<Yes, we could lure the desired species to us, then bind them to our will,>> another agreed, dripping the tang of its excitement into the water.

<<—Just a moment,>> the cousin from the Great Swamp said. <<Before we go any farther with this, are the risks fair to the unsuspecting species we choose?>>

<<Is it 'fair' to let the Umwira destroy everything once again?>> a scarred cousin countered. There was the piquant taste of collective agreement to that point.

<<And if the ones who answer our called die, what then? Will we try again? How many times?>> the swamp elder persisted.

The scarred Maker tightened its coils in anger. <<It is always like this when you join us, Amsi cousin. If all you wish to do is create dissention among us, you should have stayed in your wild swamp.>>

<<I have no wish to create discord, I only wish us to think of all possibilities,>> the Maker spat back.

The council thrashed about in frustration vomiting out its uncertainty. Before the discussion curdled beyond salvage, the oldest exerted its authority and added its placating seasoning to the communication. <<Let's not argue. Both points have value. But the Gods of our ancestors will surely bless us with a people who will not die from the Kavay Alignment or the Transformation.>>

<<So it will be,>> the others intoned as they twisted and spun themselves ever tighter about one another, in a whirling ball. <<We are of one mind in the power. We are of one purpose in the power,>> the swamp elder repeated along with the others.

And may the Gods pity and protect the one who answers our summons, Gladdris thought privately as it merged its mind with its kindred.

Chapter Two

Sagas moaned. It was happening again. The dream, no, the nightmare was sucking her into its black vortex. Fragmented images spun past. Shiny objects chased one another through the inky void. Bright rays shot from their snouts, stabbing the blackness. Blinding light, again, and again.

Sagas whimpered. She spun faster, faster—no escape. One of the shiny things came closer, exploded—burning white-hot. Ugly, flat naked faces, eyes wide, mouths agape, screaming were screaming—screaming—oh, Holy Mother, who is screaming?

Her dream-body fell whirling away from the battle, braidlets whipping, four-fingered hands flung wide, tiny claws extended, clutching at nothingness.

Then, she was no longer alone. An etheric sinewy body looped a coil of itself around her, breaking her fall. Sagas hugged her rescuer and leaned her head against its smooth neck. The creature's skin gave the illusion of a cool, rubbery solidity next to her hot face. She was safe.

A Maker! Sagas had never seen one of her people's legendary life-givers in the waking world, but in the dream she had imagined them often. Her aura pulsating with both fear and awe, she allowed it to "taste" her dream essence. <<Holy One, thank you.>>

The great head curled down to look at the slim furred creature it had ensnared in its coils. Extending its mouth tentacles, the Khutani brushed them lightly over her face and shoulders. Sagas closed her eyes and allowed the Ancient to "taste" her without protest.

When it was finished with its exam, the Khutani said into her mind, <<Little priestess, you are very brave, but it isn't wise to swim the Starry River alone.>>

<<I am not brave,>> she protested. <<The dream sucks me in—I can't control it. Maker, what is happening to me?>>

<<Hmm. It would seem that you too have been hooked by our lure for the Dream-Chosen. I am impressed, little Avairei. We were unaware of your ability to detect our dream conjurings in this manner.>>

<<I don't understand, Dream-Chosen?>>

<<Yes, a new host for our symbiont children.>> The Khutani rumbled a laugh. <<Ah, your species is so child-like at times. You can't hide the bitter taint of your lies from us forever, you know.>>

Sagas trembled; she felt ashamed. The Holy Ones *knew*.

Why was that such a surprise? How could her priestly elders have thought they could deceive their "Makers." <<We mean no disrespect—we hoped only to spare you the torment—>>

The ancient tightened its coils, stopping her babbled explanation in mid flow. <<Our bodies may have been confined to the underground water-ways since the enemy's plague, but don't underestimate us in other ways. We aren't children to be placated with sweet words and the Blood Gift. Always remember we created your species from the life-patterns we saved from the Great Destruction.>>

<<I-I know. I-I'm sorry—I've not forgotten, Holy One.>>

The coil tightened, stopping her babbled explanation in mid flow. As it tasted her mounting fear, the Khutani relaxed its grip. The Maker nuzzled her shoulder. <<You are forgiven. Come, since you are here I will show you what our angling has discovered.>>

<<Show me what, Maker?>>

Suddenly a glowing sphere floated in the blackness ahead. They swam nearer, and sagas saw misty bands of color flowing across its blurred surface.

<<The planet Dymar,>> the Khutani said.

Sagas shuddered. She'd seen this image before. The Maker was taking her back to the scene of her nightmare. Yes, there were the shiny objects spitting beams of red and blue light.

<<Don't be afraid, little priestess, we still swim within the dream. They can't harm us.>>

Sagas relaxed, grateful for the Khutani's reassuring presence. There were more of the shiny things encircling the planet now, and others were rising from the surface as they watched. They chased one another, sending out the deadly rays.

<<What is happening here?>> Sagas asked.

<<It is a war,>> the Khutani said. <<Our search for a new host led us to this world. The species that has gained dominion over this planet has been invaded by others of its kind. We have touched their sleeping minds; they are very interesting to us.>>

Sagas watched another of the shiny objects explode. <<Interesting? That wouldn't be the word I would use to describe this. To me, so much power is terrifying. The ancestors of the Umwira were said to have commanded such power—and they nearly destroyed our world. Why do you bother with these creatures?>>

<<This species has a great knowledge of destructive technology, that is true, but they are complex, not just killers. Come, we will go closer. I will help you savor them.>>

Sagas felt the vertigo reclaim her. When the images around her refocused, they no longer swam in the black Void. They floated near the planet's surface. Now she saw scorched dwellings and vegetation. Sagas squeezed her eyes to mere slits; the light was so bright. How odd, green plants? Everything was the wrong color.

Pillars of dark smoke billowed into the sky, great rumbling sounds made the air tremble. Sagas wrinkled up her nose at the stench of charred flesh and hot metal. Nearby a broken tree screamed in silent agony.

Then someone coughed; Sagas looked down. Just below them was a four-limbed Avairei-like creature wearing unusual black clothing and a metal hat confining most of its long russet mane. It crouched behind a broken wall as if hiding. Then, as if somehow aware of them, it glanced up, its blue eyes staring right through them.

Blue! Sagas stared, choking down her revulsion. Its eyes were as blue as the kavay in the deep pools under the mountains. How could such a holy sign be found upon this fearsome creature?

<<This one calls himself Dunnagh Kai. He is one of my favorites,>> the Maker explained. <<I often watch him.>>

Sagas shuddered. <<Maker, are those weapons the creature is carrying—can he hurt us?>>

Sensing her fear, the Maker gurgled a dismissal of the notion. <<True, he carries powerful alien weaponry, but he cannot harm us. We still swim

protected within the Dream.>> Mouth tentacles waving to taste the ether, the Khutani grunted with satisfaction. <<However he is a clever one of his kind and does detect my conjuring—in a limited way.>>

<<Oh, Holy One, like our Warlinga, he has the Mind Magic?>>

<<Magic?>> The Khutani rumbled a laugh. A tone of smugness colored the mental voice. <<His people call themselves Humans. And yes, his particular tribe, the Caldoni, have some skill in what *your* people call 'magic,' but their powers are limited compared to our own, of course.>>

Mind Magic or not, the creature was an ugly brute.<<Have you spoken to him?>>

There was a hesitation, then the Maker reluctantly admitted. <<His species has an instinctual fear of us in our natural form, so our communications have been—difficult. His people are losing this war, however, and must flee the planet soon.

<<We will speak to them directly then. We will aid them in their escape and guide their craft to us at that time.>>

Sagas started to ask another question, but the Maker cut her off. <<You ask too many questions. I want to savor how he deals with the problem his enemy's most recent advance will pose for him.>>

Sagas whimpered as more alien weapons roared somewhere nearby. Had their imprisonment to their underground waterways made the Khutani too desperate to see, what was so obvious to her?

As if hearing her private thoughts, the Maker growled.

<<Holy One, please don't bring these terrible creatures to our world. I fear they are death bringers not saviors!>>

<<I had expected better of you, little priestess. I assumed that with your heightened gifts, you would also have the intelligence to understand. Will you be true to your breeding and help us when we call? Or are you just another ungrateful child like so many of your kind?>>

<<You wrong me, Maker,>> Sagas protested. <<I am loyal and true to my breeding—but these creatures are alien. Can their bodies even withstand the transformation? I know there have been many failures in the past, but surely some species upon our own world can be made to serve without bringing—>>

<<Do you truly think we are fools? Of course, we have considered these factors. You try my patience.>>

Sagas swallowed further protests. There was no point. <<Your will, Holy One. I am yours to command.>>

<<Good. Let us go closer I want to savor him further...>>

Tired. Hot. Have to rest. All seems quiet. The last news from HQ said this sector might be overrun any time now. Need more information, sensory equipment limited—no good now. Risky, but must perform the Cumarsaid.

Sagas gasped. The Khutani nuzzled her neck in approval. <<Ah, you see his spirit float free on its silver cord. Now do you understand?>>

Sagas made a face. Magic or not, the creature was an ugly brute.

As they continued to watch, the Caldoni's glowing spirit body drifted above the smoky streets in a widening spiral.

<<What is he doing?>>

<<Hunting for his enemies. Let us taste him again>>

Fires, lot of them—spreading. Pain, so much pain, human, animal, all around. Hurts. Oh, Gods, the land hurts! Can't think—must go higher. Ah, better, can see the sector, no enemy nearby—where are they? Hmm, ride the wind, check by the university...

Fierce battle rage slammed into his awareness. He reeled, almost falling out of the trance. *Steady, keep the focus—where are they? There, coming round that burnt out apartment block. Passed that spot not too long ago. A patrol, no two—maybe more, the enemy is heading this way. Must go, or be cut off.*

———※※———

HIDDEN FROM VIEW, DUNNAGH crouched and wiped his face on a dirty sleeve as he came out of his trance. Breath coming in ragged gasps, he ventured a quick look round. No Creggan nearby. Safe for the moment, but over to the west of his current position came the roar of heavy artillery. Plumes of dark smoke billowed into the iron-gray sky. *Damn!*

He'd warned the Commander this was going to happen. Too bad the politicians had no faith in his Psy. The corps could have won this little war—if they'd been given the chance. But now that the peace negotiations had collapsed, his people were only covering the civilian retreat.

Heart still pounding, Dunnagh felt the skin on the back of his neck tingle. The wisps of red hair escaping his helmet suddenly writhed about his face as if magnetically charged. He was so tired, but he'd be a dead fool if he were to ignore his Psy gift sending him another warning.

Still crouched behind the broken wall, he checked the charge of his beam rifle and then drew out the communication unit from a pouch at his hip, thumbing the speaker. "Blue and Green Squad. This is Blue Unit Leader. The enemy is closing in. Everyone back to the hovercraft. Now!"

The charred sentinels of skeletal trees stood amidst the rubble and broken glass along the empty street in front of him. Keeping low, he left cover and sprinted for the rendezvous site in the plaza three blocks away. Somewhere behind him a barrage of light weapons' fire sounded. Was that Green Squad or the enemy? He'd ordered O'Neil and his wild men to cover the section west of Blue's position. Dunnagh quickened his pace.

Speaking into his communicator as he ran, he said, "O'Neil you better not be pulling one of your reckless stunts—not now. Get your arse back to the rendezvous site."

Then heavy artillery fire began again. Cursing under his breath, he quickened his pace. In the plaza ahead the hovercraft lay squat and ponderous, its engines already gearing up for a hasty retreat.

Out of the corner of his eye, Dunnagh saw his Second, Nathan Derek, emerging from a smoldering apartment block with a terrified woman and two children in tow. Swerving to intercept them, Dunnagh scooped up the smallest child, then joined Nathan in hurrying the remaining pair across the exposed ground.

At the transport Dunnagh ushered the family inside, leaping up the stairs behind them. Eyes darting quickly around the cabin's dim interior, he made a hurried check of passengers and crew. Motioning for his driver to wait, he once again stepped onto the stairs, scanning the plaza and surrounding buildings for stragglers.

Nathan remained at the bottom of the stairs, beam rifle up and ready. "See any sign of the Creggan patrols?" Dunnagh asked.

"No, not yet. Did you see them?"

"No, but I felt them with my Psy while in the Cumarsaid. They're out there all right."

Nathan grunted, and turned back to watch the plaza.

"Marnez," Dunnagh said. "Raise Commander Tizu at the spaceport. Tell him our situation. Ask him for additional orders."

A wiry woman with luminous dark eyes, Marnez saluted and tongued the control of the implant in her jaw. A moment later she said to Dunnagh. "Sir, Commander Tizu says there are no further orders. We are to collect our people and get back to the space-port."

Dunnagh looked at the laconic Rhys, sitting in the driver's seat. "Green squad hasn't called back in a while," Rhys said before he could ask.

Worry churning in his gut, an image of O'Neil's scarred face with its cocky grin appeared in his mind's eye to torment him.

Dunnagh joined Nathan at the base of the stairs. "Any sign of Green?" he murmured.

Nathan shook his head.

Thick black smoke and flames topped the skyline in Green's direction. Should he wait? Dunnagh drummed his fingers on the stair rail. Damn, that whole squad was always taking unnecessary risks.

The pavement beneath his feet shuddered.

"Marnez, any answer from Green?"

"Negative, Sir."

"Keep trying." Now Dunnagh's Psy was sending fiery shudders down his backbone. They needed to go—now! "I wonder how many Creggan units are out there hunting us."

Nathan snorted. "Who knows, the Dymarians were fools to trust them. Judging by the amount of incoming rounds we're taking today, the Creggans must have brought in half their force in secret, while the politicians sweet talked each other at the negotiating table."

Dunnagh nodded, only half listening. A fierce Psy headache was building behind his eyes. How much longer could he afford to wait? He continued to drum his fingers on the stair rail. Damn!

Suddenly pain, like a red-hot blade, stabbed deep into his gut. Dunnagh gritted his teeth, stifling a cry. O'Neil's face covered in blood flashed before his mind's eye. The man lay in a heap of smoking rubble, his lively green eyes dulled by death, his rakish smile shattered. Around him were the twisted bodies of his squad.

Was this dire sending in the past, or a future possibility that could be avoided? Dunnagh's heart pounded and his throat went dry with indecision.

The hovercraft was exposed and vulnerable in their present location, but he couldn't just abandon an entire squad if there was any chance Green could make it back to the rendezvous site. By all the gods of his people, he didn't want to leave them.

"...Damn it, O'Neil, get your arse back here!"

Tizu had warned Dunnagh not to take any unnecessary risks on this mission. Dunnagh had told O'Neil that—but did the man ever listen?

Nathan touched his arm, and pointed back across the plaza. Several armed men wearing Creggan insignia on their helmets were just emerging from behind a burned out office building.

"That's torn it," Dunnagh muttered. "Damn you, O'Neil, I can't wait any longer. Ancestors forgive me. I'm sorry." Dunnagh leapt for the doorway, shouting for Rhys to get going.

Right behind him, Nathan paused at the top of the stairs, firing several quick blasts across the plaza, making the first line of Creggan soldiers dive for cover. When the weapon's charge faltered, he tumbled the rest of the way into the transport. Dunnagh slammed the door hard.

Rhys pulled down on the throttle and the transport gave a violent lurch forward, sending Dunnagh crashing to the deck beside Nathan. They were underway.

In the next instant Dunnagh sat up, bawling orders. "Taleish, get up on that cannon and give us some covering fire. Marnez, tell Commander Tizu we're coming in hot, with the enemy in pursuit."

Dunnagh stood, bracing himself against the bulkhead as the *ka-thunka-thunk* of the cannon exploded overhead. There were a few bursts of answering enemy fire, and then they were out of range, speeding toward the spaceport.

AS THE WEAPON'S BOOM echoed within the dream, Sagas writhed. New hosts? These creatures were death bringers not saviors—why couldn't the Makers sense that? Had their long confinement made the Khutani too desperate to see, what was to her, so obvious?

These creatures, this destruction, it was horrible. *Were the awakened ancients now crazy? No, no, impossible! Go away, traitorous thoughts. The holy race is wiser than a foolish Avairei priestess. Surely they know what is best—for all of us, and yet...*

<<Holy One, I can't watch this—I can't stay here—I have to go back.>> Sagas squirmed out of the Khutani's protective coils, and was gone, spinning away into the waking world before the Maker could stop her.

Chapter Three

Sighing with relief, Dunnagh glanced around the transport's interior. "Everybody all right?" There were grunts of agreement from his squad, but only a frightened silence from the refugees.

He pushed himself off the bulkhead and walked down the aisle between the seats, his eyes expertly assessing the condition of his charges. Frightened, yes. Some tearful, others shocked into stony silence, their eyes staring blindly at nothing.

Oh, there were cuts and bruises aplenty, and that one fellow probably had a broken arm—he'd better have Williams give him a painkiller from the medical kit. But there was nothing that couldn't wait till they got on board the transport ship.

Then his eyes widened in surprise. In the shadows at the rear of the cabin a woman with green eyes and creamy skin sat next to an elderly couple. Dunnagh swore under his breath.

Was that Sairsa, his new fiancée? Yes it was—damn! What was she doing here? Stubborn woman, he'd warned her days ago to get out. Why hadn't she listened? His expression grim, he started down the aisle towards her, meaning to give her a piece of his mind.

When he was about halfway there, she looked up, saw him, and shook her head. Then ignoring him, Sairsa returned her attention to the couple beside her. Taking a closer look, he realized the two were her Caldoni mother and her Dymarian stepfather. He'd met them briefly once.

Her widowed mother resettled in Dymar after Sairsa's father died. Sairsa grew up in the Dymarian capital, her stepfather being a government official of some sort. And, being the independent, strong-willed, Caldoni woman that she was, she'd refused to desert them in spite of his attempt to convince her otherwise.

Damn it, she could have been killed. No, he wouldn't think about that now. That would make him frantic. She was right, this wasn't the time to discuss personal matters. He had a job to do; he'd better keep focused on that or they might not live past the next few minutes.

Giving added weight to his decision, flying debris from a nearby explosion chose that moment to pelt the bulkhead behind Dunnagh with a hailstorm of rock and metal. A woman screamed and burst into loud sobbing. Rhys pulled hard on the controls and the transport lurched sideways to avoid more falling rubble.

AT THE DYMARIAN SPACEPORT, every available craft was being pressed into service for the evacuation. Dunnagh's vehicle was directed to a privately-owned vessel, called *Freedom's Chance*, readying for take-off about halfway down the runway. The rich galactic philanthropist Dr. Bennett who had hired the Caldoni mercenaries of the Lann Gheal corps for this rescue mission owned the *Chance*.

Parking in the loading bay, Dunnagh's squad hurriedly ushered their passengers onto the waiting ship. As Dunnagh climbed up the ramp at the end of the procession, he saw Commander Tizu waiting for him.

Dunnagh crossed to him and saluted. Tizu's short stature, golden skin and almond-shaped eyes were an exotic contrast, compared with the tall, fair-skinned Caldoni armachda that made up the bulk of the troops Tizu commanded.

The corps had originated on the planet Caldon, and most of its members, like Dunnagh himself, were Caldoni. But Lann Gheal would take other soldiers with skill if they could pass the tests as Tizu had.

Tizu returned the salute, glanced back out the closing hatch then fixed his scowling gaze on Dunnagh. "Where's Green Squad?"

Guts churning, Dunnagh took a deep breath and forced himself to look into his commander's eyes without dropping his own. "Sir. We were hard pressed at the last. I couldn't risk waiting longer."

Tizu muttered a curse. Dunnagh tasted bitter stomach acid in his mouth and mentally braced himself for the blistering tirade he was sure was coming. But instead, Tizu turned his back to him and growled, "Anything else to report?"

Report? Was Tizu waiting for him to confess? Dunnagh felt the urge to do just that, endure Tizu's rage and take his punishment. But he couldn't force himself to do it; this place was too public. Refugees crying, galactic officers and crewmen shouting, mechanical equipment booming and banging, he couldn't speak of his shame with so many outsiders nearby. He'd tell Tizu later. He would tell him—he would.

Instead he said, "No, sir. By the time we reached Government Square, the entire western sector of C district was under enemy control. We collected what civilians we could. Then we got out. We waited for Green until the Creggans spotted us."

Tizu made a noncommittal grunt. Dunnagh felt the knot in his gut tighten a little tighter. Tizu hadn't come right out and accused him, but Dunnagh was sure that his commander knew he'd made a terrible mistake by giving O'Neil his head.

More lives lost to the war's stupidity—and Dunnagh's stupidity. Silently Dunnagh grieved for the loss of so many good soldiers. Green Squad was dead. And it was his fault. Maybe he *should* go home like his mother wanted.

Long warrior's braid tossed over one shoulder, Nathan came over carrying his helmet and pack in one hand, and Dunnagh's pack in the other. Dunnagh saw the stubborn set to his jaw and the steely gleam in his friend's gray eyes.

Stepping away from Tizu Dunnagh intercepted him and took his pack. "What's wrong now?" He glanced a warning in Tizu's direction.

Nathan motioned with a slight jerk of his chin to a thin man in a Dymarian governmental tunic talking to one of the ship's officers. Was that Sadrew, the Dymarian councilor's aide? What was he up to now? Dunnagh sighed. "Has Sadrew been spouting off again about the Caldoni mercenaries Dr. Bennett hired?"

"If that shit-for-brains makes one more comment about needing to protect Dymarian women from the, 'Caldoni savages,' on board this ship, I'm going to—"

"You're not going to do anything. Just ignore whatever he says. It isn't important—"

"It is to me," Nathan shot back. "I'm getting tired of having the rest of the galaxy always looking down their noses at us. We're here risking our lives for their pampered backsides aren't we? I've never forced a woman to do anything. And I'm not about to start now—"

"Shut up, and that's an order, Armachd," Dunnagh hissed. "This isn't the time—let it go—"

"Trouble?"

Dunnagh spun round; Tizu had focused his smoldering, black stare on him again. Then noticing Sadrew talking to some of Dr. Bennett's crewman for the first time, Tizu's mouth set into a thin line.

"No, Sir," Dunnagh said before Nathan could open his mouth.

Nathan saluted. "Everyone's on board, Sir. The Mate over there has asked us to help the crew get the refugees settled as quickly as possible so the ship can lift off."

Tizu scowled as if he knew that wasn't the whole story, but he chose not to pursue it further. "All right, let's do it. The quicker we're out of here the better for everybody."

DUNNAGH HAD JUST SNATCHED a hurried meal and was coming out of the ship's mess, when the floor under his feet bucked, slamming him hard against the bulkhead. Ignoring the pain rocketing up his arm, he dashed for the first of the refugee compartments assigned to him. At the same moment, alarms in different parts of the spaceship set up a raucous screaming.

Bennett's ship was on an errand of mercy, its cargo consisting of frightened refugees, a lot of them women and children. But that wouldn't matter to the murderous Creggans. The enemy must have sighted Bennett's ship leaving the spaceport and now was attacking to prevent them from slipping through the blockade.

Once again the floor shifted under his feet. He swayed like a drunkard, but kept moving. In the room ahead, Dunnagh heard frightened people shouting questions at anyone in a uniform they saw passing by.

Would that damned siren ever shut up?

Bracing himself against the doorframe as the ship lurched again, Dunnagh surveyed the people inside. Against three of the room's four walls, narrow bunks climbed in tiers towards the gray ceiling. Terrified refugees peered out from within the protective poly-fiber webbing. Those not fortunate enough to have secured a bunk huddled on the floor among their belongings.

These latecomers were making do with straps attached to cargo rings in the floor. The belts weren't much protection if the fighting got rough, but under the current circumstances, it was the best the ship had to offer them. There were too many people wanting to flee the war—and too few ships making it through the blockade. Dr. Bennett's ship was dangerously overcrowded.

Dunnagh hid his pity behind a mask of professional competence. "Everybody stay calm. It's going to be a little rough for a while. Secure yourselves as best you can," he yelled over the noise in the hallway.

The wide-eyed women and children huddled together on the floor were a pitiful lot. Most had escaped the enemy's advancing troops with little more than the clothes they'd been wearing. Dunnagh helped a young mother with a crying toddler fasten herself and the child to a cargo ring, then he hurried on to another chamber, ignoring the shouted questions in his wake.

He didn't know any more about the current situation than they did. Lann Gheal was a planetary fighting corps. Like Dunnagh's refugee charges, Bennett's command center aboard ship was off limits to them.

His responsibilities finished, Dunnagh caught up to Nathan and Marti, a tall, dark-skinned woman in his unit. Together they raced for the safety of their own quarters before the turbulence worsened.

As Dunnagh crawled into his bunk, his Psy warned him that Death hovered. He tried to ignore the icy chill flowing down his back. Was it his time—or Nathan's?

Blessed gods, let it not be so. Let them both survive this terrible day. He studied the high cheek-boned, strong, Caldoni features of Nathan's well-loved face. Nathan was the man who had been closer than a brother to him since his childhood.

Their bloody wrists bound together, a black-robed war priest had once chanted sacred words above them as they pledged the traditional Caldoni oath of the battle-bonded to one another.

"I hate this," Nathan grumbled and pushed brown hair off his sweaty forehead. "Bennett's crew better know what they're doing or we'll be fried."

"Now that's a pleasant thought."

"Well, I don't trust 'em. If I'm meant to die on a mission, then I want to die with a beam-rifle in my hand."

"Yeah, not like this, helpless in the belly of a ship with an unfamiliar crew in control," Dunnagh agreed.

"Damned right."

His Psy pricking him again, Dunnagh swallowed his unease, determined not to give way to his fears. His Psy wasn't one hundred percent reliable. Nathan wasn't going to die. And neither was he. His lovely Sairsa would never forgive him if he did.

Giving Nathan a lopsided grin, Dunnagh sealed the webbing around his bunk and lay back, trying to relax. The ship bucked, slamming Dunnagh against the bulkhead. Relax? Not happening, he thought grimly and eased away from the vibrating metal.

Nathan growled a curse, still wanting to vent. "Politicians, spineless carrion-eaters all! How could the Galactic Union have let things get so out of hand? They should have known what would happen on Dymar. Balls, nobody can be that naïve."

"Naïve? Maybe—maybe not, but no matter what the rest of the galaxy believes, it is our sacred duty to serve and protect them, if the cause is a just one. That was what we pledged our lives to do when we swore the Warrior's Oath."

Dunnagh's little speech only earned him another snort of disgust from his friend. "When you spout that crap, I don't know if you actually believe what you're saying or you're just trying to convince yourself as well as me."

Did he believe in the Warrior's Oath? "Damn you, Nathan, you always cut straight to the truth in ways no one else can. As a young recruit just out of the academy I would have fought anyone who claimed he didn't honor the Oath and believe in its code of service. But now..." Dunnagh let out a troubled sigh.

"Now, I don't know. I've seen too many missions since then." Remembering O'Neil and his men, Dunnagh suddenly felt incredibly sad and disheartened. "Sometimes I don't know myself what I believe."

Something in Dunnagh's tone of voice made Nathan study his face for a long moment. When he spoke again, he changed the subject as if he knew he'd touched a topic best left alone. "I hope this ship is fast. If the Creggans realize it's Dr. Bennett they're chasing, we're in for it."

Dunnagh blinked, uncertain at first what he was talking about. Then, "You're right. The bounty they've put on Dr. Bennett is a great incentive to follow us across the galaxy and back again."

"Right. So there's no point in worrying about all that now, is there? They catch us—or they don't. I think I'll take a nap."

Dunnagh chuckled. "Sure you will. Pleasant dreams."

Pleasant dreams. He could use a few of his own, come to think of it. He hadn't been sleeping well himself. But were his frightening dreams only the fault of stress? His Psy was unusually silent on the matter, so he prayed his unease was due only to the pressures of the Dymarian evacuation.

Dunnagh looked away, feeling a lump form in his throat. If they lived through this mission, could he really do it—could he really quit, leave Nathan and everything he'd worked so hard to achieve in the corps?

He closed his eyes and willed his mind into quiet. His mother was probably right; there were too many good Caldoni armachda lost in someone else's stupid war.

Maybe he should go home when his term of enlistment ended this time. His parents were getting on in years, and what new bride-to-be would want her man in active service? Nathan would just have to cope without him, if he wanted to stay in Lann Gheal.

Nathan, dependable, but frustrating sometimes, oh, by all the gods of his ancestors, how Dunnagh loved him.

In his mind's eye, he saw his cousin and best friend as a lad splashing in the creek behind grandpa Kai's orchard. They'd spent a lot of time with the old couple on the clan lands in the Black Mountains back then.

The land will heal a troubled soul, grandma had always claimed.

Green growing things, clear running water, warm sunlight and soft breezes, they had worked their magic on Nathan, giving back a frightened child his voice and his soul, after his parents' terrible deaths. How could he leave him? If Nathan were to die because he wasn't there to guard his back—could he go on living if that were to happen?

Then, without stopping to think, he heard himself saying, "Nathan, I haven't known how to tell you, but Mahir wants me to come home and help her with Shivon Ru'a and her boy."

Startled, Nathan glanced over at him. "What about Michael? He may not like you interfering, you know?"

Dunnagh waved a hand in dismissal of that idea. "Nobody cares what he wants. He's only the boy's father—and a foreigner."

"Yeah, just a foreigner. A foreigner, but did you ever stop to think that maybe Shivon wants to live her own life, too? Without the clan mothers always interfering? If you cave in to your mother's pressure and go home, you're just going to make it that much harder for her to do that. You aren't legally responsible for your nephew now that you're not on Caldon. You don't really have to go back—"

"Of course I have to go back. It's our way—and clan law. You don't understand."

"I see. So, now you think I don't understand, because my own father was a foreigner and I'm only half Caldoni? Is that it?"

"I didn't say that," Dunnagh spluttered. "Stop trying to twist my words. Of course you're Caldoni. Your mother was Caldoni; that's what counts."

Nathan gave a noncommittal grunt and closed his eyes. Exasperated, Dunnagh glared at his friend, but Nathan ignored him, pretending to sleep. Why was he acting like this? "Nathan, did Michael tell you something about their plans?"

"No, not really."

"Then why did you say that?"

"Oh, I don't know. Love seems to make all the Kai branch of the family act stupid. Why should your older sister be any different than the rest of you?"

Dunnagh felt a flush heat his face. Damn him, not this again. Affecting an air of long-suffering, he said, "Damn it, Nathan, you've spun your treadmill back to Sairsa and me again. Give it a rest—"

Turning on his side, Nathan propped himself on an elbow, the better to see him. "No. I won't give it a rest. You and I both know that you like being an armachd in active service. How long do you really think you'll last as a desk soldier, hmm? Every day it will be the same thing—no excitement—no new challenges. You can't do it. You'll only make yourself, your girlfriend, and everybody else back home miserable if you try."

"I will not. I've told you before that I was thinking about getting out. My marriage plans and the trouble with Shivon's boy made me realize it's time, that's all."

"Uh-huh, and a few weeks ago you told Tizu, in my hearing I might add, that you wanted to go all the way. Become a Commander, just like him. That, I suppose was a lie, hmm?"

Dunnagh sighed. "No. It wasn't a lie. It's just—"

The ship gave a violent lurch. "I don't want to talk about this any longer. Just forget about it—for now." Dunnagh wedged his body tight against the bulkhead at his back and fastened the last of the safety straps.

Nathan snorted. "Damned right I'll forget about it. And so should you." Lying back in his bunk, he turned away from Dunnagh.

Dunnagh settled back with another exasperated sigh. He didn't know what to do, and he didn't want to think about it either. But was Nathan right? Could he really give up his hard-won freedom and go back to the life of a desk soldier at home?

Damn it. Why was he mulling over such questions now? There were more immediate concerns to trouble his mind than Nathan and the conflicting obligations waiting for him back on Caldon.

A thread of black humor tangling in his thoughts, he decided that if the enemy blew them apart, he wouldn't have to worry about going home—ever. And that would certainly solve everything, now wouldn't it?

Suddenly Bennett's ship lurched violently upward, then plummeted downward with a sickening jolt. Someone heaved and then cursed. From beyond their compartment he heard the faint echoes of children screaming. Damn it what was going on up there in the command center?

Why was he mulling over future plans now? There were more immediate concerns to trouble his mind than Nathan and the conflicting obligations waiting for him back on Caldon. Then, he decided that if the enemy blew them apart, he wouldn't have to worry about going home.

Forcing his fists to unclench, he relaxed and smiled as a new thought came to him. He might not be allowed into Bennett's command center, but there *were* ways, Caldoni ways, to find out what was going on. Sliding into the psychic trance the warriors of his rank knew as the Cumarsaid, he merged his Psy awareness with the ship's sensors. No longer blind to the workings of the ship or the space through which they were traveling, he probed further...

FLEEING THROUGH THE blackness. All systems functioning. Enemies, circling—coming closer. Data noted. Shields up. Energy in the core building—white-hot—soon.

Dunnagh's body trembled. Power surged through his veins as he felt the ship ready itself for the jump.

What's that? Laser fire, trying to cut us off... Ship swerves away. Another blast—ship dances out of range... Good.

Two well-armed destroyers, giving chase. They will kill—faster, faster!

Dunnagh licked his lips, tasting the fear of the crew in Bennett's command center. Then, a steady voice, giving orders. Strong hands upon the controls—soothing the panic.

Nearing the jump point. Shields pulsating with new vigor.

Dunnagh's body shook violently from the awakened power in the engines.

Blue fire streamed from the enemy's weapons, bursting against the ship's shield in a rain of silver missiles. *Freedom's Chance* convulsed;

Dunnagh groaned, and groaned again as the shields absorbed yet another round.

Hurry, faster— No, need the power to make the jump. Now, yes now! The jump—taking his breath away... White-hot pain, exploded into his mind, blotting out all other sensations.

Then he was falling—out of control—agony dragging him down into the blackness of the Void.

Chapter Four

Awareness returned, but shattered, fragmented. The Psy-link he'd established with the ship was gone. A bleak, terrifying blackness engulfed him. Pain, he remembered great pain—and then, what? Nothing. But there had to be something else—something more...

Yes, now he remembered. The forward shield had taken a direct hit just as the ship made the jump. Were he and the others aboard dead? He had no way of knowing while trapped in the void, but he doubted it.

Now that he focused his attention on the matter, he could faintly detect the luminous silver cord that connected his spirit body to his living flesh somewhere in the physical world. But never having gone so deep into the Cumarsaid, he feared he might not be able to find his way back without help.

Dunnagh chanted the names of his Ancestors, hoping that one of them might be summoned to his aid. Again, and again he called without any response. The aura surrounding his spirit-body shimmered with the muddied colors of despair. He was lost—going to die—condemned to this horrible blankness—forever!

Losing hope that his prayers would ever be answered, Dunnagh was startled when a blue-green radiance suddenly materialized and sucked him down into a swirling vortex. Metallic salts and rotting lake weed stung his nostrils. Choking on the taste of fish slime and blood, he struggled, but sank deeper into the chaos. A kaleidoscope of aquatic images and unfamiliar sounds battered his mind. Alone in the maelstrom, he was out of control and helpless.

As his sanity began to crumble, the vortex spat him out into a pool of black water in a shadowy grotto. Dazed, but with a measure of his physical senses returned, Dunnagh welcomed the peace of this new refuge. Then he realized to his horror that he wasn't alone. Several massive, eel-like creatures were speeding towards him, churning the water to a luminous phosphorescence in their wake.

Cold spears of panic shot through his aura in missiles of sour yellow light. Damn, there were too many of them to fight and he couldn't out-swim them—even if he knew where to go. Recalling earlier lessons in the Psy, Dunnagh mastered his fears, and created a glowing orb of etheric matter as both shelter and shield. From within its protection he bobbed atop the water, surveying the newcomers' approach.

The great snaky-looking beasts swarmed about him in a huge, gray tangle. But in spite of their ominous appearance, when the aliens established contact with him, their communication was gentle and reassuring. <<Welcome, Caldoni warrior, we mean you no harm,>> a colorless voice said into his mind.

<<It is well that you have come, Dream-Chosen,>> another, deeper voice said. <<Your eagerness for the bonding pleases us very much.>>

<<We have been searching among the worlds of the Starry River for one such as you. You are blessed to us,>> another called to him.

Chosen? Bonding? The only thing he was eager to do was return to Bennett's ship. Their words were flattering, their Psy emanations urging him to trust them—lower his barrier. But on the other hand, their appearance reminded him of monsters cast for a horror vid. A primitive human instinct warned him to be careful.

<<Who are you?>>

One of the creatures separated from the encircling mass to coil itself loosely around his shield. Its mouth tentacles played over the barrier's strands as if testing their strength. <<We are the Khutani, warrior,>> it said, and raised its head to look him in the eye. <<Don't be afraid. Please lower your shield. Let me taste you.>>

<<Taste me?>> Dunnagh laughed. <<Eat me more like. No thanks. My shield stays where it is.>>

<<No, Chosen, you misunderstand me. Tasting is one of the ways my species communicates. I would never try to eat you; that is not my intent. I wish only to understand you better.>>

Dunnagh hesitated, his mind in conflict. Fight them to the death, swim away and hide, or just relax and surrender to the alien's sweet urging, what should he do? Well, they seemed friendly enough—even said please. What was he so worried about?

Stalling for time, Dunnagh kept his shield firmly in place, asking a question of his own. <<Do you have a name?>>

<<My name is Maker Gladdris.>>

<<Maker? What do you make?>>

The Khutani rumbled a laugh, pressing its spidery tentacles more insistently against Dunnagh's barrier. <<Life, Chosen. The explanation may be difficult for you to grasp at this time, but all will be revealed to you in due course. Let me just say for now that we are the ones who re-established life on the surface of the planet Timorna after the Great Devastation.>>

Shattered glass, mangled bodies behind a crumpled wall, blood running into a sewer with a dripping sound, the Khutani's words invoked in his mind terrible images from the current Dymarian rescue mission.

Dunnagh shuddered, feeling suddenly disorientated. Were the enemies he'd been contracted to fight, threatening another world?

<<The Umwira nearly destroyed everything,>> another Maker said. <<And now the descendants of that foul race threaten everything anew.>>

<<Umwira?>> Not the Creggans then. But what did these aliens expect *him* to do about the Umwira—whoever, or whatever that was? The sinewy mass of Khutani was blocking off any escape. Without his protective shield, they might crush him. Knowing his danger, Dunnagh still found it hard to conceal his revulsion.

<<I have to go back; my people need me. Our enemies—>>

<<Yes, yes, that is being taken care of. We know about those who pursue your vessel, warrior. When your people come to us; they will be protected from the hunter in the sky,>> an impatient Khutani interrupted. <<In exchange for your assistance we offer sanctuary for all your kin—>>

Dunnagh let out a derisive laugh. <<Take care of the Creggans? Not even the entire Galactic Union forces can do that! They are a powerful, violent people. How could you possibly—I don't understand.>>

<<Not all perhaps, only those who pursue you.>> Gladdris clarified.

<<Even if I believed you could do such a thing, why bother?>>

<<Lower your shield. Probe my mind, and you will find the answers you seek,>> Gladdris urged.

Did he detect a note of irritation, or urgency in the mental voice? Dunnagh wished the slight dizziness clouding his thoughts would dissipate. He couldn't afford muddled reasoning right now. He needed to think clearly. His life might depend on it.

Well, why not do it? He'd communed with alien species before—had even worked for them once or twice. Maybe he should lower his barrier. The damned thing was exhausting to maintain anyway, and yet...

<<It's obvious that you want something from me—though I'm not sure what. Do you want to offer Lann Gheal a contract?>> This was an odd way to negotiate the corps' services, but they were aliens. Maybe they didn't know the proper procedures.

<<Lann Gheal?>> Gladdris's mental voice sounded puzzled. Then,<<Ah, the pack of warriors with whom you hunt your enemies, is this to which you refer?>>

<<Yes. Do you wish to offer my company a contract to fight your enemy—these Umwira?>>

<<Perhaps in future we will make *contracts* as you call them with others of your species. At present, however, our interest is only in you. And it is to you to whom we offer our 'contract.' Lower your barrier, warrior, so that we can communicate freely mind-to-mind.>>

Gladdris was right about his shield limiting their Psy communications. It was certainly a risk to unshield, but they were at a stalemate. He would have to take action soon or his spirit would be sundered from his physical body permanently. <<All right, let's talk more freely, then.>> Dunnagh released his shield.

The moment the barrier vanished, Gladdris coiled itself about Dunnagh, before he could change his mind. When he was engulfed and helpless, the Maker's mouth tentacles crawled over his face and chest in a hurried exploration. Moist and tingling, Dunnagh shuddered at the alien touch.

In spite of his resolve, he instinctively started to erect another shield. Gladdris stopped him with the lightest touch of its Psy. Dunnagh trembled, but he allowed the Khutani to continue its exam without further protest.

Deciding to do a little exploring of his own, Dunnagh stuck out a tentative hand and touched the Maker's muscular neck. He sensed enormous Psy flowing under the creature's satiny hide. Pressing his hand more firmly, he next sent out a mental probe, touching the alien's mind.

Gladdris encouraged him, but Dunnagh was disappointed with the results. He saw little more than images of gloomy pools in caverns with rock formations outlined in phosphorescence, similar to the one in which he was trapped. Gladdris also shared thoughts and emotions with him, but they were all tangled about chemical flavors, some familiar, some not. He could make little sense out of what he "tasted" in its mind.

He detected no threat, but there *was* something the Maker kept hidden from him—he was sure of that, too. Dunnagh lifted his hand and broke the contact. Had Gladdris fared any better with its probe?

Still uncertain, he said, <<What do you want from me?>>

<<As we said, your help, Chosen.>>

<<I can't help you. I don't even know where you live.>>

<<Your ignorance is of no importance,>> another Maker said. <<Your vessel is being guided to our world as we speak.>>

Gladdris' head shot up, and it glared at its peer. <<Gently, cousin, don't frighten him, or you may spoil everything.>>

Spoil everything? Frighten him? Dunnagh doubted if Gladdris had wanted him to hear that little interchange, but they had underestimated his Psy, and he *had* heard.

Dunnagh pushed on the upper coil encompassing him. It was as immovable as stone. Striving to maintain his calm, he said, <<I need to return to the physical world now, before my body weakens further.>>

<<Give us what we need of you and we will help you return to your ship.>> the deep-voiced one offered.

Gladdris let out an angry hiss, then hastily said to Dunnagh, <<You are right, you must leave soon, and we will help you find your way back, but there is yet time to speak of important matters. Will you agree to a kashallan bond and aid us?>>

Dunnagh sensed more rapid communication between the Khutani, but this time he was unable to follow their drift. Maintaining his firm pressure for release on the massive coils confining him, Dunnagh kept his voice even, and asked, <<Kashallan? What is a kashallan?>>

<<Kashallan is an ancient word in the Timornan language,>> Gladdris finally said.

<<Hmm... That answer isn't very helpful I'm sure there's more.>>

<<As you might suspect from our appearance, we are unsuited to life upon the surface of our world,>> a Khutani with long scars on its flanks said. <<When you become a kashallan, you will be our representative upon the surface.>>

<<To do what?>>

<<Whatever is necessary to defeat our enemy,>> another said impatiently.

<<Heal the sick and injured, be our eyes and hands upon the land of Timorna.>> Gladdris added hastily.

<<Do whatever we tell you to do,>> another hissed.

Do whatever he was told—just like in the corps. Dunnagh barked an ironic laugh.

The agitated tangle of gray bodies writhed, whipping the dark water to a glowing foam around them. <<Don't toy with us, Warrior. Timorna needs one such as you.>> another growled.

Timorna? Dunnagh couldn't ever remember hearing of a world called Timorna before.

<<As a kashallan we can offer you the fulfillment your spirit craves,>> Gladdris enticed. <<Just as you have always dreamed.>>

<<Dreamed? How do you know what I am dreaming?>> Dunnagh shuddered as if an icy blade had just slid between his ribs. Damn them had they been mucking about in his dreams? Was this why his sleep had been so unsettled of late? What else did they know about him and his people?

Continuing to press against the coils confining him, Dunnagh said, <<Your assessment of my abilities is flattering, but I'm not interested. Release me—now.>>

<<Stop this foolishness>> the eldest among the Makers commanded in a booming voice.<<We know you, Dunnagh Kai. In your most private thoughts you fancy yourself a warrior, in the traditional sense of the word among your people.

<<You want to be a man who can, not only fight, but who can write poetry and enjoy the fine arts. These qualities are what have attracted us to you. So many gifts, so much complexity along with your destructive technology, your species intrigues us. This is why you are our Dream-Chosen.>>

<<Unfortunately there is nothing romantic or uplifting about the galactic wars in which your species engage. And we all know that, too,>> Gladdris said. <<The horrors you have witnessed, the destruction you have caused, is shriveling your soul. During this last mission, you told us, you had to get out, or be overwhelmed by guilt and despair. We are offering you the life-purpose you crave. Swear to us your Caldoni Warrior's Oath and you can achieve that fulfillment.>>

Warrior's Oath! How had it known? Gladdris' words reverberated in his mind. In a time when most Caldoni were illiterate, a sworn oath had been as binding as a written contract. Even in Dunnagh's time, an oath had a legal standing—though it was seldom invoked.

The Warrior's Oath the Maker referred to had meant something once. But now it was just a formality, something they all pledged at the academy when they took the officer's training.

I taught you better than that, boyo, Grandpa Kai's voice thundered in his private thoughts. *The oath is sacred; you have sworn it. By doing so, you have dedicated your life to helping those in need. And damn you if you take a coward's way out when challenged to do your duty!*

Dunnagh felt the presence of his ancestor's ghost hovering nearby. As in life, his long silver hair was braided into two plaits that framed a high cheek-boned face with a drooping mustache. His mind had always been quick and he'd been fierce in his opinions of a man's honor and obligations. Pale blind eyes weighed, judged him.

Dunnagh writhed as the strength of the ancient laws and his guilt tightened like a noose around his heart. What to do; oh, Ancestors, what should he do?

But was he truly seeing Grandpa's ghost and hearing his voice? Or was it an illusion, just some alien trick? In spite of their primitive appearance, these Khutani Makers obviously possessed tremendous telepathic powers for them to have ferreted out so much information about him and his clan. How could he be sure the voice belonged to grandpa?

And yet, whoever had spoken to him, spoke truth. He had sworn the Warrior's Oath and was honor-bound to uphold its code. And, in spite of all that had happened to tarnish his high ideals since leaving the academy, in his heart-of-hearts he did long to help those in need—like the heroes of old depicted in Grandpa Kai's stories.

Focusing its eerie glowing stare on Dunnagh, the eldest intoned, <<The appeal has been made, Caldoni warrior. Our world may be destroyed if the Umwira achieve their unholy goals. Will you remain true to the warrior's oath of service you have sworn? Will you become our kashallan?>>

Kashallan, kashallan, the word reverberated as a kaleidoscope of images exploded before his mind's eye. Flick...smoking rubble and human refugees bloody and crying. Flick...unknown furry aliens gazing at him with adoration and pleading in their eyes. With the thunder of war drums and Caldoni victory chants ringing in his mind, Dunnagh saw himself with a shining sword and shield locked in deadly combat with a dark and sinister foe. Flick...the same shadowy enemy lying dead at his feet. Flick...Grandpa Kai smiled with approval and love as he sang a ballad that proclaimed his mighty deeds and prowess.

Dunnagh trembled, meeting the old man's eye. *Oh, Grandpa, I know you were so disappointed when I chose the corps instead of becoming your apprentice. Why couldn't you understand how Caldon's poverty and the family were smothering me? I had to get out. I just had to—forgive me.*

No forgiveness is needed. I'm very proud of you—always have been. I know you will do what is right. Won't you, Mo Ogha?

Yes, Seanair, I will. I promise.

Suddenly a new feeling of lightness and excitement flooded into Dunnagh's heart. If he could help these Khutani—make a difference for once. Swearing the oath to serve them might atone for so much evil he'd unwillingly caused, along with the good he'd tried to do while serving in the Lann Gheal Corps.

His voice tight with emotion, Dunnagh surrendered to Khutani urging and agreed. <<If you charge me by my Warrior's Oath—and if your cause is

honorable, then I must accept. I will swear to you my Oath of Service. And I will speak to my commander on your behalf. I'm sure something can be worked out.>>

Still swept along by the tide of his dreams, Dunnagh reasoned that once Bennett's contract ended and the refugees were unloaded at their new home, Commander Tizu would be overjoyed to know Dunnagh had negotiated Lann Gheal a new contract. He could count on Nathan, as his battle-bonded to agree to the idea as well. And his lovely Sairsa wouldn't mind if they married but didn't go home right away; he could talk her round—surely he could....

<<The appeal has been made and the bond is accepted. So be it,>> the eldest intoned. <<Blessed creature, all Timorna will honor you for this gift of yourself.>>

Gladdris nipped gently at Dunnagh's shoulder. As the etheric blood welled up, the Maker stuck a tentacle in the wound. Dunnagh yelped as a needle-sharp pain sent a river a fire cascading down into his chest. A roaring sound pounded in his head; he spasmed and tried to pull away. Gladdris tightened its coils, holding him steady.

Then, as quickly as the sensations had overwhelmed him they were gone. Gladdris nuzzled Dunnagh's neck and loosened its coils. <<The bond has been shared. I accept your service. Thank you, Chosen. We will come to you in your dreams, teach you and prepare you for the Transformation.>>

<<Transformation? You never said anything about any transformation.>>

Surprised, Gladdris lifted its head and stared. <<But of course you will be transformed. How else should you become our kashallan?>>

<<I agreed to become your agent—help you—and I'll do my best to convince my commander to make out a contract, but that's all.>>

<<What is this nonsense about contracts,>> the Maker with long scars on its flanks grumbled. <<We do not make contracts with mere Warlinga. Now that you have agreed to the sacrifice, we would expect your kinsman to guard you, and fight the 'Hated Enemy' at *your* orders. It is you who must make future agreements with them.>>

<<No, you don't understand,>> Dunnagh said, determined to force the words past the impulse that urged him to relax and quit being difficult. Damn big worms—what had they done to him? *Have to—fight them.....*

<<I am only a Unit Leader in the Lann Gheal Corps. I can't commit myself, or our troops, to any action without the approval of our leaders.>>

<<Chosen, calm yourself. It is you who don't understand,>> the deep-voiced one said. <<You belong to us now. You are our kashallan. Only that is important.>>

Belong to them? Fear and rage tangled in his thoughts. What had he really just agreed to do for these enigmatic, big worms? Somehow, he was afraid he wasn't going to like the answer. <<Now that I have agreed to the service, you are implying there is more to becoming your agent than fighting your enemies. What exactly do I have to do to become this kashallan?>>

<<During the Transformation, you will become a living host for one of our symbiont children.>>

<<Host for a symbiont? No way! I agreed to help you get a Lann Gheal contract to fight your Umwira enemies. I didn't agree to become your puppet—your slave.>>

The mere thought of some slimy alien worm crawling about under his skin sent icy chills down his backbone. So, Gladdris *had* been keeping something back as he'd suspected. Tempting him with dreams of glory—damn them! It was time to leave.

<<Let me go,>> Dunnagh growled.

Gladdris stared at him unblinking, but didn't slacken its grip. He might be confined in the big worm's coils, but he still had enough reserves of etheric matter to form a long-bladed dagger. Though it would surely mean his true death if he attacked. If Gladdris didn't let go, he would do it—and would burry a spirit-blade hilt-deep in the Maker's eye, even if the rest of the brutes tore him to bits in the next instant.

<<Gladdris, You dosed him as we agreed, didn't you? The human's physical body is failing. He has sworn blood oath to us, the rest can be sorted out later. Let him go,>> the scarred one said.

Gladdris angrily hissed, and stubbornly tightened its coils, confining Dunnagh further.<<Yes. Against my better judgment I have done what

we agreed upon—but there is no need to force him to our will. He is an honorable, sentient being. When he understands I'm sure he will comply.>>

<<Gladdris, enough. We haven't much time. Release him,>> the eldest commanded.

Suddenly the etheric silver cord connecting Dunnagh to his physical body pulsed with new vigor. Gladdris unwound itself with a growl of displeasure. Focusing his attention on the cord, Dunnagh hastily pushed through the sinewy tangle, to follow his glowing lifeline.

But once out of their reach, he felt honor-bound to clarify his position. <<Just so we understand each other, I will speak to my superiors on your behalf. I will do all in my power to help you fight your enemies—but that is all. When I swore the Warrior's Oath I didn't agree to share my body with any symbiont—and I won't.>>

Only silence answered his declaration.

Dunnagh waited, unnerved by their lack of response. His natural sense of caution warred with his desire to be gone. The cord pulsed with need, urging him to hurry. Not much time left to him; he could feel the cord fraying the longer he remained. He would have to risk attack, turn his back on them—flee.

Once Dunnagh's back was turned, the deep-voiced Maker spat out a rope of etheric light. Swift as a striking snake, it slid over his head, and molded itself around his neck like a luminous silver collar. Whirling back to face them, Dunnagh howled in outrage, clawing at the restraint.

Teeth bared, Gladdris lunged at its deep-voiced companion. <<You, slimeworm. Take it off! He gave us his oath! There is no need—>>

<<Gladdris, enough, didn't you just hear his impudence?>> the deep-voiced one roared. <<The alien is barely known to us. I'm merely ensuring his future compliance.>>

<<Gladdris, it's only a loose tether. It will enable us to protect him from the Umwira should they discover our conjuring—>>

Forming a shining sword from the same etheric matter that created his earlier shield, Dunnagh slashed at the silver tether, determined to break it.<<Liars. Black-hearted devils!>>

When he was unable to sever the tether, he let out a battle cry and lunged at the nearest Maker with his sword held out like a javelin. <<Take it off me.>>

The collar flared like a star and Dunnagh convulsed, his sword fragmenting into a shower of white sparks. <<Insolent child, do you dare threaten us?>>

He screamed and shook a defiant fist at their circling gray forms. <<Damn you! Yes, I dare. I won't be your kashallan—your slave!>>

Then the fabric of the dream tore apart, and he was falling, tumbling down and down through the blackness, back to his body.

Chapter Five

Coming awake with a groan, Dunnagh rubbed his throat, and swallowed painfully. His head throbbed with a blinding Psy headache. Around him the barracks compartment on the ship came alive. As people climbed out of their bunks, he heard nervous laughter and jokes about the ship's close call.

Dunnagh took in several deep breaths, fighting for control. He hoped the pain in his neck and head would dissipate soon. *Can't be sick –not now, Tizu will want me to check on our charges soon. And, I don't want him to have to come looking for me—not after what happened to Green Squad.*

With trembling fingers, he undid his webbing and sat up slowly. Someone laid a hand on his shoulder. Dunnagh looked up. Nathan was standing over him, frowning, his gray eyes troubled. "Dunnagh, are you all right? You look so, so—weird."

Dunnagh grimaced. "I feel weird. Never mind how I look." Suddenly dizzy, Dunnagh bent, putting his head between his knees. "I'll be all right; just give me a moment to clear my head."

Nathan grunted and sank onto a nearby bunk, studying him. His hand hesitated, then he reached out and stroked Dunnagh's red-gold hair. "Dizzy?" Dunnagh stiffened, then nodded. "Take it easy for a moment. Don't rush it."

Dunnagh sat up, pushed Nathan's hand away impatiently and tossed his braid over his shoulder. "I'm all right now. Don't mother-hen me."

Nathan retreated, dropping his hands into his lap. "What happened?"
"Not much. I'm fine."

"Sure you are, and I'm a green-skinned Hatza. Damn it, Dunnagh, this is me you're talking to, you know? What happened?"

"Oh, all right, after we strapped down, I went into the Cumarsaid. I wanted to find out what was happening to the ship. But like a fool I stayed in the trance too long, and then I got caught in the vortex of power when the ship made the jump."

"Oh, brilliant."

"I know, I know." Dunnagh waved a hand in a dismissive gesture. "It was a stupid thing to let happen. I'm no green recruit, but everything happened so fast at the end. And then …I was somewhere else—" His eyes unfocused as he strained to remember. "It was dark—I was floating—"

Dunnagh cursed, rubbing at his neck. "Nathan, this is going to sound crazy, but I think someone tried to enslave me by laying a Geish on me and invoking the Warrior's Oath, while I was helpless within the void!"

Nathan barked a nervous laugh. "Yeah, that is pretty weird all right. In the middle of a jump—who? To do what?"

Dunnagh shook his head, frowning with concentration. "I don't know. I'm trying, but I can't remember much of it. They called me their Chosen—Dream-Chosen—or something like that. It was all so confusing— All I can remember clearly is waking up here a moment ago with a splitting headache."

Dunnagh rubbed his throat. His uniform felt tight. No, his neck hurt. Had he gotten tangled in the webbing somehow while he was in trance? Oh, he was tired.

"One thing I *do* know for certain; the ship took a hit just as we made the jump. I think that's why I didn't get out of the Cumarsaid in time."

Nathan frowned, looking worried. "You'd better tell Tizu about the ship taking a round. I wonder what kind of damage she's suffered."

Dunnagh snorted. "Nothing real bad or we would be dead by now, but we might have to find a nearby planet where we can make repairs."

Nathan muttered a curse. "If that's the case we better hope that Creggan ship didn't follow or we're dead meat and space-dust, no doubt about it."

Had Nathan just foretold their fate? Dunnagh shuddered and looked away, his Psy twisting a knot in his gut.

Unaware of his friend's concern, Nathan grunted, and stood up, dismissing Dunnagh's story about the Oath with a wave of his hand. "Well, just forget about the oath stuff; it's probably nothing important. Weird things can happen to your head while in a jump, even if you're not in Cumarsaid."

Dunnagh rose as well, only half listening. "Maybe."

Chapter Six

It had been hours since the jump and nothing had happened. The armachda went about their usual routine after a battle, eating, drinking, cleaning, repairing gear, and restoring their weaponry to combat readiness. As his body performed familiar tasks, Dunnagh couldn't shake the feeling that there was something wrong, no matter how normal things appeared.

In an odd way, he knew that this wrong something had to do with what had happened to him during the jump. And that unwanted knowledge terrified him. But every time he tried to grasp its meaning, fear would defeat him. Finally he decided that for some reason he was afraid to know the answer, and so couldn't get past a mental barrier of his own making.

By the time he came off duty he was a bundle of nerves. He knew he needed a distraction, something to take his mind off his unsettling thoughts. He decided to find Sairsa and see how she and her family were managing. Slipping into a clean shirt and rebraiding his hair, he headed out to find her.

Keeping in mind galactic prejudice towards the Caldoni, Dunnagh paused in the doorway of her assigned quarters, hoping to see her before someone noticed and complained to the Commanders about his unauthorized visit.

The large room was crowded, jammed with people, moving about dazed and frightened, trying to pick up the pieces of their shattered lives. No Sairsa, where could she be? He knew this was the cabin she'd been assigned...

Ah, there in the back were her parents, sitting alone, seemingly oblivious of the activity going on around them, caught up in their own little world of fear and loss. He felt sorry for them, all of them, these bewildered, frightened people, so unprepared for the war that had overtaken them and torn their bright, safe world apart.

Dunnagh hesitated. He needed to find Sairsa desperately, but after the trauma of the jump, the thought of facing her parents alone gave him a queasy feeling in the pit of his stomach.

You're becoming quite the spineless coward today, my lad, he chided himself. *Got to face them sometime, if you would name them in-laws, might as well be now.* Taking a deep breath, he squared his shoulders and crossed the room.

As he approached, he studied the pair carefully. The Dymarian man was outwardly calmer than he had been earlier, but still had a vacant look about his eyes. Dunnagh knew that look; he'd seen it before on the faces of war survivors. His Caldoni wife, on the other hand, was a different story. Rigid, jaw tight, she sat glaring, angry and embittered at the fate that had once more torn her life apart with war.

They looked up as he halted in front of them. He smiled politely and said in galactic standard, "Excuse me, can you tell me where I might find Sairsa?"

For a long moment no one spoke. The old man was blinking muzzily, and the old woman glared at him with hostility. He shifted uncomfortably and was about to leave when she finally spoke in low, angry Caldoni. "So you're the one. I knew she was seeing someone new, but she wouldn't tell me who. When I saw you a while ago with her as we boarded the ship, I knew why she wouldn't tell me about you, a Caldoni Armachd!" Her voice dripped with contempt.

Dunnagh was startled by the vehemence of her emotion, and involuntarily stepped back. In the same language he said, "Honored Mother of the Clans, you do me an injustice. By my Oath, I respect your daughter very much. I offer her no dishonor, I assure you."

She gave a derisive bark of laughter. "By your Oath indeed." The woman leaned forward, quivering with rage. "I tell you this, warrior: if you *really* honor my daughter you will forget about her and leave her alone."

Dunnagh hesitated, bewildered. "I don't understand, Elder. What have I done to displease you so? My family—"

Still glaring, she cut him off. "It's not *who* you are, warrior, but *what* you are that I object to. My Sairsa deserves better out of life than to learn to love a man who will leave her a grieving widow by his early death. And you and I both know that is your most probable fate. So I say to you again: LEAVE MY DAUGHTER ALONE!"

Hearing his wife's angry words, the old man roused. Laying a comforting hand on her arm, he soothed, "Now, Janet, I don't know what you're saying to this young man, but my dear please calm yourself."

She rounded on him snarling. "Stay out of this, Richard. You don't know. You can't understand—" A sob caught in her throat.

"What's going on, mother?" Unnoticed, Sairsa had come up to them, balancing two food trays in her arms. She set them down with a resounding thunk on a nearby table, put her hands on her hips and glared defiantly at her parent. She waited.

No one spoke, her mother met her stare but refused to say anything. Getting no satisfaction from that quarter, she transferred her glare to Dunnagh, waiting again.

At last, feeling very uncomfortable, he cleared his throat. "Your mother was informing me that she does not find one such as myself suitable for her daughter," he explained.

"I see." She turned back to face her mother, folding her arms across her chest. "Excuse me, Mother, but the last time I looked at my ID, I believe it stated that I was an adult," she said, her tone dripping with sarcasm. "And, as an adult, I'll decide for myself who I see or don't see, thank you very much, *mother*. You have no right—"

"I have every right to consider your future happiness, I'm your mother," Janet snapped. "And don't talk to me like..."

As these two strong-willed women screamed at each other, Dunnagh's mouth dropped open in shock. Glancing down at her step-father, their eyes met, the man's mouth quirked into a sympathetic grin. This was a side of his love unknown to him. It was definitely enlightening and maybe a bit scary.

Oh yes my dear, you are definitely a woman of the clans, he thought ruefully, *and may I never feel the sharp side of your tongue. I might just drown in my own blood.*

They were starting to attract the attention of the other passengers in the room, who were hungry for any diversion to take their minds off their own miseries. The mother-daughter shouting match was gathering a growing crowd of spectators. Embarrassed, Dunnagh was turning as red as his hair.

At last Sairsa paused long enough to become aware of their audience as well. With a final muttered curse, she turned on her heel and stamped back out into the corridor. Offering the elders a quick bow, he followed her.

She was waiting for him, leaning up against the wall, arms crossed, head down, hugging herself. At his approach she looked up, unshed tears in her eyes. "I'm sorry you had to witness that. Mother is so stubborn and I..." Uncrossing her arms, she blindly reached for him.

Stubborn? His lip twitched, but he prudently kept quiet. Moving closer, he took her in his arms. She blinked and a tear splashed down on his arm.

"Oh shit," she swore, as the flow came in earnest.

Dunnagh put an arm around her shoulder and guided her down the corridor to a dark corner under a staircase. He took her in his arms and held her tightly as she sobbed into his shoulder. Patiently he soothed her, murmuring softly in Caldoni, stroking her gently, and allowed her to cry.

Dunnagh stared blindly at the far wall, mind in turmoil. Gods, what a complicated mess. He wanted this woman with all his heart and soul. But a small corner of his mind kept insisting that there was truth in her mother's angry words, and maybe she did deserve better than a Caldoni armachd like him.

She was talented and beautiful and used to a much more luxurious life than he could offer her. And, looking squarely at reality, Death's shadow was always beside him. Not growing up among the clans, how *would* she cope if he were to die?

At last he felt her relax against him as she quieted down. She sniffed and blew her nose. Lifting her chin, he kissed her tenderly, tasting the salt of her tears on his tongue. "Sairsa, I've grown to care for you very much." He took a deep breath, ignoring the growing ache in his chest. "But maybe your mother is right. You do deserve better than a Caldoni warrior sworn to The Oath like me."

She stepped back shaking her head, eyes filling once more with tears. "Do I have to fight with you too? Damn you both! I'll choose for myself what's best for me," she sobbed. "I love you, Dunnagh Kai, and—and I thought you loved me too. But if you don't, then say so. Otherwise, let me decide for myself what I want to do with my life."

For answer, he pressed her to him fiercely, his whole body alive with the wanting of her. "Oh, Sairsa," he breathed, "I love you so much." He kissed her passionately again and again, intoxicated with the need of her.

When they at last came up for air, he said, "I've been thinking that maybe it's time I go back to Caldon and take up that teaching position my uncle's been offering me. Would you come home with me as my wife, my dearest Sairsa?"

Equally solemn, she nodded. "Yes, Dunnagh, I will go with you anywhere in this wide universe." Then laughing through her tears, she added, "I only ask that you be patient with me as I relearn our Caldoni language and culture."

Joining in her laughter, he kissed her deeply. "I'll be patient always, Mo Leannan." He smiled a gleam of mischief in his eyes. "And they do say that the bed is the best place to learn a new language, hmm?"

Smiling, she punched him playfully on the arm. He pulled her to him again, kissed her, and then froze. From down the hall he heard someone shout, "Anybody seen Kai? Commander Tizu wants him."

Tizu's timing is almost as great as Nathan's usually is. He sighed. "I've got to go, my love, I'm sorry."

Chapter Seven

Dunnagh stood, bemused, in the doorway of Dr. Bennett's private suite aboard the *Chance*. Commander Tizu had just ordered him to report here. When Dunnagh asked why he was being singled out for this "honor", Tizu only shrugged and told him to get going.

Feeling a shiver run down his spine, Dunnagh wondered if this summons had anything to do with the damage he'd told Tizu the *Freedom's Chance* sustained during their escape.

In the center of the room, two men lounged in comfortable chairs, tall glasses and a pitcher of drinks on the low table in front of them. When the older of the two saw him, he gave Dunnagh a smile that showed off his fine, white teeth, and said, "Come in, Armachd Kai, and join us."

His face expressionless, Dunnagh bowed and took the empty chair across from them. Bennett's suite, with its cream colored walls and colorful hollow-vid photos on the walls was a far upgrade from the utilitarian grey barracks where his people and most of the refugees were quartered.

"I'm Dr. Bennett, and this is my protégée, Dr. Philip Singey." Bennett pointed to the pitcher. "Help yourself."

"Thank you, Sir."

The pair were quite a contrast to one another. Dr. Bennett, Lann Gheal's boss and the sponsor of the Dymarian rescue mission, was an elegant man, a bit thick in the body but tastefully dressed, in dark green over tunic and cream under robe. His graying hair was worn rather long, but cut and styled carefully to enhance his tanned patrician features.

The other man was much younger and slimmer than his mentor. With his wavy black hair and ebony skin, he was handsome, Dunnagh supposed, though a bit exotic to a Caldoni's way of thinking.

Singey was plainly dressed in blue tunic and tan pants, but like the doctor's own apparel, they were expensive. And in his case, they were tailored to fit his slim build to best advantage. Unlike the doctor's exaggerated friendliness however, Singey eyed Dunnagh with a cool aloofness that annoyed him before the man even had time to say a word.

"Commander Tizu said you wanted to see me, Sir."

"Yes, I'm hoping you will be able to help us."

Dunnagh poured himself a glass from the pitcher and sipped. The concoction was a bit too fruity for his taste, but definitely good Caldoni uiskia in the mix somewhere. "If I can, certainly, Sir."

Bennett flashed him that smile again. "Good." Then sobering, he said, "The ship's instruments were damaged during our escape from Dymar. We will have to make repairs before we can proceed to our original destination.

"To make the necessary repairs, however, some of the life support systems will have to be shut down, and in order to do that we need a safe place to unload most of our over-crowded, human cargo.

"Our options in this sector were limited, but we managed to locate what we believe to be a suitable planet. What we require now is more detailed information about conditions down on the planet's surface. Unfortunately, the ship's backup system wasn't designed to give us the information needed. This presents us with a unique problem, Armachd Kai, one in which your distinctive skills can be of use to us, I think."

Dunnagh froze, his drink halfway to his lips. He quickly set the glass down, his features sliding once more into an expressionless mask. His clan elders were going to tear a strip off his hide if he'd been careless. "I don't understand, Sir. You need a good technician—which I am not. How can I possibly help you with this?"

"I think that you know exactly what I mean, armachd," Bennett challenged. "You see, I probably know much more about the Caldoni than most outsiders, or the Fir Gall, as you call us. I know about the oath you take, and the magical disciplines your warriors learn. In fact, that's why I have chosen to hire Lann Gheal so many times in the past. I have a lot of respect for your people and their traditions.

"And I also know about a particular trance-inducing technique taught to the warriors of your rank, which is called the Cumarsaid. Your Commander confirms that you are a practitioner of that art."

Dunnagh took a deep breath and let it out in a long sigh. Finally he said, "My Ca Ce'awn trusts you very deeply, if he has told you so much about our ways."

"I would like to think your Ca 'Ce'awn does, Armachd; Arde Laron and I have been friends for years. I am not asking you to betray any Caldoni secrets, but, if it is allowed, we could use the help. If we were followed—well, time could be important."

What had Nathan said about a bounty put on Bennett and his ship? Yes, Dunnagh could understand the urgency. All their lives might depend on that unknown factor. Out loud he asked, "Tell me what you need more specifically. Then I will know if I have the training to accomplish it."

"Fair enough." Bennett relaxed and once more picked up his drink. "The techs say the instruments have been giving us a wide range of conflicting readings. That has me concerned. The anomalies could be just a technical problem, as Philip here suggests, but I want to be certain.

"Oh they've told us the basics, like the chemical content of the atmosphere, and the surface soil. Unfortunately there's nothing like civilization down there, only a few primitive life forms have registered on the computator's surveillance field.

"What we need are more details about a suitable place to erect a temporary base. I'm sure you are aware that the ship is dangerously overcrowded. If the Creggan fleet should find us in our present condition.."

Bennett left the rest of his thought unvoiced, but Dunnagh knew what he meant. If the Creggans found them now, they wouldn't have a chance. But what if there was an unknown danger here on the planet as well? A danger far worse than any posed by the Creggan bounty hunters—what if?

"We have the supplies already on board for the refugee's new quarters on Gammon 5," Bennett continued, "so if this planet is suitable, we might as well set up the pre-fabs on this world—for a while. The refugees might be more comfortable and safer down there anyway."

Dunnagh gently rubbed at his neck. Bennett left the rest of his thought unvoiced, but Dunnagh knew what he meant. And yet, how could he contradict countless years of tradition and perform the Cumarsaid in front of these outsiders—even though all their lives might depend on him and what he might learn.

"Is there no other way? My clan elders—"

Bennett acknowledged his predicament with a nod. "Oh, we could take the shuttle down and have a look, but it might take days. And, this is why I think you can save us time."

"Time, which we can't afford to waste. Yes, I see. Dr. Bennett, may I ask—do you have any reason to suspect that the Creggan warships that attacked the *Chance*, are still following us?"

"Is that a wild guess, Armachd, or some Caldoni magic at work?"

Dunnagh shrugged. "Perhaps a little of both, Sir."

Bennett nodded. "To answer your question, maybe. The instruments are picking up a faint signal. But right now, and until we *do* know, we are keeping our systems output down to the very minimum to avoid detection for as long as we possibly can."

At least with a base on the planet some of us might have a chance, to survive and wait for help, *even if the Creggan ships found us.*

Thinking of Sairsa, Dunnagh said, "I will do what I can."

Bennett relaxed and smiled again. "Excellent."

"Has my Ca' Ce'awn allowed you to see the Cumarsaid being performed?" Dunnagh asked as he took another mouthful of his drink. Definitely good uiskia.

"Ah—no, I've never seen it. My knowledge is strictly secondhand. Do we need to do anything to help you—ah—prepare?"

That was unfortunate. Dunnagh would have felt easier in his mind if the doctor had been trusted enough to have witnessed such a display in the past. And the fluttering in his gut intensified when he glanced over and caught Singey's eye. The man looked down his nose and gave him a condescending smirk. He hated to perform any Caldoni secrets in front of the man's obvious skepticism.

But what choice did he have? Invoking thoughts of Sairsa to give him courage, he took in a deep breath and let it out slowly. "No, not really," Dunnagh said, "just don't touch me while I'm in the communion. I will only go into a light contact, so I can tell you what I see and you can ask me questions. Will that be what you want?"

Bennett and Singey exchanged glances. "Yes-s, that should do nicely," Bennett said.

"One more thing, if you could display a picture of the planet on the vid terminal, that would help me focus."

Singey punched a few buttons on the console beside his chair. Instantly, the lights dimmed and a view of the planet they now orbited appeared upon the far wall. Dunnagh swiveled to face it, allowing his eyes to half close. Mauve, gray, and tawny browns dominated the planet's surface in swirling bands of color.

He took in a deep breath, letting it out slowly, and allowed his body to relax. In his mind he recited the ancient Caldoni prayers that were the triggers to help him open his awareness. With another deep breath, he slipped into the Cumarsaid...

<<Honored Guardians of this beautiful world, here me and help us. We are in danger from enemy hunters. We seek sanctuary. Please help us, Holy Ones!>>

As Dunnagh reached out for contact, the guardian spirit of the planet flooded his awareness with a cascade of powerful images and impressions.

"NOW WHAT, DR. B?" SINGEY whispered. Bennett shrugged, and returned his attention to the motionless armachd. Singey drummed his fingers impatiently on his chair arm, wishing Bennett hadn't talked him into staying for this. He hated this kind of superstitious nonsense.

Suddenly Dunnagh cried out, swayed dangerously, almost falling off his chair. Instinctively, he reached out to steady him, but Bennett shook his head. When Singey glanced at the armachd again the man had righted himself, and now sat with eyes closed, his face contorted by some strange emotion. He shivered. To his taut nerves, the room seemed cooler, as if a ghostly presence was forming in the air around them.

Finally, Bennett asked, "Armachd Kai, what's happening?"

For a long moment there was only silence, then a hollow voice quite different from the armachd's answered, "Pain! Old pain now, but still—hurts." He moaned the sound welling up from somewhere deep in his inner core. Dunnagh's entire body shuddered as if suffering a great trauma.

The two men exchanged confused glances. They waited, but no further information was offered. Dunnagh continued to tremble violently, but remained stable on his chair.

"Armachd, we don't understand. Have the Creggan ships found us?"

A long pause, then the eerie voice again. "Safe... Hunters in the sky cannot be allowed to find—the Dream-Chosen...."

"Armachd, we don't understand. Please explain."

The eerie voice again. "Long ago, a great disaster. Pain, so much pain. But the Makers hid the patterns, kept life's essence safe. Now the Makers call. Must have freedom. You come. Bring Chosen."

"Makers, Chosen, freedom? Armachd, please explain."

Silence...

Singey stirred, then unable to contain his impatience, he whispered, "Doctor, this is all very interesting, no doubt, but it isn't getting us anywhere. We need to know—"

"Have a little patience, Philip. I fear these things must proceed at their own pace."

Singey made a face, unconvinced. Then, taking the initiative, he asked, "Armachd, you mentioned a disaster. Can you tell us if it is safe to land on the planet?"

"Yes-s. You are welcome. Come!"

"All right, that's one fairly straight answer," Singey grumbled under his breath, "let's try for more." Oh, how he hated this. He felt so stupid, all his scientific training rebelling at such a weird approach to collecting data. But if Bennett thought it was worth it—well, he was a rich man who could afford to indulge his fancies.

Secretly, Singey doubted they would get anything useful from this superstitious nonsense—and the doctor probably did too. But Bennett was definitely obsessed with the Caldoni, and, for him, this was the best chance he was likely to get to pry into their secrets. His eyes flicked to Bennett's face; the man was watching the armachd with rapped attention, fascinated. He was definitely not ready to call an end to this little farce.

"You say we are safe, but the instruments don't necessarily support that statement. Why is that?"

"Instruments inferior... All must come—need you—come." The Caldoni let out a long sigh, then lapsed into stillness once more.

Singey heaved a sigh and asked, "Alright, if we are welcome, then where should we land?"

From within the void, Dunnagh heard the question. He concentrated. <<Where, Mother Timorna, should we land our ship?>>

<<*Here,*>> *the voice said, slowly sending to him a stream of images and impressions.*

"To the north, there is only death. Black. Barren." He took a ragged breath. "Hurts... In the south, there is a place. High, flat, safe—a good place. On this high mesa, between the Rim Wall and the Shallow Sea, make the landing. Come. S-soo-n-n."

Dunnagh let out a long sigh. They waited, but he offered no further explanation. There was only the muted sound of the ship's activities to punctuate the stillness.

"Doctor B, he must have fallen asleep; he's just sitting there. This is a total waste of our time, I'm afraid, and not very interesting. I have work to do," Singey grumbled. "I have to go; I have work to do."

Before Bennett could object, he stood, knocking over his half-finished drink in the process. As he dove for the glass, his chair crashed to the floor behind him.

At the sound Dunnagh convulsed, nearly falling, his eyes flying wide open. Seeming disoriented, he took several deep breaths. His hand came up and massaged his throat. Then through half closed eyes, he watched them warily.

Bennett caught Singey's eye and frowned. Annoyed at himself for causing a scene and making a mess, Singey mopped at the spilled liquid and muttered an apology. He hoped that would satisfy the doctor—he could care less what the Caldoni thought.

DAMN THE MAN, DUNNAGH thought. The link was broken. But what had just happened? He felt suddenly uneasy, a cold blade of dread twisting in his gut. The Spirit was telling him something—something important when Singey had interrupted. Through half closed eyes, he watched the other men. Bennett looked thoughtful, Singey disgusted.

The dark-skinned scientist mopped at the spilled liquid and muttered an apology, but Dunnagh could tell he didn't mean it. He clenched his jaw, feeling his temper rise. Bennett caught his eye and smiled. Was that toothy grin a little forced this time?

"Armachd Kai," Bennett said, "what we heard was rather confusing. Can you add anything to what you said now that you are—uh—back?"

Dunnagh hesitated, reluctant to speak in front of Singey's obvious skepticism. Finally he sighed and nodded. "I couldn't detect any ship other than our own nearby, but my range is limited. As to the planet—" another wary glance at Singey, "This world calls herself Timorna.

"Some time ago—thousands of years, I think, there was a great disaster here. Nuclear, probably. I was shown visions of blackened, glassy rock. It was highly radioactive once, but not so much now.

"The northern continent is still uninhabitable. The smaller southern continent is different, however. There life survived. In the area I was shown for our camp, there is nothing harmful.

"On the high plateau where we should land there is only some kind of yellow moss, some shrubs, and a few small animals. Nothing either poisonous or dangerous there to worry about. No harm will come to us on the plateau. I was promised that."

Bennett turned to his protégée, raising an inquiring eyebrow. Singey shifted uncomfortably and looked down at the computator terminal now in front of him on the table. Keeping his voice neutral, he reported, "The instruments say there are two continents, as he says. The northern land mass is lifeless and shows evidence of radioactivity that is at the high margin of human tolerance."

Bennett gaped, his expression a mixture of amazement and respect. Turning to Singey, he said in a low voice, "What did I tell you, Philip? There is no way that a Caldoni armachd could have known that. Lann Gheal was merely hired for a military evacuation of the refugees. They have had no access to the ship's instruments since coming aboard."

Singey made a face, then turned back to the computator. "There is a smaller southern continent connected to the larger land mass by a wide peninsula. There is no evidence of fallout or other harmful substances that I can detect from here with this—"

Singey waved his hand in frustration at the inadequate instrument. "If there is such a place as Armachd Kai described, then it would be in the southern region."

"It is there."

In the tone of voice he might use with a particularly dim-witted servant, Singey looked down his nose at Kai, and drawled, "That may well be, but forgive me, armachd. But you see, I'm a scientist, and I'm finding all this very hard to accept. How do you *really know that*?"

Dunnagh reddened. This was what always happened when his people tried to explain to the Fir Gall. Now he was trapped and was angry with himself for getting into this predicament in the first place. No matter what the need, he should have refused to do the Cumarsaid.

"Well?" Singey persisted.

The pompous ass wasn't going to let it go, damn him. His voice hoarse with the effort to control his mounting fury, Dunnagh said, "Because She promised me."

"She, the planet? Oh, come now, Armachd—"

Dunnagh stood abruptly. Rage contorted his features for a moment, then he assumed a mask of hostile indifference. Addressing Dr. Bennett, he bowed. "If you will excuse me, Sir—I have told you all I can. I have duties to attend to." He pivoted then walked stiff-backed from the room.

For a long time Bennett sat motionless, staring at the closed door. Finally he sighed, and took a sip of his forgotten drink. "I wish you hadn't done that, Philip. The Caldoni are a proud, secretive people. I'm afraid that in one thoughtless moment you may have undermined years of patient courting of their trust on my part."

Singey gave an incredulous snort. "Surely you exaggerate. I—"

"—I don't exaggerate, Philip. I mean exactly what I said," Bennett interrupted. "You don't know them like I do. You're used to the constant sniping of the scientific community, where everything and everybody is a target for debate. What you did just now may not seem important to you—but to him, it was a betrayal of an almost *sacred* trust.

"The Caldoni *never* share their secrets with outsiders. And with good reason, I might add, judging by your behavior just now. He only agreed to do it at all because he thought his clan leader trusted me, so he felt safe enough to let me see. And now... " Bennett's voice trailed off in angry frustration.

Singey looked chastened, then contrite, he murmured, "I'm sorry, Doctor. I was letting my own private prejudices color my thinking. But it's just so unscientific. When I hear that kind of superstitious nonsense, it reminds me of witch doctors, voodoo and such like—I get—well, it's an insult to a man's intelligence." He shook his head helplessly.

Bennett gave him a disgusted look and stood up; Singey came hastily to his feet as well. "What's done is done and we'll make the best of it. At least we know now where to set up the base."

"Doctor—if you think it will help, I'll go after the man and apologize."

Bennett considered. "No, I think not. Let him cool down first. Later, when you can catch him alone, do it."

Chapter Eight

Dunnagh had no time to mull over his confused memories of the Cumarsaid trance. Like the rest of Lann Gheal, he was too busy preparing for the landing to have any time for his own personal worries.

Much to Dunnagh's surprise, when the spot for the base was located on the planet's surface, he wasn't the one heading up the patrol going to secure the site. Tizu gave Dunnagh's second in command, Nathan, that dubious honor. Dunnagh was relieved; he would have liked to stay on the ship the entire time they made repairs, but Tizu was having none of that.

Suspecting Dunnagh's request centered around spending more time with his girlfriend, Commander Tizu told him firmly that he would do his share of patrolling, like everybody else.

Dunnagh closed his eyes as the familiar whine of the shuttlecraft's deceleration pressed him firmly back into his seat. They would be landing on the planet soon. Shortly after the engine's roar subsided, a crewman moved to open the hatch and let down the stair. Dunnagh rose and, grabbing his gear, followed Tizu out into the red-gold sunlight.

Timorna—the name came unbidden into his mind as he stepped onto the yellow vegetation at the base of the stairs. Getting clear of the unloading Dunnagh paused and set down his pack, and looked around. The sun on his back, had a comfortable warmth, but he suspected it was very cold here at night. His nostrils widened slightly with the unfamiliar scent of the land, pepper and lemon, with a coppery undertone. In all his travels he'd never encountered anything quite like it before.

In the distance to the north and the east, a forbidding range of barren mountains climbed towards the mauve sky in an unbroken wall. To the south and west the land wasn't quite so precipitous. There the slopes of the mesa atop which they'd landed, ran down into a maze of tawny canyons.

Recalling knowledge gained during his trance, he knew that these "Broken Lands" led eventually to the Great Swamp and the Shallow Sea beyond.

Taking a deep breath, he slipped into a light Cumarsaid trance. Emptiness... Hunger... The sadness seeped up from the cold rock, and covered the vegetation with a film of loneliness. Ghosts moaned in the wind, their entreaties unintelligible to his alien ears.

Then, a soft tendril of thought brushed his awareness. Startled Dunnagh threw up a mental shield. His spirit crouched within its protection, trembling. He waited, unsure why he was acting so spooked. There was no fanged monster charging him with jaws open wide, either within the Dream or physical world. Absently he massaged his neck...

This is stupid. What's a matter with me? Feeling somewhat foolish Dunnagh cautiously lowered his shield, and eased out of the trance. The land felt as empty and lonely as before. The contact had been faint; had he imagined sentience where there was none? Maybe.

Before he could pursue the enigma further, Nathan touched him on the shoulder and laughed when he jumped. "Not much like home, is it? So, what do you think of this place?"

Dunnagh turned back to the scenery. His lip twitched but he didn't smile. "No it isn't like Caldon—nothing green here. I'm not sure what I think. It's beautiful—sort of, but for a planet with a temperate climate and a breathable atmosphere, it seems so, so empty."

Nathan snorted. "Wait till you've been here a while. Right now our people are making a terrible racket with the unloading. But later when things settle down, it's so quiet that it's downright eerie. Sometimes I get this feeling—" Nathan shook his head, and hastily added, "Never mind—it's just a crazy notion of mine. "Come on, let's get you settled before Tizu finds us something to do."

The camp was about a half-klick from the southern cliff face. It consisted of a number of freestanding tents, a combination prefab HQ and mess building, and across the quadrangle, a sickbay and field lab unit. A small mountain of gear to one side of the quadrangle attested to the work still needed before more of the refugees could be unloaded.

Dunnagh followed Nathan into the first tent beside HQ and dropped his gear on an empty cot. "We probably have a few minutes before anyone comes looking for us," Dunnagh said as he sat down on the cot. "So tell me what's been going on."

Nathan sat down on a cot across from him, pushing a strand of loose brown hair off his forehead. "Nothing much to tell, really. We came down and followed the usual procedure when landing in a potentially hostile zone. When we were certain we were alone, we set up camp. I have sentries posted, but so far they've seen nothing larger than a cat-sized animal creeping through the thorn bushes."

"Did you check the canyons I saw?"

"A little." Nathan began fiddling with the string tying his braid.

Dunnagh allowed the irritation of a superior officer to color his voice. "A little? I don't need Tizu coming down on me for a sloppy mission—not after losing Green on Dymar," he snapped.

"It's not like you to be so careless. What's going on? Why didn't you do a proper reconnaissance? And, more to the point, why are you so reluctant to tell me about it now?

Nathan refused to meet his eye, focusing instead on the complex problem of retying the cord around his long, brown warrior's braid. When he finished and could delay no longer he looked up. "Yeah I know I haven't followed our usual procedure, but the canyons are—ah—weird."

"Weird."

"Yeah, weird."

"Care to explain that?"

Nathan sighed, groping for words. "They're full of these tall reed-like plants. The damn things make it impossible to see more than a few feet in front of your face when you're in there."

He started to play with his braid again, caught himself, and tossed the braid back over his shoulder. "It's like—like being a rabbit caught in a hay field before its mowed. It's creepy down there!"

"That's hardly a reason for not doing a proper reconnaissance," Dunnagh said. "We've fought in jungle terrain before; the canyons couldn't be any worse. What's the real reason?"

Nathan thought about it for a moment, and then admitted, "Our communications equipment doesn't function properly down there, and we don't know why, because it works fine up here on the mesa. We lost a squad for half a day in that maze. Believe me, that wasn't fun."

He made a face and shook his head. "After that mishap, I didn't send any more land patrols in there.

"But I did take the precaution of sending the hover-sled out several times, for a radius of about twenty klicks. The instruments found nothing, but I've posted sentries near the edges of the cliff just to be sure.

"If we've missed something big and nasty down in there, it's not getting up here without a taste of our weaponry." Nathan watched Dunnagh's expression through heavy lidded eyes, and gave him a hopeful grin. "Like you and the techs said, perfectly safe, nothing to worry about."

"Yeah, but were the readings the techs gave us accurate after the damage we sustained? And you know as well as I do that my Psy isn't perfect."

Nathan's smile evaporated. "The techs thought their readings were accurate—and your Psy is better than mine—and usually right."

Dunnagh kept Nathan in suspense while he considered. Would Tizu agree with Nathan's assessment of the situation? Or would he see Nathan's departure from routine as just another example of Dunnagh's failure as a unit leader.

Then, he recalled the touch he'd experienced while in trance a while ago. Were they in danger? The information about their communications equipment not working in the canyons twisted a knot of unease in Dunnagh's gut. The touch—if it was from another sentient being—he wasn't sure now, hadn't been threatening, and yet...

No, we'll be fine. We'll only be here while the ship is being repaired; there's no reason for anyone to go mucking around down in the canyons anyway. And Nathan's right, our firepower can handle anything we might come across on a primitive world like this.

Dunnagh looked up at the roar of the shuttle taking off. Outside in the quadrangle someone swore in Caldoni and another laughed. The sounds of unloaded gear being stacked reminded him he had a job to do. He needed to find Tizu and report.

Unable to help himself, he gave Nathan a reassuring nod and inwardly winced at the naked relief he saw in his friend's eyes. "Sounds like you've done everything I would have done." Dunnagh stood. "Let's go find something to eat, before the commander sees us, and puts us to work. I'm starved. I'll unpack later."

Chapter Nine

G roaning at the unexpected weight, Dr. Tessa Farris lifted the field pack to her shoulders. "Philip, how can you stand to carry around all this heavy equipment when you're working?"

Singey smiled. "I guess I'm just a hopeless glutton for punishment." Turning his smile on the plump woman standing near them, he said, "My assistant and I are quite used to it by now. Aren't we, Gemma?"

Gemma looked up from fiddling with her pack strap. Eyes soft with her adoration, she brushed her lank brown hair off her forehead and nodded.

"Tessa, you don't have to come with us, you know. I can get one of Commander Tizu's men to carry the extra gear."

"No, really, Philip, I want to come. If I get bored watching you two," she patted her jacket, "I've brought my pocket computator full of books along, just in case."

Singey grunted. "Where are the guards that uncouth Commander Tizu promised me? He tapped his walking stick against his leg in a hurry to be gone. He was just about to send Gemma to HQ when two black-clad armachda walked around the corner of the pre-fab.

His chaperones today were a dark-haired, wiry, woman, and a tall, lanky Caldoni man with a drooping brown mustache. He sighed. Barbarians, like the rest of the Caldoni mercenaries Bennett favored. The pair saluted and told him their names were Marnez and Taleish. Singey nodded. Then, without another word, he headed out, setting a brisk pace.

Yesterday he'd realized there was something very strange about the plant and animal life on this planet. All the samples he had taken so far revealed an unknown substance in their cellular structure. Some alien enigma he'd never seen before. He didn't have the proper equipment here in the field to do a thorough examination, but if he could collect enough data before they had to leave, he'd finish his analyses in his own lab.

Unconsciously his pace quickened, as the excitement of discovery bubbled over in his mind. This unplanned layover was going to rocket his career straight to the top. All he needed were a few more samples, a hearty dose of Bennett's money for research and then the University chair he coveted would be his.

"Philip, please."

Singey glanced back, then reluctantly slowed his pace. He had forgotten about Tessa. She was a pretty woman, with a full-breasted figure, a creamy-skinned, heart-shaped face, and curly dark hair worn well below her shoulders. Like Dr. Bennett and himself, Tessa Farris came from one of the richer families in galactic society. They had run into each other socially over the years, but not enough to make them more than casual acquaintances. Their interests were too different to encourage intimacy.

Singey waited for her to come alongside him, then said, "Sorry, Tessa, Gemma and I have been making some interesting discoveries about this planet."

"That's all right. I don't understand much about biology and genetics, but I do understand about the excitement of a new discovery. We get them in my field of primitive anthropology, too, you know."

"Quite. I'm sure you do, my dear."

Tessa blinked, then a moment later laughed. "Philip, you can be such an obnoxious snob at times; I don't know how Dr. B puts up with you."

Singey chuckled. "I guess you'll have to ask him. Sorry, I didn't mean to sound so pompous. By the way, I've been meaning to ask *you*, Tessa. Why were you on board *Freedom's Chance* at this time? Surely even a woman of your wit and charm, might hesitate to embark on such a dangerous mission as the Dymarian rescue."

Bennett had only asked Singey at the last moment, because one of his doctors had taken ill shortly before launch. He'd been flattered by the great man's attention and willingly agreed. Confined to his lab so much of the time, the lure of adventure had appealed to him. He was in between projects at the moment, and his pre-med training was certainly an asset for the project.

Tessa glanced covertly at the two black-clad figures with weapons drawn, walking a short distance ahead of them, before confiding, "Actually,

I invited myself. Dr. B. didn't know I was on board until we were well underway. He was furious when he found out. But I had to come. This was my big chance."

At his raised eyebrow, she smiled. "You probably know already how obsessed he is with the Caldoni. Well, I want to write a book about them. Oh, I know they aren't actually 'primitives,' but the little we do know about them points to some very ancient folk customs among them. I've been after Dr. B. for months to introduce me to some of his contacts. And now that I have a grant... " She smiled slyly, her eyes sparkling with her excitement. "When I heard that he had hired Lann Gheal again to help bring the last of the refugees off Dymar, I just had to come."

After what he had witnessed in Bennett's suite, Singey thought the label of "primitives" fit the Caldoni quite nicely, and he doubted if Tessa would get any help from Bennett.

"Excuse me, Dr. Singey," Gemma said. "This is where we left off our survey yesterday."

Singey looked around. He recognized the view of those far peaks and the purple shrubs near the edge of the cliff. "Thank you, Gemma. You are correct; I don't know what I'd do without you."

Taking off his pack, Singey informed his two guards they would be working in this area for a while. Faces expressionless, they nodded, squatting down in the yellow vegetation where they could see the surrounding countryside.

Tessa helped the scientists unpack their equipment and half-heartedly collected a few plant samples before drifting off to bother the armachda. Relieved to see her attention occupied elsewhere, Singey dismissed her from his mind and got to work.

"HI, I'M DR. TESSA FARRIS. It's so fascinating to discover a new planet like this, isn't it? Dr. Singey is quite excited."

Taleish blinked, then nodded slowly.

"It must be an exciting life being a Lann Gheal Armachd. Have you two been in the corps long?"

They exchanged glances, then looked away, studying the landscape. Finally, speaking Standard with a thick accent, Taleish said, "I no be a understandin' ya."

Tessa repeated her question, this time speaking very slowly. He blinked and turned to Marnez. A brief conversation in Caldoni followed, then Taleish said, "I be in Lann Gheal five year."

After a few more aborted tries, Tessa gave up in frustration. Walking over to a sheltered spot near some purple shrubs, she flopped down and took out her pocket computator.

Marnez chuckled under her breath. "Taleish, you are such an amadan, asking me to translate. You knew exactly what she was saying."

"And, to be sure, I am a-knowin'," he agreed in a heavy brogue. "But I also know her type, and I don't want to be bothered with the likes o' her, don'tcha know."

"What are you babbling about?"

Taleish sighed. "Well, maybe you don't know, not having been born among the clans. She's an anthro." Seeing Marnez's uncomprehending look, he explained, "My family comes from a small village called Ar An Ra. It's deep in the Black Mountains; Unit Leader Kai's got kin up there too, I think. Anyway, mostly what's there is a lot of poor people doing some farming and herding their cattle and sheep.

"It's pretty backward by galactic standards, which is why we get a lot of the university anthro-types coming around. They want to study us like we were some kind of alien life form. That woman is one of them, and I'm not going to talk to her about Caldon and my kin."

Marnez studied the dark-haired woman and licked her lips in appreciation. "Well, you may be right about her being an anthro, but I'm glad you talked me into coming this morning. The sight of her is worth the boredom of watching Mr. Snoot and fat Miss Mousey collect plants."

Taleish chuckled. Marnez turned. He winked at her, and she gave him a wolfish grin in return. "Mmm, sweet, hmm?" Then he laid his hand familiarly on her well-muscled thigh. "Ah, but the pretty doctor is but a drab hen compared to such a beauty as your fair self."

Marnez snorted and shoved his hand off her leg. "You better leave me alone, boyo, or I'll get my woman to mop the barracks floor with you."

"But you don't have to tell her," he wheedled. "We could just—"

"*Poc mo hon.*"

"Ooo," he shivered dramatically. "I'd love to kiss your pretty ass, my love, and your tits and your beautiful—"

Marnez laughed. "Gods, Taleish, I don't know who is worse—you or McLaren. Always after me and Marti to show you our tits, or have a three-way party. Just forget it—you're not *man* enough for the job."

Taleish leaned over her, green eyes sparkling. "And how would you know that, my heart, till you try me, hmm?"

"Ahem." Singey stood scowling down at them, tapping his walking stick against his trouser leg. They scrambled to their feet.

"Yes, Sir?" Marnez said.

"I've finished here, so we'll be moving on."

"Shall we escort you back to camp now, Sir?"

"No. I've gotten all the data I can from up here, but I need a few more examples of the plant life to prove my hypothesis." He pointed over the edge of the cliff to the canyon below. "I want to get a few specimens of those reed-like plants growing at the bottom of the cliff there."

The armachda exchanged glances then Taleish said, "I'm afraid we can't allow that, Sir. Our orders—"

"I know what your orders are, Armachd Taleish. Your Commander has made his position very clear to me. But I need a few more samples, nonetheless."

His black-clad guards shook their heads. Singey sighed. "All right. Then let's go back to camp and get the hover-sled. You can fly me into the canyon from there—"

"I'm sorry, Sir, but we can't do that, either," Taleish said, cutting him off. "Armachd Ross said that the sled needed some repairs. He thinks those little rat-like creatures got into it last night. He was working on it when we left."

"Yes, those animals are a nuisance. They've been in the lab, too. You people will just have to be more careful."

As if speaking to an uncooperative servant, he said, "I'm just going down to the bottom of the cliff to collect a few specimens. I don't plan on wandering around and getting us lost, which is what your Commander is

afraid of. We'll just take the new samples and come right back up that trail."
He pointed to the cliff.

"We'll still have to report in and get permission, Sir," Marnez insisted.

"All right, do that." Singey tapped his stick impatiently while she
contacted the base through her implant. At last she turned back to him.
"Well."

"The Commander has gone up to the ship, Sir."

Singey sighed. "Look, you people have checked this area very
thoroughly, correct? You found nothing harmful, correct? What can
possibly happen to us, if we stay in sight of the cliff?"

Singey stalked off to pack his gear. Over his shoulder, he said, "You can
remain here or come with us. I'll explain to Commander Tizu when we get
back to the base, if you're worried about getting into trouble."

Taleish bent and picked up his beam rifle. "Come on. We'd better go
with him, just to make sure the fool doesn't take it into his head to go
wandering off and get lost."

"Taleish, are you crazy? The Commander will have us on report."

"Yeah, he will, but what choice do we have? The fool is going, with or
without us. And the Commander will also skin us alive if we don't go with
them, right?"

"Yeah—maybe, but—"

Taleish rounded on her, his expression grim. "Listen to me, my beauty,
this Dr. Bennett is a rich man, and this pompous arse here is his
friend—and also rich, I've heard. They could make a lot of trouble for the
Commander and the corps, if they wanted to.

"Mr. Snoot says, he only wants to go to the base of the cliff. So we
humor him and let him get his samples—then everybody's happy, right?"

"I guess so, but I still don't like it."

"Neither do I. Just tell base what we're going to do and get your rifle.
Look they've already started down."

Chapter Ten

Nathan set down his tray and flopped into an empty chair across from Dunnagh. "You look like shit."

"Thanks for the compliment, Mo Hara. I'm not surprised; I feel like shit. I haven't been getting much sleep lately."

"Is it those dreams again?"

Dunnagh sighed and rubbed a hand across his face. He was so tired. "I wish I could remember all of it when I wake up—"

"Big eels talking to you," Nathan snorted. "Too much duty time, and letting Taleish and Oglas pick horror vids for our rec-time entertainment—that's all that's wrong with you. They are just dreams. Don't you think, as your battle-bonded, I'd know if you were in danger?"

Feeling suddenly safe and protected, Dunnagh's lip twitched into a smile. "Yeah, you're right. You would. I'm sure of that."

"Damn right I would." Nathan sipped his tea, then changed the subject. "Uh—when is your friend coming down to the base?"

Startled, Dunnagh looked up from his meal. Nathan usually avoided speaking of Sairsa. Was he finally going to accept the inevitable? "She's supposed to come down later today—if her mother doesn't need her."

"Her stepfather have another heart attack? I notice he isn't with that bunch of politicos over there."

Dunnagh glanced at the boisterous table of dignitaries across the mess. "Not as far as I know. But he's still sick, and the ship's med center is so short staffed that Sairsa and her mother have been taking over most of his nursing."

Nathan went back to eating. Without looking at Dunnagh, he said, "You still plan on leaving and getting married after this mission?"

"Yes."

"How nice for you."

Maybe his friend wasn't quite as accepting as he'd hoped. Nathan refused to meet his eye, and went back to doggedly eating. Dunnagh picked up his fork, then changed his mind and put it down again. "We've been over this ground several times before. Damn it, why are you bringing this up again? I hate this, you know."

Nathan paused, fork halfway to his mouth. "Hate what?"

"You know perfectly well what I mean—I wish you would understand."

"Oh I understand, all right. You're being an ass. I understand that perfectly."

Dunnagh flushed and resumed eating before his temper got the best of him, and he said something he would regret. Maybe his secret fantasy about them marrying the women of their dreams and returning to teach at the academy was a nice fantasy, but that was all it was. When a new relationship promised to deepen into real love, Nathan always pulled back, and eventually the woman gave up and left him.

Losing all his family as a child probably did make it hard to trust, Dunnagh supposed, but damn it, Nathan wasn't even trying any more. He seemed to be content with casual affairs and whatever Dunnagh chose to share with him of his life.

Once their companionship had been enough for Dunnagh, too, but not now. "I am serious about marrying her, you know? Maybe you should try a little harder to hold on to a lover, because soon I won't be there for you when another affair goes up in flames."

Nathan flushed a deep crimson. Dropping his fork to his plate with a clang, he opened his mouth, then closed it, staring at something over Dunnagh's left shoulder.

Dunnagh turned and saw Rhys at his elbow. "Yes, Squad Leader?"

Rhys saluted both him and Nathan. "Commander Tizu wants to see you, Sirs." His eyes flicked to Dunnagh's unfinished plate. "Right now."

Swallowing down the last of his tea and a couple big mouthfuls of his meal, Dunnagh followed the two men out of the mess.

Once outside in the quadrangle, Dunnagh stopped. "All right, Rhys, what's the problem?" Dunnagh spoke in Caldoni to avoid being understood by a nearby group of refugees on their way into the mess.

Rhys glanced at the Dymarians, then, also speaking in Caldoni, he complained, "It's that damned Mr. Snoot—I mean Mr. Singey—sorry, Sir! This morning the Commander assigned Taleish and Marnez to guard the scientists when they left camp.

"But Marnez hasn't reported in since they went into the canyon. Commander Tizu wants us to go look for them."

"The canyon?" Nathan spluttered. "But I thought no one was—"

"No one *was supposed* to leave the mesa," Rhys agreed. "But the prick disobeyed Commander's orders and Marnez and Taleish let him."

"Stupid shits. They're dead meat once the Commander gets hold of them," Nathan grumbled. Rhys nodded, his expression solemn.

Singey again. Dunnagh resumed walking. He could feel his face burning just hearing the man's name. "The canyons? I haven't been down in them—why are you looking like that, Nathan? What's the matter?"

"Remember, I told you about our communications malfunctioning down in those washes? It would be easy to get lost in them—and stay lost for a long time. That's what's a matter!"

"The Commander thinks that too—" Rhys broke off as they reached the headquarters doorway. "I'll let him tell you the rest," he murmured as he opened the door and stepped back for them to enter.

Tizu sat, fingers drumming on the table in front of him, his swarthy features twisted into a mask of barely contained fury. He looked up as they entered and motioned them over. Dunnagh saluted. He'd learned to tread softly when his fiery commander was in such a temper.

"Rhys reported Dr. Singey and his party are missing, Sir."

"Yeah. While I was busy with Dr. Bennett and the Dymarians, the damned fool decides to take a stroll through the canyons, looking for lab specimens. With all that's been going on around here today, nobody remembered to tell me about it until a few minutes ago."

"Yes, Sir." Dunnagh glanced at Nathan; he was scowling as fiercely as Tizu was.

"So, Kai, congratulations. You get to go find them. Take some of the off-duty armachda with you and go bring them back. Rhys here can go with you as your tracker. I'd send you out in the hover-sled, but Armachd Ross reported that it's still malfunctioning.

"We have about six hours till dark. I want *everybody* back in camp by then. Safe and accounted for, understand?"

"Yes, Sir. Uh—what about data from the ship's satellite? Do you have directional coordinates you can give me? That would save—"

Before he could finish, Tizu shook his head. "No coordinates. The techs say there may be another vessel entering this sector. The instrument readings are a mess—unreliable. But as a safeguard the satellite's been disabled—temporarily. That's why someone with your Psy skills is needed for this mission."

Maybe there'd been something more to Dr. Bennett's insistence on the Cumarsaid than mere curiosity, as Dunnagh had assumed. Maybe they really had been followed. Dunnagh swallowed down the taste of bile and saluted. "I will do my best, Sir."

"You'd better," Tizu growled, "because I've also learned that a young society woman, someone Bennett is particularly fond of and worried about keeping safe, is with them."

Tizu made a face. "Scientists! I'd like to—damn it never mind. Singey couldn't have picked a worse time for this little stunt—and I'm going to string Marnez and Taleish up by their thumbs when I get hold of them. They'll be mopping out the latrines for a year—if I don't drown them in the bowls first."

"Yes, Sir."

Tizu grimaced then stood. "Any questions? No. Draw what you need from stores and get going then."

In the entrance Dunnagh paused, one last worry on his mind. "Commander, I hate to ask, but about my—uh—friend—"

"When she comes down on the next shuttle, I'll let her know you'll be back later. I'll see to her welfare, if need be. You just keep your mind on your assignment, Kai—got that?"

"Yes, Sir, I will, Sir, and thank you. We won't be long—don't worry."

DUNNAGH STOOD MOTIONLESS near the edge of the cliff, looking over the land spread out below him. With a deep breath, he slipped into the Cumarsaid trance...

Though he used all the power of his gift to search, he found no trace of the missing party. A Psy shield of immense power, or some natural phenomena peculiar to this world, was masking all Psy awareness of the canyons below. With such a strong interference, no wonder their technical communications equipment failed.

Coming out of trance, Dunnagh rubbed at his neck and loosened his collar. He'd never come across such a barrier before. Damn, he didn't want to go down there; he wanted to be back in camp with Sairsa. Dared he report his unease to base? No, they had to find the missing party, and he was the logical choice. He was the most experienced officer with the Psy on the entire Dymarian mission.

Not being born of the clans, Tizu's acceptance of Caldoni gifts only went so far. With Dunnagh's girlfriend expected any time, Tizu might see his reluctance to head this mission as just an excuse to spend time with her. He couldn't afford a bad report on his record—not if he wanted to teach at the academy once he returned home.

Singey, you arrogant prick. Feeling trapped, Dunnagh clenched his fist and swore softly. He'd have to descend into the canyon—there was no help for it. Putting his back to the scenery, he walked to where Nathan and Rhys squatted.

His eyes closed, Rhys's hand rested lightly on the ground in front of him. He'd slipped into a Cumarsaid to gain more information about the scuff marks he'd found. Dunnagh glanced at Nathan's impassive face, then crouched beside him.

At last, Rhys opened his eyes and said, "This is it." He pointed to the scratches. "These say they went down here. The slope's less of a challenge at this point than elsewhere."

Dunnagh stood up, peering over the edge. There was not a trail exactly, but definitely a way down for people burdened only with light equipment. If you were careful and took it slow, it could be done. "Chang."

"Sir?"

Still studying the terrain, Dunnagh said, "See if you can contact Marnez, armachd."

"Yes, Sir." Chang took a portable communications unit from his belt, and spoke into it. "Nothing, Sir."

"Put it away. We'll try again later."

Addressing the entire squad, Dunnagh said, "All right, we're going down. We don't know what's happened to Dr. Singey's party, so stay alert. We'll use the standard procedure for traveling in enemy terrain. Rhys, you take point. Oglas, you take rear guard with Marti."

"Unit Leader, someone else can take rear guard, let me—" Marti broke off when she looked into his eyes. A cinnamon-skinned woman, almost as tall and muscular as Dunnagh himself, her battle companion Marnez, was among the missing. Dunnagh would have liked to leave her in camp, but relented, knowing how he'd feel if Nathan was missing. But he also wasn't going to risk the mission on her impaired judgment. "No. Not this time, Marti."

AT THE BOTTOM OF THE cliff they found no sign of the scientists, but Rhys did discover an animal trail and some human footprints. They had obviously taken the trail, so Dunnagh motioned Rhys forward.

Moving around in the canyons *was* like being a rabbit caught in an unmowed hay field as Nathan had warned. They hadn't gone very far before the vegetation hemmed them in on all sides. The plants' central stems rose about nine feet into the purple sky, with slender brown leaves clustered around a central core. Near the base, their color changed to a pale blue, and gave off an acrid stench when slashed with the machetes.

In the close air, the odor was overpowering. Dunnagh found himself nauseated within the first few minutes. And the Gods alone knew what else was in these canyons with them. Off in the distance, he'd heard animals screeching a moment ago.

Chapter Eleven

Concealed by the tall brown reeds, four long-armed, wooly creatures of various ages, slithered on their bellies towards a nearby kavalpa thicket. Once safely inside the black-leafed tree's shelter, they stood on their short legs and moved to the parent tree's base. A small spring pooled near its arching roots. They laid aside their blowguns and lapped its blue liquid.

Thirst satisfied, they crouched in a circle to talk. "What did you see, eh?" Headman Talla said to the two young hunters.

"Oo More come, Talla," one answered.

"—got lots of pretties," the other interrupted, "Lot'a shiny things maybe."

The fourth creature, an older gray-pelted shaman, spoke then. "We can catch them, eh? Just like other ones. We'll take pretties, and magics."

Tala, grunted. "Maybe." He turned back to the hunters. "How many?"

The hunters glanced at one another. "Two or three, five, many."

Slap! "Stupid taba worms! I tell you to count!"

The young ones cringed, covering their heads against further blows. "What does it matter?" one whined. "They're stupid Umwira mutants, just like others we caught."

"They're not Umwira!" the other hunter said. "They're mans from out of the sky. My brother saw them come down in a big shiny boat that farted fire—"

"Oh, what does he know—he's stupid like you, smelly liru rat."

"My brother not stupid like me—he knows. You take that back, fart-breath, or—"

They fell upon each other, screaming, biting and kicking. With a roar, Talla sprang to his feet and waded into the fray. Roughly knocking them apart, he settled the dispute. He raised a large fist. They groveled. "Quiet. You're both stupid. DON'T MAKE NOISE!"

Thoroughly chastened, the two put their hands over their mouths, so no sound could escape.

"What are you going to do, Talla?" the shaman asked, focusing the headman's attention back on the problem under discussion.

Talla scratched the mound of his belly, thinking. At last he grunted to himself and said, "We'll take them and their pretties—just like other ones."

"And what will you do with starmans after we take pretties, hmm?"

Talla looked surprised; his heavy brow wrinkling in confusion. "I don't know. We could just leave them, and go away."

The old shaman made a rude noise. "No, that's not a good idea. Starmans might be angry if we take their pretties."

"Might hurt Begta with magics," one of the hunters chimed in.

The shaman glared murderously at the speaker. The young hunter groveled and covered his head.

"Could eat," the other hunter suggested hopefully.

Talla growled at another interruption, but the shaman raised a hand to halt his angry outburst. "Wait! We could take starmans to Gormach—let *Warlinga* eat starmans. Then maybe Warlinga will go away, and not eat poor, poor little Begta."

"Hmm." Talla scratched his belly again. "Gormach is a very bad Warlinga. Maybe he will take the meat, but not go away."

"Naw, Gormach won't do that." The old shaman raised his hand high over his head. "Starmans are very big, got lots good meat. When Gormach see them, he will want them." He lowered his hand to near the ground, "We are poor little, skinny Begta, eh? It is good plan.

"Maybe he will eat, or maybe he will sell them to Avairei priests for slaves." He snorted. "What does it matter? Starmans not hurt Begta if Gormach has them. Gormach will take them and go away, eh?"

Returning his attention to the hunters, Talla asked, "What are new starmans like? Can we catch them easy?"

The hunters looked at each other. "Maybe—"

"What do you mean, maybe?" The scout squirmed. Slap! "What do you mean, *maybe*?" the leader repeated, raising a fist in warning.

Cringing, one said, "Got a tracker, maybe got big magics—"

The old one jumped up. "Big magics, hah!" He thumped his chest. "I am Mighty Umwa; I got bigger-bigger magics. Starmans' magics are no good against Mighty Umwa's power. You'll see. I'll fix it."

"If old wind bladder got such big magics, how come he never make Gormach go away and stop eating Begta before now?" one of the hunters muttered under his breath.

His partner poked him sharply in the ribs. "Umwa is watching you," The first hunter clamped his hand over his mouth.

The shaman scowled; Talla looked indecisive. That would never do. Umwa's dream-mentor had told him the Warlinga must take the strangers to the Avairei at Sulas. It was very important. He added a final incentive. "With more pretties, Talla can buy a new wife, hmm?"

Talla grunted, and then slapped his thigh, decision made. "Yes, we catch them. We'll take all the shiny pretties and give the meat to the Warlinga." He pointed to the scouts. "Get rest of Begta. Set the trap. We'll wait here. Go!" Gurgling with excitement, the two picked up their blowguns and slipped out of the thicket.

Chapter Twelve

The weak sun of this world no longer shone into the canyon and Dunnagh was worried. It seemed like they'd been slashing their way through the undergrowth forever, and still there was no sign of the missing party. Damn Singey! Dunnagh was growing impatient. Sairsa was probably on the planet by now. Rich prick or no, if she had to go back to the ship before he got back he was going to beat the man to a pulp.

Then, Dunnagh noticed through the pain of a pounding headache that Rhys had stopped. When he came up to him, Rhys motioned him forward and pointed.

Cutting across the path they were on, at right angles was a new trail. This one appeared to have been made by something being dragged across the reeds, breaking them to form a rough path. Catching a bright spot of color out of the corner of his eye, Dunnagh crouched. At the base of a nearby broken plant was a drying red stain.

He reached out a gloved hand and touched the blot, then brought his finger to his nose. He sniffed, but the smell of the fluid was so mixed with the scent of the reed's own sap, he was unable to tell for sure what it was.

"Could be human blood, it's the right color," Rhys said, voicing his worst nightmare.

Dunnagh grunted and stepped past him into the new trail, looking both ways, searching for other clues. To the left the track twisted off into the undergrowth, disappearing quickly among the high stems. Not much help there. To the right, however, the path headed straight for another one of the black, willow-like tree thickets that stood out like tiny islands in the sea of waving brown reeds. He could just see the tree's silhouette nestled up against the canyon wall about a klick ahead.

Dunnagh reached out with his Psy, trying to discover the meaning of this new sign. But as before when he'd tried, there was nothing, only a thick, impenetrable blankness. He stepped back to Rhys's side. "Have you gotten anything through the Cumarsaid?"

His expression solemn, Rhys shook his head. "Nothing."

Dunnagh saw the worry in his armachd's brown eyes, and looked away before Rhys could see that it mirrored his own growing concern. This blocking of his Psy had never happened to him before. There was far more to this primitive world than they had assumed. Tizu needed to know about how the Caldoni "gift" didn't function here.

His uniform felt suddenly tight; Dunnagh rubbed absently at his neck. Creggan war ships or no, maybe they needed to find the fool scientists and get off this planet as soon as possible.

Motioning for the others to draw near, he said in a voice barely above a whisper, "Just ahead, Rhys has found another trail cutting across this one. It's been made by several heavy objects being dragged through the reeds, apparently heading for the black tree thicket over to our right."

He pointed towards the looming canyon wall. "On some of the broken plants, there are red stains that could be human blood."

"If it *is* human blood, we'd better follow it," Nathan said.

"I'm of the same opinion. My only question is do we all go, or do we split up. This is my first time down in these canyons. I'd like to hear from some of you who were on the original reconnaissance before I decide."

"I say we stay together and take the new track. This trail we've been on isn't showing much promise," Rhys said.

Nathan glanced over his shoulder at the new path. "I agree. This place is too dangerous for us to go off in different directions."

His freckled, boyish face wrinkled with a frown, Oglas said, "Maybe, but what if it's just an animal's track over there? We know the scientist's party took the trail we're on; it was right there when we came off the cliff.

"Some boot prints in the mud, hairs tangled on a plant leaf, there have been a few indications that they came this way. They have to be ahead of us, because there haven't been any branches off this path."

"Yeah, but even an asshole like Singey probably wouldn't have gone this far into the canyon. Not with our people along. They would have stopped him," Samuels said.

"Maybe not under their own power, but that doesn't mean they aren't still ahead of us down the trail we've been following," Marti said.

Dunnagh caught her eye and nodded. Marti had the "gift" too. Had she received a sending—did she know for certain? "What do you mean, Marti? Are you thinking they were captured by some intelligent beings?"

She shrugged. "Could be."

Golden-skinned, black-haired Chang glanced from one grim Caldoni face to the other. "But we checked down here and the instruments said—"

"The instruments told us shit!" Nathan said, his voice an angry snarl.

Dunnagh wiped the sweat from his forehead and took a drink from his water flask. His neck hurt—he could barely swallow—and his head was pounding like a drum. They needed to get out of here. Enough talk.

"All the suggestions have merit. We'll split up and follow both trails. If our people have been captured by some intelligent natives, this," he waved his hand vaguely at the cross-trail in front of them, "may have been left to throw us off the real path. Rhys, the Fe'an twins, Samuels, with me. Chang, Marti, Oglas, with Na—"

"Dunnagh," Nathan pleaded, "Give me Rhys and let me follow the new trail."

"All right, Nathan, take Rhys. But only follow the new sign as far as those trees. If you don't find anything, then return to the other trail. We'll continue on down the path we've been following about a click, then halt and wait for you to join us. If you *do* find them, or have trouble, fire off a shot and we'll come back. Understood?"

"Understood." Nathan slipped his beam rifle off his shoulder, checked the setting, and then looked at his armachda. "You ready?"

Marti looked up from checking her own gear, and gave him a grim nod. "Ready."

Chapter Thirteen

<<Nathan, report! What's happening? Where are you?>> Dunnagh focused the full power of his Psy on the etheric fog engulfing them, but couldn't free himself from its cottony folds. He knew Nathan was alive and moving somewhere among the tall reeds, but he couldn't make contact. Nathan's gift wasn't strong, but surely he would be straining to communicate with him as well.

Swallowing down his frustration, he took in a deep breath and let go of the Psy. To either side of the game trail they'd been following, his squad crouched, alert, expressions fierce, awaiting his orders. The light was fading. What could possibly be keeping Nathan? He'd had plenty of time to make it to the trees and rejoin them.

Suddenly, a beam rifle's blast shattered the silence, bringing the resting armachda to their feet. Holding up a hand, Dunnagh listened, but the reeds distorted the sound. The shot seemed to have come from in front of them. Which was crazy, because the thicket where he'd sent Nathan, was to the right and behind his present position—he was sure.

Then, he heard another shot—and another. That was no signal; it sounded like a small war. Dunnagh shouted for his squad to follow, and pelted back down the trail the way they'd come.

Out of the corner of his eye, he saw an indistinct, fur-covered body with a spear, rise up from the reeds just ahead of him. Without slowing his pace, Dunnagh brought his rifle up and fired. The creature screamed and doubled over.

Dunnagh discharged a second beam into the body as he passed, then fired again as another dark form rose out of the reeds. He heard the sounds of more gunfire, and their attackers' shrieks. Damn, it was impossible to tell how many of the natives were hiding in the vegetation.

Heart pounding, Dunnagh glanced over his shoulder to check the positions of his remaining armachda. Keeping together in close formation they were right behind him with the blond Fe'an twins at his back. Steady and dependable no matter what the situation called for, he breathed a little easier and pressed on. What had happened—where was Nathan?

Then, there was no more time to wonder. The natives were mobbing them. They popped up out of the brush with ear piercing shrieks, charging from all directions. Without stopping to aim, Dunnagh fired. The nearest creature dove headfirst into the reeds.

Missed. Dunnagh swore and brought the muzzle of the rifle to bear on a furry body carrying a club, as it pushed its way through the reeds towards him.

As his rifle discharged, something struck his cheek. It felt like a bee-sting, sharp and burning. He slapped at it with his free hand. Then, he was falling, crashing down heavily onto the trail.

Dunnagh tried desperately to get up, but he couldn't move. Terrified, he strained, but his body wouldn't obey the slightest command. He could still breathe and blink his eyes—thank the gods—but he was as helpless as a newborn, and totally at the mercy of his attackers. All his larger, voluntary muscles were now paralyzed.

He'd fallen in a heap; there was nothing in his line of sight but the reeds. He could hear crashing in the underbrush, and there was a lot of unintelligible shouting going on, but he heard no more rifle fire. That was a bad sign. In spite of the paralysis, his mind was completely clear.

Maybe the drug's effects wouldn't last too long.

Who were these savages—where had they come from? The Spirit had promised they'd be safe—and the corps teks claimed they'd checked the entire southern continent. They swore there was no evidence of intelligent life anywhere on this world.

Out of the corner of his eye, he saw two squat figures dragging one of the armachda, Moraga Fe'an maybe, like a heavy sack, down the trail to lie near him. Shortly after that, one of the creatures rolled him over onto his back and stuck its furry visage right into his face.

It grinned, displaying impressive fangs and gibbered something at him. With strong, four-fingered hands, it rummaged through his clothes.

Reaching into his tunic, it pulled out his clan medallion and his ID tags. The creature gurgled happily. With a quick tug, it snapped the chain free from around his neck. Dunnagh's head jerked up and fell back with a hard thud.

The beast sat back on its haunches and examined its prize, chortling to itself. Another of its companions noticed the booty, and approached. They babbled at each other, their voices growing louder with each exchange. Finally, the second one grabbed the coveted objects out of Dunnagh's captor's hand.

With a loud screech of outrage, the original possessor of the tags, dove for them. Growling and snapping, the two rolled around and over Dunnagh's limp body as they fought for possession of the shiny trinkets.

He grunted as one of the combatants fell across his chest, then gasped as a poorly aimed clawed hind foot missed its mark and drew blood in a long gash down his leg. If he hadn't been wearing light body armor on his torso, they could have disemboweled him without even being aware of it. He felt panic bubbling up, then he controlled it, as the sheer ridiculousness of the picture hit him.

What a way to go. A farce not a hero's ballad would be his final story. Would Grandpa Kai be amused when next they met? How would he explain this one in the Halls of the Dead?

The fight caught the attention of a third and larger creature—a leader of some sort, Dunnagh later decided. It rushed over with a roar, picked up the two combatants, one in each large fist, banged their heads together then threw them to opposite sides of the trail. The two whined and slunk away under the leader's angry tirade. Then the leader claimed the disputed ID tags for his own.

Though it was hard to tell from his present supine position, Dunnagh guessed this male might stand about waist-high or a little more if he were upright. The creature had a thick coat of brown, wool, long arms, and stubby legs with clawed feet. His head was round with no visible outer ears. The eyes were a feral yellow, set deep within heavy brow ridges. The nose was high, with flaring nostrils, the jaw heavy and jutting forward. Pouches and primitive weapons dangled from a woven belt around his ample middle.

The native picked up a long tube from the ground. A blowgun dart, that's what had hit him. How had they missed these creatures in their initial reconnaissance? Oh, Nathan, how? Desperately he reached out with the Psy, trying to make contact with his battle companion... Nothing.

Feeling his panic taking over again, Dunnagh forced himself to repeat the calming battle readiness prayer until he was under control. There was some alien force blocking his attempt that was all. It had been happening all afternoon when he'd tried to contact someone on the base. Nathan wasn't dead, he told himself sternly. If his friend was, he'd know it, no matter what the natives did to them.

He hoped that at least some of the armachda had gotten away. The savages were good, and this was their home ground. But Lann Gheal armachda were trained professionals and good at this type of warfare, too. Somebody must have made it out of the trap. Dunnagh desperately wished there was some way he could warn Tizu. The Commander must be frantic.

Oh, Sairsa, my love, will I ever see you again? More to the point, will I ever be able to move again, or is this paralysis permanent?

Before he could drift down that morbid pathway too far, the leader of the natives shouted a series of guttural orders. Two of the hairy creatures grabbed him and began half dragging, half carrying him down the trail.

Chapter Fourteen

It was full dark when Dunnagh, his squad and their captors, reached the shelter of another tree thicket. Stripped of gear, and clothing, the humans were then deposited against the arching roots of the central tree.

Careless of his comfort, the savages tossed Dunnagh down along with the rest like so much firewood. Dunnagh couldn't tell in the darkness how many of his people lay around him. Being one of the last to be brought in, he had been dropped on his side at the edge of the pile.

Under him someone grunted. He felt so helpless; he couldn't move, couldn't even offer an apology for the obvious pain he had caused, and might still be causing the person trapped under him.

The scene about him was straight out of a nightmare, the shadowed tree with its drooping, willow-like branches, and the savages, shouting and gesticulating like short hairy demons, gathered about the green flames of a large fire. Occasionally someone knelt at the spring near the tree's arching roots and drank the bubbling liquid.

A few of the boldest plucked and ate some of the large purple fungi, growing near his head. Seeing this made Dunnagh painfully aware of his own thirst and hunger. The mushrooms didn't look appetizing, but a drink of water, on the other hand, would taste very good about then.

Their captors seemed oblivious to the drugged and paralyzed humans' welfare and ignored them. And later, when he realized what "dinner" was going to be, he decided he was just as happy to skip it.

It was difficult to clearly see the activity on the far side of the thicket, but the stench of fresh gore, alerted him to the meal's preparations. They were butchering all right, but it was their own dead they planned on eating, not any game.

Over the men's shouts he could hear the women's high-pitched keening. Their grief seemed real enough, but in spite of that, he saw the carcasses being roasted. The savages were feasting on the bodies of the dead, even as they mourned them.

Dunnagh knew he had accounted for at least two of the fallen tribesmen. How many had been killed by others in his squad? And, more to the point, what type of vengeance might he and his armachda expect from these people for those deaths? Natives who cannibalized their own dead were capable of anything, he reasoned.

Sometime later, his view of the feast was interrupted when someone pulled him off his trapped companion. Not a tribesman, but Singey peered down at him—a very battered Dr. Singey. The scientist's right eye was closed completely by a dark purple swelling. On his left cheek, there was a long cut oozing blood that ran from near his eye to his chin.

Seeing the scientist's injuries, Dunnagh suddenly felt grateful for the numbing effect of the drug he had been given. When it wore off—if it wore off, and if he was as battered as Singey, his body was going to hurt—and hurt bad.

As if divining his greatest fear, Singey said, "You'll be all right in a while. The drug they shot us with doesn't cause permanent paralysis.

"If they don't give you another dose, the effects should start to wear off near morning."

Well, that's a relief, Dunnagh thought. *Then maybe we can get out of here—*

"You'll be weak and pretty shaky, though. I still can't stand."

That isn't so good. Dunnagh's hopes for a quick escape shattered.

"I can see all the questions in your eyes that you want to ask me and can't. Questions like: What happened? Why did I disobey orders and come down here in the first place?"

Singey's face contorted into a gargoyle like grin. "Will those do for starters?" He let out a bark of mirthless laughter. "See, I know them because I've been asking myself those same questions for hours now. Believe me, Kai, you couldn't say or accuse me of anything that I haven't thought of myself."

I bet I could, asshole. Then he chided himself for his lack of charity. The pampered Mr. Snoot looked a mess. It would be better to put aside blame and work together to get out of this mess as quickly as possible. But later, when they were back on the base, he and Mr. Singey were going to have a "little talk."

The scientist was saying, "... Yes, I know I disobeyed orders—and I left your armachda no choice but to follow. Your Commander said there was nothing dangerous on this world. We only planned to take a few plant samples from the growths right at the base of the cliff. But the little savages were waiting for us.

"They were hiding in the reeds. We never knew they were there, until it was too late. I think they must have been watching us for days, hoping for just such an opportunity.

"After we were down and helpless, they stripped us and divided up our things. Then they dragged us underground. Just before you came, they brought us here. Apparently there is a maze of tunnels that connect to various parts of these canyons. That's how these people get around normally, I think. They seem to go outside into the reeds only when they're hunting or food gathering."

Tunnels. That explained a lot. The teks had picked up something on the infrared equipment, but had wrongly assumed what they saw were harmless burrowing animals.

Did we leave our brains back on Dymar? And with that thought came a ripple of unease within his Psy.

He now realized that both trails through the undergrowth were part of a clever trap. The first was the lure to insure Dunnagh's squad went deeper into the canyon. The second trail they found, was deliberately planted to split them up, thus making their capture easier to achieve. It was an operation that earned his grudging, respect.

When he saw he had Dunnagh's attention again, Singey said, "I must go soon, before they discover I can move. But I'll leave you with one last bit of news that may prove our saving. With us was a Dr. Tessa Farris. Her field of study is primitive cultures.

"Tessa has a language implant. The savages seem to be fascinated with anything shiny. I suspect metals are rare on this world. So we are hoping that if we can talk to them soon, and offer some trinkets from camp, we may be able to ransom ourselves."

If they don't kill us, either by accident or design, first, Dunnagh thought bitterly.

Singey groaned and began to crawl away. "I'm sorry; the cramps have returned. I have to go and lie down now."

Damn, Singey, don't leave me yet. I need to know—tell me about Nathan, and the rest of my squad. Unable to speak, no matter how hard he strained, Dunnagh tried using his Psy to ask Singey his questions, but the man's mind was focused totally upon his own misery and remained oblivious to Dunnagh's urgent sending.

As Singey left him, Dunnagh heard a shout and two of the woolly tribesmen rushed over to them, brandishing bone knives.

Singey raised a hand, protesting weakly. "Please no; I'm not trying to escape—where would I go? Please, don't—"

The natives gibbered at him and one of them kicked him with a clawed foot. Singey groaned and curled into a ball, trembling. "I meant no harm. I was just—"

Save your breath, Dunnagh thought. *They aren't listening.*

The commotion was attracting a crowd. A third creature, the fat leader he'd seen before, listened to the gesticulating tribesmen. He yelled and shook a meaty fist at the cringing Singey, then taking out his bone knife, he cut a gash into the scientist's arm.

Singey evidently knew what was about to happen, because he cried out and tried to pull away. The native motioned for one of his men to hold on to him, while he withdrew a clay jar from one of his belt pouches and rubbed a thick brown paste into the wound with a flat stick. Within moments, Singey lay limp, his body once more overcome by the drug.

The leader started to put his jar away, then changed his mind. Coming over to Dunnagh, he peered down into his face, studying him carefully. Dunnagh stared back into the leader's feral yellow eyes with all the defiance he could muster.

The creature's brow ridges wrinkled and he made a low guttural sound in his throat. Without warning, he kicked at Dunnagh's side. When Dunnagh made no physical response, the native smiled, showing his lethal fangs. Turning his back on Dunnagh he shouted something to his men and went back to the group by the fire.

Dunnagh wished he'd been able to communicate in some way with Singey before the natives spotted him and drugged him once more. There were so many things he needed to know and the frustration was worse than an itch he couldn't scratch.

Singey was a trained scientist. His observations would be valuable. Their lives in future might depend on what Dunnagh knew about the savages and their situation. And, Dunnagh had to grudgingly admit, the scientist had courage to risk being discovered and seek him out to tell him the little he had.

Now that he had been moved, Dunnagh's view of his surroundings was limited to the flickering shadows among the branches overhead. With nothing to distract him, the fear was claiming his reason again.

Oh, Nathan, where are you? Forcing himself to master his fears, his mind automatically slipped into the discipline of the Cumarsaid. He needed to talk to Nathan—find out what had happened. And, back at the base there were other clan members who were also practitioners of Caldoni Mysteries. Maybe he could contact one of them and relay their situation. Tizu was probably worried enough to have the whole company on alert by now.

Dunnagh sent out the call, and this time—wonder of wonders—a groggy Nathan answered. A thousand questions tumbling over one another in his head, he babbled, <<Nathan, are you all right—where are you—what happened?>>

<<All right?>> A mental laugh.<<Now that's an intelligent question. Stripped naked, bloody, and stiff as a board, what do you think? I'm behind you by the tree. I heard Dr. Singey talking to you, but couldn't see him.>>

Relieved to know his battle companion was near, Dunnagh mentally chuckled. <<Yeah, that wasn't the smartest question I ever asked, I'll admit—but never mind that. What happened?>>

<<Ambushed. Same as you I guess.>>

<<How about the rest of the patrol?>>

<<They're here too. Nobody killed that I know of just battered up.>>

In a way that eased his mind, but Nathan's words also dashed any hope of someone making it out of the canyon to alert Commander Tizu.

<<Has anyone been able to contact Owen or one of the other Psy trained Armachda back at the base?>>

As Nathan was projecting an answer, a wave of angry Psy slammed into Dunnagh's mind, beating him down like a blow from a giant hammer, knocking him out of the trance.

Then from across the clearing an old gray-furred creature shrieked and came rushing over, waving a long bone in Dunnagh's face. The bone was decorated with dangling charms at one end, and the savage kept shaking them and shouting at him.

Dunnagh blinked, unsure what to make of this new development. Once again the mental assault came, but this time Dunnagh was prepared and threw up a hasty shield.

<<So you're the one that's been blocking me, you little shit. Well, let's see how you like a bit of your own in return.>> Dunnagh lashed out with a bolt of angry energy, enveloping the furry savage in a halo of crimson Psy.

The creature's yellow eyes bugged wide in surprise, as he absorbed the full thrust of Dunnagh's blow. He let out a tremendous roar and began pelting Dunnagh with a barrage of searing energy. Dunnagh's defiance seemed to have enraged the savage beyond reason.

The woolly, gray-pelted creature jumped up and down screeching. Spittle dripped from his open mouth as wave after wave of etheric energy crashed into Dunnagh's barrier, leaving him breathless.

He sensed Nathan offering to let him borrow his Psy, but in their battered and drugged condition, neither was strong enough to overpower the native. Unable to regain the offensive, Dunnagh with Nathan's help, sent off one last burst, then retreated behind his shield as he sensed another powerful wave of Psy surging towards him.

Dunnagh held up under the bombardment; the old fellow failed to breach his defenses, but the savage never allowed him an opening to resume his assault either.

Recognizing the futility of his Psy attack at last, the old savage next began physically beating Dunnagh with his bone wand. Mercifully, Dunnagh couldn't feel the blows, but he was helpless under the onslaught. Eventually, someone by the fire noticed and came over and dragged the enraged old fellow away, much to Dunnagh's relief.

Mentally and physically exhausted, Dunnagh slipped into unconsciousness, all thoughts of contacting the base forgotten.

Chapter Fifteen

Dunnagh's spirit body drifted restlessly within the dream. He needed guidance—someone to help him and his men out of the trap ensnaring them in the Waking World. As he searched for answers, a glowing ball of opalescent light suddenly appeared before him.

<<Why have you been so long in coming, Chosen,>> the voice within the orb chided.

<<Was I supposed to be somewhere? And why do you call me Chosen, spirit?>>

The glowing orb brightened with impatience. <<You ask too many questions to which you already know the answers. Come, I have been sent to guide you; the Makers await us.>>

Maker. That was a word with a disturbing association. But before he could puzzle it out, he sensed massive eel-like beings, swimming through the void to meet him. Their presence sent an icy spear of dread through his being. Without stopping to think, he erected a glowing magical shield.

<<Why do you resist them, Chosen?>> the spirit said. <<The Transformation will be much harder on you, if you aren't prepared. Let them come to you, and teach you.>>

Transformation. The spirit's words burst apart an unconscious barrier, flooding his mind with a torrent of memory that up to then had been kept hidden. <<No. I can't—liars, they are evil—I'll be no creature's slave.>>

<<Evil? Slave? You speak nonsense. But have a care that you do not create what you fear most. You have sworn an oath; the service is owing. Master your fear.>>

<<They tricked me.>> Then to the encircling pod of sinuous, gray forms, <<Do you hear me? I won't be your slave—never!>>

Suddenly a collar of etheric silver materialized around his neck, blazing like a new sun. Dunnagh cried out, falling to his knees and clutching at his neck.

Then, in the next moment he was on his feet and molding a spear out of etheric fiber. <<I WILL BE NO CREATURE'S SLAVE! I owe you nothing. You ugly worms tricked me.>>

His terror manifesting a life of its own. A giant wolf with angry yellow eyes and gaping jaws materialized as guardian in front of his shielded spirit. It stood stiff legged, head high, nostrils flared. It howled, challenging the enemy to come forward and fight.

No escape. The Khutani now encircled him in an ever-tightening coil. Ribbons of blue-white fire streamed along their sinuous backs. The ether stank of burnt copper and river weed.<<No one has tricked you, Caldoni. You gave us your Warrior's Oath. Lower your shield. Let us come to you and teach you.>>

<<Teach me? Hah! You said you were a people in need—>>

<<And we are in need. What we told you was true,>> the deep-voiced one snarled.

<<I thought you wanted to hire Lann Gheal for a contract.>> Dunnagh barked a harsh laugh. <<But no, that wasn't what you wanted, you want to own me—me, body and soul. Well you can't I won't let you!>>

<<It has cost us much to seek you out among the worlds of the Starry River and we have invested a great deal of our power in rescuing your people from their enemies. But instead of thanking us and keeping your word, you ignore our sendings so that we must employ other agents to find you, and force your compliance.>>

<<Enough of this,>> the deep-voiced one said. <<You will come to us for a kashallan bonding as you promised or suffer the consequences.>>

<<We expected better of you, Caldoni,>> another Maker chided.

Banishing the wolf with a flick of its power, the one calling itself Maker Gladdris, separated from the encircling mass and coiled loosely around the edges of his shield. Its mouth tentacles played over the barrier.

<<What is wrong, chosen? Of all the sentient beings of the universe, you and your people are blessed to us.>>

<<Blessed?>> Dunnagh projected his disgust and impatience with such drivel. <<If I am so *blessed*, then why have you put this collar about my neck? I gave you my word—there was no need—>>

<<The collar is only a loose tether, foolish human. It is meant for your protection as well as your discipline,>> an ancient said.

<<Protect me from what? All I need is protection from *you*.>>

<<You speak like a spoiled child, not a warrior,>> a Maker in the circling pod said. <<We protect you—from the Umwira—>>

<<I don't care about any Umwira, whatever, or whoever that is. Release me. I'll take my chances with the *Umwira*.>>

<<You don't know them as we do. The Hated Enemy is very dangerous—especially to you,>> Gladdris said. <<Though it has been centuries since we defeated them, the Umwira have great power even now. If the enemy were to learn of our conjuring—our bargain with you—if they knew of your arrival on our world, you and all of your people would be in great danger.>>

<<With all our technology? You're talking nonsense. We can take care of ourselves.>>

Gladdris stared at him unblinking, but made no move to uncoil itself. <<Can you, foolish child? Should we lower the shield that even now veils your vessel from the pursuing hunters? Should we do that; let you take care of yourselves? Will your people survive? I think not, and we both know I speak truth.>>

Infuriated to admit it—even to himself, Dunnagh feared the Maker might be right. Overcrowded and crippled, they would be an easy target if discovered by the war ships hunting them.

But could these Makers possess Psy so powerful? Or were they toying with him, playing on his fears until he did what they wanted?

<<Let me go. We have nothing to talk about.>>

<<You must listen first.>>

Tired of arguing pointlessly, Dunnagh used his Psy for a mental assault. The shock of the Khutani's block seared his mind as if he'd just touched live circuitry with his unprotected hand. Dunnagh screamed.

Thoroughly shaken, and with shield gone, Dunnagh sprawled moaning. Gladdris nuzzled him, making soothing rumbles deep in its throat.<<Chosen, calm yourself.>> The Khutani brushed a tentacle as lightly as a caress across his cheek.

<<Why do you continue to defy us? Do you really *want* to swallow your dreams and go home? You and your brother-friend are needed on this world. You won't have to leave him, or the female you have chosen for your mate now that you are here. Have you considered that? This too we have done for you—as a compensation for the sacrifice we have asked of you—and you have sworn to grant us.>>

How did they know about Nathan and Sairsa? What had they done to him in the Dream-Time? Had he really told these Makers so much about himself as they claimed? But if what the Makers said was true and their power had somehow rescued Bennett's ship, he and the rest of the humans *did indeed* owe them a great debt.

Then a tendril of doubt wormed its way into his thoughts. Had the Makers rescued them? Or had they caused the ship to be attacked? And against all odds, how *had* the ship's crew managed to find this world in the first place?

True, they had desperately needed a hideaway where Bennett's overcrowded ship could be unloaded while the crew repaired the damage done running the blockade. But if the rumor he'd heard was true, they hadn't needed to search very long, because, ta-da! There it was, appearing like magic on the view screen, an uninhabited planet with a breathable atmosphere.

No one had questioned their good fortune at the time. Dunnagh supposed their situation had been desperate, but that didn't explain a sloppy reconnaissance, technical equipment not functioning properly, and the failure of Caldoni Psy, once they'd safely arrived at this sweet little sanctuary. So many strange occurrences—so many slip ups—it was unnatural. They were professionals, damn it. Lann Gheal didn't make these many stupid mistakes—ever!

Dunnagh's aura shimmered with the turmoil of his thoughts. This new revelation hit him like an axe blow. At last forcing his mind into stillness, he looked the Maker in the eye, and said, <<Answer one question for me; if you want my help. Did you cause the Creggan warship to find and attack us? Did you bring us here with some alien power?>>

Gladdris returned the stare; its mind shielded from Dunnagh's probe. After a long pause the Khutani said, <<Does this matter now? You have come to Timorna. Your people's wandering has ended. You will never leave this world.>>

Never leave! <<No, not true! Damn you what have you done to me and my people?>>

<<What have you done to yourself,>> the deep-voiced one growled. <<Gladdris, stop coddling him. He is toying with us.>>

Mustering all his Psy, Dunnagh screamed his defiance. Then he was falling, tumbling into blackness.

Interlude

The glowing waters of a hidden underground pool, illuminated the Makers' bodies coiled together in a loosely tangled knot. All were present. They could begin the communion.

<<We are of one mind,>> the oldest and most powerful among them, intoned.

<<We are of one mind and one purpose,>> the others chorused.

<So it has been and so must it always be,> Qwaltamis concluded.

<<It is a pity our Dream-Chosen has proved so obstinate. What says our agent among the Begta?>> a Maker asked.

<<The shaman will do all that is required of him,>> Gladdris announced. He will obey in spite of the cost to his people. The aliens will be brought to us.>>

Then, spitting out the sour taste of its worry for all to savor, Gladdris said, <<That is good, but what of the others left on the mesa? They cannot be allowed to leave our world. We will need them in future.>>

<<True, cousin, and most of the aliens are now upon the surface.>> Qwaltamis said. <<They will be safe enough—for a time. But you should also know that in your brief absence to contact the Begta, the pod thought it best to remove the shield protecting their ship.>>

Gladdris froze. <<Was that wise?>>

<<The shield was too draining to maintain much longer,>> another explained. <<We can better use the power to protect those already here.>>

It was unfortunate for those still aboard the alien craft, but yes, Gladdris could taste the wisdom in the pod's decision. Leaving the shield in place was nearly as dangerous for the humans as banishing it. There were vile magics being conjured in the Ghostlands. And the Umwira wizards were clever at hiding from Khutani scrying.

<<Yes, cousin, all of us savor the taste of your concern,>> Qwaltamis said. The knot of bodies writhed with their collective emotion.

<<The Avairei, I fear, are proving untrustworthy,>> a Maker said, changing the subject.<<But we may have to rely on some of them when the new host is brought to a pool for the bonding.>>

<<I have already considered that,>> Qwaltamis assured its peers. <<I'm confident that at least some among them are true to their breeding and will obey our summons. Now that the Dream-Chosen is among us, we will instruct them to bring the Chosen to us.>>

<<So it will be,>> the others intoned as they twisted and spun themselves ever tighter in a whirling ball. <<We are of one mind in the power.>>

<<We are of one purpose in the power,>> Gladdris repeated along with the others. *And may the Gods pity and protect the one chosen,* it thought privately, as it merged in the conjuring with its kindred.

Chapter Sixteen

Tizu shoved open the door to HQ, his mouth set in a stubborn line. Right behind him, Bennett entered and closed the door quietly. As if continuing an ongoing discussion, the doctor said, "Commander, can't you think of anything else we can do? Surely—"

Tizu rounded on the man, fists clenched. Then, taking a deep, calming breath, he said, "Look, doctor, I've told you before; I've got my best people out looking for your colleagues. That's all I can do until it's light. Dr. Singey disobeyed a direct order from me. Unit Leader Kai has our best tracker with him. The squad I sent after them is made up of experienced professionals.

"I could sound the alarm and send half my force to go mucking about in the dark, but you yourself said, if we did that, it might start a panic among the refugees. And, 'we don't want to upset the Dymarians unnecessarily, right?'" Tizu folded his arms across his chest. "So just exactly *what* do you want me to do?"

Dr. Bennett sighed, sat on a nearby chair and rubbed a hand through his graying hair. "I'm sorry, Commander Tizu. Of course you know your job, and I'm just interfering, but—" His voice trailed off and he sighed again.

Tizu grunted and sat on the corner of his worktable, eyes flicking around the room. Goronwy was bent over the com-unit, pretending to be engrossed in his duties. Over in a shadowed corner, he noticed Dunnagh's fiancé. Tizu's eyes widened and he gave Goronwy a murderous scowl. He opened his mouth to order her out, then decided against it. She seemed sensible enough. As long as she stayed quiet and out of the way—why not let her be? She'd be as worried and anxious for news as he was.

"The waiting is hard on everybody, doctor," he said instead. "But right now there's not much else I can do, but wait."

WITH ONE HAND CLUTCHED tightly around the magical charms each wore, several woolly natives crept towards the starmans' camp. The old shaman told them they would be invisible when he gave them the talismans, but their natural hunter's caution warned them to be careful nonetheless.

Nearing their objective, they flattened themselves under the thorn shrubs and peered into the lighted clearing. There were so many curiosities to explore here, so many pretties! But tonight there seemed to be more of the tall aliens moving about than they'd seen on earlier raids into this fascinating new place.

With an impatient jerk of his head, the youngest hunter whispered, "Let's go get pretties now, eh?"

"We wait," the leader growled.

"But Talla didn't share starmans' pretties," the young one protested. "He kept all best pretties for himself. I want pretties, too."

He started to rise, but a muscular arm snaked out and shoved him roughly to the ground. The young Begta clamped a hand over his mouth to stifle a cry. "Quiet, taba worm. We won't get pretties if starmans catch us, eh? I say we wait."

Night deepened while they continued to observe the camp, but the activity didn't diminish. "Starmans aren't going to sleep, maybe there won't be any pretties tonight. We might have to come back later," one of the hunters said.

"Maybe," the leader agreed.

"No, I want pretties now," the young one said. "Old shaman said his magics would make us invisible. Starmans don't need to go sleep; we can get pretties."

"Maybe."

"When I came here with Talla, we found a place not in camp, that had a lot of pretties," another hunter said. "I will show you. We can get many pretties there, too."

The leader grunted. "You show."

Silently, the little thieves crept to a shadowed place between two buildings. A long, sleek thing stood silently in the moss. It was dark and lustrous, and gave off a faint metallic luminescence in the dim light.

"Oo, pretty," the leader breathed, running his hands in admiration over the thing's smooth surface. "Pretty!" He bent down and tried to lift it. He strained with all his considerable strength but couldn't budge it.

He turned on his companion and gave him a hard thump on the top of the head. "Stupid taba worm, this pretty is too big!"

Rubbing his head, the hunter backed out of reach. "We don't take big pretty," he whined. "Big pretty, got little pretties inside. We take 'em."

"Show."

The hunter climbed up on the thing's hard skin, pressed something, and the entire top of the object popped open. Waving to his companions, the Begta disappeared inside. Grinning broadly, the leader, followed by the rest of his kinsmen, climbed in after him.

Oh, there were pretties—so many bright, shiny pretties in many shapes and sizes. The hunters pried loose whatever pleased them and stuffed their finds into the empty pouches at their waists, gurgling with excitement. And, the nice Starmans had even left them some hard, shiny tools to help them obtain more of their coveted plunder. Greedy for the treasures this alien device contained, they forgot to be quiet.

So engrossed were they in their scavenging, they didn't hear the approach of three of the big strangers until it was almost too late. Screeching in terror, the leader and his men leaped out of the big shiny pretty and raced for the edge of the mesa.

The young one, tucking one last pretty into his pouch, found that he had waited too long. When he tried to run after the others, he was jerked roughly to a halt by a large starmans who grabbed him and held on till the other starmans could help imprison him.

TIZU WISHED HE COULD go to sleep, but the pain in his gut wouldn't let him. They had dimmed the light, but no one in HQ felt like talking. Armachda on duty came in to make reports, then left. Bennett sat half dozing over a cold cup of tea. Dunnagh's fiancé was still huddled in the corner. Someone had brought her a blanket. She'd wrapped it around herself and her eyes were closed, but Tizu doubted if she was sleeping.

He wished the hours would speed by till dawn, when they could be up and doing something. Doing anything would be better than this damned waiting. Where was that fool Kai anyway?

Damn the man? Shit, why was he getting mad at Dunnagh? The Caldoni was a good second-in-command, and he'd be damned sorry to lose him—if, God forbid, something had happened to him and his squad.

Suddenly the door to HQ banged open. "Commander, quick," an armachd cried.

Bennett jumped up, knocking over his chair. Tizu remained where he was. "Calm down, Owyn, and tell me what's going on. Has Kai come back?"

Owyn shook his head. "No, Sir, but we surprised some natives inside the hover-sled. We grabbed one of them, but the rest got away." With an oath, Tizu pushed past Owyn in the doorway and raced across the quadrangle.

By the time Bennett caught up to him, Tizu was scowling down at a brown-furred creature, being held by one of the largest of the Lann Gheal men. He was whimpering piteously, his yellow eyes round with terror.

Eyeing the creature's bulging belt pouches, Tizu suddenly realized that it wasn't the rat-like creatures that were getting into their gear, but these furry savages. "Owyn, check those bags the little thief has on his belt. I want to know what he's got in them."

By this time, the activity in the quadrangle had attracted a small crowd of onlookers. Tizu's scowl deepened when he noticed the Dymarian Councilor's aide, Sadrew, among them.

The native whined in protest as Owyn cut off one of the fiber pouches from his belt. Opening the bag, Owyn poured out into his hand a twisted assortment of parts that could only have come from inside the sled.

Tizu swore, and rounded on another black-clad figure hovering nearby. "Ross, go check out the sled. See how bad the damage is."

A cadaverous man in well-tailored clothing, Sadrew looked down his long nose at the whimpering savage. "Commander Tizu, I thought you told us this planet was safe. No harmful life forms, no dangers. I understand that some members of our party are missing, and now this 'beast' comes into our camp, right under your men's noses and does no telling what kind of mischief." The aide folded his arms across his bony chest and looked stern. "Well, what have you to say for yourself, Sir?"

Tizu glared right back; he had clashed with the Councilor's aide before, while they were still on Dymar. Sadrew had a high opinion of himself and his position in the Dymarian government, and he made sure everyone knew it. He'd been a thorn in Tizu's side ever since the evacuation started.

Highly critical of the Caldoni corps, Sadrew was very public in his opinion of Lann Gheal. Since coming on board Dr. Bennett's ship, he had been, constantly complaining about conditions on the *Freedom's Chance*, and loudly criticizing how Lann Gheal did their job. And now here he was, trying to start more trouble.

Just what I need—and how did he find out so fast about the missing scientists? Damn the man. Dymarian official or no, if he says one more word—just one more—I don't care if Bennett likes it or not, I'll—

"Mr. Sadrew, please," Bennett said. "Your outburst isn't helping the situation. We have all been working under a handicap with the ship's instruments not functioning at prime efficiency. The Commander and his people have done the best they could under the circumstances. I've hired Lann Gheal forces before. I can assure you they are well trained and highly competent. And it doesn't help the situation to be blaming anybody; we are all doing the best we can."

Before Sadrew could think of a suitable reply, Ross jogged over to them, face as dark as a thundercloud. "Well?" Tizu said.

"It's bad, Sir." Ross shook his head. "They got away with about half the stabilizer crystals, and many of the control chips are gone or damaged. The inside of the console is a disaster."

"And just how, exactly, did the little shits *get* inside the console, armachd? Just how did they manage that, hmm?"

"I think, because I left the tool box in the cockpit when I was working on it earlier, Sir."

"You did what!" Tizu exploded.

"Yes, Sir."

"Consider yourself on report, Armachd, and I'll deal with you later. Now get back over there and start repairing what you can in that damned sled. Then, make a list of parts you'll need to finish the job, so we can call up to the ship and have them sent down as soon as possible."

"Yes, Sir."

Tizu next focused his fierce glare on the crowd still loitering around the quadrangle. "Well, what are you people gawking at?" he demanded. "Get out of here. Go to bed or something. Go on, get out of here!"

When the area had emptied save for the armachda on duty, Bennett returned his attention to their prisoner. The little savage hung like a limp rag in the big man's grasp, still whimpering. "He looks so frightened. What shall we do with him, Commander?"

"I'm open to suggestions, Doctor. You got any?"

Bennett sighed, rubbing a hand across his face. "I don't, actually. I'm sorry. We could let him go, I suppose. Look at him—the poor creature is scared out of his wits."

"Mm. We could, but I'd rather not—not just yet anyway. If we let him go now, he and his friends might think they can come back for an uninvited visit any time they like, and take whatever they want."

Bennett nodded, still studying the intruder." Yes, I see your point."

"And I have another reason for wanting to hold on to this little thief. I want to keep him till I know where our missing people are. If they've been captured—well, if we hang on to him, maybe we can negotiate some kind of trade for our people."

"Captured! Is that what's happened? Do you think that's possible?"

Tizu shrugged. "Not likely for my armachda. But I told you Dr. Singey and his party disobeyed a direct order of mine. Either voluntarily or with a little *help*, they left the mesa and went down into the canyons."

Tizu was silent for a long moment, thinking. When he turned back to Bennett, he said, "Maybe Sadrew is right, though I hate to admit it. We did check as thoroughly as we could. We thought we had covered every possibility. There was absolutely no indication of trouble that we detected either with our instruments, or, with the other resources the—uh—Caldoni can use."

Bennett nodded his understanding and put a hand on Tizu's arm. "I know you did your best, Commander, and I'm certainly not accusing you of carelessness, by any means, believe me."

Tizu grunted. "Thanks for the vote of confidence, Sir. I wish I could feel certain myself that I deserved it. When everything seemed so—deserted so—empty around here, I guess maybe we did get careless." He shook his head. "I just don't know."

"So what do you want to do with this fellow?" Bennett asked.

"I've got an empty storeroom or two around here that can be locked. We'll put him in one of them for now and see what happens. That is, if you agree with me."

"It sounds reasonable enough," Bennett said. "But since we've discovered that there is an intelligent native species on this planet, perhaps we should consider shipping people back up to *Freedom's Chance* in the morning, just to be safe. The captain assures me that the repairs are almost complete. We will be leaving soon anyway. The Dymarians will just have to put up with the overcrowding till then."

"You may be right, and in the meantime, I'll post a larger guard around the camp to discourage more 'visitors.' If we start evacuating, though, I'd like to keep some of my armachda down here, until we know what's happened to our missing people."

"But of course, Commander. I'm as worried about them as you are."

As Bennett headed back across the quadrangle towards HQ, Tizu turned to the big armachd holding the native. "All right, Tarla, we're going to lock this little thief up for a while. I want you to take him over to that empty storeroom by the mess, understand? We'll put him in there for the night. I'll have Goronwy bring over the keys and help you get him settled."

"Yes, Sir." Shifting his grip on the native's woolly arms, Tarla began half dragging, half carrying his prisoner across the square. "Come on, and stop crying; nobody's going to hurt you."

Coming around the corner of one of the starmans' big houses, the terrified young hunter's nostrils flared as he caught the unmistakable smells of food. Oh, the odors were very alien, but he knew what they were, and what the starmans meant to do to him. This big beast, so like a Warlinga in size, was taking him to the kitchen to be butchered.

With a strength born of desperation, the hunter raked the big man's legs savagely with his hind claws and bit down hard on an unprotected arm. With a startled yelp, the stranger loosened his hold enough for the agile Begta to slip out of his grasp and race for the edge of the mesa.

TIZU HAD CAUGHT UP to Bennett and opened the door to HQ, when he heard a shout followed by a blast of beam rifle fire. Slamming the door on the startled Bennett, he raced back out into the night. Sidearm drawn and swearing under his breath, he headed for the camp's outer perimeter.

When he jogged up to a group of dark-clad figures, they were standing over a woolly lump on the moss.

Tizu holstered his weapon and glanced down at the twisted body of their furry intruder. Dark-purple blood oozed from a hole in his side, staining the yellow moss a deep brown. Tizu wrinkled up his nose at the smell of charred wool. "What happened?"

"I was taking him, like you said, to the storeroom," Tarla said. "He was coming along peaceable-like, when all of a sudden he just went sort of crazy." The big armachd held out his still-bleeding arm and lifted a pant leg to display the long claw marks on his legs.

"I yelled for somebody to stop him—I'm sorry, Commander, I didn't mean to—" Tarla's voice trailed off and he glanced anxiously at Tizu's scowling face.

Tizu sighed, and softened his expression. Tarla tried so hard, in spite of his mental limitations. "It's all right, Tarla. Go back to HQ and get Bennett or Williams to look at those wounds. They look deep, and I don't want them getting infected."

When the big man was gone, Tizu faced the other sentries. "All right, which one of you idiots shot the little bugger?"

A red-haired man with a drooping mustache said, "I did, Sir, I was just trying to wound him, but he—uh—swerved, and—"

"Mm." Tizu pointed to the redhead and the man next to him. "You two mangy dogs go find a tarp, and put him in that empty storeroom off the mess for now. We'll figure out what to do with him later. The rest of you get back to your posts. And keep alert! I don't want any more surprises tonight, understand?"

When he got back to HQ, Bennett was already at work dressing Tarla's wounds. Tizu came over to inspect the damage. They looked worse in the brighter indoor light than they had outside.

Shit! I hope Tarla doesn't catch some weird alien disease. With Kai's bunch gone, I might need all my fighting armachda—especially if the natives decide to take revenge for the death. After tonight's debacle, Bennett's right. We should get the civilians and any unnecessary Lann Gheal personnel out of here first thing tomorrow.

Unfortunately, Tizu's plan wasn't meant to be. A short time later, Tizu's musings were abruptly interrupted by a startled cry from Goronwy at the communications console. Moving quickly to his side, Tizu demanded in Caldoni, "Keep your voice down. What now?"

Goronwy shifted his headset and said in the same language, "Commander, I'm picking up communications from a Creggan warship. They've found us. The *Freedom's Chance* has shut down all communications and is moving rapidly away from the planet, but the Creggans are giving chase. She's under attack, Sir."

Part Two: Slavery

Chapter One

Protector of the favored lands to the south, the fortress of Tragar Keep crouched on the tawny mountainside like a massive predator, ever vigilant, ever menacing the barren slopes and thorn-choked valleys that spread out northward, below its lofty perch.

The sun was sinking into a russet cloudbank, when a sentry brought word that Begta hunters carrying long reed litters, had just arrived in the meadow below the fortress. Sitting at the head table of his hall with a full pitcher of mushroom beer in front of him, K'San Gormach Tragar was trying to drink away a particularly boring afternoon.

Listening to the man's preposterous account, Gormach's head crest flattened and his brow wrinkled into an angry scowl. "Have a care, Chi'am, I am in no mood for one of your jokes today."

Chi'am bowed at the waist, never taking his eyes from Gormach's face. "I am not joking, K'San. There are Begta in the meadow—truly there are. Send your young cousin to the wall to see for himself, if you don't believe me."

Gormach glanced sidelong at his cousin and heir. Tobrach had paused in the process of pouring the beer and was staring at the sentry with jaw agape. If this was a prank, the witless fool wasn't a part of it. Gormach's scowl deepened. He hated surprises.

"I will believe you, Chi'am—this time." Turning to his Hunt Leader, also sitting at the head table, he smiled. "How very interesting. Begta have never willingly offered themselves for the cook pots before now. Summon your men. Let us go invite our unexpected *guests* to dinner."

Warega laughed and swallowed the last of his beer. He stood. "Willingly, K'San, I am getting tired of hard cake and porridge. Begta meat will be a welcome change."

Head crests held high, whip-like tails coiled about their waists, gray-green scales gleaming in the golden sunlight, the Warlinga were a tall people, almost twice the height of the Begta. Bred by the Khutani Makers for the southern land's protection, they were heavily muscled and naturally armed with tooth and claw.

Augmenting their inherent gifts, they carried bone knives at their waists and long spears with bone or stone tips in their four-fingered hands. Gormach in the center of the hunting pack, they marched down the narrow trail to the moss-covered meadow where the Begta waited.

The Tragar Pack entered the clearing in close formation. As they halted, all the Begta fell to the ground in front of them. Gormach stepped away from his guards and gazed down with contempt at the groveling woolly creatures. Begta. Such an inferior race, but why were the little slimeworms here?

"Hmm, Begta can be most diverting, but the entertainment is in rooting them out of their holes and hunting them through the liru reeds and kavalpa thickets, Gormach said. "I wonder what they are *really* up to."

Warega laughed. "Yes, the fun of the chase is almost worth the poor eating on their measly carcasses."

Then, looking past the trembling Begta, Gormach noticed the paralyzed bodies sprawled upon the moss. They were strange creatures, the like of which he'd never seen before.

The little vermin had brought them here for some purpose, but what? Gormach glared, radiating menace. He hated riddles.

"Ah, little Begta, how nice of you to stop by." Gormach gave the fat Begta headman a toothy smile. "Staying for dinner, are you, hmm?"

The Begta clutched a bone charm to his chest, his teeth chattering. "N-no, g-great G-Gormach, we c-can't stay."

He swallowed, then went on in a rush. "But we bring g-gift to Warlinga—good g-gift." He pointed to the bodies laid out on the ground.

"Hmm." Gormach ran a clawed finger across his jaw in speculation. "Pity you can't stay for dinner. Oh, well, show me my gift then." The headman sprang to his feet and ushered Gormach around the clearing.

Several, flat-faced, nearly furless beasts were positioned, like grotesque statues, for his inspection. Some were draped face up with muscular arms folded across their chests, while others were laying face down to expose a particularly plump backside.

The Begta had handled them roughly, but that was to be expected. Begta were too stupid to care about how they damaged property. Blood and bruises aside, the creatures were a well built, if rather ugly species.

And evidently, they were so defenseless that even a Begta could capture them. Their smooth naked bodies lacked any natural protection, like scaled armor, sharp teeth or long claws.

But perhaps they did have some use. They were almost as tall as his own people, and in a slave race bred and slaughtered for its meat, their helplessness would be an asset not a liability.

"Wherever did you get me such an interesting gift, little Begta?"

"Strangers come down from sky. We see, we take, and bring to Great Gormach," the headman explained.

Gormach growled deep in his throat. "Don't insult me by telling lies, you little liru rat. I'll have none of your fanciful stories. They're some kind of escaped mutants out of the Ghostlands, aren't they?"

The Begta headman fell to the moss, groveling at the Warlinga's scaled feet. "S-s-sorry, oh, s-sorry, Great G-Gormach. I tell t-truth. yes-s. mans m-mutant, is Umwira m-mutant."

Gormach was enjoying this little farce. He prodded the quivering Begta with a clawed foot. "That's better. If you lie to me again, I might be very angry. You would not like that, I think. Would you, little Begta, hmm?"

"N-no, Great G-Gormach." The Begta stared up, his eyes pleading, but Gormach ignored him. Instead, he turned, studying the captives.

The Begta jumped up and hurried over to a young female with particularly soft, plump flesh. He held out her arm, his expression hopeful. "See! Got lot meat—good eat," he said. "Gormach eat, or trade to Avairei for slave. Gormach take nice gift and go away, eh?"

Gormach came closer to inspect the body, a rumble of a laugh deep in his throat. So that was the sly little worm's scheme, was it? He pushed the Begta away and seized the offered prize.

Claws sank effortlessly into soft flesh as he pulled the pale-skinned female roughly to her feet. She made a strangled noise in her throat, but remained unresisting, her body still helpless from the blowgun poison.

Lolling with head down, the nipples of her plump breasts pressed against his scaly torso. Gormach tangled a hand in her greasy mane and raised her face. Wide brown eyes, fleshy cheeks, small pink mouth atop a flattened jaw—what a weak and ugly creature she was.

The drug had dulled her physical reactions, but her mind was clear enough; he could see that in her eyes. His snout wrinkled at the pungent scent of her terror. She knew already what he intended, and that pleased him immensely.

Shifting her into the crook of one arm he held up his free hand for her to see. Looking into her eyes, he extended a clawed finger and tore a gash across her shoulder and onto the upper part of her chest.

Gormach stared, fascinated by the damage he'd caused so effortlessly. What tender skin these creatures had. Ignoring her strangled whimper, he probed the wound a little deeper. To his amazement, it filled with a stream of red blood. He grunted in surprise, head crest dipping. Red. What an odd color for blood.

Ah, but the smell! Exotic, and as intoxicating as the finest lamra brandy. He took in a long, shuddering breath, nostrils filling with the fragrant yet unfamiliar scent. Groaning he clutched her tighter against his hard chest. His long brown tongue snaked out and licked the wound.

Hmm. The blood tasted different—very salty, with a subtle, metallic aftertaste. It was like nothing he'd experienced before. He licked the wound again, savoring its fragrance and unique flavor. Such exotic flesh would make an agreeable change from their usual fare.

Gormach looked once more into the female's frightened eyes. Her breath came in short, ragged sobs. Part of his enjoyment was knowing that she was aware of his intent. He smiled, showing her his impressive fangs, already stained with her blood.

"Poor ugly mutant, did your wizard cast you out because of your physical failings?" He brushed a strand of hair off her forehead with a gentle touch. "Poor creature. Soon," he promised, "Soon. But first I want to savor your terror to the fullest, little mutant, yes, to the fullest."

Then as he bent to lick the wound again, a bolt of angry mental energy slammed into his mind like a lance of hot lightning. Gormach's head shot up. With a startled grunt, he blocked the next thrust. Barely able to control his mounting fury, he scoured the clearing with all senses alert, searching for this unknown adversary.

Who would dare interfere with him while he amused himself? Certainly it wouldn't be the stinking Begta still groveling on the moss—they wouldn't dare. No it wasn't them. Was it his sniveling cousin Tobrach? Gormach's head crest flattened. He fixed the younger Warlinga with a baleful glare.

Tail curling and uncurling in thought, Tobrach was staring towards the northern mountains, and paying him no attention. Gormach's lip rose in contempt. His oh so noble and perfect heir was daydreaming again.

Still aware of the hostile presence battering at his mental shield, the rumble in Gormach's throat swelled in volume. But if not Tobrach, who then? The rest of his useless clansmen, had been broken to his will long ago. Surely none of them would incur his anger so openly.

When no stronger attack was forthcoming, Gormach decided his adversary was no real threat. Sensing a new victim to toy with, he became curious. He scanned the clearing again, and soon located him. Gormach's head crest rose and his jaw gaped open in surprise. His adversary was one of the paralyzed mutants.

The mutant was lying on the ground propped up on his side, almost at Gormach's feet. He was a strong-looking male with a long, tangled, russet mane. The creature had been watching him play, and to Gormach's further amusement, the ugly mutant wasn't enjoying the show. His eyes were alight with pure hatred. And what eyes! Gormach stared, incredulous. He had never seen their like. They were blue, blue as the kavay-rich waters in the Khutani's underground pools.

Gormach displayed his reddened fangs, enjoying the male's helplessness, as much as he had earlier enjoyed the female's fear.

"You would like to rip out my throat if you could, wouldn't you, mutant? But the blowgun poison won't let you try, will it?" He shook his head in mock sympathy, then bent and licked the female's flesh again, watching carefully those startling blue eyes as he did so. "What a pity, hmm?"

The eyes widened with fury, screaming out the challenge that the helpless body longed to carry out.

Suddenly a knot of fear tightened its coils in Gormach's gut. It was unnerving to find a strong hunter's spirit in such a physically defenseless body. Who were these creatures? For what purpose had the Ghostland wizards' bred them? Gormach's tail lashed the ground behind him, irritated once again.

He *hated* riddles.

And this particular mutant needed to be taught a lesson. Such a spirit might be prized in a war-trained hunter, but it was most undesirable in a slave. Whipping his tail round, Gormach slapped the mutant hard across the chest. The mutant let out a startled grunt, the force of the blow knocking him backwards with a satisfying thud. He remained sprawled in an untidy heap, his mental attack finally silenced.

"That's for your insolence, fool," Gormach told the inert body. "Have a care how you defy me in future. I may not be so *gentle* with you next time."

Gormach watched for signs of rebellion a moment longer, then returned his attention to the female. But while he was distracted by the male's futile assault, her fear had overpowered her and she had slipped away into unconsciousness. He shook her limp body violently, but she didn't awaken. Damn the mutant; his pleasure had been spoiled.

As a vent for his frustration, Gormach roared and savagely ripped out her throat. The fragrant blood spewed out in a scarlet fountain drenching his arms. Holding her body away from him, he surveyed his spasming kill with satisfaction. The exotic, metallic scent filled his nostrils, and he quivered with excitement.

Gormach lowered his mouth to the bubbling flow, and drank long and deep, savoring its rich flavor. When he finished, he dropped the carcass to his feet, and motioned one of his clansmen to take the body away for the butchering.

Out of the corner of his eye, Gormach noticed the fat Begta headman backing away. He grinned to himself. Here, at least, was one more little game to be played out. Whipping out his tail, he wrapped its sinewy coils about the Begta, pulling the frightened little man around to face him.

"Ah, little Begta, leaving so soon? And without saying goodbye?" Gormach clicked his tongue in disapproval. "How rude, I'm crushed. And just when I was going to thank you for my wonderful gifts—*all my gifts.*"

Gormach tightened his hold and brought the barbed tip of his tail to rest just under the headman's jaw. Eyes widening, the Begta's bladder emptied its contents in a gush of pungent fluid. Gormach's snout wrinkled in disgust.

Ready to berate the Begta for his "rudeness," Gormach happened to notice a long black leather sheath attached to the Begta's woven belt. What was the little vermin carrying? Gormach reached for a black-handled something in the sheath.

Slowly he drew it out. It was a knife, and, by the Great Hunt Leader, what a knife! The blade was long, lethal, and as black as the pool of oblivion. Cool and hard, it was neither stone nor bone, yet strong and well balanced. By his ancestors, it was made of metal. Metal! He'd not known the precious substance could be used for more than adornment. But this lethal object was made from no fragment of metal salvaged from the ancients' burial mounds.

He ran a clawed finger experimentally across the blade's edge. It sliced through the tip of his claw effortlessly. So sharp! He hissed again, startled. Now *this* was a real present. It would seem the little Begta had indeed brought him a gift—a treasure.

He shook the frightened Begta roughly and demanded, "Where did you get this, Begta slimeworm? Tell me, and none of your lies!"

"M-mans h-have. We t-take from m-mans when we c-catch."

"None of your stories." Gormach snarled. I won't have it!"

The Begta's teeth were chattering with fear, but he remained adamant. Could the little vermin be lying? Probably not, not this time. The creature was intelligent enough not to try his patience that far.

He glanced at the mutant whose mental attack had startled him such a short time before. The creature still lay inert. But without the blowgun poison hampering his movements, the mutant might prove to be a more dangerous opponent than Gormach had first assumed.

He certainly had the mental training to wield the war magic. And, with such a weapon as the one Gormach now held, he could easily compensate for his physical failings.

The Khutani had bred the Warlinga to defend the southern lands from the Northerners. Traditionally it had always been Clan Tragar's responsibility to protect the border. But it had been a long time since Gormach had taken his hunting packs into the Ghostlands to challenge the Hated Enemy.

The border had been quiet for years, ever since his father's time. Gormach himself, had had little to do to maintain peace in the area, so fierce had been his father's prowess. The old K'San—damn him to the black pit—did such a thorough job, there had been no way for his son to gain the attention of the High Ones in the inner council, and thus further both his and his family's advancement.

Over the years, Gormach stayed on the border, cursing his luck, getting drunk as often as he could, and hunting stupid Begta out of their grubby warrens whenever he was sober enough, or bored enough, to bestir himself out of the keep.

And now a cringing, lowly Begta had brought him this, this amazing weapon. With such sharp, magical blades, a band of even these pitiful creatures could come down from the north and kill hundreds.

That was a most unpleasant thought. If a warband of the creatures slipped over the Jeban Pass, he and his kinsmen would be blamed for the destruction they would cause. Providing any of them lived long enough to be brought to trial, of course.

He had definitely allowed things to get out of his control if mere Begta could capture such a prize. Yes, that was plain to him now. His young cousin, Tobrach, damn his self-righteous, arrogant soul, was right. They *should* go north into the Ghostlands. But before he went up against the Umwira, he must have an advantage to counteract this new kind of magic.

He would have to extract the secrets of weapon making locked away in Blue Eyes' mind. And to gain that knowledge, he would need help. He would take these captured mutants to the Avairei at Sulas.

He wasn't well liked there, but he wasn't overly worried about a refusal of their help. The priests could be made to see, it would be in their own best interest to aid him. With their Khutani-made potions, the Avairei knew ways of extracting secrets from the most unwilling subject, ways subtler and more effective than any amount of pain he could inflict.

And once their wills were broken, and the information Gormach needed obtained, Blue Eyes and the rest of the mutants would make good slaves and good eating, as the Begta suggested.

"What have you found, San cousin?"

Startled out of his musings, Gormach looked up. Tobrach must have noticed his prize and come over for a closer look. Without comment, Gormach handed him the blade. Tobrach took it, then hissed, as he tested its sharpness and cut himself.

"By the Great Hunt Leader!" Tobrach whispered. He glanced quickly down at the cringing Begta still held firmly in Gormach's grasp. His head crest rose in silent inquiry.

"Yes, you might want to check and see if any of our other dinner guests have such pretty trinkets. We wouldn't want them to hurt themselves, now, would we?"

Tobrach laughed. "No, cousin, and yes, I will gladly check. May I have one of these knives, if I should find any more of them?"

Feeling magnanimous for once, Gormach agreed. "But of course, little cousin."

Tobrach turned away then paused. Head crest lowered, he asked, "Cousin, where would a Begta get such a weapon?"

"Who knows. They claim they took them from their captives." Gormach laughed, pretending to dismiss the idea. "But who believes a Begta's lies? Don't trouble yourself, cousin. Leave such questions to me. You just do your duty and let me handle this."

When Tobrach left him Gormach flicked the sharp tip of his tail across the fat headman's throat. There was no amusement left in toying with the little vermin now. Motioning to his Hunt Leader Warega to attend him, he started up the trail.

The Hunt Leader waved to a few of his men to follow him and fell into step beside Gormach. "Your will, K'San?"

"Bring some Loti and haul my 'gifts' up to the keep. Put the mutants in a pen by themselves for now, and feed and water them. You may have to do the feeding by hand at first. The Great Hunt Leader only knows what effect that blowgun poison will have had on them.

"We leave for Sulas in a few days, and I want the mutants well fed and pleasing, so that we can make a good trade with them. Do you understand me, kinsman?"

Warega bowed low. "Yes, K'San."

Chapter Two

Tobrach sipped his mushroom beer and resigned himself to another evening of watching Gormach drink himself into insensibility.

Green flames shivered in the sand-fire lamps hung upon the stained walls. The hall was chaotic with Loti servants, hurrying to refill pitchers of beer. Animated Warlinga sat on carved stools around stone tables, boasting and shouting rude jokes to one another at full volume.

"Why are we sitting here getting drunk, and dining on exotic flesh instead of doing our duty—the one we were trained and bred for," he grumbled, his muzzle half submerged in his drinking bowl as Hunt Leader Warega sat down beside him.

The old veteran snorted and poured himself another round. bowl raised to cover his mouth, he said, "I should be used to these debauches by now, but the sight of our kinsmen disgracing the power and name of our ancient lineage like this, always rankles, no matter how many times I witness it,"

Tobrach sighed and agreed. He felt so helpless.

Warega rumbled a mirthless laugh. "Lowly Begta the only alert guardians on the border—oh the shame!"

"Since my arrival at Tragar, I've tried to convince my cousin to take the hunting packs into the Ghostlands. But my none too subtle hints, always fall upon deaf ears. And now, these strange mutants have come down from the north with their unknown weaponry... "

Tobrach wasn't fooled by his cousin's attempts to shrug off his questions. There was something going on in the Ghostlands. But instead of attacking the problem directly, he sat here getting drunk again.

"Perhaps now you will seriously consider what we talked about before, hmm?" Warega said.

Tobrach froze, beer mug half-way to his mouth. His voice hardening, he growled, "Though it hurts my family pride to admit it, Gormach is not like his noble father who brought high praise to our clan."

Warega dipped his head crest in agreement. "A scoundrel and a drunkard—that's why you need to claim your birthright, Most of the hunters and I will support you if—"

Tobrach's headrest flattened with displeasure. "I hate being here, Hunt Leader, I will freely admit, and I hate even more, seeing my kinsmen drift, out of boredom and despair, into a life filled with abuse and debauchery, but I won't have the blood of a kinsman—even one such as Gormach upon my claws."

Warega poured more beer and stood, his own crest lowered. Lip raised, showing a glimpse of fang, he said, "Be careful, young cousin that your cowardice doesn't get us all killed."

Get them all killed. A shiver ran down his spine. Was there truth in the hunt leader's words?

Tobrach was sent to Tragar, his clan's ancient border keep, two years ago when he completed his training, because his cousin Gormach had been repeatedly denied breeding privileges. As the son of the next highest-ranking member of Clan Tragar, Tobrach was Gormach's heir, until the Ima Matri of Sulas relented and allowed him the red kavay and a mate.

After being here this long, Tobrach thought he understood why Ima Sagas had refused to consider his cousin's requests, and didn't blame her. But knowing the reasons for his "glorious exile" didn't make his stay at Tragar Keep any easier to bear.

The evening meal was long over. Tobrach desperately wanted to leave the hall and go to his room, but Gormach was in no mood to accept his excuses tonight. If he left, his cousin would take his absence as a personal criticism and be offended. And, a drunk and offended Gormach would mean trouble for some poor innocent clansman or servant, who might unknowingly get in his way. Such brutality had happened before. Tobrach had no wish to be the cause of more needless suffering for others unable to defend themselves.

A lavender foam outlining his mouth, Gormach's booming laugh echoed around the hall. Several men at the lower tables glanced up in surprise. He was overly excited about something tonight, but Tobrach hadn't bothered to discover its cause.

A kinsman said something and Gormach laughed again, His ample paunch, glistening with grease and meat drippings, shook with his mirth. Gormach gestured wildly with his bowl. Warega dipped his head crest, his eyes now glassy from drink.

The beer was flowing freely, the men becoming more agitated as they talked. *I give it two more rounds and there will be at least one fight breaking out,* he wagered with himself. I just pray that no one gets killed this time. If there is dying to be done, it should be up north fighting the Umwira, not by the hand of a drunken kinsman in the keep.

What a death—and what a life.

Gormach let out a loud belch and slapped Tobrach companionably on the back. "Drink up, cousin. You're not celebrating."

Tobrach choked. Pitching forward he spilled the contents of his half-raised bowl across the table. Slowly righting himself, he poured another bowl from the pitcher and swallowed a large mouthful of the frothy liquid.

"Ah, Cousin, forgive me, what exactly are we celebrating tonight?"

Gormach chuckled and threw a heavy arm around his kinsman's shoulder. "Why the making of our family's name and fortune, just like in my father's day."

Tobrach dipped his head crest in polite agreement. "I see. How wonderful, cousin." What was the fool going on about? He'd been muttering something all evening about mutants and big plans that would make him famous—even called to the High Council at Riath.

Tobrach assumed what he hoped was an attentive expression, but paid little attention to Gormach's drunken babble. He might as well get drunk along with everybody else in this stinking hole. There would be no early escape to his room tonight.

SOME TIME LATER, HIS senses a bit muddled, Tobrach became aware of an on-duty guardsman speaking to Gormach in a low urgent tone.

Unfortunately for the poor man, Gormach became more enraged with each word he spoke. The hunter's quiet exhortations ended abruptly, when Gormach stood and knocked the man to the floor with a bellow.

Placing a restraining hand on Gormach's arm before he could do the man more harm, Tobrach slurred, "What'sh wrong, San Cou'shin?"

"This son of a half-bred Begta is trying to tell me that the captives can't tolerate the kavay in their food. Says it makes them sick. Bah!" Gormach jerked away from Tobrach's hand.

The movement caused him to sway dangerously off balance. He righted himself with his tail and looked from Tobrach to the sprawled hunter. His red eyes gleamed with menace in the lamplight, daring them to laugh. When both remained silent and unmoving, Gormach mumbled a curse and aimed a vicious kick at the hunter's side anyway. The man scrambled out of reach and leapt to his feet.

"Begta filth! What nonsense. Kavay doesn't make you sick; it keeps you alive on this poor excuse for a world! Those damned mutants are trying to defy me by dying, before I can find out their secrets.

"Damn their worthless, naked hides!" Gormach slammed his heavy tail down on the table, sending the bowls and pitcher crashing to the floor. "I'll teach them. They'll not get away with this insolence!"

Tobrach placed a restraining hand once more on Gormach's arm. It was dangerous to cross Gormach in his present mood. But if he was clever, and brave enough to take advantage of the opportunity offered, he could finally escape the hall.

As Gormach spun round with teeth bared, Tobrach struggled to make his sluggish tongue work properly. "Please, San Cou'shin, you shouldn't trouble yourself. Dealing with insolent mutant captives is a task beneath your dig-ni-ty."

Gormach blinked, suddenly uncertain. Tobrach hurried on. "It's my duty to save you from such unpleasantness, San Cou'shin. Please allow me." Tobrach motioned for a Loti servant to bring more beer.

When the new pitcher and bowls arrived, Tobrach eased Gormach back onto his stool and served him. "Drink up. You're celebrating, remember? Don't worry about the mutants, I'll see to them," Tobrach said, and he inwardly chided himself for being such a bone-sucking sycophant. But damn—he needed to get out of here!

Gormach grunted and took a big drink. As luck would have it, a fight broke out just then, focusing his cousin's attention elsewhere. Tobrach breathed a sigh of relief and motioned for the hunter to follow him.

Outside, in the chill of the courtyard, he gulped a few deep breaths, hoping to clear his head. When he had sobered a bit, Tobrach turned to the hunter standing beside him rubbing his jaw. "All right, Chi'am. Tell me what you told our K'San in there."

"It's the mutants. They are having trouble with the food we gave them. I told our K'San that I think they can't tolerate the kavay." His tail lashed anxiously, as he scanned Tobrach's face and head crest position.

"And why do you think that?"

The man flicked his tail. "The food was good—not rotten or such like. There was no reason for them to sicken. But they *are* mutants. Who knows anything can be true with them? I just thought—" He stopped, looking away, his face turning green with embarrassment.

"That is a pretty big assumption to make, but start at the beginning and tell me more of what has happened."

"Well, we did like our K'San said. We brought them up from the clearing. We put them in the little pen near the gate so we could keep an eye on them. They seemed to be doing fine at first. The poison was starting to wear off by then and they could move a bit. So, we figured it would be safe to feed and water them—and so, we did.

"At first, they seemed grateful to be given anything, especially the kavay water. But not long after that, they all got sick, started puking, and twisting and moaning like they were in a lot of pain. We have tried twice more to feed them, each time with the same results. So I thought I'd better tell K'San Gormach." Head crest dipping, Chi'am glanced over his shoulder at the noisy hall.

"Let's go have a look." Tobrach motioned for the man to lead the way. Chi'am grabbed a lamp from the door and they headed across the darkened courtyard.

Like most keeps whose history and construction went back to the early days after the "Burning Times," Tragar Keep was built into the side of a mountain. Its main hall and living quarters nestled deep within the rock, but outside there was a large open courtyard surrounded by high stone walls. The warm weather barracks, kitchen, and the pens where the Loti peasants and other slaves were housed was in this open area.

The captives' pen, like all the others, afforded little in the way of comfort to its inhabitants. It was just an open space surrounded by a stone fence on three sides, the fourth being the outer wall itself. Against the back wall, a frame roofed over with liru reeds, gave some protection from the weather. On the floor of the shelter, was a mat of old, dry, shri moss, smelling strongly of its previous Loti occupants.

Tobrach opened the gate and stepped inside, motioning for the hunter to precede him with the light. Using his tail often to keep his balance, he lurched to the edge of the shelter and stopped, looking around.

By the Great Hunt Leader, what a pitiful sight they were. Naked, half buried in the moss and shivering, the mutants blinked up at him in the unaccustomed light. They were definitely sick. Tobrach's snout wrinkled at the strong scent of vomit and feces.

Examining them more closely, his head crest flattened in irritation. His kinsmen hadn't been gentle in their forced feedings. The captives were liberally decorated with fresh claw marks. The guards had better have a care or Gormach would not be able to sell them to the priests at Sulas.

Tobrach recalled hearing talk earlier in the hall that these creatures seemed to know nothing of the speech of civilized folk. But how could that be? Even the Hated Umwira who came south to raid, knew the southern tongue. The mutants must come from a place far to the north if they didn't know even the basics of the southerner's speech.

This was an unsettling thought, because up until now his people had assumed that beyond the large peninsula called the Ghostlands, the land further to the north was uninhabitable.

But what if the land *wasn't* dead and poisoned? Tobrach fingered the long knife at his hip. What if there was a whole tribe up there like these mutants—a race with unknown skills and weaponry?

Suddenly he wished he could communicate with the captives. He wanted to find out who these people were and where they came from. Were they a part of the Great Umwira Alliance? Or could they be persuaded to join the Warlinga in their struggle against the Ghostlanders? All their lives might depend on the answers to those questions.

Following his impulse, Tobrach sent out an experimental mind probe. Pain, lots of pain, fear, and grief for the one killed today. But when his prying was recognized by some of them, their anger hit his unshielded mind like a rock mallet.

Tobrach reeled, nearly falling. He righted himself with his tail and took in a deep breath. He hadn't expected them to know the mind magics—did Gormach know about their gift? The blue-eyed one in front of him had led a few of the others in the attack against him. Shielded now. Tobrach eyed the creatures with a new respect.

Their gifts weren't very focused at the moment—probably as a result of the blowgun poison. But the fact that they knew the magic at all, was most disconcerting.

They seemed so helpless in appearance—even the male's organs dangled from their groins without a protective sheath. But what if this vulnerability was only a ruse, bred into them by a clever wizard, hoping to deceive and unwary adversary. What other magics might their Umwira wizard have bred into them to compensate for their defenseless exterior?

Tobrach shook his head to clear it. He decided suddenly that he was too tired, and probably too drunk, to figure anything out tonight. He'd seen enough for now. He motioned for his kinsman to follow him and walked out of the pen.

Outside, he leaned on the fence and turned to Chi'am. "I don't think the problem lies with the kavay, Chi'am. Nor are they trying to kill themselves as the K'San assumed. The sickness is more likely a reaction to the damned Begta poison still in their systems. Continue to feed them, forcefully if necessary, so they don't weaken—but have a care."

His head crest flattened and his look was stern, to emphasize his next words. "They have very thin skins, and they are starting to look quite damaged. Our K'San wants to sell them to the Avairei, and if the creatures are too badly abused the priests won't trade for them. If that happens—Gormach will not be pleased—and we don't want that, do we? Do you understand me, Cousin?"

The hunter touched his jaw and dipped his head crest. "Yes, San Tobrach. I will tell the others. We will be more careful in future."

"Good. And, you had better ask the household priest for some yellow kavay salve in the morning. Some of those claw marks look deep—and clean up their pen." He turned to go, then paused as another thought came to mind. "Cousin, in future tell the kinsmen to report to me personally about the mutants. Our K'San is much too busy with other matters to be bothered with such trivial concerns. Do you understand?"

Chi'am bowed. "Yes, San Tobrach, I understand and will obey."

Chapter Three

D unnagh lay sprawled in the dry moss, painfully aware of his bruised and naked body. He wished the spasms tearing through his gut would end, so he could sleep. A chill breeze rattled the dry reeds in the thatch over his head, passed effortlessly through the skeletal frame of the shelter and cut like a knife across his back.

Green torchlight cast frightening shadows around the courtyard, illuminating, then silhouetting the lizardmen posted outside the stone corral where the humans had been tossed, while still paralyzed.

Booming laughter and the sounds of bones being cracked between sharp teeth, came wafting out from the open doors on the other side of the courtyard. In his mind, malevolent red eyes mocked him. A long brown tongue licked the blood from the young woman's breasts, before the brute killed her. Tears of frustration and helpless anger, pooled in the corners of Dunnagh's eyes.

"Choke on the meat, you black-Hearted, scaly devils!"

Within the shelter's darkness, he heard moans, and a quiet sobbing. Somebody cursed and began retching. "Oh, no—" He groaned as his own stomach writhed in sympathy with the unknown other. He rolled on his side and dug out a hollow in the moss. In wave after agonizing wave, his body tried to force something—anything up and out. Finally his effort was rewarded by a trickle of bitter, gray liquid. Breathing raggedly, Dunnagh flopped backward, dizzy, little lights dancing before his eyes.

"Oh, Gods, my guts hurt—everything hurts—better to be paralyzed with the blowgun poison than this! Where are those woolly savages when I need them? Damn, not again." Dunnagh barely rolled over in time, before the retching began anew.

When the heaving stopped and he lay back exhausted, the bittersweet taste of the alien food lingered in his mouth. Dunnagh closed his eyes trembling—waiting. The waves of burning heat and icy chills seemed to follow the vomiting.

A hand touched his shoulder. "N-Nathan?"

"Dunnagh, is that you?"

Not Nathan. Who is speaking? It hurts to think. "Yes, who's there?'

The hand slid upward and brushed the hair from his face. "It's Enghus Fe'an, Dunnagh. I heard you being sick; are you all right?"

"Stop making jokes, Enghus. If it wouldn't hurt so much I'd laugh."

"Yeah, I guess that was a pretty stupid question. I'm c-cold."

Hungry for a little warmth and human comfort himself, Dunnagh heaped more of the stinking moss over them both, then pulled Enghus's shivering body into his arms. "Me, too." Dunnagh sighed and closed his eyes. Enghus mumbled something about trying to find his sister, Moraga.

"I'm sure she's here, Enghus, and I'll help you find her. I need to find Nathan—we'll go soon—when I'm not so dizzy. I just have to rest for a moment, then..."

He was drifting off into sleep, when footsteps and lantern light on his closed eyelids roused him. "What now," he mumbled. His tongue felt thick and clumsy in his mouth, his eyes gritty and swollen. Were the fiends still hungry? Who would be next? A sleeping Enghus moaned as Dunnagh disentangled himself and rolled on his side to face this new threat.

Two "lizardmen" had just entered the enclosure and were heading towards their open-sided shelter. The taller one was a well-muscled male, about seven feet tall with thick, gray-green scales and large four-fingered hands with retractable claws. A leathery head crest rose from his high forehead to the base of his neck.

He was unclothed save for a necklace of large bone beads and a thick woven belt about his hips, holding his primitive weapons. His male organs were enclosed within a sheath of scaly hide that lay against his lower belly.

Pretending to sleep, Dunnagh watched them come, through half-closed eyes. Was the one they'd nicknamed, "The Butcher," one of their late night intruders? No. These two brutes were too thin. By all the Ancestors and Gods of Caldon, how he'd like to ram his machete hilt deep in the Butcher's fat gut.

Swaying slightly, using his tail for balance the taller of the two stopped just outside their shelter. Sighing he exhaled a smog of raw meat and alcoholic fumes in Dunnagh's direction.

Peering into the dark interior, he motioned for his companion to hold up the light. His tongue flicked out from between massive jaws as if tasting the air. The lizardman caught their smell and wrinkled his snout. Dunnagh didn't blame him for making a face. The stench of vomit and feces in the shelter was nearly unendurable.

Suddenly Dunnagh felt the invasive touch of the lizardman's questing Psy probe. He cursed, throwing up a hasty shield. Just like that other, "The Butcher," this one had the Psy, and had come here to mock and torment them. Heedless of the consequences, Dunnagh's rage lanced out, slamming into the lizardman's unprotected mind.

The man let out a grunt of surprise, and shook his head as if to clear it. Hastily withdrawing his probe, the lizardman erected his own shield, and stared down at them.

Dunnagh raised himself to one elbow—all he could physically manage—and stared right back. *Yes, you black-hearted devil, we can use the Psy, too*, Dunnagh silently told him. Dunnagh could hear muffled curses and angry mutterings from the darkened shelter at his back. The rest of his squad was awake now, and aware of their late night intruders.

The lizardman considered them thoughtfully for a long moment, then shook his head again, and motioned for the other man to precede him from the pen. Outside the enclosure they leaned against the stone fence talking and glancing back into the shelter occasionally. When they left, Dunnagh let out the breath he hadn't realized he was holding, and flopped back into the moss with a heavy sigh.

He wished he could figure out a way to warn Commander Tizu about the dangers here. They had no idea back at the base that there were sentient natives on this world with strong Psy abilities. He'd told Marnez to keep trying her communications implant; and when that failed he'd tried his own Psy, but to no avail. Each time he made the effort a smothering cloud of alien Psy enveloped him like a shroud, making any telepathic sending impossible.

Damn that fur-ball of a shaman. Was he strong enough to still be blocking his gift from this far away? Or was it someone else? At the edge of his awareness a terrifying revelation swam restlessly in the shadows. It probed his defenses, threatening to surface and reveal unwanted answers. Dunnagh shied away from that knowledge, forcing it back into the depths, determined not to heed its urgent summons. He returned his attention to their late night visitors instead.

Now that he had a moment to think, Dunnagh realized there hadn't been any real threat in the native's probe. Perhaps it was there, hidden, but all he could recall was a sense of curiosity, and maybe a little pity. And in its way the lizardman's late night intrusion was a blessing in disguise.

The intrusion had forced him to become conscious of the deepening cold and his obligation to the others. If he didn't do something to help his squad and the scientists, someone else might die.

Taking a deep breath, he spoke into the darkness. "Lann Gheal, this is Unit Leader, Dunnagh Kai. I know we're all very sick right now. But we have to keep together. We have to help each other or some of us may not make it through the night."

"Does it matter? We are all going to die anyway," a voice said. "Better to freeze than let one of the monsters tear out your throat and eat you." Murmurs of agreement to that morbid thought echoed in the darkness around him.

"Damn you, it does matter," a harsh feminine voice said. "I, for one, don't plan on giving any black-hearted lizardman a free meal on my carcass! They'll earn that meat if they want it, damn their stinking scales. I'll fight them with everything I got. And damn any of you, if you give up and let them have what they want without a struggle."

"Marti, that you?" Dunnagh asked.

"Yeah, Unit Leader, it's me—" She gagged on the last word.

Dunnagh felt his own gorge rise, but was able to control it. As he waited for her to finish, he heard someone weeping. The noise had been there, at the edge of his consciousness for some time, a monotonous drone underscoring his sickness. "Lann Gheal, who is crying?"

Silence—except for the heart-wrenching sobs. He waited....

"Damn it, somebody nearby find out who that is!"

There was a faint rustling, then a murmured conversation between a man and a woman. "It's one of Dr. Singey's people, Dunnagh. She says her name is Tessa Farris," Nathan, reported.

"See what you can do for her, Nathan, find out how badly she's hurt."

"Right."

Dunnagh continued, "Dr. Singey?"

There was a long silence, then Singey's weak voice answered, "Yes, Unit Leader?"

"Do you know what's wrong with us?"

"It's either a reaction to the drug that paralyzed us when the short woolly savages captured us, or it's something in the alien food that the lizardmen are forcing us to eat."

I knew that already, idiot, tell me something I don't know. "Can we survive it, whatever is causing this sickness?"

Singey rasped a laugh. "I don't know; your guess is as good as mine, Unit Leader. It's too soon to tell."

Thanks a lot, Mr. Snoot, Dunnagh thought, then quickly controlled his irritation, before he said something that would only make their situation worse. Already he'd heard his squad's angry grumbling and curses directed against the man. As their leader, Dunnagh had to set aside his own personal dislike for Singey and set an example of cooperation. Accusations of blame weren't going to get them out of this mess.

"Unit Leader," someone said; Dunnagh thought it was Oglas. "Do you know who was killed?" The man choked back a sob. "I couldn't see—"

"Gemma Roberts, my assistant," Singey said.

Good, that's an important question answered. "All right, everybody find a partner—or two—someone nearby. Check each other for injuries and then report."

It took a while, but at last Dunnagh was satisfied. There were no broken bones or other serious injuries. Everyone was accounted for, and had others nearby to help them make it through the night.

Chapter Four

The captives were awakened shortly after dawn when lizardmen entered their enclosure, meal buckets in hand. A few well-placed slaps of their tails had the humans out of the shelter. Four women and nine men, staggered and crawled into the daylight and sat on the bare ground near the fence, to await the unwanted feeding.

"Oh joy, breakfast," someone muttered.

Sitting between Nathan and Singey, Dunnagh assessed his people's condition. They were a sorry lot, huddling together battered, naked, shivering, fearful of what this day might bring. Fighting down his own sense of despair, he addressed them quietly. "Listen to me. There's no point in fighting this; they'll force feed us this stuff like before. Just try to eat it. Do the best you can."

Taleish shook his head, his bruised face contorting with fury. "Not me. They won't get me to eat that awful blue stuff again!"

Refusing to rise to the bait, he joked, "And wouldn't your battle be a grand epic for the bards to sing." Someone laughed and Taleish's face turned a bright red beneath the bruising.

Taleish opened his mouth, but Dunnagh cut him off. "There are long claw marks across your back and shoulders. You're swaying as you sit—can't even stand. Now you will do as I say, Armachd, and that's an order," Dunnagh said, becoming serious. "There's no point in fighting when there is nothing to be gained. Save your strength for important things, like getting out of here." Dunnagh turned to include the rest of his squad. "Do you understand me, Lann Gheal?"

"But, Unit Leader, it makes us so sick—it's poison," Oglas protested. "What good is it to save our strength for an escape, if we're poisoned in the meantime? We might as well die fighting here and now."

Oglas's argument met with agreement from the rest of the squad. Dunnagh had to admit he had a point, but was Oglas right? He'd better check. "Dr. Singey, is this native food they are feeding us going to kill us?"

Singey had been staring down at his hands, lost in his own thoughts until Dunnagh addressed him. As Singey looked up, for just a moment, Dunnagh saw the haunted look in his dark eyes. Then it was gone, hidden behind his usual mask of arrogant aloofness.

"I can't be certain, but I think, if it was lethal, we would be dead by now," Singey said to Dunnagh. Then addressing everyone he assumed his professorial tone of voice and added, "I'm not sure what's happening to us, but I think Unit Leader Kai is right. While we are still alive there is hope. It would be best not to do anything foolish at this time."

"Should have taken your own advise a few days ago and stayed on the mesa, asshole. It's your fault we're in this mess." Someone muttered.

Dunnagh hadn't seen who made that uncalled for remark but he heard the rumble of agreement that followed.

Singey made no sign that he'd heard the comment, but his skin turned an ashy gray. Dunnagh swore under his breath, and snapped, "That's enough, Armachda,"

Nathan snorted. Dunnagh hadn't noticed until then the tangled-haired woman with frightened eyes tucked protectively against his beefy side. He evidently had seen the speaker because he said, "If you're gonna pass out blame, Taleish, you better count me in. And yourself too, for that matter. It was Lann Gheal who made the bad reconnaissance in the first place."

"That's enough," Dunnagh said his voice taking on a hard edge. As his Second, Nathan was backing up his orders, but Dunnagh knew him well enough to recognize the self-blame in his friends gray eyes. This kind of talk could get them all killed. It had to stop—and now.

"We have enough trouble without blaming each other, or ourselves. We have to work together if we want to escape, so no more stupid accusations. Understand? That's an order."

When it was his turn, Dunnagh eyed the bowl of blue-gray porridge thrust at him with a sinking feeling, but he managed to choke down most of his portion. The native observing him seemed satisfied with his effort and took the rest away.

Ignored by the guards after that, Dunnagh crawled away to sit in the sun and was soon joined by Nathan.

"You got any bright ideas on how to get us out of here?" Nathan asked as he sprawled beside him.

Still watching the activity going on outside their enclosure, Dunnagh snorted. "I can barely make it to the privy corner except on all fours. I'm not ready to take on the lizards yet, how 'bout you?" As he asked his question, he turned and gave his friend a toothy smile.

Nathan blinked, then barked a laugh, which ended all too soon in a gurgle as he started to puke. Burying the stinking mess after he finished, he wiped his mouth and grinned.

"Sure, I'm ready. Just say the word, Fearless Leader."

Nathan looked pale and drawn in spite of the attempted jest. Sorry that his feeble attempt at humor had ended in more misery for his friend, Dunnagh stammered an apology. Nathan waved his hand in dismissal, but the moment of teasing had soured like the alien food in his gut.

The situation was too desperate to continue their banter any longer. Turning back to watch a group of lizardmen pairing off for weapons practice, Dunnagh said, "I hate to admit it, but until our health returns, there isn't much we *can* do but watch and wait."

Nathan had turned and was watching the weapons practice with a professional eye. "Watch and wait. I hope we have that kind of time."

"So do I. But we'd be hard-pressed to take on the brutes when in shape, so I figure when we make our move, we will have to take them by surprise—and do it right—because we won't get another chance."

Watching two of the better fighters lash out with their whip-like tails as they spun, thrust and parried with their long bone-tipped spears, Nathan grunted an agreement. "You're right about that. One chance and only one."

Eyes still focused on the match in progress, he asked, "You got any idea where we are or how to get back to base—once we regain our health and escape?"

Dunnagh took in a deep breath and let it out slowly. Unfortunately he had no answers and wished the responsibility for their safety and the success of the mission didn't lie so heavily upon his shoulders.

"I was carried face down on the litter. Mostly what I saw was the hairy arm holding the pole near my nose. Ask around and let's try to put together a possible escape route from everyone's recollections."

"Right. I'll do that."

"And even if we can't make it back to the base all the way, if anyone remembers seeing a place where we can hold up, make a fire to send off a signal, the Commander can send a squad in the hover sled to our rescue."

Nathan gave him a grim smile. "All the lizardmen's fancy moves and pointy spears won't be a match for a beam-rifle, that's for sure, Boyo."

Nathan might have elaborated on that topic, but the dark-haired woman that had been beside him at breakfast—Tessa, was that her name—called to him at that moment. She sounded so frightened and alone. Dunnagh could sense his friend's indecision.

"Go on. I have no further orders, and being a trained scientist you might get some useful information out of her—once she calms down."

"Right. Guess I'll get started on asking those questions for you then."

"Yeah, you do that." When Nathan was gone he found it hard to focus on escape plans or the lizardmen wandering about the courtyard. The sun was blessedly warm on his back—and there would be another cold night to come. Lying very still, he fought down the urge to vomit, and at last drifted into a restless sleep.

THROUGH THE TANGLED threads of his dreams, Dunnagh became aware of the afternoon chill, but resisted surfacing into consciousness, until he heard the Butcher's booming laugh. Then fear goaded him awake. He struggled to all fours, cursing, desperately trying to shake off a numbing lethargy. In the shelter behind him he could hear more awakened sleepers calling out questions in frightened voices.

Dunnagh ignored them and glanced towards the courtyard. Several of the lizardmen were over by the gate to their pen, and yes, the Butcher was among them. His hand convulsed, yearning for a weapon. If he wasn't so sick—if the damn little furballs hadn't taken his rifle, he'd show them...

Dunnagh eased himself into a better position, still keeping his eye on the group at the gate. There was a lot of tail waving and loud talk going on over there. *You black-hearted devil, what are you up to this time?*

The answer came soon enough, when a woman's piercing scream, tore his attention away from the Butcher.

Unnoticed, two of the ugly brutes had entered their pen. Striding over to where the twins lay in the waning sun, they grabbed Enghus and began half dragging, half carrying him towards the gate. His twin sister Moraga crawled after them, shrieking Caldoni curses at their backs.

The lizardmen held Enghus with claws extended, ripping great bloody wounds in his pale flesh as they tried to subdue him. Enghus was a tall blond, beefy man running to fat. He had a thick neck and bulging arm muscles. He was a weight lifter and a good hand-to-hand fighter by human standards. But, in his weakened condition, and with two of the larger lizardmen to contend with, he was steadily losing ground.

In spite of that, he wasn't making it easy for them. With a strength born of desperation, he fought them every step of the way, adding his own colorful invective to the din.

The Butcher watched Enghus's struggle with red-eyed intensity, his tail lashing the ground behind him. His lips curled back from his fangs in, what Dunnagh suspected, was a grin of anticipation. He was just like a big fat cat toying with a cage full of mice. All their fears, their pain, their struggles just added to the sadistic brute's pleasure.

Then, the Butcher tore his attention away from the struggling Enghus, and focused his malignant stare on Moraga, crawling relentlessly after her struggling brother.

He pointed to her and gave an order to one of the men leaning on the stone fence. The man dipped his head crest, vaulted the fence, and kicked her backwards into the dirt.

Moraga sprawled, landing hard, her breath exploding in a grunt of pain. Wild straw-colored hair framed her pale, frightened eyes, and her bruised face contorted with anger. Heedless of her own safety, she pulled herself back to all fours and began following her brother.

Again the lizardman kicked her, then, when she still refused to give up, he whipped her several times with his barbed tail. At last unable to go on, she lay there in the dust, bloody and sobbing.

Watching more of his people being tormented, wave after wave of scarlet rage engulfed Dunnagh like the fires of an erupting volcano, blotting out all reason. He forgot about the caution he had earlier ordered his squad to maintain. The need to destroy their tormentor, became the sole focus.

Trembling with the violence of his emotions, Dunnagh slammed a Psy shield into place, left the shelter unnoticed and crawled toward the gate.

The Butcher laughed, the sound deep in his throat as his men held the struggling Enghus out to him. Before making his kill, he paused, searching the pen for something. When he spotted Dunnagh he stared into his blue eyes, and grinned, displaying his fangs. Dunnagh sensed the challenge; the fiend was baiting him—daring him to stop him.

While still keeping eye contact with his opponent, The Butcher bent to his victim and sank his teeth into the man's throat. With a jerk of his head he ripped the wound wider, savoring the kill. Ignoring the spasming corpse, the monster sucked at the spouting red fountain, while continuing to watch Dunnagh for a response.

With a cry of outrage, Dunnagh lurched to his feet. He swayed like a drunkard, ran forward a few steps then crashed to the ground in a heap of tangled limbs. He screamed another curse, struggled to his feet once again then sprawled after taking only a few more steps.

Over and over he forced himself to rise, then fell as his strength gave out once more. At last, fury spent, and unable to move, Dunnagh lay cursing and sobbing in the blood and the dust.

The Butcher mocked him with his booming laughter. Then, with the evening's entertainment concluded, he took his dinner and left.

Dunnagh remained where he'd fallen. His tormented soul writhed in agony over another death and his failure to prevent it.

Then, Nathan was beside him, crushing him to his chest. He wrapped his arms about Dunnagh, cradling him in a protective embrace. Dunnagh clung to him, sobbing and cursing, feeling Nathan tremble violently against his bruised chest.

"Oh, Nathan, I tried—I wanted—"

"I know, I know, hush now. You stupid, stupid ass!" Nathan scolded, his voice choking on a sob of his own. "You could have been killed, too—oh, Gods, why did you do that? You reckless, stupid, stupid ass!" Burying his face in Dunnagh's tangled hair, he held and rocked him, continuing to berate him as he cried.

As he quieted Dunnagh heard a trembling voice say, "Oh, Dorothy, I don't think we're in Kansas anymore."

Who had spoken that line from the ancient literature? Dunnagh pushed himself away from his friend and looked around. For the first time he noticed Singey had come with Nathan to rescue him. Though not looking at them, it must have been the scientist who had spoken.

Through half closed eyes, Dunnagh gave him an appraising look. Following Nathan had taken courage. Maybe there was more to Mr. Snoot than his haughty exterior.

To give them some privacy, the scientist was sitting a short distance away, staring across the courtyard seemingly lost in some morbid contemplation of his own.

Dunnagh tried to stand and fell back. "Help me up, you two, and let's go see to Moraga." Singey looked startled when Dunnagh held out a hand. After a brief hesitation, he took it, and together the three men staggered back to the shelter.

When they arrived, Marti was holding her while Rhys dabbed at her wounds with a bit of clean moss. "How is she?" Dunnagh asked.

Rhys looked up, his expression grim. "Nothing's broken. She'll live—as long as the rest of us anyway."

Dunnagh's eyes filled once more with tears. Sinking down into the moss beside the weeping woman, he reached out and took Moraga's hand. She looked up at his touch, her tear-stained face blank for a moment, then she recognized him. "He's gone, Ce'awn. (Chieftain)" She choked. "My twin—that black-hearted devil killed him—" her voice trailed off on a sob.

Dunnagh enfolded her in his arms, tears streaming unheeded down his own face. "I know, my dear, I know," he murmured, his voice thick. "And I'm so sorry, Moraga, so sorry. I tried—" He shivered as Marti lifted her powerful voice in a banshee wail, beginning the keen for the dead.

All activity around their pen came to a sudden halt. The primal call sailed out across the courtyard, shattering concentration, sending chills down the spine of everyone in range. Uncomfortable at their wild display of grief, their captors looked away, but made no move to stop the keen. With a grim satisfaction for the disruption they were causing, Dunnagh lifted up his own voice in the traditional Caldoni lament.

Oh, Enghus! Solid, dependable Enghus, always doing more than your share and protecting my backside in many a drinking-house brawl and fire fight. May you know peace in the halls of our ancestors, and give your enemies a fearsome bellyache tonight!

Releasing Moraga for a moment, Dunnagh tore open a half-healed wound on his arm, and lifted his face to the sky. He swore by his blood that one day he would kill this enemy. To Enghus, and to the ancient Gods of war, he offered his blood, until that day when The Butcher could be sent to them in its place.

———————— ⟊⟊⟍⟍⟑⟑⟑ ————————

AS THE CALDONI LAMENT intensified, the sounds sent icy chills running down Tessa's backbone. The funerals she had attended in her young life were quiet, dignified affairs, nothing like this. These people's display of grief was overwhelming. Their keen was so intense, so—real.

Feeling both embarrassed and uncomfortable, she resisted the demand to surrender to its release. Nothing in her background had prepared her for anything like this. If she let the force of the lament take her, if she got sucked up into its emotional vortex, she might drown in a bottomless sea of pain and despair.

Tessa glanced over at Singey, hoping to catch his eye. He was sitting nearby, his posture rigid, his face closed behind its haughty mask. Tessa scooted closer to him. She craved someone familiar, someone from her old life—a link to that sane, normal world outside this horrible nightmare. The Caldoni open display of grief must be as disconcerting and alien to him, as it was to her. Why couldn't he see how much she needed him?

Though he hadn't said much, Tessa suspected he was taking Gemma's death very hard. He was probably blaming himself for their current situation, as well.

The only child of aging parents, he'd never been an easy man to know. Tessa now suspected that his arrogant manner was due to the fear of being rejected and scorned, rather than true snobbery, as she once had assumed. "Philip," she pleaded. Reaching out, she touched his arm.

After her third try, he finally heard her over the din and patted her hand clumsily. But it was obvious to her, he was unable to pull himself out of his own misery to comfort anyone else. Disappointed, she pulled her hand away and allowed him to sink back into his own thoughts.

Tessa glanced shyly over at the big man with the gray eyes and long, brown hair still bound in a ragged braid down his back. Last night, he'd said his name was Nathan when he'd held her close in the darkness. He came to her at his Unit Leader's orders, but he had been tender—not at all like the awful stories she'd heard about the Caldoni armachda.

She'd been shy about their nakedness, and worried he might try to take advantage of that fact, but he hadn't. Though she had been sick, like all the rest of them, he hadn't seemed disgusted by her vomiting.

Much to her own embarrassment, Nathan had helped her with some of her very intimate bodily functions, when she was too weak to crawl to the privy corner by herself. Afterwards he held her close, his large, muscular bulk a comforting human solidity in this frightening place. He had spoken to her gently in Caldoni, soothing her with his native language's rhythmic cadence till she fell asleep in his arms.

Tessa watched him wistfully, hoping he would see her distress and come to her. But he was sitting beside his leader, his eyes streaming with tears, his voice raised in the keen like the rest of them.

Tessa couldn't imagine any man of her former acquaintance weeping so openly, especially not a big, strong man like Nathan. And yet, among these people, exaggerated grieving seemed so right, so natural. Their lack of embarrassment in emotional display must be a product of their primitive culture, she decided.

Culture. The irony of her situation suddenly struck her and she tried to hold back a hysterical laugh. She'd wanted to study the Caldoni hadn't she? She'd wanted it so much that she'd hidden herself aboard Dr. B's ship, hadn't she? Well, here was her big chance. And if she lived to make it back to civilization, her career would be assured.

She giggled; why, she'd probably be famous. Tears sprang to her eyes. Oh, Blessed High One, if she lived. Taking a deep breath, Tessa fought for control. She couldn't fall apart now; she had to make those field notes, didn't she?

Through tear blurred eyes, she glanced once more at Nathan, but he was still not looking her way. Tessa found it impossible to grieve for someone she didn't know. But she could mourn; yes, she could lament their plight, and pray for their rescue. She trembled, feeling suddenly very much alone.

As if in answer to her unspoken prayer, someone touched her arm. Tessa looked up, startled. The woman who had been their guard, Marnez, was beside her. "Don't be afraid, my pretty, I will take care of you." Marnez stroked her snarled hair, and pulled her into a protective embrace. Tessa leaned into her, and unable to hold back any longer, began to cry.

Chapter Five

Worn out by his grieving, Dunnagh at last fell into an exhausted sleep. Life awake was so horrible, and they were all depending on him to get them out. Him, but what if he wasn't strong enough, or smart enough; what if he failed them? His spirit shrank away from the thought. So many responsibilities, so many worries piled upon his shoulders, at least in his dreams he could hope for escape.

Unfortunately nothing in this alien dream world was familiar. He searched, but couldn't find the path back to Caldon. Frantic, Dunnagh cried out to Grandpa Kai to help him, but there was only gray mist enveloping him like a woolly shroud.

Shouting a Caldoni war cry, he created a sword out of etheric matter and slashed the fog into shreds, but it only reformed around him in the next moment. Exhausted at last he released the sword, cursing with frustration.

Then he sensed he was no longer alone in this twilight world. Someone had heard his call and had come to help him. Ahead, half hidden in the mist was a shadowy specter. It was no alien monster, but a man like himself. The ghost was a big man, dressed in black with blond hair and a plaid thrown over his shoulder. The phantasm had its back to him, but he was sure he knew him. <<Enghus?>>

The ghost turned; the wound in his neck dripping blood. Dunnagh looked into a skull's face and shivered. Enghus held out a hand to him. Dunnagh stifled a sob; his friend looked cold, and lonely.

Dunnagh hesitated; he knew the danger the ghost represented for him. In the way of its kind, Enghus Fe'an had come, seeking a living kinsman to follow him to the underworld.

<<Walk with me a while, kinsman,>> the ghost begged. I am so far from the land of my birth—from the kin—who will remember me in

times to come. How will my ancestors find me on this alien world? Please, kinsman don't leave me alone. Come.>>

Come? The ghost's longing was so strong, Dunnagh felt his defenses weaken. He forgot all about duty, living kin, and the warrior's oath that bound him to the creatures of this alien world.

Hadn't he just been yearning to go home? Yes, it would be so easy—he could just let go and follow his friend. Why fight and struggle on, when there was such a peaceful ending right here and now. <<Wait for me, Enghus, I'm coming.>> Reaching out, Dunnagh took the ghost's cold hand and followed Enghus further into the mist.

Then, as suddenly as Enghus had materialized, he vanished and Dunnagh was once more alone, enshrouded in the mist. Confused and a little frightened, Dunnagh turned in a circle, but saw no one. <<Wait! Enghus, don't leave me alone. I want to go home, too.>>

The ghost never answered, swallowed up by the gray mists. Dunnagh waited, then picking a way at random, Dunnagh turned to his left and started walking. Unable to judge time, he trudged on, senses straining for the sight or sound of Enghus, or something to guide him back to the physical world.

Dunnagh cursed himself for a fool. What had he been thinking to come so far into the Twilight World? He was completely lost. He might indeed die, whether he willed it or not, if he couldn't find the way soon.

Then up ahead the mist thinned and he saw the husks of brown reeds, rising out of murky pools in a barren landscape. Skeletal trees along the path he walked, thrust out twisted branches to hinder him. In a hollow among huge boulders, the skulls of dead monsters grinned at him from half covered graves. Somewhere ahead he could hear the sound of waves on a rocky beach. A nebulous feeling of dread warned him to go no farther in that direction. Turning, he began desperately to retrace his steps.

Rising up beside the path his feelings of guilt and depression manifested a life of its own to accost him. A black being with a blurred form and glowing eyes reached out a clawed hand. <<Come back. Poor, poor creature, you have tried so hard and all for nothing. You can't win, but it isn't your fault. Come abide with me a while. Let me keep you safe You have suffered so much.>>

Resisting the lethargy and the Du'ach whispering to stop, rest, sleep. He grimly trudged on. He wouldn't be tempted; he wouldn't listen, no, he wouldn't... But as he felt his resolve weakening again, he snarled, <<Leave me be, Spirit, I won't listen to your lies!>>

<<Poor Creature, you don't really mean those cruel words. Come, let me take care of you.>>

Dunnagh swore a vile Caldoni oath under his breath and kept walking. Where was the path back to life? Damn, he had to find it—and soon. He didn't want to die after all.

Then, from somewhere out of sight there came a high-pitched, gleeful baying. The sound sent a spear of terror through the very marrow of his being. It was a sound he knew well from his grandfather's stories. It was the sound of a hunting pack in full pursuit of its quarry.

And suddenly, with total clarity, Dunnagh knew that he was this phantom pack's prey. Merciful Mother, he'd waited too long—been a fool—he was going to really die!

Dunnagh splashed through a fetid puddle and up a stony hillside. Long reeds, brittle as glass, slashed at his face and arms. Unseen objects in the mist tripped him. Voices out of the fog laughed and mocked him. Panicked, he fled blindly, fear clutching at his soul.

<<Come back, little human, give your soul into my keeping and I will protect you,>> the specter elongated its dark arms, clutching at Dunnagh with claws extended.

Dunnagh ran faster. No. he didn't want to surrender to his guilt and self-loathing. That fate would be a living nightmare, crueler than the end Death's hunting Pack offered. He had to keep moving—resist the Du'ach—find the way out...

Dunnagh paused as he cleared the top of the next rise, and looked back over his shoulder. He could see the leader at the head of the shadowy pack in the hollow below. Gray-green scales, red eyes and long sharp fangs, the monster resembled the lizardmen who tormented him and his people in the waking realm.

But unlike the lizardmen, this creature also had bat-like wings. With them unfurled, the monster skimmed above the ground in a long effortless stride, steadily gaining, on the floundering human.

Coming up to him at last, the creature lashed out at Dunnagh with its whip-like tail. The razor-sharp tip sliced into his back, the pain lancing through his dream body in a flaming burst. He cried out, stumbled. In the next moment he was up and running again, the agony in his back an added goad to his terror.

Suddenly the silver collar round his neck blazed white-hot. Dunnagh screamed and fell to his knees, clutching at his throat. He groped for his Psy to make a sword and shield to defend himself, but it was too late. The shadowy pack had closed in around him, sucking away his strength.

Looming over him, the pack's leader curled its tail around his torso and jerked him roughly to his feet. The monster drew him closer, staring down at him with hard red eyes and dug its claws into him, shaking him roughly. Dunnagh shouted a war cry and pounded at Death's emissary's scaly chest.

The collar blazed again, demanding his submission. The monster's voice thundered. <<Why are you here in the twilight world bordering Death's realm? Why, Dream-Chosen?>>

Suddenly the form of the being that held him changed. Where the red-eyed Lord of Death had been, now a huge, gray, eel-like creature held him within its massive coils. The Maker's head swung round to face him. Mouth tentacles brushed his face.

Dunnagh shuddered and jerked his head away. Masking his fear with anger, Dunnagh snarled, <<Just another foul trick—not death's Hunter at all.>> There was no escape from the ugly, big worms—even into death—not as long as he wore a damned slave's collar, anyway.

Its mental voice now gentle, Maker Gladdris asked, <<Chosen, is your desire to spite us so great that you would forfeit your own life rather than fulfill your obligations to us?

<<And what of those of your own people charged to your care? Are you such a coward? Do you wish to abandon that responsibility as well? In truth, we expected better of you, Caldoni Warrior.>>

<<I-I.>> Dunnagh's voice trailed off. He felt so bad at that moment that he wanted nothing more than to burst into tears. Gladdris was right; he was a failure—and a coward. What reason could he offer in his defense? Nothing. He felt shamed. Chasing after ghosts and selfishly trying to end

his pain? Damn the Du'ach. Had it managed to slip under his guard and sink its claws into him in spite of his efforts to resist?

Unable to keep the torrent of his emotions bottled up any longer, he decided to risk the Maker's derision and speak the truth. <<It's so terrible on this world—too hard. I don't know what to do—or what's happening to me. I can't save them—>> once again his voice faltered.

Maker Gladdris was silent for a long moment, finally it said, <<It is a pity; your species seems far more dependent on your technology than we assumed. We thought one such as you, with your strong telepathic ability—we thought you could adjust-»

<<And now that you see that I can't,>> Dunnagh interrupted. <<Release me. Let me—let all of us go home. Find another species for whatever this kashallan thing is.>>

<<Alas, we can't do that either. It is too late. The kavay has already begun to alter you. We cannot change what is meant to be.>>

<<Can't or won't. You claim to be so powerful—and maybe you are. But with all the ability you have, then surely you could fix things for us—if you wanted to.>>

Gladdris rumbled deep in its throat and brushed a tentacle across his cheek. So eager for the Maker's answer, Dunnagh barely noticed its possessive touch.

<<Perhaps I should be flattered by your confidence in our abilities. Unfortunately we are not omnipotent. Even we cannot replace what the kavay has modified. Timorna is your home now, Chosen. You must accept this and honor the oath you have given us—>>

<<My oath?>> Dunnagh's temper suddenly flared. <<You tricked me—I feel no obligation to honor such an oath. I told you big worms before; I will not be a slave!>>

<<Back to this again? You are only enslaved if you choose to make yourself so, Spiteful Child,>> the Khutani snapped, its own temper heating. <<Have you considered how your stubbornness has caused you and the others in your hunting pack death and torment?>>

Dunnagh felt an icy chill ripple across his aura. Had he caused the brutal deaths of Enghus and that poor young woman, because he had resisted the Maker's call to honor his oath and go to them? By all his ancestors, he was a worse monster than the creature that held him ensnared in its coils, if that were true.

<<I am tired of these games we play every time we come to you. Do you forsake your oath to us? Would you have me release you and choose another from among your kindred?>> the Khutani asked.

<<If you truly want to follow your kinsman, I will give you the death you crave. I will release you from your service. We can choose another.>>

The frost in the mental voice sent a ripple of fear shivering through his being. Was death what he wanted? Who would the Makers choose in his stead? Nathan, Sairsa, the faces of his loved ones and his armachda flashed before his inner eye.

The Maker wasn't lying to him about such a threat. They would choose another. And even if he had been a gullible fool tricked in to becoming their slave that was no reason to be cruel or cowardly enough to pass on his obligation to some other unsuspecting human. No this was his battle and he would fight it.

<<No, I don't want to die. I don't understand what is happening, but I do know that others depend on me now.>>

<<You don't understand, because you don't *want* to understand,>> Gladdris said. <<We call to you in your dreams; we try to prepare you, but you run away or fight us every time.>>

Dunnagh touched the collar at his throat. <<Release me and maybe I will listen to what you want to tell me.>>

<<I think not. You have proven to be unworthy of our trust. The tether stays.>>

<<Black-hearted devil, release me!>> The collar burned in response to his emotion. He pounded his fist against the Khutani's sleek hide.

Then, the form of the creature holding him shifted once again. A beautiful alien woman's face now looked down at him. Her features were somewhat cat-like, but her eyes were round and luminous. Atop her head, a long mane was twisted into numerous tiny braidlets. She cradled him in her arms like a mother with her babe. Dunnagh pressed his face into the silky brown fur of her breast.

The vision smiled and stroked his hair.<<My dear adopted child, I know what we ask of you, isn't easy. I understand. So much depends on you,

and you are in pain, torn apart with guilt and self-doubt. But have faith in yourself for you are indeed worthy—never doubt that. Your ancestors are proud of you—your adopted mother is proud of you.

<<This is the tempering time. And, like the fine steel of your weaponry, I have faith that you will do well. Here, life isn't easy—no, never easy. You must be strong enough to survive when at last you make the kashallan bond. Don't despair, for there will be more than pain and sorrow, I promise you that. In your future, there will be joy and love to balance the hardships. You will see, the Makers' Dream-Chosen, you will see.>>

Reaching up his arms to clasp around her neck, he whispered, <<Mother, I'm so afraid; please help me—>>

Then, in the waking world, someone shook his shoulder. The beautiful vision of Mother Timorna dissipated.

Chapter Six

Coming awake with a cry, Dunnagh opened his eyes. Singey was leaning over him. "Wake up, Unit Leader, someone's coming," he whispered close to Dunnagh's ear.

Dunnagh sat up, trying to shake off the muzzy feeling left after restless sleep. The night chill was bitter against his naked skin. "Gods, man, what are you doing awake?"

Singey grimaced. "Couldn't sleep. But look—over by the gate to our enclosure; we have company again."

Focusing his attention where Singey pointed, he saw a lizardmen open the gate, pick up something from the ground and step inside their pen. Dunnagh's first thought was that the Butcher had come back for another game; then he dismissed the notion.

That wasn't the monster's style. He enjoyed displaying his sadistic cruelty, and tormenting his helpless victims to an audience. The Butcher would hardly be sneaking into their enclosure at any time, and especially not, in the middle of the night.

No, this was someone else, and here for some other reason. Dunnagh crawled out of the moss and sat on the ground just in front of their shelter. Singey and Nathan took places on either side of him. Startled, Dunnagh glared at the scientist, but Singey refused to retreat or meet his eye. He was no trained soldier; he might get hurt if trouble started. Dunnagh opened his mouth to order the man back, then changed his mind.

Get hurt? What a laugh. They all could get hurt—or dead. He had no control over what happened to himself, the scientist—or anybody, why pretend otherwise?

And, he might need Singey's scientific advice. So, if the arrogant prick wanted to put himself into harm's way, Dunnagh would let him.

Around him in the shelter, Dunnagh heard the others waking, asking sleepy questions of their neighbors. "Stay alert, Lann Gheal, but keep quiet," Dunnagh said in a low voice.

Keeping the lantern low, the lizardman approached them slowly and stopped just outside their shelter. There he squatted, setting the lantern down beside him. He laid a small platter on the ground and pushed it forward towards Dunnagh, then sat back, looking at them expectantly.

Dunnagh ignored the tray for the moment and studied their visitor. Was he the same one that checked on them that first night? Maybe, but he couldn't be sure. All their scaly faces seemed too much alike to him for certainty.

This one probably was young; he had few of the long scars that he'd noticed on most of the others. The lizardman seemed calm and non-threatening, merely waiting for them to do something—but what?

Then, a strangled oath from Nathan made Dunnagh break off his exam of the lizardman and turn to him. Nathan's features were contorted with rage. "What's wrong?"

"What's wrong? Look at the plate, Dunnagh. See what he's brought, then ask me what's wrong. Look!"

Dunnagh looked. At the same time he caught the pungent odor of blood and half-cooked meat. It didn't take long for him to make the connection, as Nathan had. Oh, Enghus. Dunnagh took in a deep breath, letting it out slowly. Behind him he heard angry muttering and cursing as the news of the gruesome offering was passed on.

Without turning round he said, "Be quiet!" His eyes met their visitor's again. There was obviously something going on here that they didn't understand. He didn't think the creature came here to mock them with a plate of Enghus's half-cooked remains. No, he was too composed for that.

Tentatively, Dunnagh reached out with a mental probe. The touch was accepted. Dunnagh felt sadness, bitterness, sympathy maybe, but definitely not mockery or malice of any kind. And something else, but the alien thought patterns were so different from human thinking that it was hard to understand them.

Getting nowhere, he pulled back his probe. Still keeping eye contact with the other, he spoke. "Dr. Farris, Tessa, could you come up here please?"

There was rustling in the moss and Nathan scooted over to make room for her.

When she was beside him, Dunnagh pointed to the platter. "I need some help here. I believe he isn't trying to torment us by bringing us this, but I can't figure out what it means either. Dr. Singey says that you have a language implant. Can you find out what he wants?"

"I'll try. I'm starting to understand them a little, though some of the sounds in their language are nearly impossible for a human palate to create. I'm not sure he will be able to understand me."

"Just do the best you can."

A halting conversation followed, with many pauses as each speaker groped for words the other could understand. At last Tessa nodded and turned back to face Dunnagh, eyes alight with excitement. "He says it's an offering to the kindred of the dead one."

"I figured out the meat was probably Enghus, but why did he bring this to us?"

Her faint smile was apologetic. For the first time, her heart-shaped face had lost its haggard look and taken on animation. *She's quite pretty,* Dunnagh thought. Rested and away from this waking nightmare, she would be a delight to any man. Nathan was lucky, and he'd better have a care in future, if he wanted to keep her.

"...I'm sorry, Unit Leader," she was saying, "I forget that most people aren't familiar with primitive anthropology. I've read about this ceremony before, but never came across it in my field studies. In some primitive tribes, the relatives of the deceased eat a portion of the dead one's flesh. It is believed by them that, when they eat the dead, that person becomes a part of their living bodies. That way the dead will always be with their kindred and never forgotten."

She pointed to the platter. "He says it is, 'to remember.' I think he brought us this so we could honor our lost companion by partaking in such a ceremony. My language skills are still basic, so he can't tell me much. But you are right; he means no disrespect—in fact quite the opposite. His people obviously practice a similar ritual for their own dead. I'm certain that's why he brought this meat to us."

"Respect?" Dunnagh and Nathan stared at her incredulously.

"I am guessing a bit," Tessa admitted, dropping her eyes under their combined gaze. Then she rallied and said in a firmer voice, "I can't be far wrong—it has to be some type of ceremony like I read about. There is no other explanation that would fit the facts."

"Perhaps, my dear," Singey said, "But looking for an explanation that would fit the facts might be very different on such an alien world."

Tessa shot him a murderous look. "You don't know what you're talking about, Philip, you aren't a primitive anthropologist. Don't try to lecture me in my own field."

Trying to suppress a smile, Dunnagh exchanged a look with Nathan. She'd slapped Mr. Snoot down, right proper like. His friend was going to have his hands full with her once she got some of her strength back.

Then, recalling the scene he'd witnessed when they'd been captured by the little woolly savages, Dunnagh had to admit that maybe Tessa had a point about the cannibalistic funeral practices on this world. The explanation she'd offered certainly explained what he'd seen that night.

Someone made an angry comment about where the damned lizard could shove his damned offering, breaking in on his thoughts. "Quiet, everyone," Dunnagh snapped. "That's enough."

He scratched at his stubble of a beard and probed the alien mind again. As before, he sensed no malicious intent. But there was also no way to explain to the lizardman how repellant his people found the thought of eating the dead. And, if they *were* able to explain, and then rejected the offering, their visitor might be insulted.

Then, a new thought occurred to him. Why was this warrior bringing them this offering in the middle of the night? Could it be he didn't want the Butcher to know what he was doing? And, if that were true, why didn't he *want* the scaly fiend to know? What would it matter?

So many questions needing answers, he mused. Well, it didn't matter at that moment, any conspiracy against the Butcher had his whole-hearted approval—in principle at least. And, it certainly was true they needed a friend among the natives, not another enemy.

Remembering something about a lonely ghost in his dreams, Dunnagh thought, *Oh, Enghus, I would willingly take a part of your essence within me. I will gladly keep safe your memory and love, for as long as I live. And, eating a part of you, old friend, is a whole lot easier than eating the glop and blue puke juice that they have been feeding us.*

Dunnagh took a piece of meat from the plate, and addressed his people, his voice low and solemn. "You heard what Dr. Farris said. This is their custom, and Enghus's meat is offered to us with highest respect. I believe that is true. I've probed his mind, and can find no other intent. So, in that spirit, I accept the gift."

"But it's not our custom," an angry voice said, "and I don't—"

Who was that? Ah, Samuels, the new man to the squad. "No, it is not our custom, Samuels," Dunnagh interrupted. "But how would he know that, hmm? By bringing us this, he has offered us a way to honor our dead as he would honor his own, and so we will accept the gift as it is intended, and honor the giver as well."

"But—"

"No buts, Armachd. I, for one, am not disgusted by this, or ashamed to eat this." He lifted the hand containing the bloody meat. "Enghus was a good friend and loved kinsman. To help me remember, I would willingly make a piece of him part of my living flesh. But you can do as you please, Samuels." Then, putting the gruesome piece in his mouth, Dunnagh chewed and swallowed.

"When you put it like that, I'm not either," Nathan announced. He reached over Dunnagh's shoulder, took a piece and ate.

When the plate was returned empty, their visitor seemed satisfied. Next he removed a small pouch from the belt around his hips, and handed it to Dunnagh.

Dunnagh opened it, and poured into his hand several roughly carved bone beads. They were newly made, that was plain. They still reeked of blood and gore. The man had obviously spent the previous few hours making the beads for them. This, too, was Enghus and a part of the ceremony, but what were they supposed to do with them?

Dunnagh looked up from the bones, puzzled. The lizardman held up a necklace of similar but larger beads around his own neck. He said something to Tessa, and she turned to Dunnagh. "He says that these too are for the remembering."

Dunnagh bowed in acceptance of this second gift. He was quite moved, feeling a lump of emotion rise into his throat. The meat, the lizardman could have saved from his own portion at dinner. But the beads, had taken time and effort to make, even in this crude form.

This man had gone to a lot of trouble for complete strangers, treating them with respect as if they were "people," and not just living hunks of meat. "Thank him for us, Tessa, if you can."

The lizardman stood, acknowledging Dunnagh's thanks, then, taking up the empty plate and lantern he went out of the pen, leaving them alone once more.

Chapter Seven

"Unit Leader, Dunnagh?"

Dunnagh's eyes flew open. A cold hand was shaking his arm. "What?"

His face blurred with sleep, tufts of moss clinging to his matted brown hair, Oglas rose up on one elbow and peered down at him. In the moss nearby someone groaned and another head lifted, muttering a sleepy complaint. "What's wrong?" Dunnagh repeated, his voice lower this time.

"You was crying out in your sleep again—just like you did last night and the night before. Are you hurting, Sir?"

Dunnagh rubbed a hand across his face, trying to think. What time was it? It was still dark, but the sky was paling to russet in the east. In spite of the cold his brow was clammy with sweat. "I'm all right, Oglas, just a bad dream again. Sorry I woke you. Go back to sleep."

Oglas grunted and lay down, piling the moss back over his shoulders. Dunnagh rolled on his side and closed his eyes, pretending to sleep. Not long afterward, he felt Oglas move against his back for added warmth. In a short while, he heard the other man's faint snoring begin anew. Dunnagh let out a sigh of relief. He was afraid to go back to sleep himself; the dreams often reoccurred when he did, but he had no wish to include others in his private hell. They needed the welcome oblivion sleep brought.

During their captivity only mealtimes punctuated the endless hours of their misery. Dunnagh, like everyone else, fell into the routine of choking down the food and drink they were given, then crawling away to sleep as much as possible during the warmth of the day.

At night they huddled together, buried in the moss, and talked about good times back home and escape plans. By unspoken agreement, no one mentioned at such times the weakness that made a walk to the privy corner a major achievement.

Dunnagh didn't want to admit, even to himself, that their growing despair might make escape impossible by the time their strength returned. The uncertainty of not knowing when someone might be on their captor's dinner menu, was destroying everyone's will to resist.

To these powerful lizardmen, he and his people were just meat for the table—animals, with no dignity, or rights. He wasn't sure how much longer they could cling to their tattered humanity if they had to go on living like this.

The Begta—Tessa had found out what the little savages were called, had paralyzed them and robbed them of all the little things of civilized existence they'd taken for granted. Now these trivial losses seemed so important—so apart of what it meant to be human. Of course, their clothes and equipment weren't really. He was still the same man inside—or so he kept reminding himself. But each day that passed without escape or rescue, it became harder to convince himself, and the others, of that fact.

Dunnagh lay mulling over his worries till the sky lightened to amber, and his bladder felt full enough to burst. Taking care not to disturb his companions' sleep again, he eased out of the shelter and stumbled to the privy corner.

As he finished he became aware of the unusual amount of activity going on in the courtyard outside their pen. Curious, he glanced toward the gate and saw Singey leaning against the stone fence, his arms resting on its top. Dunnagh wandered over to join him. The Warlinga, another word Tessa provided for the lizardmen, were up earlier than usual this morning.

"Ancestors, man, do you ever sleep?" Dunnagh leaned against the fence and rested his chin in his hands.

His skin ashy, his black hair matted, Singey turned his head. When he recognized Dunnagh, he gave him an aloof gesture of acknowledgement and turned back to the activity in the courtyard. Dunnagh frowned, and kept his eye on the scientist. Arrogant prick. Why was he out here so early anyway? Had someone said something to him? Or refused to lie next to him during the worst of the night's cold? If so, he would find out.

Then recognizing another tormented soul, Dunnagh said in a low voice, "Let it go, Singey, this isn't your fault."

Singey's mouth molded itself into a smile that looked more like a grimace. "Is that an order, Unit Leader?"

Dunnagh flushed and tightened his jaw to bite back the angry response to that remark. Damn the man. "Yeah, if you want to see it that way, then it is an order. Whether you like it or not, *Mr. Singey*, for the duration of this operation, you've been drafted into Lann Gheal."

Singey's head jerked back as if he'd been struck. His mouth opened, then he closed it without a word and turned away to stare into the courtyard.

Dunnagh glared at his stiff back for a long moment, then let go of his anger. "Damn it, man, can't you see that I need you? I have my own ghosts to torment my sleep, but I can't let them ride me to destruction—and neither can you. We all have to work together if we want to survive this nightmare. I may need your expertise at some point. And I can't have you unable to function, because you're wallowing in self-pity."

Singey thought about it for a while, then he nodded. "Fair enough. Consider me your newest recruit then."

"Good." Dunnagh forced a smile and turned to the courtyard. There was definitely a lot more activity going on than usual out there. Warlinga shouted, and checked over packs and weaponry. The four-legged servants Tessa named Loti, hurried back and forth from the storage huts and the inner keep, carrying packs of food and other traveling gear. In the center of the open area a mound of equipment grew larger as the sky paled.

Loti were the natives that the Warlinga used as servants and, in some cases, beasts of burden. The Loti were odd-looking creatures, to a human way of thinking. They had lower bodies somewhat like a horse with a human-like torso perched atop their front legs. But rather than hooves, the Loti's legs ended in a paw-like foot with long claws and a large thickened pad. They had tails like a horse's, but their bodies were proportioned differently, more compact and muscular. Their upper torsos reminded Dunnagh of the Begta, but unlike the Begta, their fur was long and shaggy. They looked somewhat like walking rag mops.

"What's going on, do you know?" Dunnagh asked Singey.

Still staring out into the courtyard, Singey shook his head. "They've been up and busy since before first light. If I were making a guess, I'd say that someone is going on a journey."

"Mm." The man had a real knack for stating the obvious. "I wonder who's going and to where? If a large proportion of the Warlinga leave, and, if we gain back our strength before they return then maybe—"

Singey snorted. "That's a lot of ifs. And what will you do, Unit Leader, if they take us with them to wherever they are going?"

Dunnagh made a face, suddenly feeling his guts sour. That was something he didn't want to even consider.

As if reading his unvoiced thoughts, Singey said, "Do you really think we can escape? Do you have any idea where we are?"

"I was carried face down on the litter when the little savages brought us here. I don't know exactly, but I could make a pretty good guess, based on what I was shown—" Dunnagh hesitated. Singey turned once more to face him. "During the Cumarsaid trance you witnessed in Bennett's suite aboard the *Chance*."

Singey digested that information in silence, then nodded. "Well, I guess that's something a place to begin." He turned back to the courtyard. Warlinga with meal buckets were heading their way. "I can't help wondering why no one's come after us. I could understand why your commander might not want to risk another ground patrol in the canyons, but surely they should have sent out the hover-sled to find us by now. We couldn't be out of range—could we?"

"No, we aren't." What was a matter with him? Why hadn't his sluggish brain made the connection before now? Dunnagh stared at the scientist and felt a cold shiver of dread run down his spine. Too much pain, too much fear had made them all apathetic, stupid. Dunnagh wished he knew how to pull off their escape, or if not that, how to get a message to base—

Was there a base left on the mesa? With two parties missing, Singey had a point, Tizu probably didn't want to risk another ground patrol. But the hover-sled was another matter. Now that his mind was focused on the question, Dunnagh realized that he hadn't heard the sound of an engine once, since their capture. That was very strange—very strange indeed.

What if they didn't come because they couldn't. What if the Creggan warships had found the *Freedom's Chance* and maybe the base too. Were they all dead? *Oh, Gods, no, please not that—let them be alive,* he prayed silently. But if the armachda at the base were dead, or unable to come to their aid for some unknown reason, that meant, the scientists, Dunnagh and the rest of his squad were totally on their own.

Naked and stranded on an alien world, among a hostile native population, without any weaponry to defend themselves—the pain in his gut stabbed him like a warrior's blade. Somehow, they had to escape from this nightmare...

Dunnagh glanced at the tumult outside their pen again. Hoping to hide the note of desperation in his voice, he asked, "Philip, this is one of those times when I need your scientific expertise. Do you have any idea how long before we will be strong enough to make an escape?"

Singey considered, then shook his head. "I'm sorry, but I can't say. The glop and blue puke juice, as Nathan so aptly named our food and water, hasn't killed us, so I assume it won't. Eventually our bodies will adapt, but I don't know when that will be."

"Hmm. Well I hope it's soon." Dunnagh looked down at his folded arms resting on the stone rim. With a dirty finger he traced one of the purple curving lines that now wound around his arms and torso. "And what about these marks. They don't hurt, but they are disconcerting. Will they go away once we've adapted ourselves better?"

Singey glanced over at the indicated markings. They all had acquired them, but against Dunnagh's paler skin the effect was startling. Dunnagh looked like he'd been painted with alien tattoos. "I don't know that either, but once we're back on a civilized planet, I'm sure they can be erased."

Dunnagh started to ask another question, but the Warlinga carrying their meal arrive just then and a guard shouted at them to get in line. Dunnagh took a place behind Nathan and Tessa and pushed his misgivings to the back of his mind. He needed to keep his focus on one thing at a time if he wanted to remain sane. And, right now choking down breakfast was all he could manage to think about.

After their meal, their usual routine was interrupted. Instead of allowing them to drift back to the shelter for a nap, they were herded together and led out into the courtyard where the final preparations for the journey were underway. His fear had become a reality. They were going along, too, and Dunnagh was definitely not happy about the prospect.

Nathan glanced over Tessa's head at the packed Loti, and said in Caldoni, "If they take us any farther away from the mesa, it's going to be much harder for us to find our way back to the base when we're strong enough to escape."

"Yeah, I've been worrying about that too. I'd sort of hoped the Butcher and his men were going off somewhere on their own—maybe leaving our late-night visitor in charge. With Tessa to translate, we might have talked him into letting us go."

Nathan snorted. "Not likely, boyo, the Butcher might get hungry. Or he might get bored and want to torment his play-toys for a while."

One of the Warlinga officers approached and studied the captives for a moment, then shouted a series of orders. Dunnagh cursed under his breath as he saw two Warlinga lift a struggling Chang and tie him face down across a Loti's back.

Nathan barked an ironic laugh. "I see our status has slipped from meat animals to just another sack of the baggage."

IT DIDN'T TAKE DUNNAGH long to discover that being strapped down across a Loti's back, was way down on his list of interesting ways to travel. His guts ached after the first few minutes. He also found it hard to breathe in that position. He couldn't help letting out a groan of pain when he bumped into obstacles along the trail.

Unlike horses back home, his mount seemed to be aware of his difficulties and tried to help him. She often turned round to steady him or to give him a comforting pat on the shoulder. Throughout the day, she crooned soothing words to him in her own language, hoping perhaps to ease his troubles with the sound of a friendly voice.

The Warlinga set a fast pace and kept it up for hours through a rugged, mountainous terrain. And it <u>was</u> rough country; every inch of Dunnagh's body could attest to that. But the difficulties didn't seem to matter to Loti or Warlinga; their progress seldom varied.

The natives had endurance as well as strength. Dunnagh had to admit, even if he were in good health, he would never have been able to keep up with them. He just wished they'd let him ride the Loti like a horse rather than being tied across her back like an unwieldy pack.

Throughout the day they climbed steadily higher into a craggy range of mountains, whose tawny peaks faded into purple mist near the far horizon. The land was nearly devoid of vegetation at these heights, and Dunnagh was struck once more by the barren emptiness and the silence of this world. Except for the noise their company made, there was no other sound but the wind blowing off the high crags. If other creatures lived here, they were underground or well hidden among the rocks.

But one thing he *did* notice, was the distinct advantage the Loti's strange mixture of hoof and claw, had for traveling in this type of environment. With her claws to aid in climbing, his Loti was able to go where no horse or mountain goat could have gone.

From the little Dunnagh could see, the faint trail they were following was often dangerous. The Loti seemed not to notice and went on as if nothing was out of the ordinary, keeping up with the Warlinga, who were also using their own clawed hands and feet to find holds in the steep places along their route.

At sundown they made camp for the night on a wide ledge where a small blue spring seeped out of the rocks near the entrance to a cave. This was obviously a well-used stopover, because to one side of the cave mouth was a stone-fenced corral for the "stock." Along with a pitiful string of roped-together Begta, the Loti were herded into this corral and unloaded. Dunnagh, and the other captives, were unceremoniously dumped to the ground with the rest of the baggage.

Body aching, unable to stand, Dunnagh crawled over to the stone fence and sat, his back against its pitted surface. He closed his eyes and took in several lungfuls of the cool dry air. He hurt everywhere! Just inside the cave one of the green-flamed fires burned, a large pot hanging over it. Dinner. He wished he could share some of the fire's warmth too. The air at this altitude was colder than at the lizardmen's home base.

Nathan crawled over, already shivering. "It's getting colder."

Dunnagh grunted. "I noticed. We'll have to huddle close tonight and hope we're still alive in the morning."

Chapter Eight

After they ate their portions of lumpy porridge that evening, the humans crowded together in the lee of the cliff wall, while Tessa told them what she gleaned from her Loti during the day.

"It's very odd, but evidently on this planet, different species have evolved to fill specific societal functions. I've never heard of such a thing, but that's the only rationalization I can imagine that explains what Cati has been telling me.

"And, there's another species called the Avairei who live at a place called Sulas. That's where we are going, by the way—to this Sulas. But I'm not sure why or what will happen to us there. I'm sorry; my language skill is still quite limited."

"You did fine, Tessa," Dunnagh said and patted her arm to reassure her. "Without you and that implant, we wouldn't know even that much."

"Tessa, you said that these different species all function as specialized parts of one larger society. If that is true," Singey said in his snooty, lecturing tone of voice, "then it is very odd indeed. In theory, a highly sophisticated breeding program, carried out over a long period of time *might*—and I mean might, bring about such results, but this world is far too primitive for that.

"And, there is no way such a process could come about naturally." Singey shook his head. "It's impossible; it just couldn't happen."

"You may be right, Philip, but I don't know any other explanation for what Cati, my informant, told me. The Loti till the land and act as servants for the Warlinga and the Avairei, and the Warlinga," she motioned to the noisy group by the fire, dining on Begta meat, for a change, "are supposed to protect the other peoples from something called 'Umwira,' and other monsters that live in these mountains.

"The Avairei must be rulers of some sort—maybe your breeders. I don't know. Cati is a kind, gentle creature, but I doubt if she knows much more about the larger affairs of her world than most peasants on human settled worlds would know."

"What about those little devils the Begta?" Oglas asked.

"I'm not sure exactly where they fit into the scheme of things," Tessa said. "They seem to be some kind of outcast people. The Warlinga despise them, catching and eating them whenever they can.

"The Loti attitude towards them seems to vary between one of amusement at their wild tales and annoyance. They are evidently notorious thieves, stealing anything that catches their interest."

Nathan snorted a laugh. "Well, that's one thing we all can attest to. If the little furballs hadn't wanted our stuff, we wouldn't be in this mess."

"That's true," Taleish said. "And, when I get my hands on one of the little furballs, I'm gonna—"

"Keep your voice down, Taleish, before you have one of the Warlinga joining our meeting," Dunnagh snapped.

"Let them come," he said with a defiant toss of his head. "I'll tell them what I'm going to do to *them*, when I get a hold of a beam rifle again."

"Shut up, Amadan," Chang grumbled, "Your rifle's down a black hole back in the canyons with the rest of the gear the savages didn't want. And, I've seen enough of the Warlinga for one day. You want to talk to them, go over there and ask them to invite you to dinner; then you can tell the Butcher whatever pleases you."

Taleish bristled, his drooping mustache quivering with his indignation. "Don't tell me what to do, boyo, you're no officer—"

"But I am," Nathan said. "Shut up."

"Taleish, let's keep what you're gonna do to the beasties a secret, like, just so's you don't scare them out o' their wits," Rhys said. "Then it will be a big surprise, right?"

Someone snickered and Taleish flushed a deep crimson. Before he could make another angry retort, Dunnagh said, "All right, Armachda, smarten up."

Returning the conversation to the Begta, Dunnagh decided to voice something he'd been thinking about for some time. "There is a mystery about the Begta that I'm not sure even the natives understand."

"How so?" Singey asked.

Dunnagh scratched absently at the growing stubble on his chin and shrugged. "I'm not sure what I mean exactly, but the facts we know about them don't add up. They seem childlike in many ways, stealing our gear, then quarreling over the spoils, like unruly brats. Yet, they laid a very sophisticated trap for me and my squad. There was nothing childlike about that operation.

"I'd like to think that as Lann Gheal, we are not total novices at our craft, and yet we had no idea either of the Begta presence in the canyons or of the trap itself." Dunnagh caught Singey's gaze and held it. "And some of them have *other* 'gifts.'"

The scientist nodded and dropped his eyes, unwilling to respond to his unspoken challenge.

Drawing their wandering attention back to her report, Tessa said, "According to my Loti informant, the Warlinga leader we call The Butcher is named Gormach, and he has a very bad reputation. These particular Loti aren't his. They were captured by him, the same as we were.

"Cati says Gormach and his kin ate all of her people who were the traditional caretakers of his land. Now he gets Loti by raiding whenever he needs servants.

"Cati is quite pleased to be going to Sulas; she hopes the Avairei will trade for her. She would rather work for them than go back to Tragar."

"So along with all his other sterling qualities, the Butcher is a bandit and thief. Why am I not surprised," Nathan said.

DUNNAGH'S FEARS ABOUT the humans surviving the night's cold turned out to be groundless. Of all this planet's inhabitants the humans had encountered so far, the gentle Loti were the most sensitive to their plight.

When the humans finished talking together, Cati came over to Tessa and drew her away from the others. Like a mother hen, she cooed and fussed over the woman. Motioning for Tessa to lie down beside her she tucked the shivering woman close against her own shaggy warmth, and covered her with her tail.

Dunnagh felt a soft touch on his shoulder, too, and there was his Loti settling down beside him. He looked around and noticed that the others were being invited to lie next to their Loti mounts as well.

"My name Berren," his companion told him.

He nestled in close, curling up tight, and stroked her soft, long hair. It had a pungent doggy smell with a hint of lemon. He drank it in and relaxed; the scent brought back memories of childhood, his favorite sheep dog and fresh baking from the kitchen. Before his eyes closed in sleep, he glanced around one more time. Yes, everyone was safe, and Nathan was nearby. For this night at least, they would be warm. Dunnagh let out a contented sigh, closed his eyes and slept without dreaming.

Chapter Nine

The next morning, Dunnagh shrugged off the hand of the Warlinga sent to tie him down, and mounted the Loti like he would a horse. Berren shied, but at his touch and reassuring tone of voice, she settled.

He glanced back at the Warlinga determined to argue the issue if necessary. But the man merely dipped his head crest and proceeded to tie Dunnagh's legs under the Loti's belly. When he finished, he tied Dunnagh's hands in front of him, and then wound the remaining rope over the Loti's chest and tied it securely.

Judging by the natives' surprise at his action, both guard and Loti seemed unacquainted with this form of travel. Evidently no one rode astride on this world. Dunnagh had made his point and silently congratulated himself for the minor victory. More comfortably seated, he was looking forward to the trip today, while he searched the country for possible escape routes back to the base.

Though the morning began well, it ended on a sour note when Gormach came to inspect the travel preparations. The Butcher had been in a foul mood ever since he woke. He lurched around the encampment roaring his orders and knocked about anyone who didn't obey his wishes fast enough to suit him.

Several of his men carried long claw wounds down back or side as marks of his ill temper. Loti and Warlinga alike hurried their travel preparations, hoping to stay out of the way of his claws and lashing tail.

When he got around to inspecting the captives, Gormach noticed Dunnagh's unique position astride the Loti. With a bellow of outrage, he stormed over to Dunnagh with claws extended.

Sitting atop Berren, Dunnagh was as tall as his tormentor. Letting no sign of aggression show in face or posture, he outwardly relaxed, but inwardly, Dunnagh became the proud Caldoni warrior, steeped in the lineage and magic of his ancestors.

With his Psy, Dunnagh radiated his hatred and contempt, and the Warlinga felt the challenge like a slap in the face. Gormach growled deep in his throat, quivering with a deadly menace. He lashed out with claws extended, narrowly missing Dunnagh's face. Those razor-sharp weapons could have ripped his face to shreds if the blow had connected, but Dunnagh remained motionless, calling the fiend's bluff.

All the activity around them suddenly stopped. Shocked into immobility by either fear or fascination, Warlinga, Loti and humans stared at the two adversaries now battling with the Psy.

Time passed with no break in their deadly concentration. Winds moaned through the boulders up the slope. Someone cursed in Caldoni. A woman sobbed quietly.

Finally, at the edge of his consciousness, Dunnagh became aware of Berren trembling under him. Her distress made him realize what a fool he was being.

Amadan. You can't fight him tied up as you are. All you're going to do is get yourself and some of the others killed. And for what? Nothing but your stupid pride. This is hardly the time or the place to make good on your vow to the god of war. Nathan's right; you are a reckless stupid ass!

Lowering his eyes, Dunnagh ceased his attack, hoping he hadn't taken his challenge too far already. The Butcher relaxed his menacing growl, seemingly willing to accept Dunnagh's surrender.

But as Dunnagh bent over in a submissive bow, the bone bead he'd tied into his long hair fell forward, becoming visible for the first time.

The Butcher's eyes widened. He roared and grabbed for it. Dunnagh jerked his head back and the bead fell out of reach behind him. Gormach bellowed in outrage and raked Dunnagh's shoulder and chest with extended claws. Berren let out a frightened cry and jumped sideways, carrying Dunnagh temporarily out of range.

Gormach's head crest flattened at yet another challenge to his authority. A menacing rumble began in his throat once again. He bared his fangs. What had set the black-hearted fiend off this time? Dunnagh watched him warily, jaw clenched, determined to hold on to the piece of Enghus he had left, if at all possible.

Then, ignoring him for the moment, the Warlinga rounded on his men. He shouted a question and pointed to Dunnagh. Their late-night visitor stepped forward and began a hesitant reply. Suddenly the Butcher cut off his explanation with a bellow of outrage and a vicious blow that sent the man sprawling.

When the beating ended, their friend was torn and bloody. He had to be helped to his feet. Ignoring the wounded man's distress, Gormach shouted to his men and the line of Warlinga and Loti began to move.

Dunnagh felt mortally ashamed. He had no idea why his having the bone bead angered his enemy so much. But he did know, that the Butcher's fury at Dunnagh's show of defiance, had been taken out on another in his place.

But why hadn't the Butcher killed him, just now or in their earlier confrontations? He sensed that the Warlinga was holding back and Dunnagh couldn't imagine why. Whatever was going on in that fiendish mind, he knew it wasn't over between them.

The brute might be staying his hand and not killing him for the moment, but Dunnagh had no doubt that in some way Gormach would make him pay dearly for his insolence.

Dunnagh resolved that, whatever the forthcoming punishment might be, he would do nothing to endanger another person. He would submit, do penance, and bide his time.

Part Three: Sulas Keep

Chapter One

Sagas's heart pounded with a familiar sense of dread. It was happening again. In her mind she heard the Khutani call, and the dire warning of her people's doom.

<<Beware, priestess,>> a Maker intoned within the Dream. <<if you and your people fail us, we will abandon you, and return to our deep caverns within Mother Timorna. There will be no more kavays. We will wait, and create life anew on the mounds of your graves.>>

<<No, oh, please, no, don't leave us—>>

Sagas gasped and sat up, breathing raggedly. It was still the middle of the night, but there was no point in lying in bed now. She wasn't going to sleep any more that night.

Groping in the blackness for the small sack of burning-sand she kept on the wicker table beside her bed, she lifted the lid of the stone lamp and sprinkled some of the sack's contents into the opening. A faint hiss and silvery-green light illuminated the whitewashed walls and Ascetic furnishings of her bedchamber.

Light, pushing back the shadows, Sagas sighed with relief. If this torment continued much longer, she would be mad—or dead.

"The summons you hear in your dreams is a temptation from the evil ones, not the Holy Makers. The corruption has been sent to many a devout priestess. They are a test of your faith, meant to lead the unwary astray. Ignore them.

Could she trust High Matri Enaju? Though her superior, she was also one of the Dingay clan, after all, and therefore a potential enemy. Mother Timorna, what was she thinking? Even if the woman was a member of a feuding clan, she was the High Matri. In all of Avairei history no one had defiled that exalted seat with a personal vendetta. Even a Dingay couldn't be so corrupt.

All her instincts urged her to go to the pools, beg the Holy Khutani themselves to advise her, but her superiors had expressly forbidden her that course. Sagas had been warned when she'd been hauled off to Riath for "disciplining." Her back and buttocks still throbbed with the half-healed scars of that humiliation.

"Beware, Ima Matri of Sulas." Enaju had looked down her nose in that arrogant way all Dingay had, and told her. *"A Dream-Chosen One? What nonsense. The Khutani, alas, are confined to their pools, and we can do nothing to change that. You will only distress them by relating such garbage. You will obey, Ima, or next time you will face a far more severe discipline than a caning, do you understand?"*

Yes she understood. Her duty as the mistress of Sulas Keep was to obey. Sagas gave her word; she wouldn't go to the pools; she would ignore the dreams, pray harder, and be strong.

For a long time Sagas stared morosely at the whitewashed far wall, nearly hypnotized by the flickering shadows dancing in the green light. Their patterns taunted her. Secrets—there were so many secrets—and lies. Muttering a curse under her breath, Sagas flung her legs over the edge of the bed, and stood.

"I'm going to the pools—the Holy Khutani need me, and my first duty is to them. Dingay be damned."

Her decision made, she picked up her cloak from a nearby chair and fastened it about her thin, furred shoulders. Then, she hesitated once again. Burying her face in her hands, she choked out a frustrated sob. Oh, Mother, was she doing the right thing? Disobeying her superiors—breaking her sworn word. Such a rebellious act didn't come easy to her. Then, disgusted at her weakness, Sagas scowled and opened the door.

She traveled the cold passageways without mishap, until passing the main chapel she heard the frightened voice of her young maid Pela and saw a man in a long cloak leaning over someone, blocking the entrance to a tiny alcove.

"Ata, please; I can't. It wouldn't be proper," Pela was saying as Sagas hastened her steps in that direction. The man spoke too low for her to hear his next words, but she knew him nonetheless. A shiver of dread ran down her backbone like a spill of icy water. Combaron Dingay, head of the brother's council and her second in command. The last person in the keep she wanted to run into that night.

He hadn't seen her; she could go back and take another passage—no, she couldn't. Damn the little pervert; she'd warned him before about leaving Pela alone.

Thoughts of her mission to the pools temporarily erased by this new threat, Sagas marched boldly forward. "Ah, Pela, there you are."

Combaron jerked as if he'd been lashed with a discipline rod. He spun round, braidlets whipping, rage contorting his narrow features. Sagas found it hard to keep from laughing at the expression on his face when he recognized her. "Ata Combaron, up so late? What a model of devotion for the young novices."

Sagas watched the play of emotions flicker across his face and held back a smile. He opened his mouth as if to speak, but no words came out. Sagas ignored him and turned to her protégée. "Pela, my dear, your devotions finished? What are you still doing in the halls? It's getting late."

At the sound of her name, Pela stepped forward into the light. Twisting a fold of her kilt in her hand, she gave the Dingay priest a frightened glance as she brushed past him. "Ima, Sagas, I was just finishing my prayers in the chapel when Ata Combaron—"

"Since you are done your prayers you had best be finishing the duties I assigned you earlier, hadn't you?"

Pela, looked confused, then lowered her eyes and bowed. "Yes, Ima."

"Run along to my chamber now and wait for me."

When the girl was gone, Sagas turned back to the man still within the alcove. Her temper barely under control, she said, "I have warned you before, Ata, stay away from my maid. She is already promised to another."

Combaron sucked in his breath and glared. "How dare you! You insult me with such a foul insinuation, Ima. I was merely questioning the girl about her studies—and, and your sniveling kinsman can have her. Why should I care?"

Sagas's grin was predatory. "Don't insult my intelligence, Ata, even here so far from the High Matri's keep we have heard certain rumors."

"Rumors? I have no idea what you are talking about." He sniffed, looking down his nose at her. "I was only trying to be helpful, Ima. Instructing the young is a part of my duty here as well as yours."

For just a moment Sagas had seen the fear, then he'd masked it with more arrogant bluster. So, there was at least some truth in what she'd heard then about his unnatural appetites. But aside from that, he was still a Dingay and the High Matri's own grandson. She needed to be careful—very careful indeed.

"I see. You were being 'helpful.' That was very kind of you, Ata. I think in my next report to the High Matri I shall mention how 'helpful' the new Ata Leyas she sent me is being. I'm sure she will be pleased."

Damn the Dingay—all Dingay! Ata Temog should have been Ata Leyas at Sulas after Mora's death not this sniveling little slimeworm. Sagas was well aware that she was playing a dangerous game threatening him, but she had to protect Pela and the other young novices entrusted to her care, no matter what the personal risk to herself might be.

Drawing his cloak about him, he said stiffly, "That won't be necessary, Ima. I need no special praise for my devotion to the Khutani and the people of this keep."

Definitely worried. "Your humble demeanor is very commendable, Ata. But perhaps in future you should leave the instruction of female novices to me. Do I make myself clear, Ata?"

He bowed. "Your will, I am here but to obey, Ima. I'm sure when I next write to my *grandmother*, she will be pleased to know that Sulas is governed by such a diligent and *obedient* servant as yourself. Good night, Ima." Giving her one last murderous look as he bowed, Combaron stalked off down the hall toward his rooms.

Letting out the breath she hadn't known she was holding, Sagas leaned against the wall outside the chapel. When had he taken to wandering the halls late at night? She would have to order Pela to do her late night devotions in her room or Sagas's own private sanctuary.

And of all the nights to find Combaron roaming the halls, maybe she should take her own advice and return to her suite. But when she considered that course, a knot of unease tightened in her gut. No, she must continue, but she would wait a while in the chapel and give him time to get safely inside his room, before she continued on about her own errand.

Some time later as she left the chapel, Sagas noticed Ata Temog rise from his devotions across the chamber and come after her. When it was clear he was following her and not going to his own room, Sagas paused to wait for him. Trying to keep the note of impatience out of her voice, she asked, "Do you wish to speak to me, Ata?"

Motioning her into a shadowed alcove, he spoke in a low voice. "I was praying in the chapel when I heard Combaron's voice in the hall. Is there trouble, Ima?"

Sagas snorted. "Nothing I can't handle."

The priest touched her shoulder, his brown eyes troubled. "Be careful, Sagas, don't underestimate him. Combaron can be very dangerous."

She patted his arm, impatient to be gone. "Thank you, old friend, for your concern. But I believe that Mother Timorna and the Holy Ones in the pools will protect me. I need only have faith and pray."

"If you like, I will go back to the chapel and pray with you then."

Sagas laughed and stroked the silky fur of his arm. "No, that won't be necessary. I have another errand, which need not trouble you. Go back to your prayers—or to bed."

"At this late hour? What kind of errand—" understanding dawning, his eyes widened. "Oh, Sagas—you can't be thinking of disobeying the High One's orders?"

"And why not? I am Ima Matri here, and my first duty is to the Khutani, not to Enaju Dingay."

Temog took a step backward the better to see her face. "Sagas, you can't do this! Do you question even the High Matri now?"

Sagas let out a long sigh and looked down the darkened corridor, refusing to meet his eyes. He was too perceptive; she'd never been able to hide anything from him. He knew her too well after they had worked together for so many years.

"Maybe, I don't know." Turning back to face him once more, she pleaded, "Temog, old friend, I think I shall go mad soon if-if I don't do something to stop the dreams."

Temog planted himself stubbornly in front of her. He glanced over his shoulder as if Combaron might still be lurking about. In an urgent whisper, he said, "If Combaron Dingay hears of your disobedience—well, you're not a fool. Do you want to bring trouble down upon your clan, or risk arrest and trial for sacrilege or sorcery yourself?"

"Dingay be damned!" She waved a hand in a dismissive gesture as he opened his mouth to continue the argument. "I can guess what you are about to say. Don't bother. I know all about the 'unfortunate accidents' and the unknown plagues that befall those who question that powerful family?

"Do you think as a Caltia clan member, I don't know? My family has been opposing them for the past twenty years. I don't care anymore what they want or don't want. Now let me pass—go to bed."

Temog folded his arms across his chest and refused to move. They stood toe-to-toe, eyes locked, wills battling. At last he looked away and sighed. "Oh, my Ima, I am so afraid for you. I have no wish to challenge your authority; it's just—I fear. Please don't do this; the risk is too great."

Sagas reached out a four-fingered hand, and caressed the grizzled fur of his cheek. "Temog, Ever since my appointment as Ima Matri of Sulas, I have valued you both as friend, and as my wise advisor. But in this, I must be guided by my own counsel.

"Beyond all things, my first duty is to serve the Khutani and it is the Holy Khutani summoning me. I believe this with all the power of my soul. I can't ignore my duty any longer. I must go to them—no matter what Enaju Dingay has decreed."

Temog bowed his head. "Your will, Ima. But if you must do this, let me help you. There is a guard posted at the entrance to the pools. I will go first and distract him."

"There is a what?"

He nodded grimly. "Yes, a guard—I wondered if you knew. Just after you came back from Riath, Ata Combaron ordered some of the younger priests keep vigil each night by the stairs leading down to the pools."

Sagas trembled with indignation. "The sneaking, misbegotten spawn of a cesspit now he gets even the young Atas to spy on me. Oh, I know their plan. The Dingay want Combaron to catch me disobeying. They want to get rid of me, and put a Dingay as Ima Matri here in my place."

Angry tears stung her eyes. "This is intolerable! Am I not still mistress here? DAMN THE DINGAY—HOW DARE HE!"

Temog laid a cautioning hand on her arm. "Keep your voice down, please, Ima."

Taking a calming breath, she said. "You're right, Ata. I forget myself."

"Are you sure you want to do this, Sagas, after what I've told you?"

Suddenly a cold chill of premonition ran down her spine. "Yes. I can't explain why, but it seems more important that I go, than it did before I knew of this. It feels like I may not get another chance, if I don't do it now."

Temog grunted. "Very well, I will go ahead of you and get rid of the guard. Wait a few moments, and then follow."

Chapter Two

Combaron Dingay's hand lovingly cupped the long-necked, stone bottle. The pungent scent of red kavay wafted out of its open mouth. He took in a deep breath, savoring its richness, and felt a tingling under the sheath that protected his male organ. Up and down, up and down, his hand rhythmically stroked the bottle's neck. The flask was old, and the carvings had been worn shiny by his frequent attentions.

The pretty little novice tried to hide it from him—tease him with her shyness, but he knew what she *really* wanted. She would bow to his will soon. Then he would teach her not to tease.

Thinking of the girl also reminded him of her protector. Sagas Caltia. Combaron shuddered, almost dropping the precious flask. Hastily, he stoppered the bottle and set it back on the altar, then crossed to a chair and flopped down with a curse. Thoughts of the haughty priestess had soured his gut—shattered his lustful fantasy.

Then an image of a bloody Sagas groveling at his feet replaced the other. Braidlets tangled, stripped of her ornaments and kilt, she looked up at him, her eyes moist with tears. Blood dripped from a cut on her cheek as she begged him for mercy.

Mercy. The tingling in his groin began anew. Meddling old hag—like the rest of her family, he was going to enjoy her trial and execution. He caressed the bulge under his kilt. Yes he would enjoy himself very much. And then the girl wouldn't be able to hide behind Caltia protection. Sagas would be gone soon.

Combaron leaned against the soft cushion of his wicker chair and allowed his thin lips to curve into a satisfied smile. If what his assistant Dar had told him was true, and Sagas had indeed disobeyed a direct order not to go to the Khutani, then his grandmother was going to be very pleased

176

with him. They would be rid of the Caltia witch for good, and her kin and their allies could do nothing to save her this time.

Breaking off his self-stimulation before it went too far, Combaron poured himself a bowl of spice tea from the pitcher on the table beside his chair. The rich blue liquid was cool and overly sweet, just the way he liked it. He stroked the delicate carvings on the bowl's rim and surveyed the symbols of his family's wealth and position.

Richly dyed tapestries on the walls, warm rugs underfoot, finely crafted wicker tables and chairs cluttered his apartment. It was all beautiful, and *his*. He took a sip of the tea. Sulas too would be his, soon, very soon.

A knock sounded on his door. Combaron set down his bowl and rearranged the folds of his kilt to conceal his partial arousal. "Enter."

Dar shoved a cringing young brother priest in ahead of him. A third youth followed. That one closed the door behind himself; then stood in front of it with his arms folded across his chest. Dar shoved the frightened Avairei forward again. The youth staggered a few steps, then sprawled at Combaron's feet, moaning softly.

Combaron stared at the groveling youth, his face expressionless. Dar grabbed the Avairei by his braidlets and yanked him into a kneeling position. "Show some respect to the Ata," he said. "And stop whining."

The youth swallowed hard, and stared at Combaron with pleading dark eyes. "Please, Ata Combaron, I meant no disrespect to you, the Ima, or the sacred Khutani. I-I—" his voice stammered to a halt.

He searched Combaron's face, but Combaron was sure the youth could find no clue there as to what he was thinking. Dropping his eyes to the floor in defeat, the youth trembled awaiting his discipline.

Combaron let him stew for a long, agonizing moment, then said, "Your guardianship of the pools was a sacred duty entrusted to you, brother. There are many who would regard such an assignment as a great honor. A pity you aren't one of them."

"But, Ata, I was—"

Dar cuffed him, and the youth fell forward onto his hands and knees. "Don't insult the good Ata with your sniveling excuses."

Over the youth's sobbing body Combaron's look was inquiring. Dar nodded; his eyes flicked to the other priest by the door. Combaron felt the tingling begin anew beneath his male-sheath.

Returning his attention to the youth before him, he said, "Failing in one's duty to the holy Khutani is a very serious offence, brother. You have been accused of deserting your post and indulging your selfish desires for sleep, when the Holy Ones had need of you. What have you to say for yourself, hmm?"

The youth sat up. He too glanced at the priest by the door, his expression sullen. When he returned his attention to Combaron, he said, "I did leave my guard duty, Ata, that is true, but I didn't do it for the sake of my own selfish desires, as my accusers claim."

"Lying slimeworm," Dar said and hit him again. "Then why did you leave your post by the pool entrance?"

"Dar, Dar," Combaron chided, "let the brother speak."

"I-I left because Ata Temog assured me that it was all right for me to do so," the young priest said. "When he saw me on guard by the pool entrance, he said, he could see that I was tired from working in the fields all day. He said, that he wouldn't mind standing the rest of my time.

"He assured me I wouldn't be neglecting my duty. Ata, he told me—almost ordered me to go. What was I supposed to do? He's an elder!"

Combaron glanced sharply at Dar. His apprentice dropped his eyes under that glare, twisting the fabric of his kilt in his distress.

Temog....

Dar should have warned him—found out the rest of the story before coming to him. Lazy, Begta filth, Dar was going to regret this laps. Combaron would see to that—later.

An image of Dar tied to a wall, his back raw and bloody floated across his inner vision and he smiled. Dar saw the smile and shuddered. Combaron's smile widened to show more teeth.

Then he sobered. Temog was a member of a clan, as yet unaligned with either the Caltia or Dingay factions. He would have to go carefully here; he'd been warned by his grandmother not to make any more enemies for his clan at Sulas. After what happened in Riath with that girl—Grandmother and Uncle Persig wouldn't be pleased if he accused Temog without cause and angered his powerful relatives.

Combaron was sure Sagas had disobeyed and gone down to the pools, in spite of her oath to do otherwise. And, he was also sure that Temog had lured the brother away from his post to give her the chance she needed to go to the Khutani. But why had grandmother forbidden her the pools? It was the Ima Matri's sworn duty to go to the Khutani. She was *supposed to consult them often*, about the health and breeding of her charges. What was Enaju afraid of?

The old wound of deep humiliation reopened, spilling out its festering resentment. His family always treated him like a Begta slave. They didn't trust him with important matters; they never told him anything. They expected him to do his job without telling him all the facts, and then punished him when he made a mistake—it wasn't fair.

Temog. The man was Sagas's strongest ally in this keep, everyone knew it. If that one was sending young brothers to bed, he wasn't doing it for the pleasure of staring at the pitted walls late at night.

Sagas Caltia was plotting something devilish. Combaron was certain—but how to prove it? He would have to do some more digging. There were people here who owed the Dingay plenty of favors; perhaps it was time to allow them to show their gratitude.

Chapter Three

S ulas Keep at last! Shouting an order to his men to quicken the pace, Gormach strode down the trail at the head of the column. It wouldn't be long now; soon he would have it all, everything he'd ever dreamed of having.

Behind the thick stone walls of Sulas, the Avairei priesthood had lived and studied the ancient wisdom for time beyond measure. The keep had been built in the "Early Times" from the living rock, and sprawled on a high ridge overlooking the assent to the Jeban Pass.

Like all the early keeps, most of Sulas was underground. On its upper levels were the work rooms, and warm weather living quarters for the Avairei priests and their servants. Deep within the womb of the mountain itself, lay the sacred pools where the holy Khutani lived.

In the narrow river valley below the keep, a patchwork of cultivated fields followed the course of the Magre River. As they descended, Gormach looked out across the valley to the high ramparts of the Rim Wall, and touched the long black knife at his hip. On the other side of that barrier lay the sheltered crater of the Yeyen Banai valley.

It was there, in the Yeyen, that the Khutani renewed life after the "Great Destruction." Most of Timorna's people still lived there. It was also there in the Yeyen, that he, Gormach would receive the acclaim he and his family so richly deserved. Gormach smiled to himself. This would be the beginning. At Sulas he would find the key to unlock all Blue Eyes' secrets. He would make his father's ghost proud of him yet.

The party arrived at Sulas's gate just as the Loti peasants and younger priests were returning from the fields for the evening meal. Amidst a cacophony of excited shouts, they entered the courtyard and began unloading.

Ignoring the clamor and questions directed at him, Gormach focused his attention on the arrangement of his salable goods. The lesser items of trade, like the rock powder mix, used to fuel the green fires and the stinking Begta hides, he left to his cousin Tobrach to handle. The negotiations for the main item of trade, the new mutants, he delegated to himself.

As he waited for his kinsmen to finish the unloading, Tobrach limped past with a Sulas guard. Gormach's lip curled with satisfaction. Teaching the insolent spawn of a Begta his place had been most satisfying; the lesson was long overdue.

Thinking of the incident, sent a stab of fear into his gut that he quickly suppressed. He was being foolish. He wasn't going to die—not now—and definitely not at Blue Eyes's hand. The bone bead wasn't a symbol of blood debt to the mutants. It meant nothing to them—how could it? They knew nothing of Warlinga customs, so why was he scaring himself with childish fantasies of his doom?

As he continued to wait, Gormach's tail curled and uncurled with his impatience. He wished one of the head priests would come so they could begin the trading. He wanted one of the Atas; the priests were much easier to deal with—either Combaron Dingay or Temog—anyone but the Ima Sagas, damn her to the black pit.

It was the Ima Sagas, the accursed hag, who had refused him the red kavay for breeding, time after time. It was she, the haughty witch, who had told him right to his face when last he'd asked, he was a disgrace, and would never be allowed that privilege, if she had any say in the matter. Which she did—damn her. The Ima Matris and their Khutani advisors always had the final say about breeding privileges.

Up until now. But with the Dingay clan's rise to power times were changing. If he gave the Dingay clan something *they* needed, then maybe he could get something *he* wanted in return.

Gormach prayed his host and negotiator would be the Dingay; that little pervert was the easiest to handle. He patted his rumbling belly; he was getting hungry. A little exotic flesh tonight might sweeten the deal, and interest Combaron in the larger, long-range plan he had in mind.

Yes, the meat—that would be a good thing, but he wanted no trouble. Especially not the screaming fuss the mutants made, the last time he wanted a good meal. He couldn't afford to have that nonsense now. And that troublesome Blue Eyes was likely to start a disturbance if he figured out what Gormach intended.

Thinking of the insolent mutant made him growl deep in his throat. Since his submission to Gormach's will back on the trail, Blue Eyes *appeared* to have learned his lesson and become a paragon of docile obedience, but Gormach didn't trust him.

He should have killed him that day—would have, too, if he hadn't backed down when he did. The Warlinga touched the long blade at his hip again. But his real reason for repressing his response to kill Blue Eyes, lay in the secrets he knew, not because Gormach had a forgiving nature.

Blue Eyes was obviously the leader of this little bunch and therefore, Gormach reasoned, the one most likely to know the secret of making their weapons. Gormach hungered for that knowledge, but he was also smart enough to know that no amount of pain he could inflict would loosen the creature's tongue. Gormach had felt the iron will of the mutant in their little mind-games. He suspected the man would die rather than talk.

No, the male would not break like that, but there were other ways—drug-induced ways—to loosen unwilling tongues and give Gormach what he wanted. That was why he had brought the mutants to Sulas in the first place. Someone like Combaron Dingay would be most useful, if he could interest the priest in his plan.

The Dingay clan's star was on the ascendant. How they obtained the High Matri's seat and kept their hold over the other clans wasn't talked of openly. Not if a person valued a healthy, long life, that is. But with more of these new weapons—and the *right* Warlinga to use them on their behalf, the Dingay would be most grateful—most grateful indeed.

But there were certain "difficulties" that must be overcome first. These creatures knew nothing of civilized speech. The mutants must learn to speak the common tongue, for there would be no profit in trying to pry secrets out of Blue Eyes, if all he heard was gibberish.

Gormach glanced around the courtyard. While there was still a lot of confusion, he motioned to his Hunt Leader Warega to come to him. "Separate the mutants into three groups. In the first group put all the females. In the second, put the males best suited for breeding."

He considered. "The two tall ones, Blue Eyes and the brown-maned one, should make good breeders. Hmm, that dark skinned one and, maybe that golden-skinned one with the dark eyes, he is smaller than the rest, but he has unique coloring, and the Avairei may like that.

"The rest of the males are culls. Tie them up separately, and well away from the others. We will offer our hosts one of these culls for the evening meal."

Warega bowed and would have left, but Gormach stopped him as a new idea came to mind. "In my pack is a bottle of sedative powder. Take it, make a small wound under the culls' armpits, and rub some of the powder into the cuts. Be careful of the dosage; give them just enough to make them tractable. I don't want the priest to get suspicious—understood?"

Warega showed his fangs in appreciation of Gormach's slyness. "Yes, K'San kinsman, it will be as you say. The Avairei are stupid—very bad traders. I will see that they never suspect."

"Good." Gormach smirked, baring his own fangs. "Ah, very good indeed—here comes the priest now, and, the Great Hunt Leader be thanked, it is the Dingay." Gormach hurried to intercept him, bowing as low as his protruding belly would allow. "Ata Combaron."

"K'San Gormach, what an unexpected—*pleasure.*" Combaron took a step backwards wrinkling up his sharp nose as if he smelled something overly ripe.

Gormach gritted his teeth and bowed once again to hide his irritation. *Arrogant slimeworm.* "Ata, the pleasure is all mine."

"Yes, quite." The Ata preened, never suspecting the mockery in his comment. Combaron glanced around the busy courtyard as if noticing the activity for the first time. "I see you have brought things to trade again. We didn't expect you quite so soon."

"Yes, Ata, it has not been long since my last visit, but on my latest expedition north to protect our land and peoples, I discovered some interesting new wonders." He stepped close and lowered his voice. "I thought them of such importance that I returned to share them with you—and the good Ima immediately."

"Indeed," Combaron said, affecting boredom. "Well, you will have to show me your wonders. Ima Sagas Caltia has received a summons to attend the High Matri in Riath."

This is even better. Without the old witch around, things are bound to go well. Gormach dipped his head crest. "What an honor for her."

The Dingay smirked. "*Perhaps.* And now, San Gormach, enough of the pleasantries, show me some of your interesting wonders. You can tell me the rest of your news over dinner."

"But of course, Ata, come this way. I believe my Hunt Leader has the new slaves ready for your inspection."

Gormach guided the priest to a place near the gate, where two of his hunters stood guarding the females. "As I was saying, on our patrol north we came across this band of strange new mutants."

Combaron paused, causing Gormach nearly to bump into him. "How 'strange' are they?"

"Mm, a bad choice of words perhaps," Gormach said hastily. "They are a benign mutation, I assure you, Ata, quite pitiful. They are harmless, and easily managed by any Warlinga." He pointed to the women. "These are the females."

Combaron studied them through narrowed eyes for a moment then said, "They do look defenseless as you claim—and quite ugly."

"Their naked faces are ugly, true, but they do have rather *enlarged* female charms, don't you think?"

Gormach's tail switched, he had just noticed the similarities between the two species. The Avairei were slimmer than the mutants, but in general body shape they were much alike. Focusing his attention back on the priest, he said, "Perhaps in other ways they are more pleasing as well?"

Combaron licked his thin, black lips, studying the females again; this time with more interest. Gormach dipped his head crest and turned away, scandalized by the growing bulge under the folds of the priest's kilt.

Well, well, Combaron, you sly little pervert. I see the stories whispered about you are true. You are using red kavay to heighten your lust, and for the sake of your own pleasure, not for breeding, as is proper. Perhaps these tasty morsels will amuse you and sweeten our deal.

Before the priest could become too absorbed in his fantasies, Gormach suggested that they move on to the next group. Reluctantly, Combaron agreed and followed him to a shed on the other side of the Warlinga's warm weather barracks. Four males of various sizes and skin color, were tied together against the shed wall.

"We have also captured, along with the females, several males. Because they are so defenseless and yet so large, it was in my mind that they could be bred for work and for the table." He bowed to the priest.

Combaron grunted in a noncommittal manner and turned his back on them. "You said there were others. Let me see the rest now."

"There are four other males, culls really," Gormach said as he steered the Avairei to the last bunch over by the kitchen entrance. "I thought to offer you one of these as my contribution to our evening's repast. The flesh of these mutants is quite delicious, with an exotic flavor that is most delightful." Pausing in front of the bound, half-drugged men, he waved a hand expansively. "Pick one, Ata, and he is yours."

"Hmm... Perhaps the brown-maned one there. He looks the meatiest of this lot—he'll do."

"An excellent choice. I'll have one of my kinsmen take care of the butchering immediately." Gormach raised his head crest in query. "And the others, Ata? Shall I have them put into your slave pens?"

"Yes, I'll take them all. We can discuss the trade over dinner." Combaron turned to leave, then paused. Rounding on the Warlinga, he said, "And I'll have most of those Loti as well—and young ones, mind, not like the last bunch you traded us. Those were good for nothing but the stewpots. I'll check myself this time, so no tricks."

Gormach bowed. "My humblest apologies. My worthless young cousin has disobeyed my orders once again. I shall have him disciplined."

"Yes, you do that," Combaron drawled, giving the Warlinga a sardonic look. Then changing the subject he said, "I shall expect you in my private quarters for our meal. I will send someone to fetch you from the guest house when it is time."

As the priest strode away, Gormach bowed deeply, hiding a triumphant smile.

Chapter Four

Dunnagh breathed a heart-felt sigh of relief, as he was untied and pulled off Berren's shaggy back. Unable to stand after the long hours confined to such a difficult position, he collapsed in a boneless heap on the ground at her feet. Berren made a cooing noise in her throat and helped him up. "Thank you." He leaned against her side to catch his breath. "Sulas?" he asked.

Berren murmured an agreement, and patted his head, smoothing down his dirty red hair. She said something else, but it was too hard to concentrate on the few words of the local language he'd learned. Every bone and muscle in his body ached from being tied down across her back like a sack of grain each day.

After their confrontation that second morning on the trail, Gormach had ordered him retied in the face down position. And just so Dunnagh didn't miss his point, the scaly devil had the rest of the humans retied in the astride position Dunnagh preferred.

Dunnagh had suffered his penance in silence, which irritated the brute immensely, he was sure. Knowing that, was his one satisfaction as he endured the hours of torment their travel inflicted upon him each day.

So this was Sulas. He breathed in the smells of burnt porridge, dung and an unfamiliar musky spice. At the moment the courtyard was crowded, bustling with activity. Mud-caked Loti peasants with bone tools and baskets tied to their backs trudged through the gate, mingling with the Warlinga from Tragar unloading their goods.

As Dunnagh watched, a type of native he'd not seen before, came swarming out of an inner door, to add to the congestion in the courtyard. He touched Barren's arm, drawing her attention back to him. He pointed with his chin. "Avairei?"

"Yes, Avairei." She stroked his tangled hair again and cooed to him. "Avairei good people. You will like."

"Maybe."

"Yes, yes," she assured him, "you will like."

To ease her mind, Dunnagh smiled and patted her shoulder. "Me like." Berren gave him a searching look, then seemed satisfied with his answer and turned back to watch the activity going on around them. Berren tried so hard to help him—and he was eternally grateful for her effort, but she was a simple, trusting person at heart.

He didn't know enough of her language to explain his misgivings. Any being who owned another wasn't to be trusted, as far as he was concerned—and that included the Avairei.

The Avairei were an upright species, about the height of a short person, like Marnez or Chang. But unlike his people, they were covered with pelts of sleek brown fur. Their bodies were slim, and the physical differences between male and female seemed less obvious than among humans. Atop the graceful necks of these folk, were round heads, with high, intelligent foreheads.

The rest of their faces were rather cat-like in appearance, but unlike any cats Dunnagh had ever seen, the Avaireis' eyes were a warm rich brown in color. A mane of long hair grew from the top of their heads to a spot between their shoulder blades. They braided this flowing mass into several thin plaits, with ornaments of many colors and shapes, woven in among the strands.

Here at Sulas, Dunnagh saw, for the first time, natives on this planet wearing clothing. Some wore cloaks and a kilt-like garment that varied in length between the sexes. Clothing and ornamentation among them, however, seemed to be a matter of artistic display, or a show of rank perhaps, rather than for warmth. Dunnagh shivered and glanced towards the vanished sun. They certainly had no need for protection from the weather with all that sleek dark fur.

The Avairei thronged the courtyard, babbling excitedly to one another in high musical voices and gawking at the humans. Tucked against Berren's solid bulk, Dunnagh stared right back, just as curious. They looked harmless enough—but looks could be deceiving. He rubbed absently at his neck; there was something about this place that made him feel uneasy

Suddenly one of the Butcher's Warlinga grabbed his still bound wrists and hauled him roughly away from Berren. Growling a warning for him to behave, his guard led him to another part of the courtyard. Nathan and Singey were already there, tied to one another. Dunnagh was shoved in beside them and made fast to Singey's left wrist and ankle. Shortly afterwards, Chang was roped to Dunnagh's other side.

"What's going on, Unit Leader, do you know?" Chang asked quietly.

Dunnagh shook his head. "I'm not sure. Where are the rest of our people, do you know?"

"I was at the end of the column today. When I was unloaded, everybody else was gone."

"I saw them separating out the women just before they dragged me here," Singey said.

Dunnagh glanced at him, hoping for more details, but the scientist only shrugged. "This is obviously the Butcher's doing," Dunnagh said. "I wonder what he's up to now?"

"Nathan snorted and leaned across Singey to talk to him. "Who knows what goes on in that fiendish mind? But whatever it is, he's keeping us tied so we won't make trouble for him with these Avairei. Won't get a good price for us if they think were hard to handle, I bet. Scaly devil, I'd—"

A heavy hand shoved Nathan back into line, before he could finish his threat. He let out a grunt of pain as his head slammed into the stone wall. Head crest flattened, the Warlinga bared his fangs and growled a warning for them to keep silent and behave.

When their guard stepped away, Dunnagh said, "You all right?"

"I've been better," Nathan grumbled.

Dunnagh turned back to the scene in the courtyard. Over behind this mud and thatched building, he couldn't see much of the activity going on in the rest of the courtyard. He listened, heard no screaming, but that didn't necessarily mean everyone was all right.

Where were the women and the rest of his armachda? Feelings of anger and frustration clawed at his insides. He hated this! He'd never felt so helpless in all his life.

When the Butcher eventually showed up, an Avairei wearing a red kilt was walking by his side. The slim native seemed weighed down by the weight of the ornamentation on his chest and neck.

"Here comes our prospective buyer, no doubt," Singey murmured.

"No doubt," Dunnagh agreed.

The personage was someone of high rank if the Warlinga's fawning behavior was any guide. It was sort of amusing to watch the massive Butcher toadying up to this small, narrow-chested little man.

Dunnagh wished he could understand what they were saying to each other, because the Butcher's behavior didn't bode well for their future. Gormach was definitely up to something more than a quick sale of his "merchandise."

Suddenly pricked by an undefined fear, Dunnagh studied the newcomer through half-closed eyes. He didn't like the native's narrow weasel-like face, or the unpleasant look to those feverish dark eyes.

Unlike the others of his species Dunnagh had observed, this Avairei made Dunnagh's skin crawl. Was it a sending, a warning of trouble to come that he felt? Gods, his neck hurt. He rotated his head, hoping to ease the sudden pain.

Dare he risk a Psy probe? Better not. The Butcher would probably catch him at it, and who knew what the Avairei himself might do if he felt the touch of his Psy. Dunnagh let out a breath he hadn't realized he'd been holding as the pair moved on.

"I wonder what he's asking for his prime studs?" Nathan said.

"Who cares—I don't like the look of the little ratty one any better than I like the Butcher," Chang muttered.

"Nathan, what makes you so sure we are the Butcher's prime 'studs,' as you put it?" Singey said.

"Have to be," Nathan said, showing his teeth in a smile that was almost a grimace. "Handsome, good looking armachda like us—why else would he have separated us from the rest? Except I don't know why he's included such an ugly little runt as Chang there, in our exalted company."

"Why, Nathan, it's my sparkling eyes and pleasing smile that proves my superior worth, don't you know. For once, I have to give the black-hearted devil credit for having good taste."

"Good taste?" Nathan snorted a laugh. "Is it his good taste that put you here, or only that he thinks you'll taste good, hmm?" Chang grinned ghoulishly and Dunnagh chuckled.

Singey looked from one to the other of his companions, a confused expression on his ebony face. "It's obviously Chang's racially unique features that put him with us—if Nathan's surmise is correct. Surely you know that?"

Nathan looked disgusted and turned away. From Dunnagh's other side, Chang muttered a Caldoni curse under his breath. Singey stiffened, his face assuming his habitual aloof mask.

"Yes, we know that, Philip," Dunnagh said quietly, "but sometimes when everything's bad, it helps to joke about it a little."

Singey relaxed and smiled tentatively at Dunnagh. "I see. A most sensible notion, Unit Leader, when you put it like that."

IT WAS DARK WHEN THE Warlinga untied them and herded them to one of several pens located in a row near the outdoor kitchen. Dunnagh peered into the dim interior of the pen's thatched shelter. He counted the shadowed lumps lying half buried in the moss. One. Two. Three, where were the rest of them?

His heart pounding like a hammer inside his skull, he knelt and shook the nearest comatose body. It was Rhys. At first there was no response to his shaking; then a groggy voice mumbled something unintelligible.

Dunnagh looked up, frantically searching the dimness for Singey; he needed help. "Philip, come here please!"

Singey crawled into the shelter, feeling his way in the darkness. "What's wrong, Dunnagh?"

"Something's the matter with Rhys—I can't wake him,"

Singey reached out, groping for the flaccid body. After a hasty exam, he murmured, "There's a cut under his armpit with a gooey substance on it. He's been drugged."

Dunnagh swore in Caldoni. Yes, he knew what Singey meant. They'd experienced this method of receiving unwanted dosages before. "I was afraid of that. Nathan, Chang, check who else is here and see if you can rouse them. Dr. Singey says Rhys here has been drugged."

"It's Oglas and Taleish," Nathan said a short time later. "And they're drugged too."

Where were the women, and Samuels? Dunnagh rubbed at his neck. He shook Rhys again, harder this time. "Rhys! Damn you, wake up and tell me what's happened."

It took some doing, but finally a slurred voice answered him. "Butcher—they got—Samuels-s-s." Rhys's head lolled back into the moss.

Frantic now, Dunnagh jerked him up again. "Where are the women? Rhys, don't sleep now. Answer me, damn you."

"Don' know," he mumbled, "Didn't see 'em."

Dunnagh allowed Rhys's limp body to fall back into the moss. It would be useless to question him further. Samuels that was another one gone. And where, oh where, were the women? Dunnagh stared off into the darkness, tears stinging his eyes. He could hear Nathan swearing, a monotonous litany in Caldoni. Singey murmured something, but he ignored them both.

Feeling like he might explode if he didn't do something, he lurched to his feet and staggered out into the darkness of the pen. When he reached the west wall near the Begta corral, Dunnagh leaned against its cool surface, and pounded his fist on its pitted stone.

Never in his life had he felt so helpless. All his training and instincts told him to do *something*. As Unit Leader, it was his sworn duty to get them out of this mess—but how? At the rate they were being butchered, there wouldn't be anyone left to escape by the time they were strong enough to leave. He had to make a move—and soon.

Some time later he heard footsteps and then Nathan joined him. "Hey you all right?"

Dunnagh snorted. "Stupid question, Mo Hara."

"Yeah, I'm worried, too." Then more hesitantly Nathan voiced his real concern, "You don't think the natives are having some kind of feast day, and killed all the women along with Samuels, do you?"

Dunnagh choked down a laugh. "To honor the Butcher? I doubt it."

Nathan chuckled. "That was pretty silly. I saw how most of the Avairei looked at him. The Loti were right; he isn't well liked here, but what other explanation is there for the women being missing?"

Watching their still limping late night visitor being led away from the guest house by an elderly Avairei, Dunnagh shrugged. "I have no idea. But I'm sure the Butcher is behind whatever is going on tonight."

Nathan mumbled an agreement and fell silent, staring out into the courtyard. A couple half-drunk Warlinga carrying a jug lurched out of the barracks and headed for the gate. Without looking at his friend, Dunnagh said, "You're becoming quite fond of Tessa, aren't you?"

Something in Dunnagh's tone of voice must have alerted Nathan to his mixed feelings about the woman, because he turn to face him. "Yes, I guess maybe I am. She's educated, intelligent, pretty, and she likes me, too, maybe. When we get back home—"

"You'd better be careful, Mo Hara, take it slow with her. I don't want you to get hurt."

"What?" Nathan put a hand on his shoulder and spun him around to face him. "Dunnagh, damn you, look at me. What are you talking about; what do you mean be careful?"

What *did* he mean? Dunnagh wasn't sure why he'd said that. The words just came out of his mouth, before he knew he was going to say them. "I mean be careful that's all—she's not one of us, you know, being educated, a foreigner—and rich—"

"I see." Nathan's eyes sparked with anger. "So, you're telling me that because a woman is rich and not Caldoni, she could never fall in love with a dumb, savage like me, is that it?"

"Nathan, you know that isn't what I mean. Taleish says she came along on Bennett's ship in the first place, because she wants to study the Caldoni. I just don't want you to rush into something and get hurt later."

Nathan threw up his hands in disgust. "I don't believe this. You are a real ass, you know, a real ass. Not too long ago, as I recall, wasn't it *you,* who kept telling me to grow up, have a *mature* relationship and get married? And then when I find someone that I could really care for, you have the gall to tell me to 'be careful.'"

"I meant find a woman of the clans—a Caldoni woman—"

"Like Sairsa, I suppose?"

Dunnagh was feeling his own temper flare. "Well, yes, like Sairsa if you put it that way."

Nathan snorted. "Just what I said before, you're a real ass."

"Nathan," Dunnagh warned, "don't say something we'll both regret."

"Oh, shut up for once. You've already said more than enough that I regret. And, as for Sairsa, she may have been born on Caldon and have a Caldoni name, but she's hardly what I'd call a 'true' Caldoni woman.

"She was raised on Dymar, remember? She knows nothing of her land or people—she's as Dymarian as you can get—especially with her talk of 'mature relationships.'"

"Nathan, that isn't fair—she never said anything about you having a mature relationship—that's only me talking."

"Sure it is."

"Damn it, it is!"

Nathan folded his arms across his chest and glared. "You know what your real problem is? You're jealous, that's what."

"What? Now you're being the ass."

"Am I? All the times I've watched you fall in love. It tore my heart out, but I never tried to stop you. And now here you are—alone—not knowing if your girlfriend is alive or dead.

"You see me starting to care about a woman, and you're scared shitless I really might find someone this time. Suddenly, it's you that's worried our warrior's bond will be broken. What a laugh, how does it feel, hmm? As I said before, you're jealous. "

Be careful what you wish for, Grandma Kai and Mahir had always said. And there was truth in their warnings. Seeing his dearest friend with his arm around another made Dunnagh ache with longing for their earlier close relationship.

And maybe, yes, be honest, the sight of Nathan's happiness—even in the horror of an alien world's slave pen, made him feel resentful—and a little afraid. Shocked nearly speechless by the revelation, Dunnagh mumbled an incoherent, half-hearted apology.

Nathan snorted and stalked back to the shelter, unconvinced.

For a long time after Nathan left him, Dunnagh stared blindly into the darkness. Along with all his other failings, was Nathan right? Was he jealous? For the past few years, had he been so unthinkingly cruel to someone whom he loved and whom he knew loved him in return? He was such a monster.

"Oh, Nathan I'm so, so sorry. Maybe I need you more than I let myself admit. What a mess we've made of things."

Chapter Five

Gormach tilted his stool and leaned his bulk against the wall of Ata Combaron's sitting room. At the moment, he was drinking a particularly fine liquor and felt quite content with his world. Combaron Dingay did well by himself that was for certain. The finest tapestries covered all four walls of his private chamber. There were thick carpets on his floor and his worktable and cabinet were inlaid with polished stones and slivers of precious metals. Yes, he'd done very well by himself, and wanted everyone to know it.

They had dined well, the priest enjoying the taste of the exotic mutant flesh as much as his guest. Over the rim of his bowl, Gormach studied the Avairei through half-closed eyes. Combaron sat back in his chair, relaxed, replete, his eyes a bit glazed from too much strong liquor and a heavy meal. Gormach touched the knife at his hip for luck. It was time.

Combaron set down his bowl with a thunk on the table beside his chair. He steadied it, then folded his hands across his full middle, and gazed owlishly at his guest. "Well, friend Gormach, you told me earlier that you had some interesting news?"

"Yes, Ata, but first a little gift to aid you with your *devotions*." From the end table beside him, he took a small leather-wrapped bundle and handed it across to his host.

Combaron took it, frowning. When Gormach offered no further explanation, he unwrapped the bundle and drew out a small bone-handled knife in a leather sheath. Combaron held it up to the light turning it over and over in his hands. The priest's eyes widened when he saw the silver studs decorating the sheath. Metals were rare on Timorna, the sheath alone was worth a small fortune.

When he finally slid the knife partway out of the sheath, Combaron gasped as the shiny metal blazed with green fire in the lamplight. He sat a little straighter in his chair. His eyes gleaming with excitement, he pulled the blade free of the sheath, the leather dropping to the floor unheeded.

Holding the blade once more to the light, he tested the knife's edge with a careless finger. Combaron cried out in surprise as a thin line of purple blood welled up in the cut.

"Have a care, Ata, the blade is very sharp," Gormach said, and lifted his bowl to hide his amusement with a pretense of drinking.

Combaron looked up. "Where did you get this?"

Gormach took another drink of his liquor before answering. "The blade, along with several others," he touched the sheath at his own hip, "came from our little mutants."

Combaron gasped. "Sorcery!" he breathed, dropping the knife as if it were poison. It hit the edge of the table by his chair with a clang, bounced once then fell to the floor, where it lay cold and menacing between them.

"How dare you endanger this keep by bringing devilish mutant sorcerers here! You fool, I'll—" The priest quivered with outrage.

Gormach ignored the outburst and poured himself another bowl from the pitcher at his side. Raising the bowl with studied calm to his mouth, he drank. He needed a moment to think. By the Great Hunt Leader himself, he had forgotten what a pack of superstitious fools these Avairei priests could be. Hidden by his bulk, the tip of his tail twitched in agitation behind him.

The Avairei were always ranting about evil magic and sacrilege. They were as bad as the stupid Begta, and he mentally kicked himself for forgetting that.

Setting down his bowl at last Gormach said, "Ata Combaron, I'm sure the Avairei, and your holy self, especially, are much wiser about these matters than a simple Warlinga such as I am. But, Ata, you saw them tonight—did they look dangerous?"

He forced out a bark of laughter, waving his hand dismissively. "They seem quite pitiful creatures to me. If they possessed the evil powers that you mention, would they have allowed me and my kinsmen to capture them? And, if they were indeed sorcerers, would they have allowed one of their number to grace our dining table tonight?"

Gormach dipped his head crest. "I think not, Ata Combaron. They have knowledge, very useful knowledge perhaps, but dangerous? Hardly. Why, any Warlinga can handle them, you need not worry."

"What sort of useful knowledge?"

The Warlinga held out his hands. "Who can say for certain? Right now they don't speak a civilized Tongue. But once they learn our language; there may be many interesting things they could be *persuaded* to impart." He touched the hilt of the blade at his hip. "Such as how to make these fine weapons."

"Perhaps," Combaron said. He reached down and picked up the fallen gift.

"Such new weapons are very fine," Gormach said. "One could almost wonder if they were sent from the Gods themselves. Put into the right hands—to be wielded in the service of the *right* clan, they could prove to be most useful indeed."

Combaron grunted, and studied the blade in the lamplight. Gullible little pervert. Gormach could almost see the idea that he'd just implanted take root in the priest's mind. Combaron would help him with his plans. And now, it was time for a little "dessert" to sweeten the priest's dreams.

Gormach stood, stretched and yawned. "Ata, you have been a most gracious host, but I fear the hour grows late and I, for one, would like to seek my bed."

As he turned to go, he paused. "But perhaps, Ata, you would care to take a short walk with me after such a fine meal?"

"My Hunt Leader has kept the females apart from the others. Would you care to inspect them again with me—just to see that they are bedded down and comfortable?"

Combaron put down the knife he had been studying and drained his bowl. He stood, pulling on a cloak. "Yes," he said. "I'd like that."

Gormach bowed deeply, hiding a triumphant smile. "As you will, Ata."

TESSA SHIVERED AND moved a little closer to her companion. The sacks piled against the wattle wall where they were housed, offered some insulation, but it still was cold in this horrible storage hut. Outside she could hear a noisy dice game in the Warlinga barracks, and over by the kitchen someone was throwing garbage onto the midden.

It was getting late; why were they being kept apart from the men? Earlier a collared Begta slave brought them food and water. Then they had been left alone to crouch in the darkness and worry.

Tessa had asked their Warlinga guard why they were in here, but he only growled at her to shut up. When Marti cursed him and started an outcry, he slammed her against the wall and loomed over her till she quieted. After that they were ignored.

The darkness and the waiting were becoming unbearable. Tessa found herself trembling, and she wasn't sure if it was from the chill night air or her growing fear. "What d-do y-you think they're going to d-do t-to us?" she asked the darkness.

Marti snorted. "Who knows, with those black-hearted lizards."

Reaching a bound hand across Morag, Marnez stroked Tessa's hair. "Don't worry, little one, it will be all right. I tell you before, everything's going to be fine."

Marti snorted in disgust, and muttered something to her partner in Caldoni. Marnez laughed.

"Do you think they are going to eat one of us, Marti?" Moraga asked, her voice solemn.

"If they think that, they better be ready for a fight. But I doubt it. I think they have something else in mind."

Thinking of the others, and wishing that her big Caldoni Nathan was there to make her feel safe, Tessa said wistfully, "I wish I knew where the men were."

"Me too," Marti said. "I think the Butcher has separated us because he's up to some devilment. Right now I'm more worried about our men-folk than our own situation."

"Why do you say that?" Marnez asked.

"Didn't you see how that skinny Avairei looked at us? It's way past dinnertime, my love—think." Marnez was silent for a moment; then she began to swear in both Standard and Caldoni.

"What do you mean?" Tessa said. "I don't understand—"

"She means it's for the fucking. That's why we be kept separate," Moraga explained to her less-worldly companion.

Tessa gasped. "Oh God, surely not—the Warlinga have never touched us. So, why would you think that! They're aliens—how could they—" She broke off, her whole body shaking uncontrollably.

Oh, God, to be raped by one of these horrible, ugly aliens. It would be bad enough to be forced by a man of her own kind, but to have to do *that*—with one of these awful creatures. Oh, God, no, she'd rather they killed and ate her than to do *that* to her.

Moraga patted her hand and said, "Now, now, no sense in a-worrying. Maybe they don't want the fucking. No sense getting upset before something happens, because we no be stopping it by worrying about it."

"I think Tessa is right, Marti, that idea is too crazy," Marnez said, but there was no conviction in her words and Tessa knew it.

Like so many times before, Tessa thought about her situation and berated herself for her stupidity. Why had she hidden away on Doctor Bennett's ship? Why, oh, why had she done it? No university grant was worth all this suffering. If she could just go back in time...

Tears dripped silently down her cheek and splashed onto Moraga's hand. Moraga pulled Tessa against her side and hummed a Caldoni lullaby until Tessa lapsed into an uneasy doze.

When Marti heard Marnez quietly snoring beside her, she spoke in whispered Caldoni. "Moraga, you awake?"

In the same language, Moraga answered, "I am, what is it?"

Marti hesitated, then said into the silence, "I have a bad feeling about this, and if something should happen to me, will you take care of my woman for me?"

For a long time, there was only the sound of their breathing in the chilly darkness. Marti waited. At last, Moraga whispered, "Have you had a sending then? Is it your time?"

"I'm not sure, but I know when they come for us; it will be me they take. So, will you do it for me, Moraga?"

"I will. And if you don't come back to us, I will demand your bones for our necklaces to remember you by."

"Good. I'd like that. I want to stay with my friends and kin. Yes, do that for me, too."

Chapter Six

C ombaron leaned against the doorframe of the hut and surveyed his new purchases in the torchlight. Now that he had gotten rid of that troublesome witch Sagas, he felt like celebrating. The Warlinga jerked the females to their feet and pushed them against the far wall. They stood blinking in the light; their guards hovering nearby.

Which one of these ugly brutes should he choose? Then, an image of his grandmother's face rose up in his mind's eye to torment him. Hard piercing eyes, cruel mouth smiling, she loomed over him, a discipline rod in her hand. She had warned him, if she were to find out...

No, he wouldn't spoil a perfect evening by thinking about *her*. As the Ata Leyas here, he could do as he liked, and no one would *dare* question him. It felt good to be in charge, to have things his own way—yes, it would be nice to celebrate such an event with a little pleasant diversion.

Which one should he choose?

The little one on the end, with the pale skin and dark, wavy mane, had amazing breasts. Round and pendulous, like overripe fruit, he'd never seen anything like them before. Perhaps she might be interesting to play with. No, not tonight, she was terrified; not much of a challenge there. Some time when he just needed a quick release, she would do. Next to her was the big female with the pale eyes. He dismissed her out of hand; he found her odd eyes and light coloring repulsive. The darker female next to her looked at him defiantly enough to be worth his interest, but she was too short, no taller than an Avairei—perhaps another time.

Combaron licked his lips. Ah, the last one—the big dark-skinned one—she was the most exciting of the lot. Such a huge, powerful brute. It would be a pleasure worth savoring to master her. Catching his eye, she through back her head and glared, as if she already knew what he wanted, and would fight him for it. She would be the perfect entertainment to conclude a most satisfying day.

Combaron became aware of Gormach hovering obsequiously at his elbow. "The large, dark female on the end looks promising. Have her brought to my chamber."

Gormach bowed. "Your will, Ata."

Combaron appraised the woman's bulk, then handed the Warlinga a small bottle he drew from a pouch at his waist. "Scratch her and rub about half of the contents of this into the cuts. Only half," he warned. "I don't want her too drugged, do you understand me? I want an amusing diversion, not a piece of dead meat."

"I will see to it personally, honored Ata. It will be done properly."

Combaron grunted, still intent on his prize. Then he wrinkled up his nose in disgust. "And have your kinsmen wash her down before they hand her over to my Warlinga. She is filthy, and she stinks. And, tell them to have a care. I don't want blood in my bed."

A SHORT TIME LATER, a dripping and cursing mutant female was half dragged, half carried by two of Sulas Warlinga into Combaron's bedchamber. Combaron put down the scroll he'd been pretending to read and rose slowly to meet them. Faces and head crests unreadable, the Warlinga stood with the mutant held firmly between them. He approached her with care. She bared her teeth, and growled something, no doubt obscene, in her barbaric tongue.

He came closer, baring his own teeth. She was such a big strong brute; it was going to be a rare pleasure to break her to his will. Combaron picked up a carved stone bottle from a nearby table. He toasted her; then raised it to his lips and drank.

Lowering the flask, he said to the Warlinga, "Hold her head still." Then he pinched her flattened nostrils closed with his fingers. When she could hold her breath no longer and opened her mouth to breathe, he poured the rest of the red liquid down her throat. She bucked, and gagged, but swallowed most of it.

Combaron stepped back, a smirk of satisfaction curling his lips. "That will change your mind about fighting me, I think. Soon you will be more than eager. You will be begging me for something else—yes, very soon."

He pointed to his bed, a sturdy structure set against the wall. "Tie her to the posts." Then he pointed to a couple of ragged blankets tossed carelessly in the corner. "Bring those over; set them on the floor by the bed. She can use them when I'm done with her for tonight."

The Warlinga lifted the mutant female and placed her, legs spread, in the middle of his bed, then tied her wrists and ankles to the posts. Afterwards they paused, uncertain what to do next.

His audience forgotten for the moment, Combaron gazed down at her; he could already feel a tingling in his groin. The red kavay was arousing his interest. He reached out a hand to touch her, then stopped, remembering the Warlinga still hovering wide-eyed nearby. "What are you waiting for? Get out."

They looked at one another, hesitated, then the senior of them said, "Our Hunt Leader wishes us to stay to protect you, Ata, should the female prove difficult."

"She won't. Now get out."

When they still hesitated, he turned on them, eyes feverish, his lips curled back in anger. Their tails lashed the air behind them, but the Warlinga made no move to leave. Combaron glared a moment longer, then his anger deflated like a punctured ball. "Very well—if your Hunt Leader is that concerned, then stand guard outside my door. If I need you I'll call."

When they were gone, Combaron sat down on the edge of his bed and studied his prize. He had the time now, and the mounting anticipation was part of the pleasure. He marveled at her size and her odd mutations. Like the others of her kind he had seen, she was almost naked of fur. Where she did have hair, on her head and crotch, it was as thick and matted as a Begta's wool.

Combaron stroked her head. She muttered some kind of gibberish at him, but he ignored it. Unlike a Begta's coarse wool, this creature's hair was soft and silky to the touch. He plunged his hands into it, his heightened senses enjoying its strange texture.

Tiring of her curly mane at last, he sat back, and devoured her with his eyes once more. Her size was the main reason he had chosen her tonight; she was so different from the delicate women of his own people.

Why, she was almost as big as one of the Warlinga females. Though none of those scaly creatures had such enlarged feminine charms. Still, the similarity to a Warlinga intrigued him. Secretly, he had always wondered what it would be like to couple with other, forbidden, mates and now...

What an interesting fantasy. He stroked the swell of her bulging arm muscles and shivered. Undrugged, she could probably break him in two. She was as dangerous as any Warlinga. He moaned, feeling the red kavay in his blood singing to him. The tip of his enlarged organ poked out of its protective sheath, staining his kilt with a thick gray liquid.

The drug Gormach had administered, was dulling the fight in her, but Combaron could still see the defiance in those smoldering, dark eyes. He chuckled. Reaching over he cupped one of her large, heavy breasts. He kneaded her flesh, enjoying the feel of its firm roundness under his hand.

At his touch, the woman gasped. Combaron let out a throaty laugh, bent, and ran his tongue around her dark nipple. When she moaned; he nibbled at its firm erection.

Looking up from his play, he caught her eye and smirked. He lowered his head and nipped her again—a little harder this time. She trembled with rage and sexual excitement in nearly equal measure. "Yes, I know, you big brute. In your mind you want to rip out my heart. Ah, but your body betrays you, my wild savage."

Extending his claws, he allowed them to play lightly over the swell of her belly and thighs, teasing her, a knowing smile on his sharp, face. The mutant struggled feebly against his will, but she was panting now. Her body was on fire with need as the red kavay aroused her own lust.

He laughed. "Yes, you don't want to fight me now, do you? But I won't give you what you really want—not just yet. You must learn to obey your new master, hmm? You will be begging me for it, before we are done."

Chapter Seven

Just as Dunnagh was about to give up hope, a tearful Marnez, Tessa, and Moraga were shoved into their pen. The men who weren't drugged rose immediately and hurried to meet them.

The women were shivering and incoherent—even stolid Moraga. Pulling the big woman to his chest, Dunnagh stroked Moraga's hair and made soothing noises, as he guided her back to their shelter. He sat her down and began heaping moss about her shaking body. Glancing up, he saw that Nathan and Chang were also helping Marnez and Tessa.

A sensible woman, Moraga was already calming. Tucked against Nathan's side, Tessa too was settling down. Chang, on the other hand was having quite a bit of trouble with Marnez. The woman was hysterical, cursing and lashing out with her fists one moment, then breaking down into uncontrollable sobbing the next.

Like a blow to the gut, he suddenly realized why she was acting so crazy. In the confusion and the dim light, he hadn't noticed until then, Marti wasn't with them.

Another one of their number was gone.

Jaw tight and eyes stinging, Dunnagh looked away. No more, no more, he couldn't stand much more of this. Noticing Singey hovering by one of the roof posts, looking uncertain, he said, "Philip, bring that bucket and dipper over. Maybe a little water will help calm Marnez down." Without a word, Singey crossed to the wall and returned with the bucket.

Dunnagh stood and Singey handed him the sloshing bucket. "I noticed Marti didn't return with them. Is that what's wrong?"

Dunnagh took it and filled the dipper. "Thanks. You're more observant than I am tonight. I don't know how I missed her absence."

"You had your hands full. Were they good friends?"

"Lovers actually."

"Oh... Like you and Nathan are then."

Dunnagh glanced over at his friend holding the still weeping Tessa. "Like Nathan and I were—once," he clarified.

"Oh. I wondered about that, too."

Choosing not to satisfy the scientist's curiosity further, Dunnagh motioned for Singey to follow him with the bucket and waded through the moss to crouch beside Chang and Marnez. He held out the dipper. "Calm down, Marnez and drink this."

Chang gave Dunnagh a grateful look and put the dipper to Marnez's lips. "Whisky would be better, Sir, but I guess this will have to do." When she tried to turn away, he persisted. "Come on drink up, Carol—that's right, drink it all."

It took a while before Dunnagh could get anything sensible out of the women, but at last they'd calmed down enough to answer his questions. "Start at the beginning and tell us what happened."

Moraga sniffed, then spoke in her thick Caldoni drawl. "We was awful worried 'bout you men when they split us up. We didn't know what to think when they put us in this smelly storeroom. We waited and waited—and we was getting sore worried.

"Then, the Butcher and the Avairei in charge here come back a few minutes ago. The Avairei looks us over and points to Marti. Before she can make much of a fuss they grabs her and takes her away. After that, the Butcher's men brings us back here."

"Damn them all," Marnez said, choking on her tears. "Marti, oh, Marti. Unit Leader, you know how it was for us. We've sworn the oath of the Battle Bonded, like you and Nathan—and now she's gone!"

Still holding the half-empty bucket, Singey patted her back with his free hand and muttered something soothing. Marnez aimed a punch at his head and jerked away from him.

"Don't touch me, Bacach. If it wasn't for you, she wouldn't be gone, and none of this would have happened. I could kill you for this, damn you, kill you—" She aimed another punch in Singey's direction.

Chang caught her wrist and pulled her back. She struggled for a moment, then covered her face with her hands and burst into tears again.

"That's enough, Armachd, smarten up. Get a hold on your temper. You aren't going to bring her back acting like a hysterical fool." Marnez dropped her hands and glared; she nodded. Dunnagh turned to look for Singey, but he had disappeared into the darkness, leaving the bucket in the moss.

Dunnagh took in a ragged breath and decided to let him be, for the moment at least. "Tessa, were you able to get any more information through your implant than Moraga told us?"

Tessa stared at him blankly with wide, frightened eyes, pressing herself even tighter against Nathan. When he repeated the question, she said, "N-no, Dunnagh, Moraga has told you all we know."

"Thank you." Turning to the rest of them, he said, "We better get some sleep. The Warlinga will have us up with the sun. We'll try to find out more about what happened tomorrow. The Loti will know something about this—or the Begta will."

After the others had settled into the moss, Dunnagh scanned the shelter and found, as he'd suspected, Singey wasn't among them. Leaving Marnez tucked up against Moraga, he rose and walked towards the privy.

As he relieved himself he saw Singey leaning against the stone wall, staring out into the empty courtyard. Dunnagh crossed to him and leaned companionably next to him.

The stone had already absorbed the night's chill. It felt rough and icy cold against his arms and chest. Singey was shivering. "It's getting late, Philip. Come back with me and get some rest."

Refusing to acknowledge Dunnagh's presence beside him, Singey continued to stare straight ahead. Dunnagh waited, unfazed by the rebuff. On his way over, he'd used a light Psy probe. The man was tearing himself apart again, replaying Gemma's death and Marnez's cruel words over and over in his mind.

At last recognizing that Dunnagh wasn't going to leave without an answer, Singey said, "I'll be along. Go to sleep yourself."

Dunnagh forced himself to remain against the stone and gave the scientist a toothy smile. "I'd like to, but you see, I can't—not yet."

Singey turned to him, scowling. "And, why not? I'm not your child; you don't have to hover and fret over me. I'll come to bed when I'm tired."

Dunnagh took in a slow, deep breath, letting his irritation dissipate. *You may not be a child, Mr. Snoot, but you definitely need a babysitter.*

"I know that and I'm not your mother—though being a unit leader, sometimes I feel like a mother—to a bunch of spoiled brats." Singey stiffened, and Dunnagh plunged on. "But in this case," he gave Singey another smile. "I'm your bed partner for the night. And, I'm getting cold. So, even if you're not sleepy, humor me. Come to the shelter and lay down."

Singey stared at him for a long moment, then turned back to the courtyard. In a voice barely above a whisper, he murmured, "I can't—"

"You aren't going to bring Marti back by getting hypothermia, you know?"

Singey sighed. "Yes, Dunnagh, I know—I'll be along—soon."

"Soon. Marnez has always had a temper. Keeping her, Taleish and sometimes Chang from blowing up, and doing something stupid, even when we were back home, is one of the joys of being their unit leader. What Marnez said was crap.

"And, you need to tell her that—or any of the rest of them, if they blame you for being here. Don't just walk away and choke up inside. Tell them to shut up. I can't keep fighting your battles for you; they will respect you more for standing up for yourself—that's our way in the corps."

Singey let out an ironic bark of a laugh. "Oh, yes, I'd forgotten; I am a member of Lann Gheal now. But unfortunately, I'm a recruit who lacks much physical training in personal violence—"

"Are you worried one of the armachda will resort to serious physical violence against you?"

"A little, I am to blame after all—"

"Damn it, man, that's what I've been trying to tell you. You are no more at fault than I am or Nathan or Taleish or Marnez for that matter. Most of us on this mission can look back and say, 'If I only did that, instead of that, none of this would have happened. You've lived a very sheltered life indeed, if you have never told yourself that before."

Singey thought about it for a while then chuckled. "May the High God help me, I guess I have, when you put it like that."

Dunnagh took his arm and began steering Singey back across the darkened pen to their shelter. "I sense that Gemma's death touched you very deeply, but you can't let her ghost haunt you forever. I wish we had her bone bead to add to Enghus's, but we won't forget her. She will live on in our memories and be honored. Let her go, Philip, and rest in peace."

Lying down beside Singey at the back of the shelter, Dunnagh heaped moss over himself and the shivering scientist. "What about Marti?" Singey murmured.

"That's my worry as this squad's unit leader, remember? Come a little closer and try to get some rest."

Unable to take his own advice, Dunnagh heard Singey's quiet snores, but continued to stare wide-eyed into the night. He'd put on a brave facade for Singey's benefit, but his heart ached with his grieving and the shame of his helplessness. So many lost—when would it end?

In the cold emptiness of a sleepless night, something changed inside him. With a deadly calm born out of the darkest despair, he made his resolution. *Two more gone, by my Ancestors and all the Gods of Caldon, I'll sacrifice myself first before I let them take another.*

Chapter Eight

Shortly after the morning meal, Sulas's overseer divided them into groups and put them to work doing the kind of hard physical labor a slave would be expected to do in a technologically primitive society. As he joined the Loti heading for the fields, Dunnagh saw the Butcher and his men packing up to leave Sulas. Gormach looked up as he passed.

Dunnagh gave him a thin-lipped, smile. *Want to say good bye? Don't forget to fall off a cliff on your way home, you sadistic devil,* Dunnagh wished him silently as their eyes met.

The Warlinga returned the smile, displaying his impressive fangs. There was such a calculating look in his malevolent red eyes that Dunnagh felt a cold chill run down his spine. *It's not over between us, is it? And what evil scheme have you been planning with the Avairei?*

A Sulas Warlinga shouted at Dunnagh to keep moving. With one last look, Dunnagh hastened to catch up with Berren and Nathan.

DUNNAGH SAT DOWN BESIDE Nathan and began wolfing down his portion of the heavy gray bread a Begta slave had handed out to him as his midday meal.

"Having fun?" Nathan asked.

Dunnagh leaned back against a mossy boulder by the trail and closed his eyes. The bread lay like a stone in his gut. "Great fun, ha, ha."

Nathan finished his bread and lay down beside him. "You gonna ask one of the Warlinga about Marti again?"

Without opening his eyes, he said, "Berren is going to see what she can find out for me from the Loti. I'll wait and see what she has to say before I tackle them again."

"Good." Nathan took a finger and traced the line of a long claw mark running down Dunnagh's chest. "Your body don't need any more of those."

Dunnagh grunted an agreement. They fell into a companionable silence. The sun was warm on Dunnagh's closed eyelids, and the loti singing was nice—

"I see Mr. Snoot still thinks he's too good to come sit with the savages," Nathan said.

Startled out of a half doze, Dunnagh sat up and looked around. Singey was sitting alone with his back against a boulder on the other side of the trail a little ways from them. The bowed figure looked so forlorn that Dunnagh felt his heart lurch.

Then in the next moment, his sympathy changed to annoyance. Damn the man; he was too tired for this.

Dunnagh rose and started over to him. "Hey, where are you going?" Nathan called. Dunnagh kept walking. "You're not his babysitter, you know. Come back and rest; leave the snooty prick be."

"Shut up, Nathan; get some rest yourself," Dunnagh snapped. "I *am* his babysitter. Just like I'm yours and everybody else's around here. It's my damned job!"

Nathan got to his feet and in two quick strides, caught up to him. Putting a hand on Dunnagh's shoulder, he spun him around to face him. "Hey, Dunnagh, go easy."

Dunnagh balled up a fist, ready for a fight. Nathan let go his hold, but continued to stare. "Dunnagh, what's wrong?"

"Stupid question, everything's wrong," Dunnagh said and hated the quiver of emotion he heard in his own voice. Why did Nathan have to bring up Marti? Why did he have to tell him Singey was brooding again? Damn it! By all the Ancestors, he was so tired.

When Nathan said nothing, only continued to watch him with a troubled look in his sooty, gray eyes, Dunnagh's annoyance dissipated. "Sorry, Mo Hara, I'm just tired."

"We all are. Come back and sit down. Rest break will be over soon."

"I know—and I will, in a moment." Turning his back on his friend, Dunnagh crossed to the scientist and sat down beside him.

"Why are you sitting here alone?" Dunnagh asked. "Why not come join the rest of us?" Dunnagh pointed with his lips to Nathan and the rest of the group of exhausted humans lounging beside some friendly Loti. "Are you sick again?"

"No. I just needed a little time by myself to think—that's all."

"Mm, to think. You scientists like to do a lot of thinking—what are you thinking about?"

Singey's expression hardened. "Don't patronize me, Unit Leader, as I told you before, I'm not going to become another burden for you to carry. I'm fine. As fine as any of us, that is."

"Unit Leader? So we're back to the formalities again. I'm counting on it, 'Mr. Singey,' but that still doesn't answer my question."

Singey rubbed a hand across his face and sighed. "Sorry, Dunnagh; I didn't mean to snap at you. I'm thinking about the Avairei mostly."

"The Avairei and their damned cook pots. I know, everybody's thinking about it. The worry is what's wearing away at our will to survive. The natives could take another one of us at any time, for any reason—a religious festival—an important guest—boredom. It weighs on my mind too

"But we'll be leaving soon—have to!" Dunnagh rubbed at his neck. Damn what was causing this periodic pain?

Singey watched him for a moment, his eyes following the motion of Dunnagh's hand. Dunnagh sensed him watching, felt his face heat and dropped his hand into his lap.

"It's more than that. Avairei cook pots do trouble me, Dunnagh, but they are only a part of the problem. This world, technologically speaking, is very primitive, true, but I suspect that these people know much more about genetics and biochemistry than our own scientists.

"No, don't look at me like that; I am serious. It's their pharmacological knowledge that worries me most of all."

Dunnagh thought about it for a long moment, then grunted an agreement. "Ye-es, you might have a point. So what you're saying is that these Avairei might use drugs to get whatever they want from us."

"Precisely. They can put it in our food, or rub it in to any open wound. They can do what they like to us, kill one of us anytime, and if we are drugged—like Samuels—we would be powerless to stop them. The Avairei,

I fear, are far more dangerous to us than the Warlinga, in spite of the lizardmen's strength."

Was this why Gormach had brought them here? But if so, what did he hope to get from them with Avairei help that he couldn't get with brute force? Dunnagh had no idea. "Yes, I see what you mean. And if we're caught trying to escape, what would the Avairei do? Torture us in some way with a devilish potion that would cause great pain?"

"Perhaps, but I suspect they would be more likely to keep us drugged and tractable so it wouldn't happen again."

Such a fate was too awful to contemplate. Drugs! How he hated them. To submit without a struggle, a silly grin on your face, a slave to another's will—it was one of the deepest fears of his soul.

"My own thoughts have been wandering down similar paths since we got here," he admitted. "Sadistic brutality I can fight. I may not win—but even if I lose, my spirit would remain untarnished. This other—to be shamed in such a way—helpless," He touched his neck again and shuddered.

Singey had murmured an agreement and the two men fell silent. Soon after that, the Warlinga had called them back to the fields. During the rest of the afternoon's work, there had been no private moment to question the scientist further on the subject, but the images his words had evoked in Dunnagh's mind continued to plague him.

By the time the field crew finished for the day and was led back to their pen and fed their evening ration of the monotonous "glop and blue puke juice," Dunnagh was exhausted, and too tired to question the Loti about Marti or consider seeking Singey out for further discussion. All he wanted at that moment, was his bed in the moss.

He'd just lain down, when a commotion over by the gate brought him to his feet. Beside him, Chang sat up, too, moss clinging to his dark hair. "What's going on, Sir?"

Still looking towards the gate, Dunnagh said as he got to his feet. "I don't know, but I'd better go find out."

"Me, too," Chang said.

Singey rose, as well, and joined them. "More of your nursemaid duties, Unit Leader?"

Dunnagh barked a mirthless laugh. What were the women up to over there? "You're catching on, Philip." Dunnagh paused and turned to him. You don't have to come with me. Stay here if you like."

Singey shook his head and fell into step with him. "I'll come; you might need your scientific advisor."

Dunnagh smiled. "I might at that." Alerted as well by the noise, Nathan and the rest of the men rose to follow them to the gate.

As Dunnagh approached, he could hear the women talking animatedly to the Warlinga overseer. As the conversation continued, in broken snatches, Marnez's angry high-pitched cursing, in a variety of tongues, dominated all the rest.

The argument was starting to attract attention. Several of the Avairei were drifting over, including one older man, who seemed to be a person of some authority to judge by his apparel. Dunnagh quickened his pace,

As he feared, Marnez's temper overran her good sense and she took a swing at the overseer. The Warlinga flung her away, his claws tearing a long gash down her shoulder and upper arm. The woman never noticed. Marnez leapt to her feet, screaming her curses.

She would have gone right back to the attack, probably getting herself killed, if Dunnagh hadn't arrived just then and grabbed her from behind. He embraced her, pinning her arms to her side and lifting her onto her toes. "Settle down, Marnez, that's an order, Armachd, settle down," Dunnagh murmured fiercely next to her ear.

She fought him for a moment longer, then collapsed against him, sobbing. Over her bent head he glared at the other women, and demanded, "All right, what's this all about?"

They looked at him with frightened eyes, but there was an air of grim determination in their manner that told him they weren't going to back down either. He waited, staring them down.

At last Moraga took a deep breath. "Marti was a good friend and one of the kin. And, though Samuels was a new man, he was one of us too. We wanted the bones, Ce'awn, that's all—we just want what's our right.

"Tessa was translating for us, but the Warlinga there was pretending he didn't understand us, even when we shows him." She held out Enghus's bone bead on its hair-cord around her neck.

Behind him, there were some growls of approval from the men. Amazed, he found himself agreeing with them, too.

By my ancestors, what have we become? Cannibals of our own dead, demanding their bones as if it were our right, no less. Then flying into a murderous rage when denied them. Gods! We're all about to snap with the strain of this dreadful existence, he thought.

Over Marnez's head he studied the gawkers in the courtyard. How much had they understood of the dispute? And, more to the point, what were the Warlinga going to do about this? Knowing a bit about the Warlinga by now, he thought the overseer was unlikely to let this insult to his authority end here.

Hoping for some assistance, Dunnagh scanned the onlookers and saw an elderly priest watching. Maybe he could do something to help. "Tessa, that Avairei with the gray in his pelt and all the necklaces, he looks like someone in charge. See if you can make *him* understand."

She nodded; then in halting sentences, addressed the Avairei. Seemingly startled at being spoken to directly by a slave, the old fellow hesitated, then came a little closer to the fence. As he listened to Tessa's halting request, some of the onlookers pointed at her and laughed, mimicking her pronunciation of their language.

Dunnagh heard Nathan cursing under his breath, and scowled a warning. Nathan had become very protective of Tessa. It was obvious to Dunnagh that his old friend didn't like seeing her efforts ridiculed by a bunch of young lay-about furs.

If they persisted, Nathan was likely to make an issue of it. *No more trouble—don't you dare,* Dunnagh silently told him.

Fortunately, before the situation heated further, the elder said something to the onlookers and they quieted, much to Dunnagh's relief.

Understanding Tessa's request at last, the elderly priest seemed surprised. Then a rapid conversation ensued between the priest and the overseer. It seemed to Dunnagh that the Avairei didn't look happy about the explanation he was getting, either.

Returning his attention to Tessa, the priest pointed to her bone bead, and said, "No slaves I've heard of practice a warrior's death custom. We didn't know. I will look into this." Then, he hesitated. Holding up one four-fingered hand; he extended two delicate fingers to make his point. "Two deaths, two beads?'

Tessa nodded emphatically. Pointing to herself, she gave the native word for woman, then pointing to Dunnagh she gave the word for man.

The Avairei looked thoughtful, then his jaw tightened. He rounded on Hanno, asking a series of rapid, low-voiced questions. The overseer's tail lashed the ground, and his head crest drooped as the interrogation continued. At last he gave the Avairei a grudging answer that satisfied him.

Dunnagh saw an expression that might have been anger distort the priest's features, quickly controlled. Turning back to Tessa, he said, "I will see what can be done."

The priest was about to leave when Dunnagh stopped him. Using some of the few native words he knew, he looked into the Avairei's eyes. "Thank you, Ata."

Meeting Dunnagh's blue stare for the first time, the old fellow's eyes widened. Tearing his gaze away from Dunnagh's at last, he hurried off, almost running in his eagerness to get away.

Dunnagh stared after him bemused, scratching at his growing beard. What in the world was that all about?

"Dunnagh, I always knew you were an ugly cuss, but did you have to scare the poor fur half to death?" Nathan said as he came up beside him.

Still watching the retreating priest, Dunnagh barked an uneasy laugh. "He did look like he'd just seen a ghost, didn't he? But all I said, was thank you Ata."

Chapter Nine

Maker Gladdris settled its bulk onto a rock ledge deep within the bedrock of the Sulas pools. Its mouth tentacles moved lazily, sampling the unseen currents in the depths. All was well; no enemy had breached Khutani defenses.

In the phosphorescent water above, its descendants went about their normal daily routine. Gladdris couldn't help gurgling with pleasure. Even down here, the subtle vibrations of the young one's play flowed along the subterranean currents to brush against it sensitive skin. In another context such delicious sendings would give it great satisfaction, but not today.

Gladdris reluctantly dismissed the familiar tastes of home from its mind; there were other matters far more important to sink its teeth into and gnaw upon. The maker laid its head atop its coils, gulped in large mouthfuls of black water and composed itself for the dream.

The Begta shaman had made the sacrifice. His kinsmen had suffered and some had died, but the Chosen was coming to Sulas. Gladdris's mouth tentacles writhed with the pungent flavor of its frustration. It could almost taste the Chosen; he was so near—but where was the little priestess who had agreed to help them? Why hadn't she come to its descendants in the pools above for more instruction? Had she betrayed them?

The spirit body of the Maker floated up from the ledge. It swam the etheric currents, its mouth tentacles questing for answers. Within the blackness of the void, it vomited up the bitterness of its desperation. What was the enemy planning? And, where, oh where, was the Dream-Chosen... ?

Tasting nothing familiar, Gladdris halted its search and floated, thinking. Never mind a search for the priestess, finding the willful human who had agreed to make the bond was more important. Intent on its search, Gladdris became careless.

Suddenly the blackness about the Khutani exploded with snarling monsters. In mockery of the form chosen by the Khutani, the Umwira had given themselves long, snaky bodies with the addition of ropy arms ending in bony clawed, hands. Massive horned heads topped their necks. Their red eyes glowed with malice as they watched Gladdris warily.

<<What have we here?>> the massive leader said to its pack-mates.

<<Lunch,>> one of them growled.

<<A slimeworm awakened from its nap and come to play,>> said another.

Gladdris bared its teeth, snapping at an unguarded tail. The pack howled with laughter, but drew back out of range nonetheless.

So many, the Umwira were circling to surround it. Gladdris created a shield of etheric matter. To come across it so easily, the Umwira were either very lucky or they had been waiting for just such a mistake as Gladdris had offered them.

Swimming into the dream—unthinking, truly the Makers had slept too long. These creatures must have been sent to patrol Khutani defenses. But why? Were the wizards aware of Khutani conjuring for a new host? Gladdris swallowed its fear and shifted its shape to that of a creature with armored sides and sharp spikes along its backbone.

It must not be killed or they might taste the truth in its dying essence. No matter what had alerted them or what they might suspect, the enemy must not find out about the Dream-Chosen!

<<You are alone, Khutani filth, shields and shape-shifting will not save you. You are mine and you will die,>> the leader taunted.

Gladdris wasted no time on verbal challenges while the pack circled. Etheric fire spewed from its mouth in a blinding flash of white light. The monster next to the leader screamed, its body engulfed in a ball of flames.

With a roar the pack attacked. Gladdris coiled and twisted away, bolts of flame shooting from the spikes of its backbone. Bellows of pain accompanied the volley.

The Khutani spat more etheric fire and more of the Umwira burst into flame and incinerated. But others swam past its guard to snap at Gladdris's sides and belly. There were too many of the foul beasts for Gladdris to win this battle. It must flee, but if it hurt them enough, maybe they wouldn't follow it back to the Sulas pools.

Gladdris grunted with pain, as the leader spat a stream of flame along its more vulnerable belly. Glowing ichor from the wound flowed into the ether. The pack howled in glee, closing in once more. Gladdris whirled out of range, the enemy snapping at its tail.

Two of the enemy kept pace, trying to catch Gladdris between the lethal flames of their fire. The Khutani twisted away, barely missing another salvo. Then, the leader was right in front of it. Gladdris coiled and struck, sinking its teeth into the leader's neck.

The Umwira choked out an agonized roar, raking Gladdris's belly and sides with its long claws. Gladdris caught the bony hands in its own created hands, and ground its teeth deeper into the soft flesh in its jaws.

Ignoring the blows hurled against its armored sides and back by the enraged pack, the Khutani shook its prey, opening the wound wider. Violet ichor spewed from the wound in a torrent that stank of sulfur. It fanned out about hunter and prey alike.

Gladdris tore at the wound one last moment, then drew back, incinerating the spasming corpse. Spitting out another volley of etheric fire at the milling pack, Gladdris fled into the void.

When the Khutani was sure it wasn't being followed, Gladdris halted and resumed its true form. It had been wounded and was nearing its limit of endurance, but Gladdris couldn't afford to turn back.

The Council had been careless, blindly sending out their call for help to any sensitive Avairei among the priesthood. The Umwira suspected something; there must be a traitor among the priests. Now more than ever, it was important that it find the Chosen.

After resting for a time and renewing its strength, Gladdris recalled his taste and soon located the Dream-Chosen's tether. Gladdris had been enraged by such trickery when Dievris ensnared him, but now it had to admit—*privately*, Dievris had known what was best. The alien was proving to be most unpredictable.

Not long after locating the tether, Gladdris's mouth tentacles brushed against the glowing aura of the Chosen's partially formed shield. The Dream-Chosen was awake, his mind occupied with other matters. If its touch wasn't too invasive the alien wouldn't be aware of Gladdris's prying. Slowly, very slowly, the Khutani slithered through the alien defenses and inserted a gentle probe...

Gladdris gurgled with pleasure as it looked upon the surface world once again. Through the Dream-Chosen's eyes. The Maker saw jagged tawny mountains encircling fields of blue-gray, shrubby plants. Massa root, it was a staple in the diet of both the young Khutani and the other intelligent species of Timorna. Loti farmers and Begta slaves were harvesting the ripe tubers from the red soil. They placed them into reed baskets which others were hauling to the keep.

SUDDENLY A WAVE OF sickness tore at Dunnagh's gut. He staggered, and fell forward onto his hands and knees. The basket of roots he'd been carrying landed beside him, gray tubers spilling onto the path. He cursed under his breath and hung his head, waiting for the dizziness to pass.

Just behind him Berren bent down, picked up the fallen roots and hurriedly put them back into the basket. She glanced over her shoulder as she worked, making anxious cooing noises, urging him to get up.

Dunnagh heard an angry shout from one of the supervising Warlinga and saw the man heading their way. "I know, I know." He blinked, trying to clear his vision and reached out a hand to the Loti. "Berren, help me up."

He'd spoken in Caldoni, too exhausted to think of the Timornan words, but she understood his gesture and pulled him to his feet. By the time the Warlinga reached them Dunnagh had his basket back on his shoulder and was trudging along beside the Loti. The Warlinga glared at him with head crest flattened, but made no move to discipline him again.

Dunnagh's back still stung from the lashing he'd received the last time he'd fallen; he quickened his pace in case the man decided to repeat the reprimand. All the humans had learned a healthy respect for the Warlinga's stinging tails.

Unlike the Butcher and his men the Warlinga of Sulas weren't cruel or sadistic, but they did expect their slaves to work, and work hard, which wasn't easy for the humans, while the alien sickness still limited their strength. Of course if they were strong enough to do the work expected of them without trouble, they'd be strong enough to escape, too.

Up ahead of him, Taleish shouted a curse in Caldoni. A Warlinga hit him with his tail and Taleish sprawled in the dirt. Dunnagh quickened his pace, fearing more violence. Damned fool—the man had a hot temper and no sense. Dunnagh rubbed at his neck. Escape. They had to get out of here somehow—and soon...

GLADDRIS WITHDREW ITS probe more troubled than ever. Where was Sagas? The Maker forced itself to remain calm. Drifting once more upon the etheric current, it summoned the priestess's flavor. The memory was piquant, rich with subtlety and texture, but it remained only a memory. The woman herself was gone.

Dead? Perhaps. Gladdris trembled; if that were true what would become of their hopes for the Dream-Chosen? Gladdris swallowed its growing anxiety and focused harder, hoping to detect the truth of her disappearance.

<<Sagas, what has happened—where are you?>>

Suddenly its mouth tentacles brushed against a barrier of fear and despair, so intense that it seemed as solid as stone. Startled the Maker paused, and explored the curiosity. Was this barrier a part of the mystery? The taste was vile—Umwira perhaps. Gladdris tore at the loathsome mass, hoping to bite a hole through it. <<Priestess?>>

<<You will not break through like that, Amsi. >>

Gladdris jerked its head round teeth bared. Qwaltamis, the oldest among the Makers floated nearby, mouth tentacles waving. <<The priestess—is she beyond this wall? Have you tried to reach her?>>

<<Yes, I have tried to breech it many times; it cannot be penetrated.>>

Gladdris's tentacles brushed the barrier once more, then it returned its attention to the other Khutani. <<What is this mass made of?>>

<<That is a very interesting question, Amsi. It has the taint of Umwira sorcery about it. But it was partially created by the priestess herself; which is why it is so strong.>>

<<Has she betrayed us then?>>

<<No I don't think so. Taste the barrier again. It is loathsome, but I taste only fear and despair rather than treachery. See if you agree?>>

Gladdris spat out its reluctance, but did as Qwaltamis suggested. When it finished its exam it said, <<It is as you say; Amsi, I detect no treachery. But you should also know that I was attacked just now as I searched for the priestess.>>

<<Yes, I sensed the struggle and came to aid you.>> The maker brushed a tentacle along Gladdris's healing wound. <<How badly are you injured, Amsi?>>

<<I must return to my body soon to rest, Amsi. But what shall we do? The Chosen is at Sulas; I just tasted him. He is thinking of escape again, and still refuses to come to us in his dreams. Without the priestess to guide him, he might succeed with his escape plan—>>

<<Or die in the trying. Without their off-world weaponry, these humans are no match for our Warlinga. But if the priestess, for whatever reason, can't serve us, then we must contact another. Perhaps her Ata Leyas will prove a useful servant in her place. In the meantime, you must go back and renew yourself. We will tighten the Chosen's tether and wait a little longer.>>

Gladdris dripped the sourness of its impatience into the silence between them. Qwaltamis was right; it must go, but what of the alien? <<I hope we have that kind of time>>

Qwaltamis rumbled in annoyance and finally, Gladdris burped up its acquiescence. <<So be it then, I will leave you to guard him and warn the Council of the Umwira threat.>>

Chapter Ten

Today Dunnagh was assigned the task of hauling bags of the rock powder the natives mixed and used for fuel, from a storeroom behind the Warlinga barracks to another nearer the kitchen. A commotion at the gate made him pause with a bag on his shoulder and gawk.

Someone had come calling; the on-duty guards were already opening the gate. But before he could see the new arrivals, the guard assigned to his crew growled a warning, and Dunnagh hurried on with his load. Had the Butcher returned so soon? A quick glance told him no.

Dunnagh deposited his load and quickly returned to the courtyard. When he stepped outside the storeroom, their Warlinga guard was nowhere in sight. Taking the blessed opportunity to rest, he leaned against the wall and looked around. Taller than the Avairei, Dunnagh was able to see over their heads, without attracting undue attention to himself.

Evidently these new arrivals weren't expected, because there was a lot of gesticulating and excited chatter going on among the people hurrying by. He listened, but was unable to distinguish many words. Finally, he gave up and tried using his Psy, to capture the subtle nuances of their talk

He detected a note of fear in some voices, and anger in others. There seemed to be no overt threat to him or his people by these unexpected visitors that he could sense. That was a relief, but the newcomers had definitely peaked his interest.

The arriving group consisted of several very badly injured Warlinga guards and four exhausted Loti carrying a covered litter.

"Well, well, those Warlinga have been in a scrap," Nathan said as he set down his burden and joined him. "Someone—or something has roughed them up pretty good. Maybe some of the stories the Loti and Begta have been telling us were true. Those Warlinga have certainly earned their keep today."

"Yes, it would seem so. Nathan, look at some of those claw marks! No Warlinga we've seen could have done that."

"Yeah, makes me a little weak in the knees when I think about us meeting up with that kind of beastie when we make our escape. We wouldn't have much of a chance without our beam rifles."

"Don't think about it then, we'll figure something out. You'll make it out—I promise."

Dunnagh could feel Nathan's eyes upon him, but he pretended to be absorbed with the activity going on in front of them.

The elderly priest who had helped them with the overseer, was assisting a very shaken Avairei female from the litter. Her kilt was covered in grime and maybe blood. She didn't seem as old as the Ata helping her, but there *were* strands of gray in her mane and around her mouth. She leaned heavily upon him for a moment, then straightened. Giving the crowd a haughty stare, she pointedly ignored their shouted questions.

Hearing another commotion over by the entrance to the inner keep, Dunnagh glanced in that direction. The Avairei they nicknamed, "weasel-face" hurried through the entrance, hastily straightening his cloak and adornments. He was definitely not pleased, by their untimely arrival.

Dunnagh's lip twitched. "I wonder what the little devil's been up to? He looks like a kid that's been caught with his hand in mommy's purse, and he's awfully pissed about it."

Nathan's laugh was low, mirthless. "Who cares—but the show's a good excuse for taking a rest."

Dunnagh grinned in sympathy, then returned his attention to the courtyard drama.

When weasel-face reached the people surrounding the litter, he bowed to the stately woman, but there was a hint of insolence in his manner that was plain enough even to Dunnagh's alien eyes. After listening to him for a few moments, she cut him off and brushed past him, striding angrily into the keep. A formidable woman, Dunnagh decided, and quickly revised his opinion of who was in charge at Sulas.

Chapter Eleven

S agas closed the door on the clamor in the hall and breathed a sigh of relief. Her reception chamber was a simple room with its whitewashed walls and plain wicker furnishings. After her recent ordeal, it was such a welcome sight—and one she'd never hoped to see again.

Murmuring a prayer of thanks to the Mother, she sat the lamp on her work table. She needed a drink to calm her nerves. Crossing to the sideboard, she pulled out a bottle and retreated to her favorite chair. Her finger traced the geometrical carvings on the flask. This had belonged to her mother; she'd never thought to see it again.

Sagas poured the rich purple brandy into a bowl and took a big gulp of the fiery liquid, leaned back and closed her eyes. By the Mother of them all, she was so tired. Every muscle and bone in her body ached. The events of the last few days had shaken her mental and physical equilibrium to the core.

If she had been asked before this, she would have said that her people were basically loyal to her. Now she knew from bitter experience that was not the case. She had to face it. The Dingay star was on the rise, and her clan, along with others who rigidly kept to the old traditions, were a minority within the circles of power in Riath.

For years Sagas thought of Sulas as *her* keep, to manage as she saw fit. This treachery had devastated her, because it meant that Combaron's hold over her people was much stronger than she had imagined.

Somehow, in spite of all her care, Combaron found out about her late night visit to the pools. By some sorcery that she didn't understand, he had been able to send word of her defiance to Riath, more quickly than a Warlinga messenger could run the Jeban Pass.

When a hunting pack of the High Matri's own Warlinga arrived with an order for her to appear before the High Council at once, Sagas read the scroll like the death sentence it truly was. And, she couldn't even warn the Khutani to find another to care for their Dream-Chosen—not with the guard Combaron had placed outside her door.

When she left the keep, the morning after receiving the summons, she thought she was leaving Sulas for the last time. Combaron thought so, too—she saw it in his gloating eyes.

Resigning herself to the inevitable, Sagas accepted her fate and allowed them to take her without protest. If the Great Mother needed her help to further the Khutani's' plan, then She would have to do something to get her out of this mess.

Sagas chuckled to herself and took another drink of the brandy. And, the Mother had. By all the holy Khutani in the pools, she had! Sagas drank more brandy. Oh, the look on Combaron's face when she showed up unexpectedly this afternoon. That had been priceless.

Idly she wondered what the slimeworm had been doing in her absence. She yawned then finished her drink. She was too tired to think—maybe just a little rest. Stumbling to her bed in the next room she lay down and was asleep within moments.

Sagas was awakened some time later by a knock at her door. Sitting up, she rubbed her gritty eyes, and called, "Enter."

Her personal attendant Pela, entered the reception chamber balancing a meal tray in one hand. From far down the corridor Sagas heard the evening singing in the main chapel. Great Mother, she hadn't meant to sleep so long. Pela closed the door quietly, then set the tray down on the small table by Sagas's favorite chair. The rich fragrant odor of hot stew and newly baked lamra cakes filled the room.

Sagas smiled gratefully at her protégée, sat down in her chair and picked up her spoon. "Thank you, Pela, this was very thoughtful. I hadn't realized I was so famished."

Pela bowed. Sagas took several hungry mouthfuls; the stew was very rich tonight, with a unique flavor. "This is wonderful. Give my compliments to the cook." She took another mouthful, savoring the taste. "I don't think I have had such a dish before. Has Tasi found some new recipes in one of the old tombs?"

Pela giggled. "I think not, Ima. Cook has been kept busy preparing all Ata Combaron's favorite dishes. It's probably the taste of the mutant meat that you are enjoying."

Sagas looked up from her bowl, puzzled. "What mutant meat?"

"San Gormach has been here again, and Ata Combaron, has traded with him for some new mutant slaves. The Ata, it is said, has plans to breed them, both for their labor and as meat for our table."

Sagas dismissed Pela's account of the new slaves as unimportant. She was too weary to be curious. Later, when she looked back and recalled this conversation and the events that followed, she would marvel at her dull-wittedness.

"So, this is where that spawn of the black pit, Gormach, has been hiding, what a laugh."

"Ima?"

Sagas chuckled and took another bite of stew. "I never thought I'd be grateful to that drunken, bandit Gormach for his laziness, but now I am. If he'd been doing his duty, that warband of monsters from the Ghostlands wouldn't have been there to meet us in the pass, and I would have had to answer the High Matri's summons."

Sagas took a few more mouthfuls of her meal, enjoying Pela's wide-eyed expression. "Oh, I know I'll have to answer the summons eventually, but even Combaron and his grandmother can't expect me to go till the Tragar packs hunt down the monsters and make the journey safe once more." She smirked. "I have my reprieve. And there's nothing Combaron can do about it."

I just hope I can find a way to warn the Khutani, before they drag me away, because next time, I'm sure, I won't be back.

Taking a deep breath, Pela asked, "Ima, what happened> Where are the High Matri's hunting pack? Did they go after the Umwira?"

Sagas paused, the spoon halfway to her lips. She shuddered, remembering. "No. I think they are all dead, as are about half my escort from Sulas."

Pela gasped, her hand flying to her mouth. "Ima, how terrible! You must have been frightened nearly to death. Was anyone captured?"

"I don't know; there was no time to count the bodies or look for survivors. With a small number of loyal Sulas Warlinga about me for protection, we just ran.

"And, yes, I was terrified. I'd never experienced anything so frightening in all my life. They came on us so suddenly, just this side of the pass. And they were so vicious, howling like the demented, and covering themselves with the blood and entrails of the fallen as they fought. Our Warlinga were equally fierce. Many died so the rest of us could escape."

Sagas went back to eating, not wanting to remember any more. The fight and its aftermath were going to give her nightmares for the rest of her life. Which, might not be long if the Dingay could arrange it.

Sagas doubted she would ever reach Riath for a trial. There were too many unaligned clans that wouldn't accept the flimsy evidence arrayed against her. No, a "tragic accident" somewhere in the mountains was more likely to be her fate next time.

Pela watched Sagas eat a while longer, then she ventured, "Will there be anything else, Ima? If not, may I go?"

Sagas looked up, startled. What was wrong? Pela was usually very talkative. Had she been frightened so badly by her account of the massacre, or was she afraid to be seen with her, like so many others? Disloyal? Surely not Pela. She sighed and nodded. "Yes, of course, if that is what you want, Pela. You may go."

Pela bowed and began a slow progress to the door, her movements stiff and graceless.

"Wait."

Almost to the door, Pela paused but didn't turn. Sagas rose from her chair and walked quickly to the younger priestess's side. Stretching out a hand, she lifted the folds of Pela's long kilt. The woman's buttocks and upper legs were crisscrossed by a series of ugly welts.

Sagas scowled. A thorned discipline rod had caused those marks. Why? Pela was the gentlest, most obedient of creatures. Why had she been given the harshest of disciplines in Sagas's absence?

Sagas let the cloth drop from fingers suddenly gone numb. Trying to keep her voice neutral, she said, "What is this about, Pela?"

Without turning to face her, Pela said in a voice barely above a whisper, "I was found remiss in my duty by the Ata Leyas. I have been given discipline and penance for my transgressions."

"Remiss in your duties, is it, hmm?" Sagas's face contorted with impotent rage. *Oh, my poor child, was your lack of obedience a failure to do your duty to the Khutani, or was it a failure to climb into his bed when he demanded it.*

Damn the Dingay—all Dingay! She clenched her hands into tight fists, trying to control her temper.

Choosing Pela, of all the young priestesses, for his perversions was a doubly offensive insult. She was all but promised to one of Sagas's own family. Combaron knew this, of course, so the outrage was planned and deliberate. How certain Combaron was of his family's power that he now dared defy their traditions so openly.

Sagas drew a tired hand across her eyes. So much to think about, so much to do and so little time. She touched Pela on the shoulder; the young woman was trembling. "Go now," she said, "and have Ata Temog see to those cuts."

Before Pela could protest, she added, "I know it is not the custom after a discipline, but do it. If anyone questions you about it, say I ordered you to do it. Understand?"

"Yes, Ima. Your will, Ima."

Sagas had returned to her chair when Pela poked her head around the door once more. "Ima, I almost forgot. Ata Temog wishes to speak with you about a matter of importance."

What now? What else could have possibly gone wrong in my absence? "Did the Ata say what he wished to speak about, child?"

"He said to tell you, if you should ask, that he has seen Blue Eyes."

Sagas felt the meal she'd just eaten sour in her gut.

Oh, Holy Mother, help us!

"Tell him to attend me at my prayers in my private chapel tonight."

Chapter Twelve

The humans had just been returned to their pen for the night, when Oglas cried out, "Well, the Gods be praised. Look! Tis herself it is!"

A disheveled, but very much alive, Marti Gretoc was roughly pushed into their enclosure. Marti staggered as the Warlinga shoved her through the gate. When she caught her balance, she turned and gave them the finger, adding a colorful Caldoni insult for good measure.

In spite of the language barrier, the guards took her meaning, but instead of disciplining her, they only laughed and made a few rude gestures of their own in return. Marti spat on the ground and shouted more colorful invective at their departing backs. When they were out of sight, she pushed herself off the fence and limped stiffly over to her comrades.

"Is it you, Marti, or is it a ghost we be seeing?" Taleish said as she settled herself among them.

"Yes, it's me—no ghost." She smiled, as if enjoying their surprise then hugged her lover to her fiercely.

Impatient for her news Chang blurted, "So, what happened? We thought you'd been added to the stewpot for sure."

With a teasing glint in her eye, Marti glanced at him, then gave Marnez a passionate kiss, making them wait. "No cook pots for this piece of brown sugar, boyo. That high lord in there has a real sweet tooth, he does!"

Rhys muttered something under his breath and glared back towards the inner sanctum.

Tessa looked from one angry Caldoni face to another, puzzled. "I don't understand, Marti. What happened to you?"

Marti looked disgusted. "What do you think happened? What usually happens between a man and a woman?"

"You mean that horrid weasel-face raped you?" Tessa's eyes grew round with shock.

Marti smiled, but there was no amusement in her eyes. They remained as hard as obsidian. "Not exactly. When he picked me I sort of figured what was the game. I was all set for a tussle, but the Butcher's men were ready for that. They pinned me, then the Butcher cut me and rubbed some foul smelling stuff into the wounds.

"Soon after that, I started feeling sort of dizzy-like. Then, up in weasel-face's room, he made me drink this red potion of his." She shrugged. "After that, I was willing enough—more than willing." She gave them a throaty laugh. "That potion's the strongest aphrodisiac I've ever heard of. You could make a fortune with that stuff on the black market."

Addressing Tessa directly, Marti affected an air of boredom and added, "Can't say that he was one of the better lays I've had, but he certainly was an energetic little rabbit."

Tessa blushed, noticed other eyes upon her, and looked away.

"Funny, he was just getting it on with me again this afternoon, when someone called him away. He was real mad, but he went. The next thing I knew, a couple Warlinga were pulling me out of the bed and hustling me down the hall.

"The black-hearted devils tied and gagged me, then threw me in a storeroom somewhere. I was there for hours it seemed like. Then, just now they came and got me and brought me back here."

Nathan laughed and turned to Dunnagh. "Just like you said, mommy came home and nearly caught him."

"What?" Marti glanced at her comrades. "All right, you mangy dogs, what did I miss?"

They grinned, but no one spoke, making *her* wait this time.

"Come on, what happened?"

"The real mistress of this keep came back today, as best we can figure," Oglas said. "I think his high lordship didn't want her to find out what games he'd been playing in her absence." Marti laughed her big booming laugh, enjoying the joke with the rest of them. Then she gave her lover another long kiss.

Dunnagh glanced surreptitiously at the two scientists; they seemed shocked by Marti's cavalier demeanor. Rape disgusted him, but he also understood Marti's attitude, and approved. Marti was a professional soldier.

In choosing a career where war and rapine usually walked hand in hand, she had better have such a sensible attitude or she wouldn't remain sane.

Then, looking down at several ugly bite and claw marks on her breasts, Dunnagh touched Marti's arm. Still troubled, he asked in a low voice, "Are you all right, Marti, really?'

Marti glanced at her breasts in surprise. Lifting one large globe she examined it critically. "I'm all right, Sir. I guess he got a little excited near the end. With that red drink in me, I never even noticed." She shook her head in amazement.

"Chang said something about cook pots. Why did you think that they'd eaten me?"

"Samuels never came back, either; we thought we'd lost both of you."

Chapter Thirteen

The hour was late when Sagas at last ventured out of her suite and went to the sheltered alcove that formed the Ima Matri's private sanctuary. Kneeling on her prayer rug she faced the stone altar and lit the votive lamp in its center. She watched silently as the green flames rose, casting their flickering shadows upon the painted frescos of the little room.

Sagas allowed her mind and body to settle into the familiar pattern of relaxed openness. This night, more than any other time that she could remember, she desperately needed the comfort and guidance of her Gods.

When she felt centered and composed, she picked up the ritual stone blade from the altar and made the required cut. Her blood dripped into the bowl resting upon the stone slab. As she felt the draining away of "life's essence," making her dizzy, she applied the clotting agent, and sat back on her heels to pray.

Oh, Great Ones, please accept my gift this night, and give me your guidance. O Mother of all life, O sacred Khutani of the pools, help me. For a long time, she knelt on the cold stone, listening to the silence and pouring out the hopes and fears of her soul into the darkness.

Sagas looked up as a hooded and cloaked figure slipped into the sanctuary. He knelt beside her and took up the ritual knife and bowl from the altar. When his devotions were complete, Temog spoke softly, still keeping his eyes fixed upon the holy flame. "I have seen him, Sagas, the blue-eyed one that the sacred Khutani spoke of."

Sagas glanced at him sharply, then returned her gaze to the altar. They were probably being watched. "Where?" she breathed'

"If I'm right—and I truly believe I am, he is here in our slave pens."

She stared, incredulous, a word of impatience already forming on her lips. But one look at his glowing, feverish eyes and she checked herself. Something had obviously happened to get him so worked up. And the

Khutani *had* said they would send the Chosen to her—but surely not as a lowly slave? She took a deep breath. "Start from the beginning and tell me what you have discovered."

"San Gormach was here while you were—*away*."

"Get on with it, Temog!"

"Yes, quite right. The Warlinga brought with him a band of captives, creatures like nothing we have ever seen before. When asked, Gormach said they were a new strain of mutants he captured on a raid into the Ghostlands, but the Begta also brought for sale tell a different story."

Sagas snorted. "Gormach and his clan of drunken lay-abouts up in the Ghostlands, actually doing their job? Hardly! I doubt if the fool even knows which direction is north."

Temog let out a low companionable chuckle. "Yes, I would agree with you. That is why I am more inclined to believe the Begta. They whispered to me, out of the Warlinga's hearing of course, that these new creatures he brought came down out of the sky."

Sagas blinked. "You believe the Begta! Who believes the Begta about anything?" Then, seeing him frown, she relented. "All right, you must have your reasons. Tell me. Why?"

"The Umwira mutants who come down from the North are deliberately bred by the Ghostland wizards to be dangerous monsters. These creatures aren't like that at all. They are well-formed, intelligent and completely sane."

"I gather you have given this some thought, but I still don't see—"

"Wait, let me finish. There is more. One of the Warlinga—Gormach's younger cousin, I think, was badly injured when they arrived. Later that evening, I sought him out and offered him my services as a healer. To give him credit, he wouldn't say how he came by his wounds, but Gormach has a reputation for abusing his own folk when it suits him—and I know a claw wound when I see one.

"I got this Tobrach to talking about the captives while I patched him up. Like his K'San, he said they were Ghostlander mutants, but he was also very evasive about where they captured them.

"When I asked him, he admitted to knowing the Begta's stories about the captives coming from the sky. He didn't believe the Begta, but he *did* let slip, that the Begta slaves they'd brought to trade, were with the new mutants when they were captured.

"There are other things about the new slaves that strengthen the Begta's tale, in my opinion. For example, their lack of knowledge of our language and their sickness after eating our food.

"But there is only one other fact of supreme importance that you need to hear for now. There is one among them—their leader, from what I can gather—who has blue eyes, Sagas, as blue as the kavay in the deepest, richest pool under the mountain.

"There are others that have odd light-colored eyes, but this male also has hair the color of the sun's flame, and none of the others have that. His description fits the somewhat poetical message you were given, does it not? I believe he is the one—truly I do."

Sagas was silent for a long time, weighing his words.

Temog watched her with growing impatience for a time, then blurted, "What will you do now, Ima?"

"I'm not sure," she said slowly. "I need time to think."

"Will you go to the Khutani, tell them what has happened?"

Sagas shook her head. She would like nothing better than to toss this complex situation into their mouths and have them vomit out the correct answer. "I dare not, old friend. If this blue-eyed one is the Dream-Chosen, then I must be very careful. I will be watched even more so now.

"I can't afford to arouse further suspicion. No one, especially Combaron Dingay, must suspect that I have any interest in the Khutani or Blue Eyes. Do you understand me, Temog? This is very important. As my advisor, you yourself will be watched, too, so have a care yourself. All the lives in this keep—in all Timorna may depend on what we do in the next few days."

Then, she buried her face in her hands and sighed. "Leave me now, my friend. I must pray for guidance. When the time is right, I will go to him."

Chapter Fourteen

A fter the midday break, Dunnagh was untied from the mill wheel where he'd been working all morning. He was given a long handled bone shovel and a basket, and then he was sent to the fields to harvest more purple roots.

The red-gold sun felt pleasantly warm on his back as he worked. He wished he could crawl off into a quiet corner and sleep on a soft rug like a cat, instead of mucking about up to his knees in sticky leaves and dust, but there was no chance of that.

The red-eyed Warlinga were as vigilant as hawks, and he had no wish to feel their whip-like tails across his back. The barbed tips of their tails drew blood from his thin skin as neatly as a knife.

Today he refused to be rushed. He kept up a slow but steady rhythm throughout the afternoon, and that seemed to satisfy them. Surprising himself, he found he liked the feel of the dry crumbling earth between his toes; it reminded him of working in his grandma's garden at home. Home. The hopes and fears of that other life seemed as unreal now as if they'd happened to a character on the vids. The edges of those memories were blurred, fading into the emptiness of the past, the life of someone else in another time—on another world.

Home. Best not travel down that road. Instead he concentrated on listening to the roar of the nearby river and the singing of the Loti also digging in the mounds of gray blue-foliage.

Their alien speech helped him focus his mind on escape plans. Never mind the nostalgic reminiscences of Caldon, he told himself. He needed to stay focused on what was important. They had to escape before the Butcher returned, or Weasel-face decided to murder and eat another.

As Dunnagh bent over his task, he manage to steal surreptitious glances at the surrounding landscape. To the north and east jagged peaks of brown and gray rock rose like an impenetrable wall into the heavy amber sky. Was the base in that direction? He'd been face down for most of the journey here, but surely they hadn't crossed over that mighty barrier. He would have noticed, in spite of his suffering.

No, the base had to be in the opposite direction. Perhaps, their best route of escape would be to the south. They could head down the narrow river valley, and then cut westward somewhere in the rugged moss and thorn brush country beyond. That way was easier, but it was also the way their captors would look, for exactly the same reason.

Their escape would have to be planned very carefully. They would only get one chance, and if they were discovered...

He didn't want to travel down that road either. Thinking of a possible failure, and the punishment that would follow, would make him even more despondent than dreaming of home. They would just have to do it, and do it right the first time.

When he'd filled his basket, Dunnagh showed it to one of the guards, lounging at the edge of the field. The man grunted an approval, and Dunnagh immediately started up the steep trail to the fortress. As he panted and climbed towards the gate, it finally registered on his dull mind that the path in front of him was stained liberally with red blood.

Dunnagh's head shot up, searching for the cause. That was human blood. Had Taleish angered a Warlinga again and been punished for it? The man was going to give him a seizure with his stubborn bravado if he didn't settle him down soon.

No, it couldn't be Taleish; Dunnagh hadn't seen him in the fields this afternoon—and the blood was fresh. Not far ahead, he saw Singey burdened with a similar load to his own. The man's dark torso was gleaming with a sheen of sweat, and stained from bare buttocks to feet with a flaking crust of mud.

He was limping badly with each step. Patches of blood from his torn feet stained the rocky path in his wake. Soft city feet were a rich man's luxury, and in their present situation, a curse. The man never complained, but obviously the condition of his feet was worsening each day.

In the slave pen at Tragar, when they'd been so sick, no one had worried about their lack of shoes. Nobody had been walking anywhere, only crawling to the privy and back. On the journey to Sulas the cold at night had been their prime concern. Shoes were still not important. But now that they were here, and expected to work, the lack of proper foot gear could become a serious problem for some of his squad.

As a boy, Dunnagh had spent his summers running barefoot all over the clan lands in the Black Mountains. Later, a certain amount of martial arts training had kept the calluses on his feet fairly thick. Like himself, Chang as their hand to hand combat expert had calluses in plenty. Taleish had spent his youth shepherding his clan's sheep; his feet were all right, too. Nathan was coping and would manage.

But Oglas, Marnez and the two scientists were urban-raised. They had probably worn shoes all their lives. And what about Marti, Rhys, and Moraga? He had no idea how their feet were holding up. He'd better check on everyone tonight. Maybe they couldn't have clothing under Avairei law, but damn it, if their "masters" wanted them to keep working, they'd better give them some shoes or they might become too lame to function.

And that got his mind worrying again about what might happen to anyone who got injured or too sick to work. Would they be killed and eaten? The overseer was going to have to listen to him this time.

As he returned from empting his basket in the large storage bin and headed up the stairs Dunnagh saw Singey silhouetted against the open door at the top. "Philip, wait up a moment."

Singey looked back over his shoulder, saw Dunnagh, and paused. Leaning heavily against the doorframe, he glanced around nervously, to see if he was being observed. Dunnagh hurried up the stairs to join him. "Let me see your feet. How bad are they?"

"I'll manage," Singey muttered, and made a feeble attempt to push past him.

"Let me see them, damn it," Dunnagh insisted. When Singey complied and lifted a grimy foot, Dunnagh cursed. Under the caked blood and dirt, the entire sole was an angry mass of raw bleeding flesh. "Gods, man, how can you even walk?"

Singey grimaced. "Do I have a choice?" he moved to push past him again. "We need to get back before someone comes looking for us."

Dunnagh followed him out into the courtyard, his eyes quickly scanning the area. Singey was right about someone coming to look for them, but in this case that was exactly what he wanted. If the man went lame on him, that would mean more of a delay for their escape.

Spying Hanno the overseer by the gate, talking to another Warlinga, Dunnagh took Singey by the arm, and over his protests, marched him over.

Hanno broke off his conversation when they stopped in front of him. "Go back to work," he growled.

Dunnagh stood his ground and pointed to the trail of blood, then to Singey's feet. "Feet—soft. Man no can work good. Need—" He couldn't think of an appropriate native word, so he said, "Shoes," in Caldoni and mimed putting a covering over his feet and tying it.

Hanno growled another warning, looming over the smaller Dunnagh with a threatening gesture. Grimly Dunnagh refused to back down and repeated his argument and the shoe miming. Like an exhausted beast, the dull-eyed Singey gripped his empty basket and watched the byplay, making no move to interfere or speak on his own behalf.

Dunnagh was afraid at one point that he'd pushed the overseer's patience too far, and he was in for a whipping, but he stuck it out. Damn it, he needed all his people healthy, so he had to make the Warlinga understand. "When feet bad, man no work good. Hanno want man work? Hanno need give man 'shoes.'"

At last the overseer saw the wisdom in Dunnagh's argument and barked out an order to one of the Warlinga lounging nearby. The man pushed himself off the wall and came over. Hanno spoke to him too fast for Dunnagh to catch any of the meaning, except the word kitchen. The Warlinga grunted and led Singey away in that direction.

Relieved, Dunnagh shouldered his basket and using his shovel like a walking stick, he headed out the gate. As he stepped out onto the path he happened to glance back and saw the overseer glaring at him, his tail lashing the ground behind him in a most menacing way. Dunnagh inwardly shuddered and quickened his pace. He'd made himself another enemy—he was sure of it. Well, with a little bit of luck they would be gone before the man figured out a way to take his revenge.

AFTER THE EVENING MEAL that night, Dunnagh conducted his
survey of the humans' feet. Tessa and Marnez also had tender spots, but
being smaller in stature, they'd been assigned mostly to doing kitchen work,
chopping vegetables, stirring big pots of gruel and the like. Their feet
weren't in too bad of shape—yet. Singey was the worst, though Marti had a
bad stone bruise, and Moraga had an ugly looking slash on her ankle.

Over his protests, Dunnagh made Singey sit beside him and began
dabbing at his raw feet with a bit of damp moss he dipped in a water pail. As
he worked, Nathan wandered over and sat down beside them. He whistled
softly when he saw the mangled condition of the scientist's feet.

Singey's grin was a bit lopsided as he looked up. Then he winced as
Dunnagh probed a deep slash. "Wealth does have its privileges, but I wish
I'd spent more time doing uncouth things like running barefoot through
my parents' garden."

Nathan smirked. "Yeah, being a Caldoni savage has its benefits
sometimes."

Singey winced again. "Yes, quite."

Dunnagh flashed him a warning look out of Singey's line of vision and
Nathan turned away to watch the women.

All four of them were leaning against the rock wall of the next
enclosure chatting with the Loti women housed there. The occasional laugh
and mimed gesture spoke to the intensity of their involvement. When the
women conversed like that, all the men, including Dunnagh himself, eyed
them with a mixture of curiosity and maybe a little envy.

Nathan turned back to his companions shaking his head. "Gods,
women, will I ever understand them? You'd think they were back home
having a chat with the neighbors after getting the children away to school
and picking the roses from the garden."

Dunnagh chuckled, and opened his mouth to add to that observation,
when he caught sight of two of Hanno's underlings approaching. He
dropped the moss clump back into the bucket. "We have company
coming," he said and rose to his feet.

"What now," Nathan muttered, and stood up beside him.

Singey made an effort to stand as well, but Dunnagh gestured him back. "Stay put or you'll undo all my efforts. I don't think I need my scientific adviser this time. We'll go see what they want."

The Warlinga in front opened the gate, and held it open for the man behind him carrying a leather bundle. Dunnagh with Nathan just behind him stopped a few paces in front of them. The one in charge said a native word Dunnagh hadn't heard before. Dunnagh looked at Nathan who shrugged.

The Warlinga made an impatient grunt and tossed the bundle at Dunnagh's feet. Dunnagh hesitated, then picked up the bundle and unrolled it. Inside, were a number of rawhide squares, wooly Begta fur still intact on one side. A ball of leather lacing rolled out onto the ground. Nathan bent and picked it up. Dunnagh wrinkled up his nose at the smell of his treasure.

The Warlinga laughed and repeated the unfamiliar word again. When Dunnagh still didn't get it, the Warlinga pointed to Dunnagh's feet. The light dawned, and Dunnagh bowed in thanks.

By that time the event at the gate had drawn everyone's attention. Smiling to himself, Dunnagh returned to the shelter, a bemused Nathan trailing in his wake. "What did they want?" Singey asked when Dunnagh sat down beside him again. Dunnagh showed him the contents of the bundle. "For our feet."

When Singey smelled the half cured hides, he made a face. Dunnagh chuckled and selected two of the finest squares from the bundle, then gave the rest to Marti, to pass around to the others. While she was doing that, Dunnagh dampened the skin side of the squares with his moss sponge and dried off Singey's feet with another bit of clean moss.

"I hope you won't get an infection from these; they aren't all that clean, but they will give your feet some protection till you heal, I think."

When the rawhide softened, Dunnagh molded them around Singey's feet, wool side in, and tied them in place about his ankles with the lacing. Dunnagh sat back on his heels. "There, that should do it."

Singey stared down at his feet for a long moment, then he looked up and met Dunnagh's eye. "I know you risked a beating for me today, and I'm grateful. Thank you, Ce'awn."

Dunnagh blinked at the scientist's use of the Caldoni title.

When Singey noticed Nathan scowling at him, he stammered an apology. "I'm sorry, Dunnagh, I meant no offence by using that word. It means leader or some such in Caldoni doesn't it? I've heard the others call you that since our capture—I thought—I'm sorry if I gave offense."

"The word means a traditional clan chieftain, and I don't know why these amadans are calling me that," Dunnagh said. "And, you have nothing to apologize about. I'm honored and I'm glad I could help."

He stood and patted the man on the shoulder. "Rest well, Philip. We're going to get out of here—all of us—and soon, I promise."

Nathan got up as well and followed him over to the privy corner. As Dunnagh held his penis and urinated against the wall, he glanced at his friend. Nathan looked grim; he must want to talk. Dunnagh braced himself for more trouble. "What's wrong?"

Letting his own stream of urine spray the stone, Nathan looked up. "Nothing's wrong; why did you think there was?"

"Because I don't need any help taking a piss. You must want to tell me something without making it too obvious to the others. So, I repeat, what's wrong? Is it Taleish again?"

Nathan made a face, then shook his head. "He's an amadan, but no more than usual."

"Then, what?"

Nathan stalked away from the privy corner, Dunnagh following. Over by the gate, he stopped and stared out into the courtyard. "Come on, Nathan out with it," Dunnagh said.

Without looking at Dunnagh, he said, "You're getting awfully friendly with Mr. Snoot. Calling him your 'scientific adviser' in front of the squad, fixing his feet, including him in our talks about escape, sleeping with him most nights now—yes, getting real friendly aren't you?"

Dunnagh blinked, his mouth dropping open in surprise." What? Damn it, you can't be serious? I don't treat him any different than the rest of you."

In a falsetto voice, Nathan mimicked, "Oh, Philip, I'm honored. I was glad to help."

Dunnagh felt his temper spark and clenched his jaw to hold back an angry retort. Then, he let go the anger and began to laugh.

Nathan folded his arms across his chest and glared. "And, just what's so damned funny?"

Dunnagh fought to control his mirth. "Oh, Nathan, it's you that is so funny. Over the years you've never said anything about my affairs with women—as you pointed out the other night. But the first time you think I might be interested in another *man*, you get jealous."

"I am not jealous!"

"Sure you are. But you have nothing to worry about—truly. You are the only man I've ever cared about in that way. Don't look at me like that. You are jealous—and so am I—of you.

"By swearing the Ca'Companachda oath we've had such a powerful bond for so many years, it would be strange if we didn't worry about someone coming in our lives to make us loose that intimacy."

Nathan thought about it for a while, then began to chuckle, too. "Maybe you have a point. That was pretty silly."

"Mm, hm." Dunnagh put an arm around his shoulder. "I partner with him so often, because most of the armachda won't, unless I order them to, you know. Let's go back; I'm getting cold."

As they started across the pen, Nathan said, "That stuff about Singey. That wasn't what I really wanted to tell you. It just sort of came out."

"Mm, go on."

"I just wanted you to know that when we get out of this, I'll go home with you to Caldon for a while." Dunnagh stopped and stared, mouth agape. "Close your mouth before a fly jumps in it."

That saying had been one of grandma Kai's favorites. "My, my, you're full of surprises tonight. I'm both relieved—and happy—but what changed your mind?"

Nathan shrugged. "It seemed like a good idea that's all. Don't you want me to come with you now?"

"Of course I do, but—"

"I'm your battle companion aren't I? If you feel that going home to help Shivon is so important, then maybe it is. And, I figure maybe you'll need some help with the brat." He barked an unconvincing laugh. "Between Uncle Nathan and Uncle Dunnagh the boy won't have a chance, right?"

"Right. Your decision doesn't have anything to do with Tessa and her research, would it?"

Nathan shrugged again. Dunnagh stopped walking and turned Nathan to face him. They were nearly at the shelter, so he kept his voice low. "Nathan, don't do this, please. I've been watching you two as our health improves.

"One moment you two are a cooing pair of love birds and the next moment its verbal warfare between you. Maybe you think if you help her she'll be more likely to stay with you—even marry you. But you'll for sure get the clan mothers angry with you if you tell her Caldoni secrets. Is she worth the risk of a banishment?"

"Maybe she is. And, I'm not going to tell her any Caldoni secrets, so don't worry." Nathan snarled as he pushed by Dunnagh and walked back to sit beside Tessa.

Chapter Fifteen

D unnagh sat down beside Moraga, leaned his head against the shelter's back wall and closed his eyes. His evening portion of glop was a heavy weight in the pit of his stomach, making him feel listless and uncomfortable. He farted and let out a sigh of relief. He was so tired.

As a revenge for the incident of the shoes, Hanno had put him back on the millwheel today, knowing his strength was barely up to the task. Every bone and muscle in his body ached. It felt good just to sit and do nothing for a change.

Not long ago there had been some beautiful singing coming from inside the inner sanctum of the keep. Evening hymns to their god Tessa said. Whatever it was, it sounded nice. He couldn't understand the words, of course, but the songs had a haunting drum beat, and a lot of poignant, three part harmonies in a minor key. The music matched his mood perfectly

It reminded him of home and brought a tear to his eye. Images of his mother, his fiancée Sairsa, his sister Shivon Ru'a and her troublesome boy, floated across his inner vision. What were they doing now? Would he ever see his love and home again?

When shadows bathed the courtyard in cool violet light, the concert ended abruptly. Two young priests came around and closed the doors and shutters to their portion of the great fortress. Now all he could hear was someone shouting at a Begta slave by the outdoor kitchen, and the Warlinga arguing and joking over jugs of purple beer in their barracks. He shivered and wished they'd shut up.

"You look so tired, Ce'awn," Moraga said, breaking in on his thoughts.

"Mm, I am," he said without opening his eyes.

Moraga heaped more of the dry moss over herself and him. "I heard you crying out again in your sleep last night. My mother has the gift. If she were here, she could just touch your closed eyes with a finger and take away the torment, so you could sleep."

She sighed. "I wish I could help, but I don't have that kenning. Me and Enghus were always jealous of our cousin Jean because she had that gift and the 'sight,' too."

Dunnagh opened his eyes and studied her carefully. Moraga's face was solemn, with new lines around her beaky nose and wide mouth, but her pale eyes were clear and calm as she watched him. Her talk about her dead brother often unnerved him. She'd bring up Enghus so casually, as if he were still alive, just somewhere else on another mission for the corps.

"I had a grand aunt, who people said could stop bleeding and take away pain with a touch. She died when I was very young; I don't really remember her much." He laughed softly. "I wish she'd passed that one on to me many a time. It would come in handy."

Moraga nodded. "That would be a blessing for us to be sure, though not much help for your own self."

"Mm, I was forgetting that." He gave her a lopsided grin. "The gifts are both a blessing and a curse for those who inherit them, my grandma always said. She also used to say that you couldn't use a gift on yourself, they were given only to help others."

Moraga nodded. "That be what I always heard, too. But I don't have any, so I don't know for certain."

A giggle from Tessa made him glance over to the far side of the shelter. Nathan was sitting with his arm protectively round the woman's shoulder and bending close to her ear. He said something else too low for Dunnagh to hear, and she laughed again.

Dunnagh made a face and looked away. He hoped Nathan knew what he was doing. Settling back once more, he closed his eyes. It was getting cold already. Damn the stinking lizards!

A few days after coming to Sulas, Dunnagh had suggested to the Warlinga they be given some blankets or the cloaks like the Avairei wore. The brute had become enraged and knocked him flat for his trouble. Dunnagh hadn't understood most of his angry shouting, something about insolent slaves and lessons needed. Nathan had pulled him away and together they'd crawled back into the shelter before his abused body suffered more damage.

Later, Tessa said something to him in her lecturing, professorial voice, about only high-ranking people like the Avairei being allowed to wear clothing "in this society." When she acted like that, Dunnagh wanted to answer back with something cutting, but so far he'd managed, for Nathan's sake to restrain himself.

He suspected that behind her haughty exterior there lay a very fragile, frightened little girl, not half as sophisticated as she wished everyone to believe.

"I wonder what time of day it is back home. You got any idea, Rhys?" Oglas said.

When Rhys made no answer, only burrowed deeper into the moss next to his bed partner for the night, Dunnagh opened an eye to consider him more closely.

As time passed his laconic tracker had become even more withdrawn. He obeyed orders, but would answer a direct question—only if he thought it important. He never volunteered any information or joined in a conversation unless prodded. Dunnagh was worried about the man's sanity—and maybe Rhys's friend Oglas was too, but Dunnagh didn't know what he could do about it. They were all suffering under the strain.

"Now if it was evening like it is here," Oglas continued his freckled boyish face suddenly dreamy. "I'd walk down to the bakery at the end of the plaza and buy one of those chocolate cream cakes like me brother and I liked so much."

Taleish groaned. "Not again. Shut up about food, Amadan."

"Those cakes were a wonder, more than a hand's width high with smooth dark chocolate icing on top as creamy and rich as fudge. Inside was a thick cream cheese filling between the layers that tasted of almonds. So good! My brother or myself would always bring one home for tea, whenever we visited the parents."

"Oglas, bakery treats, really? Didn't anyone in your family ever cook?" Marti said.

"Well now, me mother and me da both worked at the space port. They were busy people. Nobody had much time for the domestic chores like baking in our house."

"You missed out," Marnez said. "My father wouldn't let my mother work. He was old fashioned that way. When I used to come home on leave, the house always smelled like fresh bread or some kind of baking. Spiced yamina root pie was my favorite. Nice flaky crust baked to a golden brown, and the smooth orange root with all the cinnamon and ginger, mm, it was so good."

"I never like sweets much," Chang said from Rhys's other side, "but I'd love to taste some of my wife's gottasey right now."

Nathan snorted. "I'll stick to glop and blue puke juice. Raw, seya fish and noodles isn't my idea of dinner."

"Barbarian," Chang said. "You have no appreciation of a civilized cuisine, Sir."

"I had gottasey once when my parents took me to Shampore," Singey said. "It was very spicy as I recall."

"Will you people shut up about food," Taleish complained. "My gut hurts enough as it is without you blabbering on all night about treats we can't have. So, just shut up!"

"If your gut aches so bad, Taleish, go take a crap. Maybe it will sweeten your sour mood. Your grumbling isn't an improvement on the conversation, you know," Marti said.

"Poc mo hon."

"Kiss my ass?" Marti let out a throaty laugh and hugged Marnez a little closer. "Dream on, Amadan." Oglas and some of the others joined her in her laughter. Taleish swore a particularly vile oath that made them laugh all the harder.

Ignoring Taleish, Oglas persisted, "How about you Dr. Singey, Dr. Farris, any favorite foods you want to have when we get back to civilization?"

"Lemon ice cream," Tessa said without hesitation. "I love its tart flavor and cool taste in my mouth. On a hot day after a swim and a sunning on the beach, there's nothing like it."

"Dr. Singey?" Oglas said.

"Hmm. Well I certainly will be glad to go back to civilization as someone put it, but I can't think of anything I particularly want for my first meal. As long as it's 'real food,' and not blue or purple in color, I'll be happy with anything."

Dunnagh chuckled. "I would agree with you there, Philip, especially about the blue and purple part. I don't even know if I can stand blue berries in my oatmeal from now on."

There was a chorus of agreement to that as well. "What about you, Rhys?" Oglas repeated, this time giving his companion a gentle poke in the ribs for emphasis.

Before Rhys could answer, Taleish snarled, "Oglas, shut up. I'm sick of your blather. Let it drop, or I'm going to toss you into the Warlinga barracks over there, and ask them if they want a late night snack."

Into the shocked silence that followed, Nathan said, "That wasn't funny, Taleish. Keep your own mouth shut if that's all you got to say."

Taleish's mouth opened, then he saw Nathan's grim expression and closed it again. He balled up his fists, his eyes sullen. "Don't push it, Amadan," Nathan warned. The potential for violence suddenly hovered in the cool air between the two men.

"That's enough. If you want something else to talk about, then stop arguing and start thinking about escape plans," Dunnagh said.

Surprising them all, Rhys said, "Did you have something in mind, sir?"

"Not specifically," Dunnagh said. "But now that we are getting over the worst of the alien sickness, it's time we start thinking seriously about getting out of here."

"It's going to be hard for us without weapons," Marnez said.

"The Warlinga keep a vigilant watch on their weapons," Chang said, "but there are the heavy handled farm tools that can be used like clubs, and possibly we can steal a few stone knives from the kitchen to add to our arsenal."

"Maybe," Marti said. "The Warlinga just collect the farm tools at night, count them, then they put them in an unlocked outdoor tool shed until they're needed again."

"It's the same with the knives in the kitchen," Tessa said. "The head cook hands them out in the morning and collects and counts them after the evening meal. But they aren't locked up."

"Now that you mention it, Tessa, I've not seen any locks on this world," Singey said. "This isn't surprising on such a primitive world if you think on it. Locks are rather complicated mechanical items really. They also usually are made of metals, which I haven't observed in use since coming here either."

"That's true, Nathan said. "There aren't locks of any kind on the storage places as far as I've seen."

"Thievery seems to be relatively unknown among these people—or at least if they're around, the thieves are interested in other items," Singey continued.

"Or they follow a different set of rules," Dunnagh said.

"What do you mean, Sir," Oglas said.

Dunnagh piled more moss over a bare knee before answering, trying to get his thoughts in order. "I'm not sure exactly. But the Begta are said to be notorious thieves, yet since coming to Sulas I've seen no evidence of it."

"Perhaps they're sufficiently cowed by the Warlinga presence here to mind their ways," Chang said with a smirk.

"Yes, they have been behaving like model slaves—always groveling at the Warlinga's feet," Singey said. "They're not acting like the fierce little hunters who captured us in the canyons at all, are they?"

"No, they're not—for whatever reason," Dunnagh said. "I wonder if we can persuade some of the little furballs to go with us and act as our guides back to the base on the mesa. We could promise to give them a whole arm load of "pretties." That should be a sufficient inducement to win them over, shouldn't it?"

"Maybe," Oglas said, "but on the other hand, they're terrified of the lizardmen."

"They'll do it," Taleish said, "because they're greedy bacach at heart."

"Maybe." Dunnagh glanced around the circle of humans, assessing their strength. Could Singey, Tessa and a couple more of the sick ones like Rhys survive the brutal forced marches they would have to maintain to escape the Warlinga sent to retrieve them?

"I wonder if Berren and some of the other Loti could be persuaded to go with us, too. If we could ride, we just might be able to out run the search party that will be sent after us."

"We would have a much better chance of making it if the Loti would go with us," Moraga agreed. "But it will be hard to persuade them to leave Sulas. They be a liking it here. And after they help us what would they do? They will be back in Tragar territory, remember. Gormach might catch them again—"

"And, that fate would be a terrible way to repay such kindness. I hadn't thought of that," Dunnagh admitted. "Hmm."

"Maybe we won't need them, Dunnagh," Nathan said. "If we raided the storage shed for farm tools late one night, we can surprise the gate guards and kill them with no one the wiser till dawn. The Warlinga won't be expecting an attack from what they considered defenseless slaves, so we can probably manage it without too much trouble.

"Once the guards are out of the way we'll gather food and supplies and be long gone by daylight."

"They might not even come looking for us," Tessa said, "if we make our disappearance look like something magic. I think the Avairei especially, are very superstitious."

"Hmm. Everyone give this more thought and we'll talk tomorrow night," Dunnagh said. "But now, we'd better get some sleep. The Warlinga will have us up with the sun to work. We all need to rest while we can."

As he lay down, Dunnagh heard rustling in the moss, then, quiet footsteps heading towards the privy corner. Dunnagh raised his head to look, then he sank back his lip twitching into a faint smile. Singey. Though the man had never openly complained, Dunnagh suspected that their enforced nudity and lack of privacy was a real trial for the man.

There was nothing they could do about it, for as Nathan so aptly put it, "The natives themselves aren't shy, so why should they expect their slaves to care about modesty?"

Dunnagh followed Singey's progress with a critical eye. He was walking better, the skins were helping. Though not exactly a friend, Singey's quiet competence had demonstrated to Dunnagh on more than one occasion that he could be counted upon in a tense situation.

As Dunnagh was settling at last into sleep, he heard someone groan, then a few moments later he heard the sound of vomiting. He raised up on an elbow, who? Gods, not Taleish or Rhys again. Dunnagh fretted, because the continued weakness of some of his people would only postpone any escape attempt. He wouldn't even consider leaving someone behind, but Dunnagh found it hard to curb his impatience to be gone, now that his own strength was returning.

When Rhys came back to the shelter, Dunnagh asked in a low voice, "How are you doing, really?"

Startled, Rhys paused. Without answering, he crawled back into his moss cocoon, then muttered, "I'll be all right, Ce'awn. It's no worse than usual. Don't worry about me."

Chapter Sixteen

In his dream, Dunnagh slipped out of his physical body and floated on the etheric currents. There was peace and freedom in the solitude of the void, a welcome relief from the waking nightmare his life had become. Even more than peace, Dunnagh wanted, for the few hours his masters let him sleep, to be among familiar things, and people who loved him.

But each time he sought escape into his dreaming fantasies, his efforts were blocked. As always before, he could swim only so far, and then his etheric body would bump against an impenetrable barrier.

Dunnagh glared at the massive wall confining him. Tonight it was made of huge gray boulders, so high that its rim disappeared into the otherworld's mists. After a careful exam he decided that there seemed to be no way to go around it or under it; the thing was endless.

Swallowing down his frustration, he reached out a hand and touched it. It had been made of etheric matter; so in theory, it should be possible to push his way through...

The stone was cold and hard under his hand. It felt as rough and pitted by wind and weather as any rock he'd encountered in the physical realm. Suddenly angry, he pounded his fist against it, growling a curse. Why? Why were they doing this to him? When his fury subsided, Dunnagh leaned his head against the stone, and licked the etheric blood from a skinned knuckle.

Tears of frustration stung his eyes; he brushed them away impatiently. *No sense crying—done enough of that—doesn't help. Have to think, damn it—think.*

Dunnagh wished he was a boy again. At home. On Caldon, where his childish troubles could be set right by loving parents or other helpful relatives. Thinking of his boyhood brought to mind his maternal grandfather, Grandpa Kai.

Refusing to live with relatives, grandpa had returned to the family land in the Black Mountains after his retirement from his duties as a shenahi (traditional storyteller). He'd said he preferred the "wild places," to city comforts. Dunnagh had gained a deep love for the land and his people's traditions, while spending his summer vacations with him. Dunnagh had missed him man terribly after he passed on.

In his mind an image of the old man formed. Dressed in a faded plaid, his long silver braids framed a weathered high cheek boned face. Deep blue eyes met Dunnagh's own, and the firm mouth under the drooping mustaches twitched into a smile. <<And, what be ya snivelin' bout, boyo?>>

A wave of relief and love flowed through him. Grandpa Kai had known he was in terrible trouble and had come all this way to help him. <<Grandpa, I'm so glad you've found me. I want to go home—please, take me home.>>

The old man leaned up against the wall, his expression quizzical. <<If you want to go home, boyo, then why don't you go? What's stopping ya?>>

Had the old fellow gotten senile with his death? A note of irritation coming into his spirit voice, Dunnagh pointed to the wall, and said, <<That's stopping me—can't you see it? That damned, hard, stone wall is stopping me! I can't get past it.>>

<<Wall?>> the shenahi placed his palm against the stone and pushed against it. His hand disappeared, passing right through the barrier, as if it were made of nothing more than fog. <<You mean that one?>>

Dunnagh gaped, speechless. The old man chuckled and withdrew his hand and showed it to Dunnagh. <<So, have you forgotten everything I taught you?>> When Dunnagh still continued to stare, the old man's expression softened. <<Well, maybe you have for the moment. It hasn't been easy for you, has it, boyo?>>

<<No.>> Dunnagh felt the tears gathering again. He wanted to curl up in his grandfather's lap and cry, until there was no more water in him. But he wasn't that red-headed little boy anymore, and even here in the dream, a web of duty and obligation kept him from that final surrender.

<<Love, boyo,>> his grandfather said. <<The way home isn't out there.>> He waved his hand at the wall, <<but in here,>> He pointed

to his chest. <<You aren't alone, grandson. Your memories keep us alive in your heart. The way home is an inward journey—and the gateway is love.>>

Love. The word echoed in Dunnagh's mind as the shenahi's image disintegrated in front of him. Grandpa Kai was gone, but Dunnagh now knew how to follow him back to Caldon. Holding a golden shield of memory and love before him, Dunnagh passed through the barrier with ease. Home...Not his parents' crowded apartment in Caldon's capital his spirit had flown back to his clan's land in the Black Mountains.

Dunnagh now stood in a grassy field, the sun warm on his back. Sheep grazed further down the valley, cream and brown lumps in the hazy summer heat. A line of dark willows traced the course of Shina River, towards a dark range of mountains on the blue horizon. The air was rich with the scents of pine resin, lavender and freshly baked oat bread. Dunnagh took in a deep breath, laughed and through his arms wide. Home, he was truly home.

Gray and weathered, the Kai family's rambling log house sheltered under an oak and a tall cedar. Young rowan bordered the drive, their berries turning from a pale green to vivid orange. Behind the house, roses and runner beans fought for space along the garden fence.

His father's battered air car was in the drive, parked next to the barn. Dunnagh smiled to himself and hurried across the field towards the house. Good, his parents, and maybe his older sister Shivon and her children were visiting his grandfather, too. He desperately wanted to see them; he'd waited so long.

As he neared the house, he heard a child shout a greeting, and then race for the porch, his brown legs pumping. "Look, oh, look! Uncle Dunnagh has come home," the boy yelled as he banged open the door and hurried inside. A chorus of excited cries greeted his news.

Feeling a lump swell in his throat, Dunnagh stepped onto the porch and followed the boy inside. The place smelled of wood smoke, raw wool and fried onions, just as he remembered.

Ignoring the empty front room with its ragged leather armchair and quilt-covered couch, he hurried down the hallway towards the large country kitchen at the back. He could hear voices ahead of him; the family was in there, probably having tea.

Dunnagh paused in the doorway, trying to control his pounding heart. Tears streamed down his cheeks, blurring his vision. A log popped in the woodstove, and a chorus of welcomes greeted his arrival.

Yes, he could tell by their voices; they were all there, sitting around the massive oak table, Mahir and da, his younger brother Kenneth, Shivon, her noisy children and the old shenahi himself. Someone took his hand, his da maybe—he couldn't see for the tears, and guided him to a seat.

Shivon asked him what he wanted in his tea. Mahir kissed him and brought him the first piece of soda bread fresh from the oven. They sounded so happy to see him. He groped for a napkin to wipe his eyes; he wanted to see them, too. Dunnagh found the rag, and wiped at his face.

When his vision cleared, he let out a strangled cry and leaped to his feet, knocking over his chair in his haste.

<<Dunnagh, what's wrong,>> the furry brown creature with Shivon's voice said.

<<Leaving so soon?>> the thing with his father's voice and an alien scaly face said. It dipped its head crest and pointed with its tail to the fallen chair. <<Pick your chair up, son, before someone trips over it.>>

With hands trembling so bad he could hardly grasp the chair back, he righted the chair, but remained standing, leaning on it for support.

The Mahir creature, brushed the braidlets off her sleek brown forehead and poured more tea in the da thing's cup. When she finished she looked up at him and smiled, displaying dainty, sharp white teeth. <<Sit down, Mo Vic, and drink your tea before it gets cold. I made the farl especially for you. Won't you try some?>>

Unable to speak, Dunnagh shook his head and looked away. His eyes turned to the open window, but the lush green valley was gone. Yellow moss and scarlet thorn bush baked under a mauve sky. Trembling Dunnagh put his hands over his eyes to blot out the view. <<No!>> he roared. <<Why? Why are you doing this, damn you?>>

<<You wanted to escape into your fantasy and die,>> a hollow voice accused him.

<<No! All I wanted was to go home—just for a little while—I just wanted to go home.>>

<<You *are* home, Chosen.>>

He knew that voice. It belonged to one of the big, slimy worms that continued to torment his dreams.<<No, this ugly, cruel world isn't my home. I'll NEVER call this place home!>>

<<Timorna is your home now. You can have no other. The kavay has re-created your body in preparation for the bond. When you chose life over death at Tragar, you forfeited the chance to change your mind. There is no turning back now.>>

<<No. that isn't true—can't be true!>>

<<Stubborn, self-indulgent child, why do you persist in these fancies. Your pampered life among the stars is over. You have given us your oath of service. Your ship is gone. Accept and be content. Let us teach you, before it is too late!>> the shenahi thing said in the Maker's voice.

<<How dare you assume the form of my grandfather!>> Dunnagh's dream-body pulsed with his fury. <<Coward,>> he screamed. <<Show your true form. You mock his memory with your trickery. Damn you—lying devil!>> The collar around his neck burned white-hot, cutting off his rant Dunnagh clutched at his neck, falling to his knees on the kitchen floor, the chair toppling beside him.

The image of his home shattered. Massive sinewy coils engulfed him. A sleek gray head turned to glare at him with glowing eyes. The Maker's rubbery lips pealed back to show its sharp, triangular teeth. It squeezed its coils tighter about him, to emphasize its next words. <<Have a care, insolent child, how you speak to ME,>> the Khutani's voice thundered in his mind. <<I sought only to ease your troubled heart with my magics. No offence to your ancestor was intended. We have never lied to you.>>

<<You collar me, and demand my obedience without telling me what I am to do. If that isn't trickery and lies it is close to it,>> Dunnagh said.

<<When your superiors give you an assignment, do they have to tell you everything before you will obey?>> The Maker countered. When Dunnagh remained silent, it rumbled a laugh. <<I thought not. We would have told you before now, about our symbiont child and the transformation you will need to undergo to make a kashallan bond. But when we come to

you in your dreams, as now, you persist in fighting us. In keeping with your warrior's oath, we require your service. You will obey.>>

<<Slaves have no need of oaths. Take this collar off and tell me true about this service you require and my transformation, then maybe I will help you.>>

<<The tether stays. It is as much for your protection as your discipline, Foolish Child.>>

<<I will never obey unless—>> Dunnagh broke off as the image of the Khutani faded.

<<I tire of arguing with you, Warrior. The transformation has already begun—you cannot change what is to be. If you will not keep your word and honor your oath to help us, then you will make the sacrifice for love of your own. It doesn't matter now. You will come.>>

The Khutani suddenly loosed its coils and released him. Dunnagh cried out as he tumbled helplessly into blackness.

Chapter Seventeen

D unnagh came awake with a gasp. Damned nightmares would they ever leave him alone? He was about to go mad from lack of sleep and worry. To the east the sky was paling to rich shades of rusty brown and amber. It would be morning soon. Shivering in the cold pre-dawn air, he moved closer to the sleeping Nathan at his back, pulled more of the moss over his exposed shoulder and sighed. There was no point in going back to sleep now, but no point in waking Nathan either.

He and Tessa had had one of their disagreements again last night. She'd gone off to sleep with the women, and Nathan had sought him out as a sleeping buddy for a change. Nathan hadn't wanted to talk, but Dunnagh was glad all the same he'd come to him. When the dreams troubled him—like this morning, his old friend was a comforting presence at his back.

A chill breeze blew suddenly down from the peaks, tangling in the reed thatch above his head. <<Geish-sh-sh.>> The wind seemed to whisper the ancient Caldoni word that signified a type of obligation or compulsion. <<Geish... >> It reverberated back to him from a shadowy corner of his nightmare.

Suddenly, a deep foreboding filled him with a sense of urgency and unreasoning panic. It was a sending; one of the strongest he'd ever felt. Something terrible was coming. Coming to devour him—and there was no escape! Dunnagh took in several deep breaths, willing himself into stillness. If he moved right then, he'd start running, and the only way the Warlinga could stop him would be to kill him.

Then, Nathan stirred, shattering the fear, bringing Dunnagh's awareness back to his current surroundings. He let out his breath slowly, and whispered, "Thank you, Mo Hara."

"Huh?" Nathan yawned, and rose up on one elbow to look around. Seeing that Dunnagh was awake he brushed the hair off his forehead, and smiled. "You're up early. Just can't wait for another fun, fun day at the mill-wheel, I bet."

"Oh yeah, I can't wait." Dunnagh looked away, afraid Nathan would see the fear in his eyes. Nathan frowned.

"Dunnagh? What's wrong?" When Dunnagh didn't answer, he reached up and took hold of his friend's jaw, forcing him to look at him. "Is it the nightmares again?"

Pushing his hand aside, Dunnagh nodded, and then looked away again. "Mm—hm."

Nathan sat up. Feeling the draft at his back, Dunnagh sat up, too, and pressed his back against the shelter's wall. Nathan mounded the moss around them and put an arm about his shoulder. Dunnagh unconsciously leaned against him with eyes closed, trembling. After a few moments of tense silence Nathan asked, "You cold—or sick?"

The sending squeezing his throat, Dunnagh shook his head not able to speak out loud.

"Good. You—uh—think this brooding you're doing is going to help?"

Dunnagh let out a deep sigh and rubbed his neck. "No, but I can't seem to help myself."

"You? Our mighty savior, our fearless leader that would fight the Butcher with bound hands? I find *that* hard to believe."

Dunnagh chuckled in spite of himself. "You made your point about that stupidity at the time. Don't press the blade in any deeper."

Nathan chuckled, too, then becoming serious once more, he asked, "Dunnagh? You're not thinking of doing anything stupid again, are you?"

Startled, Dunnagh opened his eyes and turned his head to stare at him. "Like what?"

"You know—*things*. I've seen you in this type of mood before, and you always do something really stupid, when you're like this."

Silence

"So, are you?'

More silence...

"Dunnagh?"

"Nathan, if something happens to me, it will be up to you to get everybody out."

Nathan stiffened, shifting his position round to face his friend. "Oh shit! I knew it, damn it. Dunnagh, I swear if you're going to do something heroic and stupid *again*, I swear—"

"I'm not going to <u>do</u> anything, Nathan," Dunnagh snapped, "so stop hassling me, all right?" Then Dunnagh's voice lost its edge, and grew distant and introspective. "I just wanted you to know that if, and I mean *if*, anything should happen—well, you're my Second. You'll have to get them out. You *can* do it—and you know you can."

"Nathan's smoky gray eyes took on a haunted look. "Don't do this to me." he murmured. "Don't, please don't, Dunnagh—and there's nothing going to happen to you, so stop this—"

The Sending goading him to speak, Dunnagh laid a hand on Nathan's arm, and looked deep into his eyes. He said quietly, "You're not a helpless child anymore. Let go of the past. What happened to your family wasn't your fault. You couldn't have saved them if you'd come out of hiding.

"They wouldn't want you to keep feeling guilty for surviving. I've seen you in combat when things were rough, remember? You're stronger and much more courageous than you let on. So stop running away from yourself and accept what I'm telling you."

"You always have thought more highly of me than I deserve, you know?" Nathan said in a shaky voice.

Dunnagh chuckled. "No I don't. You just try to wiggle out of your responsibilities whenever I let you."

Nathan snorted, then muttered, "Do not."

"Do so."

The sky was a fire with gold and salmon pink now; the Warlinga would be here soon to get them up for the day's work. Dunnagh rubbed his neck again. "Nathan?"

"What now?"

"There's one other thing, and I want you to promise me." Dunnagh touched the bone bead that was Enghus around his neck. "If something should happen—don't leave me here alone. Take me with you, if you can."

Nathan blinked rapidly several times, rubbed his eyes, and got to his feet. "All this is too much to take with a full bladder."

Then, caught by Dunnagh's uncompromising stare, he said, "All right, all right, you win, I'll promise. But damn you, don't you dare do anything to make me keep that promise." Without waiting for an answer, he turned and walked across the pen to the privy corner.

Satisfied, Dunnagh watched him go and smiled. A moment ago he had been angry and frightened. Now he was pissing away as bold as you please, and exchanging rude gestures with a passing Warlinga. Dunnagh stood up and stretched. Nathan was right, all this was too much to think about with a full bladder.

When Dunnagh heard the rumble of the meal cart he walked to the fence and took a place in the forming line. While he waited, he watched the latecomers stumble sleepily into the cue and frowned. To Nathan, right behind him, he said, "I wonder why the women are taking so long this morning. They're usually up and visiting with the Loti in the next corral before now."

Nathan glanced around. "Moraga and Tessa are coming now."

"Good. We don't need any more Warlinga 'help' like yesterday when Chang kicked the Begta who dropped hot porridge on his foot."

Nathan grunted. "You got that right. He and Taleish both are becoming a real pain in my arss. If Taleish questions an order I give him once more, I'm gonna save the Warlinga the trouble of a discipline and beat the shit out of him myself."

Dunnagh's lip twitched. "Better not, unless you can do it when the guards aren't watching. A fight would cause more trouble—maybe get somebody killed."

"Stupid ass," Nathan grumbled. "I'll be careful, " His eyes following the big blond woman's stately progress to the gate, he said, "Moraga's doing good since the death of her twin, isn't she?"

"Yes, and I'm glad. I hate to admit it, but I was worried that she'd become a burden on us—they were so close. That thought shames me now; she's an inspiration to us all."

"Moraga's coping better than the rest of us and that's a fact," Nathan agreed.

"I'm also glad she's befriended Tessa since you two aren't exactly a cooing pair of love birds at the moment." Dunnagh watched his friend carefully, inviting further comment on that mystery, but Nathan ignored him and turned to scan the waiting line again.

Nathan sucked in his breath and said in a low urgent voice, "Dunnagh." When he had his attention Nathan motioned with his chin toward the far corner of the shelter. "Something's wrong over there."

Dunnagh peered into the shelter's interior, trying to see in the gloom. "Who is in there—Marti and who else?"

"Want me to go check on them?"

"No, stay here; I'll do it. If both of us go over there, it'll draw too much attention to the problem, whatever it is."

Dunnagh pushed himself off the fence and walked back to the shelter. He heard the cart stop to serve the Loti in the first pen. They hadn't much time.

When he came close enough to see the interior clearly, he saw Marnez lying curled up on her side, breathing raggedly. Marti shook her gently, urging her to get up, but it was obvious the woman was too ill to even stand. His guts spasmed—what was he going to do? He didn't want to think about the consequences when the overseer found out about this.

Shifting his body to block them from eyes in the courtyard, Dunnagh said in a low voice, "What's wrong with her, Marti?"

"She said last night her shoulder was hurting her. I could see she was holding it kind of funny-like." Marti pushed her matted hair off her forehead and stared at him with troubled eyes. "She's in a lot of pain—I know it. T-told m-me t-to mind my own b-business, s-she did. The little b-bitch." Her voice choked on a sob. She sniffed, and rubbed at her eyes.

Dunnagh laid a comforting hand on her arm. "What happened to her shoulder; how did she hurt it?"

"That black-hearted overseer Hanno was after her again yesterday, Oglas told me. He's been out for revenge ever since that incident at the gate. Yesterday she did something—"Marti shrugged helplessly. "I don't know what—but he grabbed her by the shoulder and threw her down." Marti cursed and balled up her fists. "If I'd been there..."

Marti, being almost as tall as Dunnagh himself, and as strong as any of the men, had been working yesterday, strapped to the spokes of that damned grinding-wheel along with him and a couple Loti. It was just as well she wasn't there or the Gods alone knew what might have happened.

"Don't worry, Marti, I won't let them take her. I promise."

And he would keep that promise too. At that moment, something fell into place inside him. He *knew* with a quiet certainty that it was his time. What he had been resisting, could not be avoided any longer. Suppressed truths exploded into his consciousness with blinding clarity.

He'd given his Oath to the Khutani; he would make the sacrifice and do whatever was expected of him, to save the lives of those for whom he was responsible.

Chapter Eighteen

When Sagas climbed with Temog and their apprentices to the outer wall's walkway, the sun was barely over the horizon. Its flaming red-gold light set the distant gray peaks afire. Patchwork fields of gray-green, brown and crimson glowed in the dawn light along the river. It was a lovely sight, yet there was a whisper of the Sorins' breath in the chill morning air.

In a couple moons or so, it would be the last harvest, and then the Sorin storms would come down from the North forcing everyone indoors for the Long Confinement.

Still, it was a beautiful morning, and how many more of them could she expect to enjoy? Sagas took in a deep breath and let it out slowly. No sense dwelling on that now. She was alive; there was blood flowing through her veins and she had a task to complete for the Khutani.

Turning her back on the scenery she surveyed the activity in the courtyard below her. Soon the Warlinga would have the Loti workers and the new mutant slaves, out of their pens and assigned to their chores for the day. She took in a deep breath to control her excitement. Was the Chosen really here? If so, this might be her only chance to see him without Combaron's meddling.

In spite of Combaron's insistence, she had refused to resume her journey to the capital until she was sure the Umwira threat was over. The High Matri's Warlinga were dead, and Combaron was only her second in command. He couldn't force her to go, especially in the face of such evident danger.

Finally recognizing that fact, the Dingay priest took half the remaining Warlinga hunters in the Sulas barracks yesterday and stormed off to Tragar Keep to find Gormach.

Thinking of Combaron's impudent rage made Sagas smile. If it wasn't such a deadly game they played, it would have been amusing. The look on his face when he left—it would not go well for Gormach once he reached Tragar Keep. Not that she felt any pity for the lazy, drunken bandit. Being the disgrace to his house that he was, he deserved worse for his laps than a spoiled brat's temper tantrum.

Sagas looked across the courtyard at the slave pens and felt a shiver of dread run down her spine. Flat naked faces, five-fingered hands, yes they were the ones she'd seen in her dreams. She'd been told how pitiful and helpless they were, but she knew better.

She'd seen the power they'd wielded in that other world, knew what they were capable of. Had they brought their magics with them? Would they destroy Timorna too if given the chance?

Have faith in the Khutani, she told herself. *The Makers are wise; they know what is best for all of us. And if their Dream-Chosen is among these strangers, then it is right for you to be true to your breeding and obey.*

"Temog, where is this blue-eyed one? I don't see him."

Temog pointed. "You can't see him well, but he is in the shelter."

"Mm, I see him now. Let's go down. I want to have a closer look at him before Hanno puts them to their tasks for the day."

DUNNAGH GLANCED OVER his shoulder. The Warlinga overseer and two of his men were entering their enclosure. "What are we going to do?" Marti whispered. "I won't let them kill her, Ce'awn. They'll have to kill me first if they try."

"I know how you feel, Marti, but wait—don't do anything foolish yet. Let me see what I can do first; maybe I can talk Hanno into letting her rest for today."

Noticing Dunnagh and Marti weren't in the feeding line, the overseer smiled and started across the pen towards them. He kicked aside the moss in his path and came into the shelter. The smile still curving his gray lips he focused his malignant stare on the kneeling Marti and supine Marnez lying in the moss. "Lazy slaves get up or I *make* you."

Dunnagh stepped forward to meet him, blocking his way. He heard Marti utter a curse as she rose in a fighter's crouch beside her lover. "Easy, Marti," he said, never taking his eyes off the Warlinga.

Head crest flattened, tail raking the ground behind him, Hanno growled. Looming over his shorter adversary, he said, "Move or be disciplined, too!"

Dunnagh held his ground. "No kill woman—no eat—"

Hanno drew back a muscular arm, and, with claws fully extended, aimed a blow at Dunnagh's head. Dunnagh dodged, managing to deflect most of the blow's force, while still blocking Hanno's path.

When he was balanced again, he touched his face; his hand coming away bloody. Dunnagh clinched his fists and stubbornly repeated, "No kill. Woman sick. Need rest today. Better soon. You no kill!"

Outside the shelter he heard Nathan bark a low-voiced order to the armachda. Was that Tessa crying? Without taking his eyes from the Warlinga's face, he knew his people were readying themselves for a fight, and suspected that the overseer's men were doing the same. Feeling strangely detached, Dunnagh stood his ground, waiting.

So, this is how it will end, he thought. *It's as good a day as any to die.*

"STOP!" a commanding female voice shouted.

Everyone in the pen froze. The Avairei woman in charge at Sulas, whom Tessa said was named Ima Sagas, stormed through the gate, the elderly priest Dunnagh had asked for help and a couple of their attendants, trailing in her wake.

In a high temper herself, she folded her arms across her chest and demanded, "What's the meaning of this?"

Hanno growled something under his breath and bowed to her. "It is nothing, Ima, just a minor problem of discipline with one of the slaves. It need not concern you, Ima, I can handle it."

Sagas continued to stare, and at last, the Warlinga dropped his eyes, tail tip curling and uncurling with his emotion. "I will not repeat myself again, San Hanno," sagas snapped. "What is going on here?"

The Warlinga refused to meet her eye or answer, the angry movements of his tail increasing.

"Well?"

Humiliating him publicly like that seemed to Dunnagh like a very dangerous game. Why was she doing it; what did Marnez's injury matter to her? When after a tense pause Hanno still didn't answer, she turned to Dunnagh. The Avairei gave an involuntary shudder as she looked into his eyes for the first time.

Dunnagh gave her, what he hoped was a reassuring smile. Slowly, searching for the right words in her language, he said, "Woman sick." He stepped aside so she could see the huddled figure in the moss. "Me tell—" he motioned to Hanno—"No kill, no eat."

Sagas grunted to show she understood him. Then, addressing the elderly priest she'd brought with her, she pointed to Marnez. "Temog, go look at her. See if you can tell what's wrong with the slave."

The priest called Temog stepped past her, already reaching in a pouch for something, but he'd taken only a few steps, when Marti stopped him. "Let him look at her, Marti," Dunnagh said. "He's the one who helped us get Samuel's bones. He won't hurt her and he may be able to help us."

Marti's glare was murderous, but at Dunnagh's repeated assurance, she moved aside so the priest could make his examination.

When Temog finished, he returned to Ima Sagas's side and spoke to her in a voice so low only she could hear. Dunnagh caught the words woman, Hanno and bones and assumed he was telling her about Marnez's confrontation with the overseer.

When he finished, Sagas rounded on Hanno and spoke to the Warlinga in a haughty voice that made his tail start lashing the ground again. Dunnagh suspected he was being disciplined, because the big Warlinga didn't look very happy.

Dunnagh wasn't sure what the priestess was talking about, but when she mentioned weasel-face's name and then a moment later something about slaves and breeding, Hanno's head crest rose in surprise.

Well, well, Dunnagh thought, that got his attention; he hadn't expected her to know that little tidbit of information—whatever it was. The Warlinga's head crest flattened again at her next string of words, but after a moment's hesitation, he bowed in acceptance of her chastisement. "Your will, Ima," he muttered.

Dunnagh saw how Hanno's red eyes smoldered with resentment, and even to his alien eyes, it was plain that the woman had made a dangerous enemy. Why? Why was she doing this for creatures she must consider just mindless slaves? Did she really care? Or were Marnez and maybe Dunnagh himself, merely pawns in a larger game that he couldn't fathom?

He wished he knew more of the local language. Dared he draw attention to Tessa by asking her to translate right now? Catching Nathan's eye for a moment, he decided against it. His friend would never forgive him. Nor did he wish to endanger her, or anyone.

Turning once more to Dunnagh, Sagas pointed to the sick woman. "No one will kill her. But you must come with me now."

He blinked and pointed to his naked chest. "You want me go—you want eat me?"

"No!" Sagas shook her head, horrified. "I don't want to eat you, but I do want you to come with me. You must go to the Khutani now."

"Khutani..." Dunnagh shuddered; the released memories that word invoked hit him with the force of a hammer blow.

In the next moment the Khutani's implanted compulsion was triggered. It sang in his blood, slipping his conscious mind into trance. He remembered his nightmare, and the Sending whispered to him that morning on the wind.

The Geish enfolded him in its unyielding coils, calming his fears and whispering to him of wondrous secrets yet to be revealed. Bond, bond, Kashallan Bond. He had promised, and with his surrender to Khutani will, came an odd kind of freedom and peace.

Yes, he would have to go with her—it was time. He had given his word, but first he needed to do all in his power to ensure the safety of his people. "Nobody kill—" his eyes flicked to the Warlinga—"my people—" he motioned to the other captives—"if no kill, then me go with you."

Sagas smiled, revealing dainty sharp teeth. She had understood his game. "Yes, you come. Nobody kill them. I swear it!" Dunnagh bowed.

Sagas turned to the Warlinga. "Do you understand this? The sacred Khutani themselves have need of this one." She pointed to Dunnagh. "He has willingly come forward to honor them. He asks for the safety of his kinsmen in return. You will not harm them while he is with the Holy Ones. Is that clear, San Hanno?"

"Your will, Ima." Tail lashing the dust in his wake, he growled an order to his men and they marched from the pen.

When the overseer was gone from the enclosure Dunnagh, nodded to the priestess and stepped forward.

"Dunnagh, wait a moment. Surely there is some other way to resolve this," Singey pleaded.

Dunnagh hesitated. He glanced at the waiting Avairei, then turned back to face his companions. But their affairs had little meaning for him now. They were like paper cutouts pasted in a book. From within his trance, he sensed their fear. It flowed over him like the waves of a retreating tide, leaving him unmoved.

His smile was sad; he wished he could comfort them, but he couldn't. The power of the Maker's Compulsion controlled him, pulsing through his body and soul, insisting—demanding—that he heed only its voice.

As he turned to go Nathan grabbed him roughly by the shoulders and spun him around to face him. "What are you doing?" he demanded in a low angry voice, his gray eyes sooty and pleading. "Dunnagh, I agree with Singey. This is definitely one of your stupidest plans. The Gods alone know what they'll do to you if you go with them. Don't do this!"

Dunnagh gently removed Nathan's hands and kissed them. "It will be all right, Nathan. I've already promised them, remember? I told you after the jump aboard the ship. I'm their Chosen. It's time; I have to go."

Nathan blanched. "Oh, by the Gods, Dunnagh, no! That oath thing you told me about—that was just crazy talk—you don't really believe it?" Over and over he shook his head. "Don't do this to me—don't leave me."

Dunnagh reached out a cool hand, caressing his cheek, forcing Nathan to stop shaking his head and look at him. Eyes slightly unfocused he gave Nathan a dreamy smile. "Keep them safe for me, Mo Hara, and don't be afraid. You will see me again, I promise."

Dunnagh let his hand fall slowly to his side, then turned, and without a backward glance, he followed the priestess from the pen.

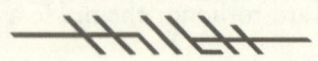

TEMOG GLANCED AT THE retreating Sagas, hesitated, and then pulled a small vial from one of his belt pouches. He handed the medicine to the female that spoke his language best. "This is for the injured one. Give her three drops on her tongue now; it will let her sleep and dull the pain. I will come back later and see to her wounds myself. Do you understand me?"

She nodded and repeated his instructions. He smiled with approval, then hurried after the departing Sagas.

HANNO WATCHED THE IMA and her retinue walk back into the inner keep, the impudent mutant among them. He was in no mood for defiance of his will today. He resented having to stay behind supervising worthless slaves, when he wanted to be with the hunters tracking the Umwira. Damn Blue Eyes and Sagas both to the black pit of oblivion.

Khutani indeed. What was the old hag really up to with the mutant? Hanno's claws flexed in agitation. How dare the witch humiliate him like that in front of his hunters. She would pay for that, he vowed. Her time here was ending; it was the Dingay clan who had the power now, not dried up old husks like Sagas and her clan.

When all was quiet tonight, he would send a fast runner to find Ata Combaron. Then *she* would see whose will is to be obeyed. "You old hag, Combaron Dingay will make you pay," he promised.

Part Four: The Kashallan

Chapter One

At the entrance to the pools Sagas paused, curious to see Blue Eyes's reaction to the Khutani's underground world. Ahead of them dark water lapped against the rim of the walkway. Patches of luminous mist trailed above its surface in ragged clouds. Spears of rock crystal hung down from the shadowed ceiling, ropes of phosphorescent fungi clinging to their shafts. Blue Eyes breathed in the moist, fragrant air, his eyes wide. Sagas waited, allowing him to experience it to the fullest.

At last, he let out a deep sigh and turned to her. "Beautiful!"

By the Great Mother, his eyes *were* as blue as the kavay, like Temog claimed. Was that why the Khutani favored him? Did they believe him holy because of his odd colored eyes? In spite of her fears and misgivings about the alien, she couldn't help wondering if it were true.

"Yes, Chosen, it *is* very beautiful. Are you ready; shall we go on?"

"Ye-ess."

"Come then." Sagas took his hand and stepped on to the first bridge.

As they moved along the lattice of interconnecting walkways, the Khutani sensed their presence. Trails of bright phosphorescent foam kept pace with their progress. The air seemed to vibrate with their excitement.

When Sagas and her entourage reached the Ima Matri's private Gifting Pool, she halted, suddenly unsure what to do next. To her dismay, only the young Khutani swam nearby.

Just having finished the morning meal, it was normal to see only the young at play near the stairs to the keep, but this day of all days, she desperately needed one of the elders to advise her about this Chosen they had entrusted to her care.

True, she hadn't given the Khutani any warning of her intentions, but Combaron's vigilance had made it impossible for her to come here before now and receive any guidance.

She glanced at Temog—no help there. He looked as bewildered as she felt. Sagas sighed. There was no help for it. The Khutani would have to do the best they could to make the bond with him unprepared. She'd gone too far now to return Blue Eyes to the slave pen. Combaron would return soon, and then she would be hauled off to Riath for her execution.

But the adult Khutani would come, as soon as they realized she had brought him. Think, she ordered her dazed mind. What must be done first? The Khutani would have to taste him to make his symbiont—she knew that much. How could she make him understand what he must do to help them create a compatible partner for him? He was so alien, and his language skills were so poor. He knew little of their ways.

Sagas crouched beside the pool's rim, drawing him down beside her. "This is my pool," she explained. She pointed to the young Khutani below them. "See the Khutani? Khutani taste me—then you. I will show you how to do it; watch me."

"Khutani." He nodded solemnly, fixing her with his eerie blue eyes.

Sagas's stomach churned. So alien, would she ever get used to those eyes or the ugly, hairless look of him? To hide her discomfort, she turned and took a small stone bowl from a niche in the rim of the pool's containing wall.

Pausing, she next chewed on a claw tip and considered. It was forbidden for anyone but an Avairei to form the link directly with the sacred Khutani. But if Blue Eyes didn't make the link, the Khutani couldn't taste him to make the symbiont.

In her dreams, she had seen him use the magic. Should she show him how to communicate with them? No, there was no need to make things worse by breaking another taboo. The Makers didn't need to *speak* to him to make the symbiont child. They only needed to taste his bodily fluids. He was the Dream-Chosen, true, but he was still just a slave and an alien stranger, after all. The sharing of fluids would be enough, she reasoned.

When she was sure she had his attention, she said, "Watch me."

Sagas lifted the bowl to her mouth and spat into it several times. Next, she shifted the bowl between her legs and dripped her urine into it. Sagas watched him carefully as she did these things. His eyes opened in surprise, when he saw her urinate, but he nodded his understanding when she asked.

Next, she set the bowl down on the walkway, unsheathed her knife, and made a shallow cut along one arm near the wrist. Sagas showed him the dark blood welling out of the wound as she tipped her forearm over the bowl. Opening and closing her fist several times, she encouraged her blood to drip into the vessel. When she felt she had given enough, Sagas lifted her arm and sprinkled the clotting powder over the cut. The bleeding stopped abruptly.

Sagas held up the bowl to show him. "This is my gift to the Khutani."

Taking the bowl in one hand and a ritual beating stick in the other, she tapped the stick rhythmically on the rim of the pool, while pouring the contents of the bowl into the liquid below. When the bowl was emptied, she set it down and pointed with the stick into the water.

"See, the Khutani come. They taste the gift; then they know me—and the news I bring them."

Her gift lay like a dark bruise atop the pool's luminescent surface. He leaned forward, fascinated, watching the gray, sinewy bodies swarm around the gift, tasting, then devouring the dark stain. When the Khutani departed, he studied her solemn face. So many questions, she could see them in his eyes, but he had no words with which to ask them.

Smiling in sympathy, Sagas touched his arm. "Soon, Chosen, you will know all the answers. Very soon. The Holy Ones will reveal to you many secrets when you have made the bond."

If you survive the transformation, that is. Sagas shuddered and made a sign against evil.

"No understand."

"I know." She patted his arm again; this language barrier was so frustrating. Picking up the knife and bowl, she rose to her feet, motioning him to follow.

Sagas led her entourage through the maze of walkways deeper into the cavern. When they went beyond the well-traveled paths, they stopped while Temog's apprentices scraped some glowing fungi into the empty lamps they'd taken from the shelf by the stairway.

In this abandoned portion of the cavern, no joyous Khutani play relieved the gloom. Their lanterns did little to ward off the feeling of despair that now enveloped them like a shroud. Temog glanced around uneasily, behind him, nearly lost in the mists and gloom, he heard his apprentices and Pela talking in hushed voices.

"Where are we going, Sagas?" Temog murmured. His voice sounded flat and muffled through the fog. When she didn't answer, he shuddered and repeated his question.

"Quiet," Sagas said, "I'm trying to remember." They had stopped at a T intersection. Mumbling to herself, Sagas held her lamp high. "Ah, this way," she said and turned to her left. Blue Eyes followed without question. He was a pale, hulking presence at her heels, even more alien and unnerving in the gloom. Temog shivered, then hurried to catch up.

At last, the walkway down which they'd been traveling, ended at the base of a massive rock wall. From somewhere beyond water splashed into an unseen basin. Blackness and the slumbering weight of the mountain pressed down upon them. Long ago, when this place was in use, an alcove had been hollowed out of the rock and made into a chapel.

Sagas stopped at the edge of a dark pool. Though it had been years since she'd been here, her memory and her instincts told her this was the place. Here, in this out-of-the-way, half-forgotten part of the cavern, was the Kashallan Birthing Pool.

To her people's sorrow, it had been long unused. The ghosts of the pool's many failures still hovered in the obscurity to torment her. Sagas shivered and made the sign again to ward off evil.

This time, it would be different—the Makers had foretold it. This time, the transformation wouldn't kill. This time, the bond would be achieved. She repeated the litany over and over in her mind, hoping to convince herself.

"Chosen—" She touched him gently on the arm. When he turned to face her, she motioned for him to crouch beside her near the pool's edge.

"What place this?"

"It is the Kashallan Birthing Pool."

His eyes told her that he didn't understand again. How expressive his flat, alien face was. It was almost possible to hear his words, by just looking at his ugly face.

Sagas tried through a series of gestures and accompanying words, to make him understand, but it was hopeless. His knowledge of the Timornan language was still too limited for her to get her meaning across. Finally she gave up in frustration.

He offered her a crooked smile and patted her hand. "No worry." Turning away from her, he focused his attention down into the water. Sagas sensed him reach out within his trance, trying to discover for himself, the answers she couldn't give him. At last, he turned back to her. In an eerie, far-away voice he said, "This *my* pool."

Sagas reached down with one hand, and then held her dripping fingers to his lips. He licked her fingers, then made a sour face at the taste. Amused, Sagas chuckled. "Yes, Chosen One, this is your Birthing Pool."

She handed him the ritual blade and bowl. "Dream-Chosen, it is time to make your gift to the sacred Khutani."

Blue Eyes lifted the stone bowl and spat into it as she had shown him. Next, he set the bowl down and took up the knife. Placing the sharp edge against his left forearm, he drew the blade slowly across his skin, making the ritual cut for the first time. He held the bowl under the wound and allowed his blood to drip into the vessel.

When she judged the amount enough, Sagas stopped him. Turning his arm over, she applied the clotting agent. He hissed in surprise. "You didn't expect the pain, did you, Blue Eyes? You will learn. Nothing comes easy on Timorna."

For just a moment, she felt a stab of pity for this blue-eyed alien. How much did he really understand about the transformation? Could he endure what was to come? Did the Khutani have the right to interfere with another being's destiny by making him a part of their plan?

Then, Sagas dismissed her misgivings and hardened her resolve. In some way she could not fathom, he must have agreed to this. To make the kashallan bond was the reason he and his kindred were here. He was the Dream-Chosen, and the Khutani sent him to her for this very purpose. She would be true to her breeding and do her duty.

Whatever came next, she and Blue Eyes were powerless to change the flow of their destinies now. They were caught up in the whirlpool of the Khutani's' making. Their personal wants or desires meant nothing anymore. Only the survival of her world, and will of the Makers was important now.

Cradling his arm, Blue eyes returned his attention to the Kashallan Pool. Sagas touched his shoulder and motioned for him to complete the gift. He blushed, then held the bowl between his legs and filled it to overflowing with his urine.

Sagas removed an ancient beater, carved with now-forgotten symbols from a niche. As Blue Eyes poured his offering into the pool, she dredged up from racial memories a song and began to sing "The Call." Her voice rang out across the cavern in a high-pitched, rhythmic chant that was swiftly taken up by the other Avairei. Blue Eyes set down the empty bowl and stared, mesmerized, into the pool below him. His body swayed to the chant's haunting cadence.

For the first time in so many centuries, "The Call" for a Kashallan rang out, to push back the darkness in the cavern. As the Avairei sang, the pool below them brightened. It swirled with a rainbow of opalescent color; the Khutani were coming in answer to the priestess's summons.

Relieved, Sagas watched as one of the larger Khutani in the Sulas pod, brushed the Chosen's gift with its feathery mouth tentacles, and then devoured it.

The gift was given and accepted. Sagas sat back, letting the beater stick fall from her numb hand. Now that it was over, she felt totally drained. For a long time, she remained motionless, staring off into the darkness. The transformation of a kashallan had begun.

Temog touched her shoulder. She looked up, her sluggish mind trying to focus once more on the world around her. "What?"

"Sagas? Are you well, Ima?"

She took a deep breath, letting it out slowly, then patted his shoulder. "I'm all right, Temog, just tired."

"But what do we do now, Ima?" Temog whispered. His eyes flicked nervously to the Dream-Chosen, crouching beside the pool as motionless as a stone.

She rubbed a hand across her face, and, taking Temog's arm, she got shakily to her feet. "There is nothing we *can* do now, but wait. The Khutani need time to prepare the symbiont child to bond with him. Maybe they will need to call a Maker to help with that—I don't know. Who can say?

"I wonder if even the Makers know what will happen. Don't look so scandalized, Ata; how could they know? Bonding with an alien hasn't been tried before."

Temog looked contrite. "Yes, of course, you have a point. Will you stay with him now?"

"No, I must return to the keep above. They will be wondering what is happening down here. I saw many shocked faces as we passed through the keep. I must explain. I must tell them *something.*"

"Is that wise? We still don't know how most of the Avairei feel about the Dingay. If you tell them what you are doing, many will turn against you. It might be very dangerous."

Sagas barked a laugh. "It's too late to worry about that now. It's already *dangerous.* Anyway, it's out of my control. The Holy Ones have made their will known. I can do no more than obey—no matter what the cost to me personally."

Temog glanced at the motionless Blue Eyes, still gazing down into the pool. "What about him? What will you do with him while the Khutani prepare the symbiont?"

What to do with him indeed; she hadn't thought that far ahead... "He can stay in the little chapel over there." She motioned to the alcove carved out of the stone wall behind them. "He will be safe enough. No one will look for him out here. Few of the Avairei even remember this place exists. Yes, here will be best.

"I will have Pela stay with him and see to his needs. Perhaps some of your apprentices can keep a discreet watch as well?"

"I think Orlan and Timma here would be glad to do that. They are good apprentices." He smiled at them fondly. "And I think they are quite overwhelmed at the moment by the honor of being a part of this—as am I."

Sagas touched Blue Eyes' shoulder to get his attention. Startled, he glanced up. "Come."

He rose to his feet, towering above her. "No stay here? Where we go?" He looked wistfully back into the pool, as if reluctant to leave it.

Sagas patted his hand to reassure him. "We go only in there." She pointed to the chapel. "You must wait now. You will need to rest and prepare yourself for the Transformation."

Blue Eyes nodded, accepting her proposal without understanding all her words. He studied her for a long moment, then reached out his free hand and gently caressed her cheek. Focusing on her those eerie, kavay-blue eyes of his, he said, "You rest too. Don't be afraid."

Sagas hadn't expected that. She reached up, covering his hand with her own, a sob catching in her throat. Turning away from the pool, she led him into the alcove.

Chapter Two

L ater that day, as Temog approached the sick slave, his way was blocked by a wall of grim-faced aliens. Confused, he stopped. Why were they acting like this? He was a healer. What was wrong with these people? He could almost taste their hostility.

Suddenly he felt afraid. Maybe these creatures *weren't* as harmless as the Warlinga claimed. Catching sight of the female who spoke the Timornan language best, he addressed her. "Please tell them I mean no harm. I am a healer. I came back, as I said I would, to treat the injured one among you."

When the translator finished, the dark-skinned female looked up at a large gray eyed male who had just walked over to them. Her black eyes seemed to ask his opinion. The male said something to her in their own language. She hesitated, then moved back, but continued to hover near the sick one, glaring suspiciously at him as he put his bag down.

Feeling a shiver run down his back, Temog slowly opened his bag and took out a small jar and a long needle made from a thorn. The female's eyes narrowed at that, but he surprised them all, by jabbing the needle's point into the tips of the two middle fingers of his own left hand. When dark purple dots of blood appeared, he rubbed green kavay salve into the punctures, and touched his sensitized fingers to the injured area on the woman's shoulder.

Still anxious, Temog glanced at the slaves again, then closed his eyes and allowed himself to "*taste*" the injury as the Holy Khutani had taught him. When he opened his eyes once more, his audience seemed puzzled and maybe a bit curious rather than hostile. Evidently a healing diagnosis was done quite differently in their far-off world.

After completing his exam, he knew the cause of the poor woman's distress. The fool Hanno had dislocated the woman's arm bone, as well as giving her several deep claw marks.

Treating the claw wounds would be easy, but re-aligning the bone might be painful. He didn't want them to get the wrong impression if she cried out—especially the cold-eyed female staring so menacingly.

Their lack of knowledge of his language was a frustrating barrier. It took a while, but with a mixture of word and sign, he finally got them to understand. Temog directed his students to raise the injured slave to a sitting position.

"Now hold her firmly while I put the bone back," he said. Temog extended her arm and with one swift movement popped it back into place. The slave cried out once, then sighed in relief.

Temog patted her uninjured shoulder, then pushed her back down into the moss. Speaking to her in a soothing voice, he removed a jar of yellow kavay salve from his bag and liberally covered the claw marks with the sticky paste.

Finished, Temog sat back on his heels and breathed a sigh of relief. Now he only needed to wait while the mixture dried and formed its own airtight scab over the wounds.

The dark-skinned male who had been watching the procedure with growing excitement, bobbed his head in evident satisfaction. Sensing Temog's regard, he looked up, his eyes brimming with questions.

Temog smiled. "I know—you have so many questions. But we are working on this language problem. The Khutani will make something to help you. Soon you will be able to speak our language better, and then I will answer whatever questions I can."

After the kavay was dry and he'd put away his things, he touched his patient once more. Her eyes opened, focusing on his face with difficulty. Speaking slowly, he said, "Is there anything more I can do for you?"

"C-cold," she said, "always c-cold."

Startled, Temog glanced at the rest of the Chosen's kin. Yes, some of them were shivering too. By the Holy Khutani, why hadn't they thought of this before? Of course the aliens were cold, all of them—they had no protective fur to keep them warm.

Turning to his apprentices, he said, "Quickly now, go to the storeroom and bring blankets for all of them. And bring good ones, mind."

"But, Ata," one protested. "It isn't fitting for slaves to have—"

Temog cut him off with an impatient gesture. "*These* slaves are well favored by the Holy Ones. What is *not fitting* is that they should take a chill and sicken. Now don't argue with me, go do as I say."

"Your will, Ata."

As Temog was about to leave, the tall gray-eyed male, who seemed to have taken over as their leader, stopped him.

"Where Dunnagh?"

"Dun-na?" Temog frowned; he didn't know that word. Who or what was a dun-na? The big male tried to explain. This was obviously important to him, but Temog couldn't figure out what he wanted.

Temog glanced around for his students for help, then recalled he'd sent them off for the blankets. He held up his hands and started for the gate, but the big male put a hand on his shoulder to stop him. A mixture of fear and anger, welled up inside Temog at the touch. How dare the slave lay a hand on him!

Then, he remembered these creatures were ignorant and alien. He must be patient with them, because they also had the blessings of the Holy Ones. Maybe they knew no better. Curbing his outrage, Temog lifted the male's hand from his shoulder, and stepped back. "I'm sorry. I don't understand. I must go."

NATHAN MUTTERED A CURSE in frustration. "Help me out here, Tessa," he begged. Tessa repeated the question.

The priest nodded his understanding at last, then smiled. "You mean the Dream-Chosen. He is well. He is sleeping at the moment, I think."

Nathan clenched his hands into fists. Dunnagh said the voice in the trance called him Chosen or something? And, just what exactly were the Avairei going to do to this *Dream-Chosen* of theirs?

"Nathan?" Tessa whispered, "What's wrong?" She grabbed his arm, looking frightened.

Nathan avoided her eye; he felt too uneasy himself to offer her meaningless comfort. "Wrong? I'm not sure." Then his heart began to pound as a new thought struck him.

"Tessa, these Avairei are priests, right?" She nodded. "They wouldn't be going to sacrifice Dunnagh to some bloodthirsty, god, would they?"

Tessa put her hand to her mouth, her eyes growing wide. "Oh, Nathan, I don't always understand them—I don't know!"

Nathan growled a curse and rounded on the startled Avairei. He loomed over the smaller man, his hands balled into fists. "You kill Dunnagh—Chosen, me kill you!"

The priest gasped and stepped back. "No kill! He is Chosen."

Tessa listened, then said to Nathan. "He's saying something about the Khutani. I think they are some kind of deity to these people—anyway, he says, the Khutani chose Dunnagh. And, he also says, he would die to protect the Dream-Chosen."

Could he trust the old fur? Had to for the moment. Nathan grunted, then addressed the priest again. "When Dunnagh come back here with us?" He waved his hand around their enclosure.

I hope soon, so we can all get out of here.

"I don't know—"

The priest was saved from further awkward questions, by the arrival of his students with the promised blankets. The captives knew immediately what they were being offered, and hurried forward to receive them.

Nathan fingered the rich brown fur of his prize, then pulled it around his shoulders. It was a little short for someone his size, but it felt good.

The blankets weren't made of woven fibers, but were a double thickness of light, furry hide, pieced together to form a dense, soft covering. Where had the Avairei gotten such wonderful pelts? They'd seen no large game animals on their way here, nor had either the Begta or the Loti mentioned any that would fit the blanket's description. Did they trade for them—and if so, with whom?

"Tessa, I'm curious; ask him where he got these blankets."

The priest took one of the blankets from the pile, and tucked it in around Marnez. When he stood once more, Tessa rubbed her hand across her new blanket and asked, "So soft—where come from, this?"

"Why, from us,"

"No, not who gives, but how are made?"

"The answer is the same. They come from us," he repeated. When she still didn't understand, he lifted her hand, and placed it on the soft warm fur of his own chest. "From us."

She reddened, and quickly removed her hand.

Watching the Avairei depart, Singey shook his head in amazement. "What a strange world this is. Nothing is ever wasted. Not even the dead are allowed to rest undisturbed."

Nathan snorted. At a warning glare from Tessa, he gave them both a disgusted look and strode off into the darkness. He was in no mood to argue with her, or anyone else right now. Dunnagh was gone. He'd had enough of the Avairei, the scientists, and the whole damned lot of them for one night.

Feeling sorry for himself, Nathan sat against the shelter's back wall in the deepening twilight. This had been one of the worst days of his life. Damn Dunnagh anyway! How could he just go off like that? Why had he left him alone, expecting him to keep them all alive—and sane?

"I can't do it, damn you, Dunnagh, I can't!"

Nathan blinked rapidly, eyes stinging, fear knotting in his gut. When he recalled that awful look in Dunnagh's eyes after the priestess said he must go with her, Nathan wanted to punch something—scream. What were they doing to his friend in there? And why, oh why, did the fool think he had to go with them? Nathan punched his fist into his other palm again and again till his hand grew numb. He wouldn't cry—he wouldn't...

Chapter Three

Tessa sat huddled in her new furry mantle and stared out into the night, uncertain what to do. She was exhausted and wanted to sleep, but the new blankets had changed everything. In the far corner of their shelter another sleepless figure huddled. She knew who it was—but she knew what the big Caldoni wanted from her, too.

As their health returned, he had made that very clear. Nathan wasn't obnoxious about it, and he never tried to force her. He understood, that when she said no to his advances, she meant it. But he never gave up trying, either. In *his* culture, she supposed such casual sexual unions were normal. She couldn't fault him for being what he was, and yet... Oh, it was so complicated.

Tessa was finding out to her dismay, that it was much harder to *live* in an alien culture, than it was to read about it in her textbooks. And, it was even harder still, to share that life with people from still another ethnic background than her own.

Tessa wished Moraga would come lie beside her. The larger woman's bulk was almost as comforting as a man's would be, and far less threatening. But Moraga was with her Lann Gheal comrades at the moment; and Tessa was too shy to disturb her.

Someone might get the wrong idea about them. Just thinking about it made her blush. And maybe, with her new blanket, Moraga might not want Tessa to cuddle up to her, anymore. Oh, she just couldn't tell with these people. She just didn't know what to think or do anymore.

Lost in her own misery, she was unaware of another's approach, till a soft touch on her shoulder startled her. "Tessa, what are you doing sitting here?" Moraga asked.

"I-I was waiting—for you."

Moraga chuckled and sat down beside her. She arranged several clumps of loose moss over her exposed legs, tightened the wrap of her blanket and let out a contented sigh. "And why would you be a-doing that, my dear, when there's another needing his bed warmed tonight much more than me?"

Tessa felt her face heat again, suddenly grateful for the darkness that hid her embarrassment. Her eyes flicked to the brooding figure by the wall. She knew what the Caldoni woman meant, but chose to ignore it. Instead, she focused her attention on the part of the shelter where Marti and Marnez lay huddled together.

Marnez had been very kind to her; perhaps she should go sleep with them. And if Moraga was worried about Nathan, surely he would be better off with one of his own kind, than with her, wouldn't he?

When she voiced those thoughts to Moraga, the big Caldoni clucked her tongue in disapproval. "No, Tessa, I don' think you really know what you're saying. True, Marnez has been nice to you, but it's because she *likes* you, and maybe Marti does too. They be sworn to each other, but they often share other lovers. Do you like them in that way, then? Is that why you don't want Nathan?"

Tessa gasped. She'd never dreamed—she shook her head violently—appalled. "N-no," she stammered. "No."

"I thought not," Moraga said. "And that be why, when I seen how it was for you and Nathan, I brings you to sleep with me."

"Thank you," Tessa murmured, still stunned and a little frightened.

"Now don't you be thinking bad things about those two. Just cause I told you what you should have already guessed," Moraga said as if she'd heard Tessa's thoughts.

"They no be forcing anybody to play games they don't want to play. So don't be afraid, all right?"

"All right," Tessa said, just to please her.

Moraga was silent for a while, staring out into the courtyard, and listening to the noisy bone game going on in the Warlinga barracks. Then, returning to her earlier topic of discussion, she asked, "Have you no lain with a man before? Are you a virgin, my dear?"

"I've had other lovers," Tessa admitted, "but that was different. We had things in common. Nathan, I think he just wants me for—you know?" Her voice trailed off, unable to continue with such a delicate subject.

Moraga chuckled, and put an arm around the embarrassed woman. "What nonsense are you talking girl? You and yon laddy over there, have a lot of things in common. The most important of which, is needing each other's comfort, and a-wanting to stay alive. Music, art and books you like or don't like, they no be important, not here, not now. Can't you see that?"

Yes, put like that Tessa could see it. And yet, she still hesitated. Every ounce of her training and background urged her to be appalled at the thought of just letting the big Caldoni have her. What would people say, if they found out later?

Maybe she should— "Moraga, I know Nathan's upset with Dunnagh gone, but maybe you *should* be the one to sleep with him."

"Well, I will, if you won't, but it's not me he be a-wanting, now is it? And besides, there is another lonely outsider among us that could use a little human companionship tonight. If you sleep with Nathan, I can offer *him* some comfort perhaps."

"Who—Philip? You're talking about Philip, aren't you?" In spite of herself Tessa began to laugh. Oh, she just couldn't imagine it!

"And why not," Moraga said. "Do you think an ignorant Caldoni like me, isn't good enough for the likes o' Mr. High Society Singey?"

Realizing she'd given offense, Tessa sobered. "Oh, Moraga, I'm sorry, I didn't mean it like that. You're a beautiful person, so wise and kind. No, it's not that—it's just—I've known Philip *socially* for a long time. He's such a cold, impersonal man, I just couldn't imagine him doing—you know—*that!*"

Moraga smiled slyly. "Well now, that be all the more reason he be a-needing someone like me, to warm both his bed and his blood for him, ain't it?" Then, persisting with the subject under discussion, she said, "So, my girl, who will it be? Nathan, who has just lost his closest friend and is in bad need of another. Or yon Mr. Scientist, who is in need of his blood heated?"

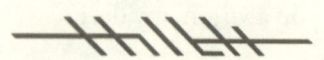

NATHAN GROWLED A CURSE under his breath. Would those damned Warlinga ever shut up so he could get some sleep? He was tired, so tired; every bone and muscle in his body ached. That devil of a Warlinga overseer had worked them mercilessly after the priests left that morning. Oh, Hanno had kept his filthy claws off them, all right. But he'd exacted his own sweet revenge nonetheless. He'd let them know, in a thousand other painful ways, how he blamed them for his humiliation.

Sleep? Who was he fooling? Even with the new blanket and quiet, he wasn't going to sleep. *Dunnagh—oh, Gods, Dunnagh, why?*

With brutal clarity, he realized how dependent they had become on each other over the years. *A stupid thing to let happen—you should know better, boyo. They always die or leave you.*

Since his family's massacre, Nathan had grown accustomed to ignoring and pushing aside any unwanted emotions when they surfaced to torment him. It had been easy. Dunnagh was always there, as friend and stabilizing anchor in an ever-changing world. And now, this strange compulsion—whatever it was, had ripped them apart.

For Nathan, it was like experiencing the cold emptiness of his parents' death all over again. Only this time, there was no Dunnagh to reach out to him. No Dunnagh, to save him from his inner demons...

Some time later, Nathan was startled out of his brooding when someone sat beside him.

"Nathan?"

He sighed. "Yeah, Tessa, it's me." Then, unable to keep a sarcastic note out of his voice, he said, "Why aren't you asleep? Moraga's probably cold—go back to bed."

"Moraga has a nice new blanket to keep her warm, you beast. I—" She halted herself in mid-scold. "Oh, Nathan, please don't. Don't get me angry, and push me away. I know you're worried about Dunnagh. I'm worried, too—about Dunnagh—and everything."

She reached up and caressed his cheek. "Please, love, I'm so frightened; I need you, too."

Nathan stiffened, then with a strangled sob, he pulled her roughly into his arms. Holding her close, he buried his face in her hair. "Oh, Tessa."

Tessa laid her head against his chest; she could feel him trembling next to her skin. Slipping her arms about his neck, she raised her face, lips parting for his kiss.

Chapter Four

Wrapped in a furry blanket, Dunnagh lay curled up on a pallet like a caterpillar in its cocoon. Earlier the young priestess, Pela she said her name was, gave him something to drink that cleaned his system out quite thoroughly. The full bucket in the corner could attest to that. Now he felt emptied, content just to drift in the dream-like state that followed the second draft she urged upon him.

He smiled to himself; it was peaceful in this place. There was no pain in his body, or troubles to worry his mind. Ancient echoes vibrated through the rocks—tales of other times, other places, the lives of creatures so different from his own kind. When he opened his eyes, changing patterns of rainbow colors swirled before his vision. Beautiful! The ghosts and the colors danced and sang of their hopes and longings.

Dunnagh watched and listened, but focused on none of it. He just wanted to drift. He was free; he could do as he liked. He could sleep or stay awake, move or remain motionless, it didn't matter. Thanks to the priestess's potions, his awareness went beyond mere physical reality. He laughed to himself—or was it the other? Idly, he wondered where the self that was Dunnagh began or ended now.

Then, his blissful peace was shattered like breaking glass. Someone from outside his dream, was calling to him. The summons was pulling him back into physical awareness. He whined, resisting, but the someone insisted—wouldn't let him escape back into the dream.

Dunnagh reluctantly opened his eyes. *She* was beside him again, the priestess who was also ensnared within the Khutani's compulsion.

He smiled up at her, his eyes soft with compassion. Poor creature, like himself, she was bound to obey the will of those black-hearted Makers. He put out a hand and touched her face. Soft, and so very beautiful, his smile widened.

The priestess took his hand and helped him to sit up. "It is time, Chosen," she intoned.

"Time?" The word floated out of his mouth in a pink cloud, hovering in the air between them. Dunnagh repeated the unfamiliar Timornan word slowly, puzzling out its meaning.

She held out a brimming bowl to him. "Yes, Chosen, it is time. The little one awaits you." She placed the bowl carefully in his two hands. He stared down at it, becoming engrossed in the kaleidoscope of colors that only he could see in its depths.

"Drink!" she urged.

He licked dry his lips. "Drink?"

"Yes, Chosen, if it is still your will to make the bond—then drink."

He looked once more into the bowl. "Ye-s-s, drink... Thirsty."

Lifting the bowl to his mouth, he drained the vessel of its gelatinous contents. Dunnagh shuddered at the unfamiliar taste and let the empty bowl slip through his fingers.

"The Transformation has begun. He has accepted the Shalla," Sagas said to the others.

Ignoring the Avairei, Dunnagh fell back onto his pallet, anxious to return to the other-worldly visions that so pleased him.

IN THE MOIST DARKNESS of the host's body, the infant symbiont awoke. This was a good place, warm and safe. It uncoiled, and began to feed. Ravenous, it gorged, hollowing out a dark cave for itself within the living flesh about it.

Pain jerked Dunnagh out of his dreamy lassitude. Barely able to breathe, but completely conscious and sober, he rolled onto his side, clutching his belly. "What is happening to me! What have you black-hearted creatures done?" He writhed. "Why, why did I ever think I could trust you— Damn the slimy big worms! Oh, Merciful Gods of my ancestors, HELP ME!"

There was no escape—the pain went on and on. It felt as if white-hot agony was tearing him apart. From the depths of his soul the sounds came, swelling, vibrating through his being, then bursting out in scream after heart-wrenching scream.

"Temog, help me hold him," Sagas cried. "TEMOG, HELP ME!"

Jerked out of his paralysis by Sagas's shout, Temog knelt beside her, motioning for his apprentices to join him. Dunnagh spasmed again. In the corner, Pela sank to the floor, covering her face with her hands, as the agonized cries continued.

OVER THE NEXT FEW DAYS, time had little meaning for the man going through the Transformation or for those who cared for him. Dunnagh drifted in and out of consciousness, his body attuning itself to the rhythms of his internal bondmate. When the symbiont rested, he fell into exhausted sleep. When the symbiont awoke and fed, torment was his only reality.

He knew nothing of his surroundings, or of the Avairei who tried to console him. Only the fire that consumed his belly was real. He tasted the feel and sound of pain—and only the pain told him he was still alive. With each aching breath, he prayed for death, so the agony would end.

As the symbiont's body matured, the memories encoded into its genetic patterns were triggered. The blind instincts that guided it at first faded. It remembered, and knew its purpose. It was Tani, the first of the Khutani to undertake a bonding with an alien host. Once it completed the adaptation of its host's body, it would be the first of its kind, in long measures of time, to leave the confinement of the pools.

Nestled safe within its host, Tani would experience the surface world again, through the shared use of the host's physical senses. The symbiont (Shalla) delighted in its new awareness, endlessly sending out tendrils of itself to merge with every part of its bondmate. But it wanted something more; it wanted to share a psychic bonding with the host, too.

Eagerly, it sought that communion. Tani reached out to the host—its Kasha, but his spirit was no longer in their shared body. Where had he gone? Was he playing a new game?

Confused, Tani searched and searched, at last finding the host's battered spirit, hovering in the twilight shallows of the etheric void. Tani was ecstatic. But no matter what it said or did, the host rebuffed its overtures. All the symbiont could taste was the creature's anger and fear.

Why was he behaving so strangely? Curious, Tani swam closer. But the host wouldn't respond to its repeated questions. Instead, he fled blindly, deeper into the void. This was not good—Timorna needed them. They would both die, if he didn't come back to their shared body.

<<Kasha, please wait,>> the symbiont wailed as Dunnagh's luminous spirit-body disappeared into the gloom. <<Please, Kasha, I'm afraid, too. Don't leave me.>>

Suddenly alone in the nothingness, the young symbiont cried out, begging for someone to help it. Where were its kindred, where oh, where, was its Kasha?

Then, Tani tasted the presence of massive gray forms swimming towards it from out of the gloom. <<Don't be afraid, little one, we are here with you. Together we will find him.>>

<<Gladdris, I warned you the creature was willful and stubborn,>> a deep-voiced Maker said to its peer. <<Be grateful I have collared him or all would be lost.>>

<<Be silent, cousin,>> the one called Gladdris hissed, <<or you will frighten the Shalla. We have enough trouble without that.>>

<<We must hurry,>> another Maker said. <<An Umwira wizard's creation, set to watch the void, has discovered our wake and follows. If the phantasm calls to others of its kind and they find him—>>

<<I don't understand,>> Tani cried, its luminous snaky body pulsed with apprehension. <<What is wrong? What is happening? Is the Hated Enemy going to kill my Kasha—>>

Gladdris nuzzled the young Khutani, making soothing gurgles deep in its throat. <<Be easy, little one, no foul Umwira monster is going to harm your Kasha.>>

<<No,>> someone growled, <<the willful creature can do that for himself.>>

Gladdris hissed another warning and the Maker fell silent.

Though still frightened, Tani was comforted by maker Gladdris's nearness. The symbiont wound itself about the great neck and laid its head against the Maker's sleek hide. <<Are you my Amla (parent?)>> Tani asked.

<<We are all your amla, little one," Gladdris said, "But hush now. There will be time for questions later. You must focus on your link with your Kasha, so that we can find him, before it is too late. Yes, that's the way – There, see the silver cord of his tether? We will follow it.>>

Together Tani and Maker Gladdris, brushed the cord with their sensitive mouth tentacles. With the young one clinging to its neck, and the other Makers beside it, Gladdris swam faster. They had little time. The host was in trouble.

DUNNAGH COULD HAVE formed a sword of etheric matter and slashed the little worm following him to shreds. He might have, too, but the slim, silver creature cried out to him so piteously. The tiny Khutani was looking for its Kasha—whatever or whoever that was. It seemed almost as lost and as frightened as he was himself.

But if it was lost in the void, it would have to call upon the Makers for help, not him. He couldn't bring himself to help, but he also felt a strange reluctance to harm it. So he ran blindly onward, hoping it wouldn't follow.

He knew he was lost and might never find his way back to the physical world, but he didn't care. He didn't want to return. He'd rather die than go back to the torment.

Dunnagh heard the chorus of voices calling to him to stop. He stopped, but only long enough to form a sword and shield. <<Liars, deceivers, devils, you won't trick me again. No, I won't come back!>> Dunnagh shouted over his shoulder and kept on running. <<I won't listen; I won't—>>The collar around his neck blazed like a star. Dunnagh cried out, and sank to his knees clawing at his neck.

<<Oh no, please, amla, don't hurt him!>> Tani cried. <<He's my Kasha, and he's frightened—please.>>

The pain ceased and Dunnagh was up and running again, before they could encircle him. Up ahead a pulsating cloud of etheric matter appeared. With the Khutani's howls of protest at his back, he dove into the luminous fog and disappeared.

Suddenly, the formlessness about him was replaced by a vast, gray plain, punctuated by islands of obsidian rock as smooth, as black glass. Overhead, angry russet clouds boiled in the murky sky. Up ahead, a great mountain spewed up geysers of flames. Dunnagh sprawled upon scalding sand, choking on sulfurous fumes.

He staggered to his feet. Damned Khutani illusions! He gritted his teeth against the pain and kept moving. They wouldn't force him back this way. He couldn't see them now, but he sensed he was still being pursued. The vibrations of heavy feet pounded the ground both behind and in front of him. They were trying to cut him off.

Dunnagh shouted a Caldoni war cry, sprinting for a large outcropping of the black rock. Reaching this temporary sanctuary, he placed his back to the stone and raised his sword.

The earth under his feet, shuddered as the mountain heaved up more molten rock and flames. Damn the makers; why were the big worms teasing him like this? <<I won't be fooled by your illusions. Show yourselves, cowards, and fight me.>>

<<The Plain of the Poison Fires is no illusion, traitor,>> a gravelly voice said. <<You know it exists in the waking world as well as here in the Dream.>>

<<And we will make your grave in both,>> another speaker said.

What Dunnagh saw next, startled him into nearly dropping his sword. From behind his rock, lumbered a pack of large, shaggy creatures with ugly, a-symmetrical faces. The pack's leader, a massive, bear-like monster, stood on its hind legs and took an experimental swipe with its dagger-sharp claws at Dunnagh's face.

Dunnagh parried the blow with his shield, and slashed at the shaggy arm with his sword. Blue-white sparks exploded from its edge as the blade struck its mark. The creature roared and jumped back.

<<Foul mutant! You reek of Khutani. You will die for your betrayal of your own kind.>>

Betrayal? Own kind, what were the monsters talking about? It suddenly dawned on Dunnagh that maybe the creatures he now faced, weren't Khutani-created illusions as he first had assumed. He'd stumbled into something far more dangerous. This was a deadly game, where he didn't understand the rules.

Dunnagh held his shield up and sword at the ready. He wished he'd had the good sense to create a beam rifle rather than such an archaic weapon as a sword. With a beam rifle he could—Too late to change his mind now. If he dropped his guard for a moment, they'd be on him.

<<Betray my own people? Never! What are you talking about.>>

<<More Khutani lies, Mutant Slime. You will die for your treachery!>> Howling their fury, the pack charged.

Dunnagh shouted a war cry of his own and lashed out with his sword. They were coming at him from three sides, snarling and snapping at any exposed part of his body. Dunnagh fought, grimly lashing out with his sword, then retreating to put the rock at his back.

The monsters were fierce, but didn't know how to work together to bring him down. He killed some and wounded others, but there were so many of them. For each one he felled, another seemed to pop out of the blistering ground, to take the fallen one's place.

Dunnagh felt himself weakening. It wouldn't be long now before they had him. He lunged aiming for the neck of one hairy beast, then out of the corner of his eye, he saw another massive brute take a swing at his head. Dunnagh lurched sideways, and felt a burning pain as the creature's claws tore down his sword arm in a trail of fire.

Dunnagh cried out, dropping his weapon. He fell to his knees, raising his shield to ward off the next blow. With a howl of triumph, the pack lunged towards him.

Suddenly bolts of blue-white lightning rained down upon the charging monsters. With cries of terror, they burst into flame, then incinerated into small mounds of fine, gray ash. Puzzled, Dunnagh looked up to see whom his rescuers might be. Glowing Khutani Makers with bat-like wings unfurled, circled in the murky air above him. They kept up a deadly fire of lightning, until the plain was clear of monsters.

The illusion of the fiery plain shattered, and Dunnagh found himself once more in the featureless void. Before he could get up, the massive eel-like bodies encircled him, blocking off his escape. Clutching his wounded arm, Dunnagh got stiffly to his feet and faced them.

<<Rebellious creature, the Umwira almost killed you. How many times have we told you the collar was for your protection, not just for your discipline. It was to save you from something like this that I insisted you wear it,>> the deep voiced Maker said.

<<Maybe if you had left me alone in the first place, I wouldn't have needed the collar or your meddling,>> Dunnagh sniped.

<<You are a fool, but there is no time left to coddle you.>> The collar blazed again. Dunnagh shouted a curse, and once more fell to hands and knees.

<<Chosen,>> Maker Gladdris said. <<Please, we have no wish to hurt you—but we haven't much time. You are wounded—>> Gladdris pointed a mouth tentacle at Dunnagh's arm <<and your body is dying in the physical world. You must go back with us now, Dream-Chosen.>>

Still on his hands and knees, Dunnagh laughed, his spirit body pulsating with black amusement. <<Dream-Chosen? You may have chosen *me*—but I haven't chosen *you*. If you won't take this collar off—maybe I would rather die.>>

<<Obstinate creature, you would kill yourself, and the little one to spite us?>> the deep-voiced one said. <<You are both a coward and a spoiled child. If it wasn't for this young one—who will die too—if you persist, I would say good riddance. You are unworthy to serve. We can choose another from among your kindred.>>

<<Little one? What are you black-hearted monsters talking about now? What little one?>>

The tiny silver creature he'd ran away from rather than hurt, detached itself from the circling tangle and swam closer. <<Kasha, please don't be angry—or afraid. You must come back now. I love you.>>

Dunnagh shuddered, his mind in turmoil. <<Love me?>>

<<Yes, Kasha, I need you and love you>> the little one said.

In spite of his anger with the Makers, Dunnagh felt strangely drawn to the little Khutani. He wanted to touch—to caress— He reached out a hand then hastily drew it back.

What am I doing? The damned fiends are messing with my mind again. I won't—I won't! Oh, Gods of my ancestors, help me!

<<Do you foreswear your oath to us, warrior?>> a Maker asked.

Dunnagh got slowly to his feet. He touched the collar at his neck again. <<Take this off me, and then talk to me about oaths,>> he said.

But there was little power in his demand. Blood was still dripping from the wound he'd suffered in the battle with the Umwira—whoever they were. And he could also feel the life thread connecting him to his physical body, growing thinner as they spoke. Either could kill him if he didn't do something soon.

<<Kasha, please,>> the little Khutani said. <<If you waste time arguing, you will die—and I will die, too. Kasha, I don't want to die.>> The little Khutani glided towards him, and coiled itself about his spirit body, resting its sleek head on his shoulder. Its mouth tentacles caressed his face.

Dunnagh trembled, but this time made no move to rebuff the little one. He studied the young Khutani for a long moment; then lifted a hand and stroked the satiny skin. <<Who are you?>>

<<I am Tani, Kasha Dunnagh, I am your Shalla, your bondmate. Don't you remember? The Makers asked you to help them and you agreed to come to us. Together we form a kashallan—please remember, Kasha.>>

Silence. <<All I remember is the pain,>> he said and couldn't keep the bitterness from his voice.

<<The pain. We never meant for you to suffer like that,>> Maker Gladdris said. Detaching itself from the circle of Makers, it wrapped both host and symbiont in its coils. Gladdris touched Dunnagh's neck with a mouth tentacle and the collar vanished.

<<The bonding with an alien host, is a new thing—for all of us, Chosen, and alas, not without its difficulties. You should have been brought to us in the pools. We could have helped you endure the Transformation, while your Shalla was too young to know how it hurt you.

<<But you were so unwilling to accept our touch in the Dream-time, always fighting or running from us, so, rather than have you resist further, we had to try the bonding in another way.>>

Tani nuzzled his neck anxiously. <<Please, Kasha, it will not be so bad when we return to our body. It was only our birth pains; they will not last. I am old enough to help you now. But we cannot stay here within the void much longer, or our body will die.

<<Kasha, come back with me. There are so many things to taste and explore, so many things we can learn from each other, so much work to be done. Will you come? I need you, all of Timorna needs you. Please come, Kasha, please!>>

Dunnagh hesitated, at last he said, <<I don't want to die—so I guess I'll come. But I'm still unsure about this kashallan bond. And maybe I'm afraid—of you.>>

<<I know, Kasha, I am afraid, too—both of you, and of the bond. Let's give ourselves time—time to learn and to grow together, agreed?>>

A long moment of silence, then, <<Agreed, Tani-Shalla.>>

Chapter Five

Darkness. No sun, always the mists and the blackness, would he ever get used to it? Dunnagh floated in the inky water, trying to catch his breath. He was too tired and sore at the moment to obey his young bondmate's urging to swim faster.

<<Kasha, hurry. We will miss all the fun; the cousins must be playing the new game already.>>

<<I know you're anxious to play, little one, but Tani, my body—uh—our body's tired. Don't you feel it? We have to rest a moment.>>

<<But I want to play with our amsi—it was so much fun.>>

<<Tani stop. Pay attention to my body; what does it tell you? We—>>

<<You are tired, because you—we swim too slowly. Arms and legs all wiggling, it feels wrong. Let me help you—like this.>>

Over his protest, Dunnagh felt his arms pressed to his side and his two legs straighten and clamp together. Then his body tried to propel itself through the water in the ungeulating motion the Khutani used. <<Tani!>>

Dunnagh's body slid forward for a few strokes, then his head sank beneath the surface. When he began to choke, Tani released its control of their shared flesh and allowed Dunnagh to swim up for air. Dunnagh surfaced gasping, then vomited up the unwanted liquid he'd swallowed.

<<I'm sorry, Kasha, I forgot our growing gill-slits aren't mature enough for us to swim like that.>>

Dunnagh let out a long sigh. <<Tani, Shalla, I know this is as hard for you as it is for me. Your Khutani instincts tell you things should be a certain way, but that way doesn't always apply to us. I—we can't swim like the cousins. You'll just have to accept that. You're different.

<<Someday, when you're—we're, mature enough, you'll be able to walk on the ground outside the pools. You'll see the mountains, and the sky. None of your—uh—amsi, cousins, will ever be able to do that. Instead of worrying about how fast we swim, think about all the new things we'll see and do, when we get out of here, all right?>>

<<Mm. If you put it like that I guess maybe you're right.>>

Dunnagh inwardly sighed with relief. Another crisis resolved—for the moment anyway. <<I am right, and Tani, next time, give me some warning before you just take over our body like that, please.>>

<<I'm sorry, Kasha, did I frighten you? I just wanted to catch up to the amsi and play with them.>>

<<I know. You didn't exactly frighten me, but it was disconcerting, and choking like that wasn't at all fun, now was it?>>

<<No, it wasn't,>> the symbiont admitted.

<<Well, something like that can happen again if you do things without consulting me,>> Dunnagh warned. <<After all, this body was mine alone, until just recently. I do know how it works and how to use it.>>

<<Mm. You do know some things about our body, but I'm amazed at all the things you *don't* know about it. However did you survive in your far away home? That is a mystery even to our elders.>>

Dunnagh chuckled. <<Well, you have a point there; I did sort of take its inner workings for granted. And, now I have you to 'taste' everything and see that it's functioning properly.>>

<<Yes, you do, and I will make sure we both stay healthy.>>

<<Thank you, Shalla.>>

In a private corner of his mind, Dunnagh stifled a scream. Nowhere to escape, nowhere to hide—the symbiont was always there. He tread water and glanced around, trying to get his bearings. Where had Tani's playmates gone?

The water was a comfortable temperature, but the air above was cool, and scented with a pungent spice that reminded him of copper and vanilla. Heavy mists often hovered above the pools' surface, enshrouding the Khutani's watery world in almost total blackness. Only the glowing fungi on the rocks, and the phosphorescent one-celled creatures in the water, gave any definition to the gloom.

The pounding of a beating stick and the sound of Avairei singing, focused his attention on the distant glowing lights by the stairs up to the keep. Playtime was over.

It was feeding time for the cousins. In his middle Tani stirred. Dunnagh felt his hunger awake; Tani's need overwhelming his revulsion to the feeding process. Where were his always-watchful nursemaids when he needed them?

The symbiont was eager to follow the rest of the young Khutani, but Dunnagh's back still tingled with the remembered pain of the nursemaids' savage attack when he tried to go over there once before. After he was back in the water by the little chapel, they eased the pain of his injuries, but he had been warned never to try that again. The Khutani said he was too young, and it was too dangerous.

Dangerous, for whom, and why? Like any young child, he wasn't given an explanation, when he ask. He was just expected to obey his elders or suffer the consequences. Dunnagh had tried to explain to them. He hadn't been trying to escape—how could he?

He was just worried about his armachda and the scientists. He'd no idea how long he'd been down here, but Nathan was probably frantic with worry. All he'd wanted was for one of the priests to tell Nathan—

Tell Nathan what? That he was all right—was he all right? Dunnagh's spirit writhed with his fears.

What can I tell them? And what will they think—or do when they discover that I've made a kashallan bond? I'm not even all human any more. Will they hate or fear me? I couldn't bare that—not that.

<<Kasha, are you sad again? Don't be sad, Kasha, I love you.>>

Dunnagh sighed and rubbed a hand across his middle. The symbiont's coiled body stirred under his touch. <<I'm all right, Shalla, don't fret. And, I love you too. I was just thinking of Nathan. Did you—uh—taste my worry?>>

<<Yes. Please don't worry, Kasha, our elders won't let anything bad happen to him. And when we are older and weaned, you'll see him again. I want to see him, too. A new cousin to play with, it will be so much fun.>>

<<Mm, yes it will be fun.>>

A sinewy body brushed against his legs in the blackness below him. The image of a scaly monster rising out of the deep to eat him, came unbidden into his mind. Dunnagh shuddered, then forced himself to float quietly as the Khutani wrapped a heavy coil around his waist.

Tani evidently caught the image—or a fleeting taste of his anxiety, because it said, <<Kasha, it's just Amla Gladdris here to feed us.>>

<<Yes, I know, the feeding.>> The image again, he pushed it away. <<I'm not afraid.>>

Suddenly his bondmate's urgent hunger bled over into his awareness, blotting out all inhibition. Dunnagh through his arms and legs around the Maker's neck and pulled his face close to the Maker's. He stuck his mouth next to Gladdris's rubbery lips, and made urgent whining sounds in his throat.

When the feeding tube appeared he clamped it between his lips and sucked greedily at the thick, rich fluid the Maker regurgitated for him. His body quivered with excitement, and gurgling sounds of pleasure accompanied his meal.

After the first frenzy of Tani's hunger passed, Dunnagh resisted the current of their shared emotion and crawled away into the darkness of his own mind. The symbiont's attention was occupied elsewhere, maybe he could be alone for a while.

SLIPPING INTO A LIGHT trance, he drew some etheric matter to him and began constructing a walled off area, where he could finally think his own thoughts without interruption. The room was more like a door less prison cell, rather than a homey sanctuary when he'd finished, but it would do. He was free to be *human* and himself within its confines.

Now what? He stood in the middle of the room staring at the blank stonework. He had his blessed privacy, what was he going to do with it? He gave an etheric equivalent of a sigh and sat down on the smooth floor.

So much had happened since they'd left Dymar—so much. And, now he was here, in a pool under the mountain, cut off from all human companions, an alien symbiont child curled in his middle. What was he going to do—what could he do? It was so hard, so awful.

Ever since he'd arrived on this planet, he'd felt so out of control. He'd gotten caught up in a whirlpool of alien making and, in the end, he'd been powerless to resist its vortex. Dunnagh covered his face with his hands wanting to cry—but dare he, even here?

Tani. The symbiont was always there, curious, like any child, asking questions, tasting his responses; he had no privacy. Could he go on living like this? Have to—no way out now. Tani was so young. He couldn't blame it. The symbiont was as much a victim as he was himself. But its elders on the other hand...

Dunnagh balled his hands into fists. Damned black-hearted, controlling monsters, if they had been honest with him—told him what they truly wanted before they put the compulsion in his blood while he'd been in the Cumarsaid aboard Bennett's ship...

If they hadn't wrapped that tethering collar around his neck. Damn them, damn them, if only—if only what? If he'd known, would things have turned out any different?

He'd sworn a warrior's oath of service on Caldon—long before Khutani meddling disrupted his life. The Makers kept saying they needed him to help fight someone, or something called the Umwira—whatever that was. Maybe they did, too, if his battle with the monsters on the burning plain was any indication.

He hadn't understood what was happening there. Why had their leader called him a traitor? Who did the creature think he was? So many unanswered questions and no one was telling him anything! If grandpa Kai were here, he could figure it out, help him—

Suddenly images of his grandparents, his parents, and his home in the Black Mountains on Caldon, welled up in his mind, leaving him trembling. With a grieving heart he conjured a vision of his sister and her children. He loved them all and he had a duty to them.

Then the realization hit him like a hammer blow. He was never going home, never again. They were lost to him forever—forever! Those horrible monsters had stolen away all that he held dear.

Even if the ship was waiting for them, and the rest of the humans were rescued, he couldn't go with them—not with Tani curled in his gut. His beautiful Sairsa, the scientists and the rest of the armachda would climb aboard Dr. Bennett's ship and leave him in this dark, alien place.

Oh, Nathan, what a laugh. You didn't want me to go home, and you're going to get your wish. Now you will go and I-I can't. You will leave me here—forever—and go home.

Thinking of the ship brought Sairsa's lovely face floating into his mind. Her green eyes smiled at him, her warm lips parted for his kiss... Would he ever see her again? Would she want to stay here with him if there was a way to get a message to her?

No, that was a stupid notion. Why would she or Nathan, or anyone want to stay. It was too much to ask even of those he knew loved him. He wasn't the Dunnagh his family and friends had known—not any more.

That Dunnagh was dead.

Dunnagh's spirit choked on the taste of his misery. And, what about Nathan, and the rest of the humans in the slave pens at Sulas? If they weren't already gone, what would they do if he *could* go back to them, and then they found out about the symbiont? Gods, he wasn't even human anymore! Dunnagh rocked, engulfed in his pain, keening.

Suddenly part of his sanctuary's wall dissolved. The symbiont's glowing eel-like form swam through the hole. Tani wrapped itself around his quivering body whining with its distress. <<Kasha, oh, Kasha, don't cry; what's wrong?>>

Dunnagh's first impulse was to shove it away, but it hugged him so tightly, cried so piteously, that he couldn't. Instead he hugged Tani back. Still rocking and sobbing he clung to his bondmate, resting his cheek on the symbiont's head.

<<Sorry, oh, Tani, I'm so sorry. I don't want to frighten you, but I can't help it. I have to grieve—you should have just left me alone—not come here—sorry, sorry, little one, sorry.>>

<<But I had to come,>> the symbiont protested, <<you're my Kasha. Don't be sad; I love you, please Kasha. You aren't alone, you are a part of me now, and I of you. We have lots of family—our Khutani family! I need you—we all need you—I'm so sorry, too. Don't cry anymore, Kasha.>>

Chapter Six

Maker Gladdris poked its head through the breech in the etheric wall and surveyed the grieving man and his frightened bondmate. Something would have to be done about this. The host's overwhelming emotions might destroy the bond yet, if not diluted in some way. That couldn't be allowed to happen, too much depended on them.

When the bondmates were once more quiescent, their emotions spent, Maker Gladdris dissolved the rest of Dunnagh's sanctuary and enfolded them in its coils. The host submitted without protest, lying back in its coils and closing his eyes as if asleep.

Gladdris studied the host with mouth tentacles quivering. Now that the symbiont child had lapsed into an exhausted slumber, the Maker had time to consider the problem this man represented. He was lying with his head resting upon Gladdris's sinewy neck. His eyes were closed, but he wasn't asleep, and they both knew that.

<<This cannot continue, Chosen. The bond will sour, if I allow your unchecked emotional displays to continue.>>

The man made no response, but Gladdris could sense that he was listening. <<My peers would counsel that I should ensure your compliance, by changing your biochemical nature, so that you will no longer be a problem to us.>>

Gladdris felt Dunnagh's body tremble at that. Yes, he understood the consequences, and was afraid, but he still kept his eyes tightly closed, feigning sleep.

<<The Council has given you into my care,>> Gladdris continued, <<and I will only use such dire measures as a last resort. It is my personal opinion that we have made many mistakes with you. I don't wish to compound our errors by committing another.>>

This time his eyes opened and he looked Gladdris in the eye. For just a moment Gladdris sensed the power of his bitter hatred, then, as if remembering Gladdris's recent warning, he veiled his emotions behind a tight mental shield.

<<We have made mistakes in part, because you belong to an unknown alien species. Creating a bond with humans is something that has never been tried before. Unfortunately, experiments seldom work out without some complications.>>

Dunnagh's mouth hardened into a thin line. Once more Gladdris tasted his anger.

<<The other reason for our mistakes, is perhaps because you seem so young to us, a mere infant, like our symbiont. No one needs explain dangers or important matters to a child. We give love and nurturance to a child and teach it discipline and obedience, but we do not explain. That is the way of all loving parents, I believe.

<<But what we have forgotten, is by your own species' standards, you are an adult. We must remember that, and treat you accordingly. Perhaps you will be more content with your new life if I explain why we have need of you.>>

<<That would help in part, elder, I admit. If I am forced to give up everything and everyone I love at home, it would be comforting to know it was for some greater good.

<<You Makers have mentioned the Umwira, but I only know what I saw on that fiery plain, when they attacked me for no reason.>>

Gladdris rumbled a laugh. <<They had their reasons, your involvement with us. They could sense our tether; that would be all the reason they needed to attack you.>>

<<That damned tether again. But I don't even know who you Khutani are, or why you couldn't have asked one of the Avairei or Warlinga to host Tani if it was so important.>>

<<Those are excellent questions needing much time and explanation to savor. We will talk about the answers in more detail later, but I will give you the simple explanation now, in hopes that it will ease your mind.

<<The Umwira are the mutated descendants of the ancient species that had dominion over this world, before the Great Wars. These people nearly

destroyed all life on this world, and their descendants, we believe, still carry the taint. Even now, they scheme and plot to corrupt or destroy all we have achieved.>>

<<I saw some of the destruction while in trance, before coming down to the surface.>>

<<Then you can appreciate why we struggle so hard to prevent such destruction from happening again.>>

<<But how could it? Our ship's instruments detected no evidence of an advanced civilization on this world. Surely these Umwira are no real threat to you—or anyone.>>

<<Ah, but they are, nonetheless. At present their technology may be 'primitive' as you think, but we Khutani savor the entire meal, not just one life time's serving. The land to the north suffered greatly in the old wars, forcing the survivors underground.

<<Some of the old technology has survived, however, though fortunately for Timorna, their wizards—people you might call scientists, don't know how to use it properly—at the moment.

<<That is not to say, they can't 'learn' to develop it again, if given a chance.>>

<<Is that likely?>>

<<Can we afford to gamble on that? And, what they have retained is dangerous enough. As you experienced, they have retained a strong Psy ability, like your own people. The Umwira wizards have also salvaged, a knowledge of genetic manipulation.

<<For the time being, they have chosen to breed a race of monsters to attack our lands, rather than focus their powers on redeveloping the old mechanical technologies.

<<Unfortunately, we are now confined to our watery world underground, but they are not. Our influence can be only minimal in the surface world above. It takes tremendous stores of our Psy energy to affect events in the surface world directly. That is why we need a host species to carry our symbionts and act as our agents in the world above.>>

<<But, if you had the genetic knowledge to re-create life after the wars, why didn't you create a host species for yourselves?>>

<<We did. Until about seven hundred of your years ago, we had such a species. Then the Umwira developed a plague that killed off our native host species, and many more of our reintroduced populations.

<<It was a terrible time, Chosen. In trying to help, some of my peers lost their lives as well. With those deaths, many of the genetic patterns we had saved from before the old wars, were lost—including the genetic patterns of our host species.

<<Oh, we tried using Avairei and Warlinga—even the Begta as you suggested, but always the bonds ended in death and failure.

<<For a long time we despaired. We left the stewardship of our world to the Avairei and swam away into our deep lairs to sleep the 'Long Sleep' and dream of our lost freedom among the stars.

<<That too, I fear was a mistake, because in our absence the Avairei have been corrupted by too much power. And the enemy has grown strong again and now threatens to destroy all we have remade. In our desperation we searched the planets within the starry river, seeking a new host to aid us. By swimming the dream, we found your people, and you in particular.>>

Dunnagh snorted a laugh. <<Should I be honored by your choice?>>.

<<You may not be able to appreciate our regard at the moment, but yes, you should.>>

<<But if you are so worried about technology that can destroy a world, why choose us? Humans also have such abilities.>>

<<Granted, your people aren't a perfect match. There is a destructive wildness in your species that reminds us of the ancient race on this world. But you have many intriguing and admirable qualities that we felt could outweigh your species' faults.

<<When we touched your mind in the trance aboard your ship, Dunnagh, we knew you had the gifts we needed. You were our Dream-Chosen. Your intelligence, your courage, your loyalty and sense of honor, all were qualities we knew our young child would need in its host. We understand your sacrifice, and we honor you for this gift of yourself.>>

<<I-I don't know what to say. I never dreamed— You honor me with your praise, but I'm not sure I am worthy.>>

The Maker nuzzled him. <<I disagree, which is why I am telling you all this.>>

<<Thank you, Elder.>> Dunnagh's smile was conspiratorial. <<Are you going to get into trouble with your—uh—amsi, for telling me all this.>>

Gladdris rumbled another laugh. <<Probably. Some of the old mud-crawlers among them won't be pleased. Most of the learned among the Avairei don't know all I have told you.

<<But the council left you in my care, so the dissenters will have to accept my judgment of the situation. I hope you now understand a little better why we needed you? Later, if you want further information, Tani can recall from its genetic memories, more details of what has been lost.

<<You have said more than once that it is important to you to fight for a just cause. I believe ours is just, and I hope you will, too.>>

<<I wish you had explained all this to me at first.>>

<<It was my plan to explain, but you were so stubborn and then we ran out of time. I wish things could have been different.>>

<<...I wish things could have been different, too.>>

<<Yes, it would have made things easier, but that is the past. We must consider the present and your raw emotions now. You are a warrior, Chosen; death is no stranger to you. Your own death could have come to you at any time—surely you know that?

<<I taste your sadness at giving up all you hold dear in your old life, but death could have forced you to do that as well. We offer a new beginning, and a chance to make the difference that your soul longs for. Can you not accept and be content?>>

Dunnagh thought about it for a long time, and Gladdris allowed him the privacy of his own thoughts. At last he nodded. <<Put that way it does make it easier to accept and understand. I will try.>>

<<That is good to know,>> Gladdris said. <<And yet I still taste a hint of sourness in your flavor. Spit out what is still bothering you lest it corrupt and spoil your sweetness over time.>>

Trembling Dunnagh rubbed at his eyes, and Gladdris tasted the overwhelming bitterness of his grief once more. <<My family will be mourning for me, thinking I'm dead, but I'm not dead. I feel like I failed them, my mother, my sister and her son—I didn't want to go back—not at first, and then Nathan said...

<<But now it doesn't matter because I can't go back—and I can't even tell them I love them or why I can't come.>>

Gladdris considered, aware of the man's silent grieving while he lay within its coils. This unresolved emotion was at the root of his resistance. His love of his family was spiced with the tang of guilt for his failure to complete a family obligation, and his secret joy at being spared that task.

<<If it will ease your mind, Chosen, I will use my gifts and allow your spirit to go home one last time to make your good byes. Would that help you to set aside your grief and become the willing host this young one of our making, needs to grow and prosper?>>

Dunnagh looked up, meeting the Maker's eye. Gladdris tasted the sharp spice of surprise and the poignant longing in the mental voice, when he asked, <<Could you do that for me?>>

<<I can and I will, if it will ease your transition.>>

Dunnagh stared at the Maker for a long moment, searching for the truth of its words in the alien visage. <<Will I be able to talk to them; will they see me?>>

<<Yes. You will not be able to stay long, but they will see you, and you will be able to communicate with them.>>

<<So much power, I sensed that in you before—from the beginning. I would like to go back to Caldon, one last time. But who, or maybe I should say, what are you that you can do this for me?>>

<<As I have told you; I am a Maker.>> Gladdris sensed the man's impatience with that evasion and chided itself for falling back into the old habit once more. <<I'm sorry, I was treating you like a child again, wasn't I? But explaining who and what we are, is a complex problem, because we ourselves don't know all the answers anymore.>>

When the host remained skeptical, Gladdris nuzzled his shoulder affectionately. <<It is true. I was born here on Timorna, but my genetic memories tell me that our ancestors came from somewhere else. Another dimension, another galaxy perhaps, I don't know. They came as the potential guardians and healers of wounded worlds in this universe.

<<They could travel the starry river and shape-shift into many forms. When some of these wondrous beings arrived on Timorna, they found a world in conflict. Timorna was a world needing their protection, because

its dominant species, like your own, had mastered the great technologies. And, that species had the potential to destroy themselves and all life on their world.

<<For many years my ancestors labored to collect the genetic patterns of as many life forms as they could. But unlike your own species, they mistrusted machines. To them, technology only brought with its use great disharmony with the life force.

<<For that reason they created for themselves a bodily form in which they could store the patterns. As the amount of genetic material increased, their bodies changed, until they settled upon the form we now have.

<<This body configuration is well suited for the task of storing such material, but it came with many limitations. Somewhere in the long past the old ones died off and their children lost the ability to physically shape-shift. Only now in our dreams, can we shape-shift, or communicate with those like us on other worlds.

<<This limitation is a great sadness to us. But Timorna has need of us, and so we are comforted. We strive always to re-create the beauty and diversity that was lost in the Great Wars.>>

<<Thank you for telling me, Elder. I don't understand it all, but I sense your own great sacrifice, and it humbles me. My own petty fears and grief seem trivial in comparison.>>

<<They are not trivial in my opinion, Chosen, which is why I have agreed to help you. Lay back now and relax.>> As Dunnagh complied, Gladdris slipped one of its mouth tentacles under the skin of his neck to strengthen the link between them. <<We will enter the dream together so that you can say your good byes to your family.>>

Chapter Seven

Floating atop the dark water, Dunnagh felt lazy and content. Yesterday a Maker not well known to him had come forward to feed him, which was a little disconcerting, but today it had been Amla Gladdris again, and he liked that better.

Sometimes, visions from his old life floated into his mind like translucent dream bubbles. He would see Nathan's well-loved face, taste the sweet flavor of Sairsa's kisses, or smell the acrid stench of the war on Dymar. Then, pop, pop, pop, and the memories were gone. It all seemed so far away; it was almost as if those people and events belonged to another person entirely, which, in a way they did. That Dunnagh no longer existed; he had died during the transformation.

Here in the pools he was loved and fussed over by everyone. It was like being a child among the Caldoni clans again. Because of the reptilian appearance of their long snaky bodies, Dunnagh had expected the Khutani to be emotionally cold. But his new "relatives" weren't like his imaginings at all. In their way, the Khutani were a very tactile and loving species.

While engulfed in their vigilant care, he could eat whenever he was hungry, or he could play tag with his age mates, or dive deep into the depths, then float lazily back to the surface, the warm, bubbling liquid flowing sensuously over his skin. He could do whatever he chose, until he was pleasantly exhausted—like now.

But no, there was more to life than this; he must remember. . . .

<<Tani.>>

<<Mm.>>

<<I think we should get out of the pool. Our body is tired and needs sleep. We should go to the chapel like Amla Gladdris wants us to do.>>

<<Can't we stay here, where it is safe and warm? Surely one of the Elders will wrap us in its coils while we sleep.>>

Dunnagh sighed. <<No, I think not. I would like to stay here, too, but our Amla Gladdris says we are too old now for that. It might be cross with us if we disobey.>>

<<But I want to stay here. It's cold in the chapel—and the bed is lumpy. We could—>>

<<Tani, no. You told me earlier that our gill adaptation is still weak. If we try to sleep by ourselves in the pool, we will sink and wake up choking. That won't be very pleasant, and we won't get much rest, either.>>

<<Hmm, all right.>>

Dunnagh chuckled and took hold of the pool's rim. Careful not to put any pressure on the tentacle casings that were growing from the tips of the two middle fingers on each hand, he eased himself out of the pool. On the walkway Dunnagh rested a moment, allowing the vertigo to pass, then got slowly to his feet. Dunnagh hated feeling like an invalid and hoped he'd regain his strength soon.

Inside the tiny chapel, he sat down on his pallet and studied his hands. In the green light coming from the votive lamp on the altar, he could see his fingers were swollen. He already knew how tender they were.

<<How long will our hands remain like this anyway, Shalla?>>

<<I'm not sure.>>

<<Well, it's damned inconvenient, that's for certain.>>

<<I know, Kasha, but this adaptation is important. In order for me to do my healing work, I must be able to touch and taste my patients.>>

<<Right, well can you send a painkiller into my brain so I can sleep? I must have banged my hand getting out of the water.>>

<<Yes, I taste the pain now. I will do that for you, Kasha.>>

Sharp new triangular teeth, gill slits, tentacled hands—where will the changes end? —And, what will Nathan think when he sees these adaptations? Human, am I still human? Best not think about that now—keep the good feelings—sleep, blessed oblivion.

———✕⚮⧵⧸⚮✕———

DUNNAGH JERKED AWAKE with a yell, his warrior's instinct suddenly warning him, he was no longer alone in the chapel. He started to rise, then sank back, feeling a little foolish. It was only the young priestess Pela.

Pela's eyes widened. She let out a startled cry of her own when she saw him on his pallet. He smiled hoping to reassure her; then he yawned. "Hello. Sorry if I startled you by yelling."

She bowed. "I am sorry that I woke you, Kashallan. I didn't know you were here."

"Mm. My elders wish me to sleep here now—if it is all right?"

"Yes, oh yes, it is all right. My Ima sent me to see to your needs. How can I serve you?'

The poor girl seemed so flustered and nervous finding him here. She was standing there, clutching the pleats of her kilt as if he might eat her. "There's nothing I need at the moment." He brushed a damp wad of hair off his forehead and yawned again. "But tell the Ima, I thank her for her concern."

"I will tell her if you like, but you can yourself. She hopes to get down to see you later."

"Mm. I would like that."

Pela turned her back on him and began rearranging things on the altar. When she had the altar set to her liking, she moved to the serving table in the corner and pretended to dust. Next, she shook out the prayer rug, and puffed up the cushions on his bed. Her movements were brisk, agitated, and she avoided eye contact whenever her work caused her to look in his direction.

When she finished, she glanced around the tiny stone room, frantically looking for something needing her attention. Finding nothing, she stood in front of him, twisted a fold of her green kilt in her hand and surveyed him out of half-closed eyes.

<<Kasha, why is she so nervous do you think?>>

<<I don't know. As best I can remember, I've done nothing to upset her. But you're right; she does seem to be uneasy in our company.>>

<<What do we do now?>> Tani asked.

<<I'm not sure—this is all new to me, too. Anything in your encoded memories about pretty young girls who are nervous? Is there something

we've forgotten, Shalla, that the Avairei might expect us to be doing right now?>>

<<I don't think so. When I'm older, they will come for healings and advice about breeding and other matters, but not now—I'm too young.>>

Growing uncomfortable under her gaze, Dunnagh asked. "Is there something wrong, Pela?" At the sound of his voice, she jumped. More of her kilt crumpled into a wad under her hand. "Come now, tell me, I won't bite you; what is it?"

The cloth fell away from her hand. Taking a deep breath, she said, "Kashallan, if it is not too bold of me to suggest it, may I fix your hair for you? You have a beautiful, long mane. It is such a pretty color, but it has gotten all tangled. If it is not cared for soon, it will be beyond saving. It would have to be cut off, and that would be a shame."

Surprised, he pulled a clump of the damp, red mass forward and examined it. Yes, it *was* looking particularly disgusting. She was right; it *would* have to be chopped off, if it was not combed soon. "I would be honored and most grateful if you would do that for me. Do you have a comb here or must you come back later?"

For answer, Pela walked to a small niche in the far wall and drew out a long-toothed, bone comb, and other hair grooming materials. "Earlier, when I was waiting with the Dream-Chosen, I brought them with me—for something to do with my time. I forgot about them when—" She broke off and looked down at her kilt.

For just a moment, Dunnagh's thoughts became ensnared in those painful memories. Then, he forced himself to push them away. He patted the mattress beside him. "Good, you can begin right now; that would please me very much." He winked mischievously. "And I promise not to cry like a baby if you pull too hard." Pela giggled. Sinking down beside him, she picked up the first matted clump and began.

It didn't take long for Dunnagh to understand Pela's nervousness once they got started on the grooming. The poor young woman held him in some kind of religious awe. Dunnagh's attempts to "chat her up," as he would have with any pretty young woman back home, only seemed to make her anxiety worse. He gave up, and they lapsed into a companionable silence. Secretly relieved not to be obliged to make conversation, Dunnagh was content to drowse and just let her comb and braid his long, red-gold hair.

Finished, Pela sat back with a satisfied smile on her pretty Avairei face. He shook his head experimentally and laughed. Rather than braiding his hair in the thick, four-strand, warrior's braid Dunnagh was used to, Pela had braided his hair in a myriad of long, tiny braidlets, as the Avairei wore their own manes. She'd had a few hair ornaments in her pouch, too, and she'd woven them into the braids as well. He shook his head again, delighting in the feel of these little talismans as they brushed against his back and shoulders.

"So much work!" He sighed. "Thank you, Pela, that was very thoughtful of you."

Shy again, her eyes slid away from his alien face. On an impulse, he put out a hand and tentatively stroked her silky fur. Startled, she looked up. "Pretty Pela, don't be so shy with me," he coaxed.

Unable to stop himself, he caressed her cheek. He drew in a ragged breath as a wealth of unexpected physical sensations flooded through his Kashallan-heightened awareness.

The image of Sairsa's lovely face took shape in Dunnagh's inner vision, and he hesitated. <<Tani? Maybe we should—>> Pop! The image disappeared, and he was once more enthralled in the symbiont's need to explore the exciting new, and very pleasing sensations coursing through their shared body.

"So—soft... pretty Pela," he breathed. Gently, he pressed her down onto his pallet.

"K-Kashallan?"

"Shh. Don't be afraid. I won't hurt you—I just want to...." His voice trailed off in a dreamy sigh as his hand slid down over her shoulder.

Pela shuddered, then held herself very still, making no further resistance. Breathing shallowly, she closed her eyes.

<<Kasha, I feel so—strange. What is happening to us?>>

<<It's sexual arousal, little one, I've felt it many times before, though never so strong.>>

<<Now I understand. I remember; this sensation is in my encoded memories. I want to play this new game, Kasha, will you help me?>>

Tani's curiosity about what their shared body could experience was endless. And, he would be enjoying this, too—so, why not? This was rather like coaching a youngster with his first seduction. Only in this case, the "coach" was along for the ride.

A blurred image of, someone who would be unhappy if he did this, tugged at Dunnagh's memory again wanting him to pay attention, but he dismissed it. His awakening arousal was all that mattered. He would think about anything else—later.

Pela's silky-furred Avairei body was slender and lithe, delicate by human standards. <<So soft to our touch—so beautiful, oh, Kasha!>> The Kashallan let his hands glide onto Pela's chest, trailing sensitive fingers around her tiny breasts, feeling their smooth contours. He bent and licked a round, erect nipple.

Pela gasped.

"Do you like that, Pretty Pela?"

She didn't answer. Face turned partially away from him, she kept her eyes squeezed shut, remaining motionless. He never noticed. Aware only of his own mounting excitement now, he continued to explore. Touching, tasting, caressing, he reveled in the feel of her soft pliant body, and the way she made his own flesh respond. Inhaling her rich, fragrant musk, the Kashallan let out a shuddering sigh.

Pushing aside her kilt, he traced the curve of a velvety thigh, and gently parted her legs. His hardening organ was growing insistent now, impatient for its own release. Awash in a flood of sensations, he glanced quickly up at Pela's face, to see if she was ready for him yet.

He couldn't tell; she had turned away, but she had made no objection to his explorations, either. He could feel her body trembling under his skillful hands. She must be liking it or surely she would tell him to stop—wouldn't she?

He gazed hungrily at the secretive mound of her sex. Slowly, he reached down and parted her long, protective outer labia, exposing the aromatic darkness within. With a cautious finger, he investigated its moist, hidden mysteries. Mm, he brought the digit up to his nose and inhaled. Shuddering with anticipation, he let his breath escape in a long ragged sigh.

"Ah, so sweet," Tani murmured, using Dunnagh's voice. "So very, very, sswe-e-et." Tongue extended, the Kashallan bent to sample her tempting juices. He savored the warm, rich flavor of her, while his hands caressed her belly and thighs. The Kashallan licked, then began to suck... Drowning, he was drowning in a flood of pleasure.

Suddenly, Pela let out a strangled cry. Violently jerking her hips upwards, she tried to pull away from him. When she found that impossible, she lay back, body rigid—sobbing.

The Kashallan let out a startled yelp, and jerked his head up from her crotch. Gingerly he rubbed the bridge of his nose, waiting for the little sparkling lights to clear from his vision. Sitting back on his heels, he wiped a trembling hand across his wet face. Awash with conflicting stimuli, he strove for control over his own arousal.

Under his hand, he had felt her body's growing excitement, climbing to match his own, and now this. What had they missed here? Dunnagh studied the young priestess, but she refused to look at him. Pela was lying with her face turned away from him, one hand over her eyes, her breath coming in shuddering gasps.

The Kashallan closed his eyes, taking council with the two parts of himself. When he opened his eyes again, Tani said, "Pela, sweet one, my Kasha Dunnagh says what we are doing is making you sad. I don't want to stop, but my Kasha is right. If you don't want to continue, then we won't. I don't want to *force* you to play this new game with me."

Pela lowered her arm and murmured, "I am sorry, Kashallan, I know it is my duty to please you and serve you, but I didn't know you would ask this of me. I-I haven't been properly prepared by my Ima. You do me a great honor, but I am not ready."

Prepared—duty—what was she talking about? Dunnagh was about to ask her to explain, when he became aware of another person in the chapel with them. Looking around at almost the same moment, Pela let out a startled cry and sat up. Ima Sagas stood in the entrance watching them, an unreadable expression on her face.

The Kashallan glanced down at his semi-erect phallus and blushed furiously. The host, at least, felt suddenly like a little boy caught with his hand in the cookie jar. Sagas's eyes flick to the offending member, then back up to his face.

Dunnagh felt his face heat even more. "Uh—Pela was fixing my hair." He held out a few of the tight, well-wrapped braidlets for her inspection.

"Mm." Turning to her protégée, Sagas said, "Come see me later in my rooms. Now leave us." Pela leapt to her feet, collected her things, and hurried from the chapel.

Watching her go, the Kashallan sighed. "Will you punish her? I hope not. This was more my doing than hers, I—"

Sagas cut him off with a dismissive gesture. Pushing herself away from the rock wall, she came and sat down cross-legged in front of him. "There is nothing to punish, so don't concern yourself. Neither of you did anything wrong."

She patted his hand. "No, that is of no importance right now. I came to talk to you about something else—something far more serious, and dangerous."

"I am listening, Ima. Please continue."

"I am not sure how much of the current situation among the Avairei, is known by the Holy Ones in the pools. What have you been told?"

The Kashallan shrugged. "What is there to know? I am here now, and when I am older; I'll begin my work among the clans."

"I was afraid your answer would be something like that. Unfortunately, things aren't that simple, and the Khutani need to know it, because soon I may not be here to help either you or them, any longer."

"Why not, Faithful One? Explain."

Sagas dropped her eyes under his intense stare and took a deep breath. "Just prior to the arrival of the Chosen at Sulas Keep, a message came for me from the High Matri at Riath. She ordered me to the capital. Though the summons didn't exactly say, it was clear from the behavior of the Warlinga sent to escort me, her command was in fact a death warrant.

"I was here to help you complete the bonding, only because we were attacked by Umwira between here and the Jeban pass. All of the Warlinga from the capital were killed, as were many of the guards from Sulas. When the fight was over, I refused to go on to Riath till the Umwira were hunted down and killed."

"I remember when you came back," Dunnagh said. "Weasel-face wasn't pleased."

"I'm not sure what a weasel-face is in your host's language, Kashallan, but I gather the word is not a compliment. That one is Combaron Dingay, and you are right. He was not pleased. In fact, he is the one who arranged with his kindred to have me arrested—and I believe killed."

"But why, Ima? What could you possibly have done to deserve that?"

Sagas's lips twitched in an ironic smile. "What I *did* and what the High Matri, Enaju Dingay, feared I *might* do, was to help the Khutani make a kashallan. I don't know why that fact should distress her so. As the High Matri, Enaju should have been more willing than anyone to help the Makers. She was not, and that makes little sense to me. What I do know, however, is she has done everything in her power, to stop me from heeding the Khutani's summons and bringing the Dream-Chosen to the pools."

"I see." He stroked his new braidlets absently, deep in thought.

She touched his hand again, bringing his attention back to her. "I am telling you this, Kashallan, because Combaron Dingay may return any time now. He went to Tragar to make Gormach rid the pass of the Umwira. When that is done, they will come for me, and I will be forced by my oath to go with them, no matter what my fate."

Dunnagh felt the anger bubble up at the mention of *his* hated enemy, Gormach. Misunderstanding his expression, she said quickly, "It doesn't matter what happens to me—I have done what I was charged to do. My life isn't important now. But unless Combaron can be persuaded to accept you as the new kashallan, it might be very dangerous for you to remain here once he returns."

He let out a bark of mirthless laughter at that. "That's hardly likely, if my instincts are right about that one. Are they, Ima?"

"Yes, it isn't likely."

He stroked his braids again. Speaking as if to himself, he said, "This is not good for us. There is so much growing and changing yet to be done to this body, and to leave here so soon—And where would we go?" The Kashallan swore angrily in Dunnagh's Caldoni language.

Go? Why not back to the base? "Ima, what has happened to my people?" Dunnagh asked.

Sagas stared at him in confusion. "People? We are all your people, Kashallan. I don't understand."

Dunnagh curbed his impatience and tried to explain, "What I mean, Ima, is what has happened to my host's kindred who were being held in the Sulas slave pens, when Dunnagh came here for the bonding? Have they escaped yet?"

"Escaped?" Sagas look shocked. "Of course not—how could they? They are here, Kashallan, but why do you ask?"

Dunnagh breathed an inward sigh of relief. Thank all the gods of Caldon and Timorna! *You crazy amadan, Nathan, were you waiting for me?* "I ask because my warriors will be of use, if I have to leave Sulas. Can you get a message to them; tell them I am well—and tell them to be ready to leave soon?"

Sagas looked dubious. "I can do that, Kashallan, but I fail to see how those naked, defenseless creatures can be of any use to you now."

"Defenseless? You of all people should know that is not so, Ima."

Sagas dropped her eyes. "I will see what can be done."

Good." Returning to their earlier discussion, he said, "No, I don't think the kindred knew that things had gotten so far out of hand among your people. But they will hear of it now." As he rose to return to the pools, he helped her to her feet, and touched her cheek with a reassuring gesture. "Try not to worry, Faithful One. We are not defeated yet!"

Chapter Eight

<<K asha, I'm frightened.>>

Dunnagh slipped into the dark water, before answering. Patting his middle, he crooned soothing noises deep in his throat. Where were the Elders? As he swam out into the pool, he looked ahead into the dimness, trying to pierce the mists that always hugged the water's surface. He couldn't see much. Only their young cousins were here now, and at any moment, they would be swarming round him, wanting to play.

Damn it, he didn't need Tani distracted now. Where were the Makers when he needed one of the big worms? He was getting hungry; surely someone should be anticipating his need and be hanging around.

<<Kasha?>>

His bondmate's frightened wail, finally got Dunnagh's attention. He stopped swimming and focused on the symbiont. <<It's all right, Tani, don't fret. The Makers will think of a way to get us out of this mess.>>

<<But what the Ima said—it was so terrible—I can't help being afraid.>>

<<I know, little one, I'm a bit frightened, too.>>

<<I know you're afraid, I can taste it—and that makes me even more frightened.>>

To distract the Shalla, Dunnagh said, <<Tani, we need to find Maker Gladdris, or one of the other Elders. Can you—uh—taste where they are. I can't see them anywhere around us.>>

Directing the host to open his mouth and swallow several mouthfuls of water, the symbiont tasted the liquid and considered. <<No, I can't find them!>>

Dunnagh felt the echo of Tani's mounting panic in both his mind and body. He resisted, and tried another ploy. <<Can you do something to make *them* come to us?>>

<<Yes.>>

<<Then do it, little one—quickly now!>>

A moment later, the Kashallan vomited an odorous liquid into the water around him. "Yuck." Dunnagh wiped his mouth, the stuff tasted horrible. <<What was that all about?>>

He got his answer soon enough. As the liquid flowed out around them all the adults within range swarmed the bondmates, wanting to know what was wrong.

Not long after that, the familiar bulk of Maker Gladdris wrapped them in its protective coils. When he was secured, Gladdris turned and nuzzled him affectionately. <<What is it, young One—what has happened?>>

Instead of answering, the Kashallan whined deep in his throat and twined his arms tightly around the sleek, gray neck. He trembled violently. Too upset to speak coherently, the Kashallan frantically nipped and licked at the Khutani's mouth, demanding to be fed.

Gladdris curbed its impatience, placed a rubbery feeding tube between his lips, and regurgitated up a meal for the distraught symbiont. Perhaps when he was satiated, it could get some sense out of the host. Just before this, he had been resting in the chapel; what happened to distress him like this?

Replete and soothed, the Kashallan leaned his head back on a gray coil and gurgled with contentment. Gladdris placed a delicate tentacle inside the host's cheek to form the link. <<Now, young one, before you get too relaxed and fall asleep on me; tell me what upset you.>>

Dunnagh sat up a little straighter. <<Now that the Shalla isn't pouring all those strange chemicals into my bloodstream, I remember what we needed to tell you, amla Gladdris. Ima Sagas had some very disturbing news for us. She thinks she will be arrested soon, and she fears for our safety if we remain here without her protection.>>

Gladdris listened as the host relayed in detail, Sagas's news. Much to the bondmates' dismay it had no quick resolution to this problem. The Shalla was too young to leave Sulas. Tani still needed the nourishment and the knowledge that only its Elders could provide.

Gladdris could feel its temper rising to the boil. How dare these misbegotten Avairei threaten a child of the pools—how dare they! Then, sensing Tani's growing distress, it changed the flavor of its sending. <<I have no answers for you yet, si'am,(child) but don't worry, we won't let this Dingay priest or the Warlinga K'San hurt you, never fear.>>

The symbiont relaxed, drifting back into a contented doze while the Khutani questioned the host more carefully. <<Chosen, tell me more about this Combaron Dingay and the Warlinga K'San you mentioned. We know only what the Avairei *choose* to tell us.>>

<<I wish I could help you more, Elder, but as a newcomer to this world, I know very little. As a slave, who couldn't even speak the language before the bonding, I can only give my general impressions, based on my own experiences.>>

<<Your warrior's eyes and your opinions are of value to us, Chosen, anything you can tell me will be of use to the Council.>>

Dunnagh then gave the Maker a detailed report of their capture, Gormach's cruelties, and how Combaron misused the red kavay and other drugs that the Avairei controlled. By the time he finished, Gladdris was finding it hard to dilute its rage so as not to upset the Shalla once more.

<<I need to counsel with the other Makers about this matter. We had no idea things were so bad in the world above. Truly these loathsome creatures have forgotten their breeding and the laws they were given. Perhaps we should abandon them—refuse to make the kavays for them, and let them die off. Then, we can begin breeding life anew at a later time.>>

Dunnagh shuddered. Gladdris could sense his distress through their link. He was probably wondering what would happen to his people—and him personally—if the Khutani abandoned their created species. Both were good questions, to which the Maker had no answer.

<<Elder, I don't think it is as bad as all that, I'm sure there are many who haven't—uh—forgotten their breeding and are still loyal. Please wait till Tani and I have a chance to discover the truth, before the Council takes such a drastic measure.>>

<<If what the priestess says is true, you might not get that chance, young one.>>

Dunnagh grunted an agreement. <<That's true enough, but there still might be away out of this mess. If we could leave Sulas, Elder, are there other pools we could go to and be safe?>>

Distracted from its thought of vengeance, the Maker considered, then said, <<Possibly. There are other Makers below the Keeps in the Yeyen Banai, but I think going there would be as dangerous as staying here. If what the priestess says about the Dingay clan is true, there would be little help for you there. Ticca Keep, at the edge of the Great Swamp would be a better choice—if you could get there—but how would you get there?

<<I'm sure you are aware by now the Shalla controls all your internal bodily functions. It is too young to digest adult food. If the Warlinga didn't kill you; you would die of starvation long before you could travel so far.>>

<<Well, that is a sobering thought; still, there must be a way... Elder, My warriors are waiting for me in the Keep above. And back at our base camp on the mesa, there may be other companions waiting, too.

<<If there was another way out of here—that would give us a head start on the hunters, I'm sure my people and I could make it back to our base. Once we were re-armed with our weaponry, we could go on into the Yeyen to deal with the Dingay, or go to Ticca if we had to. All this hinges on one big question, however.>>

<<Mm, and that is.>>

<<Our food. Back home if a mother isn't able to feed her baby herself, for some reason, we give the infant an artificial formula that will take the place of the mother's milk. If the Khutani could make me such a formula while we were away from our kin, then I could leave Sulas with my warriors, and travel to a safer place.>>

<<Hmm...That is an interesting proposal, Chosen, and one we probably would not have thought of. Such a thing has never been tried before. The young have always stayed with their kin, until they were old enough to fend for themselves.

<<But to answer your first question, yes there is another way out of Sulas that the Warlinga wouldn't know about. It lies along the course of an underground river. The main path bypasses the Magre River Falls, and heads into the Yeyen.

<<There are also side tunnels that lead back into the Broken Lands. One of those would take you near your base. If you took some of the Begta with you, they could show you the way. Hmm, you might make it.>>

<<And the formula?>>

<<That is another question all together. I will have to consult the Council of Makers. I don't like the idea, but we will explore the possibilities, in case it becomes necessary.>>

Gladdris nuzzled him affectionately and uncoiled itself. <<You need to sleep now, young one. Here are some of the kindred; they will stay with you until I return.>>

Dunnagh reached up and caressed the Maker's smooth neck. <<Thank you, amla.>>

Chapter Nine

Sagas relaxed in her favorite chair, watching the flickering green lamplight shape threatening shadows upon the far wall. Beside her on the low end table, was an unaccustomed flask of rich lamra liquor. She poured a good measure into her bowl and drank again deeply.

She felt so tired, so damned bone-weary and drained. So damned empty—of strength, of hope, of fear, even of prayer. The shadows of her doom gathered in the room's dim corners and mocked her. The liquor felt good on her tongue, sliding effortlessly down her throat, untangling the knots in her gut and dulling the ache of her fear.

She could see no escape—no escape for any of them. Combaron would come soon. She would be hauled off to her death, and the Kashallan—what chance did *he* have, with the keep turned against him by Combaron's madness? He was right; he was too young to leave the Khutani's sanctuary. And where would he go if he did leave?

If he was turned out of Sulas, he would be outlawed. No other keep would dare accept him, even if he could get there. And how was he going to do that—alone, ignorant of the world outside Sulas? He would be hunted down and killed by the Warlinga within sun marks.

Ah, Mother, why have you let me come so far in this path, only to see it all torn apart in failure now?

The Kashallan had confirmed her worst fears. The Khutani weren't aware of how bold the Dingay clan had become. By forbidding her—and, she supposed, other devout priestesses access to the pools, the Dingay had contrived to keep the Khutani only partially informed.

It was a devious plot. One that must have taken years, maybe even generations to achieve. But it had been a successful ploy, this slow, patient manipulation of people and events. And now that they had obtained the

High Matri's chair for one of their own, the Dingay clan was in a position to rule Timornan society.

They controlled the products of the pools. All the healing medicines, and the red kavay needed for fertility—everything. Not even the most powerful Warlinga clan would dare stand against them. They would risk too much, if they did.

After his successful transformation, Sagas had tried to win her people's support for the new kashallan. But when her news was met by a stunned, fearful silence; her exuberance had shattered. Whether they believed her or not, she didn't know, but they were too afraid of Combaron's growing power, to openly oppose him by supporting her outrageous claims.

She took another drink. Combaron would return soon, and she had signed all her allies' death warrants with her failure.

There was only one hope left to her now, and that a slim one indeed. The idea came to her when she recalled the little scene she stumbled upon at the Birthing Pool chapel. That had been most informative, and an option she wouldn't have considered possible before today. But now. Well, Pela would be her last desperate gamble.

Hearing a light tap at her door, Sagas called, "Enter,"

Her young protégée stepped quietly into the room. Eyes cast down, Pela hesitated in the doorway, looking frightened.

Sagas's mouth twitched; was she expecting to be disciplined for her part in that sweet tableau at the chapel? "Come in, child, and close the door. And don't look so glum. You're not going to your execution. Only I am." Sagas drained her bowl, then poured another for herself from the bottle at her elbow.

Pela saw the bottle, her eyes widening with her surprise. Sagas laughed and took another drink to steady her nerves. This wasn't going to be easy.

Pela hurried to kneel at her feet. "You wanted to see me, Ima?"

Sagas looked down at her owlishly. "Yes, I did. I have something for you." She reached down to the floor by her chair and picked up a stone bottle carved with intricate designs. "Of all the young Avairei here, you are special to me. This was mine when I was young; I wanted you to have it."

Pela took the gift reverently, turning it over and over in her hands, studying its beautiful workmanship. At last she looked up her eyes bright with excitement. "What an honor to have your own marriage flask, Ima. I never expected this." She hesitated, glancing back at the flask, her finger tracing its design.

"Are you sending me to my promised earlier than expected, because of Combaron's attentions? I want to be with my beloved, but I don't want to leave you, either."

Sagas grimaced and took another drink. The Ima Matri of the main Avairei keep in a district always had the right to decide when a mating would occur, and with whom. It was her duty to consult the Khutani, then together they would decide the most advantageous partnerships for the health and strength of the Avairei, Warlinga and Loti clans under their care. Yes, it was her right to decide a mating—and under the circumstances...

Pela's glowing face was going to make her next words even harder than she'd thought.

"Today at the birthing chapel, I saw how the Kashallan looked at you—how he wanted you. It is time you took a mate. I give you this now, so that you can prepare yourself for him."

Pela gasped, almost dropping the precious flask in her surprise. "But, Ima, I can't mate with that ugly alien—I've already been promised—"

"Promised and formally pledged are two different matters, daughter. In your case the betrothal ceremony has *not* been performed. It is within my right to make other arrangements for you if I see fit." She drank a little more brandy. "And, in this case, I do."

Sagas watched the play of emotions across Pela's expressive face. This was a terrible blow for the young priestess, but she hardened her heart against all feelings of pity for the girl. There was too much at stake here—for all of them. She couldn't allow herself to be foolishly sentimental. If the Dingay clan did manage to kill the Kashallan—and how could they not, then Pela's child might be their only hope.

Pela looked up at her with moist eyes. Sagas sighed. "I know you hoped for another; I have my reasons, daughter. Now, do you accept both the gift and the obligation?"

"But, Ima, is this possible? He is so—alien. Would he even be fertile with me?"

Good point, daughter. One I hadn't considered till now. But you won't get out of this so easily. "He is not so alien, with the kavay in his blood and the symbiont coiled in his middle. No, he is not alien at all. And if there were any incompatibilities, the Khutani symbiont would correct them." Sagas leaned forward, holding her protégé's gaze with the strength of her will. "Stop playing with me and making excuses, will you do this for your people, or do I find another to receive my favor?"

Pela looked down at the flask in her hand. She let out a ragged sigh and murmured, "Your will, Ima. I will do as you say."

Sagas sat back, inwardly relieved. Maintaining her uncompromising facade, she said, "Good. Report to Ima Alam in the morning to be properly prepared for the first bedding. Now, leave me, daughter."

Chapter Ten

In the privacy of her own room, Pela knelt by her small altar, staring blindly at the lamp's green flame. After leaving the Ima's chambers, she had made it back to her cell by instinct alone. Her vision blurred as she looked down at the marriage bottle of red kavay she held. A large oily tear fell onto its beautifully carved surface. This was the beloved Ima's own marriage flask. This mating was a great honor—and it was her duty...

This should have been the happiest day of her life. The day which she and her Promised had prayed for since their childhood, and now...

"Oh love! Oh my dearest, how can I bear this?" She set the flask with its precious contents down on the altar, before she might drop it. The silent tears wouldn't stop flowing. Hugging herself, she rocked back and forth grieving for her lost dreams.

Unbidden, the vision of the Kashallan, floated behind the curtain of her streaming eyes. She saw his ugly, flat, alien features, his pale, alien, five-fingered hands—reaching out, touching. Touching her in all those special places. Places where she had longed for another's beloved, four-fingered hands to touch.

And now, the Ima had given her to him—to him! This half-Khutani, half naked, blue-eyed stranger, now she must take him to her bed, and suffer his unwanted lovemaking forever! Pela's stomach twisted into knots at the thought. This unnatural creature—she was expected to— She shivered, suddenly afraid.

Having the attention of one of the Holy Ones, was disconcerting enough, but that other—he was so big and so unpredictable. Would the Kashallan hurt her? She didn't know. And that was one of the worst things about this arrangement. She didn't know what to expect; nor did anyone else. A union like this had never happened before.

Oh, this was not the first time in Avairei history that a planned breeding had not been to the liking of one, or both, of its participants. And that at least, was another blessing of the red drink. The potion in the flask would take care of her reticence. Once she began to take it, she would not mind anymore. In fact, she would encourage and welcome his caresses.

But here, tonight, in the privacy of her own cell, in silence, she would mourn. For her lost lover, for shattered dreams and what was not to be.

Later, as she lay exhausted and emptied of tears, she thought once more of the Kashallan. Recalling the events of the previous afternoon, she admitted to herself that he'd been very gentle with her, in spite of his arousal. Inexperienced as she was, it had been clear that he wanted her. He could have forced her, yet when he finally understood that she was unwilling, he stopped.

She had been so afraid to offend and anger him. His penetration would have hurt terribly, but she would have let him enter her without complaint if he'd insisted. But he had *not* wanted the coupling, if she didn't.

And, she also remembered what the Khutani had said. It was the host, not the symbiont that counseled restraint. More disjointed memories flooded into her mind, the pain of the Transformation, his childlike joy at his braided hair, and the tender way he touched the Ima's face once, as if he could see into her very soul and didn't blame her for what must be done.

Dunnagh came here from his home so far away. He had *chosen* to come to Timorna, just to aid the Khutani and make a Kashallan bond. That took great courage and sacrifice. Did he leave behind clan and love to do this? Perhaps. She had never considered that idea before, but surely he must have. He *must* have had ties of friendship, loving ties among his kin in his home so far away.

Even though the ancient lore-books taught that people from the stars were supernatural beings, he was no spirit after all, nor a character out of an old story. He was a flesh and blood person—and, though an alien, to be sure, he was not *that* different from her own race.

Would she have had the courage to do so much—especially for an alien race that she didn't know? Compared to such an offering, her thwarted desire for a childhood sweetheart seemed insignificant indeed. Somehow this new revelation was a comforting thought.

She might not be going into this mating with love and eagerness, but she could bring into their relationship both compassion, and respect for the partner who would share her life now.

Chapter Eleven

The door to Sagas's bedchamber slammed open with a resounding crash. Wrenched out of a troubled sleep, Sagas sat up, blinking. The Warlinga Hanno and two of his men stood just inside her door.

Sagas shook the sleep from her clouded mind and glared at them. "HOW DARE YOU? GET OUT!"

Hanno smirked, giving her an impressive view of his fangs, and remained defiantly where he was. The men on either side of him, flicked their tails nervously and dropped their eyes. Picking up her cloak from the bottom of her bed, Sagas swallowed her panic and stood. "I said get out!"

"They're not going anywhere on *your* orders, Ima." Combaron Dingay sauntered through the door. "They will leave only when I tell them to."

"You!" Her voice dripped with scorn. "Combaron, you overstep your authority here. How dare you. Take these Warlinga of yours then, and get out of my bed chamber."

"Do I overstep my authority?" He shook his head. His eyes had taken on a triumphant glitter. "I think not. I say, rather, that it is *you* who overstep your authority. If half of what I've been told since my return is true, then you have not only *overstepped*, but you are guilty of sacrilege and abomination as well."

"I've only obeyed the will of the Khutani. I have done nothing wrong."

Combaron stared, incredulous. "Ah, you are so very proud of yourself, are you? Yes, and that blue-eyed Umwira demon, who is your new master, is proud of you too, no doubt."

His eyes feverish with his conviction, he stepped closer. "You obey an evil sorcerer. Don't lie to me. I have been told how you created an abomination. You blaspheme our ancient laws—and you corrupt the minds and bodies of other Avairei placed in your care. Your crimes are numberless, witch, and your evil beyond belief!"

"I should have these Warlinga kill you right now—but I won't. Gormach and his clan will be here soon, and you and all those you have corrupted will go with him to Riath, to receive the deaths you so richly deserve."

Sagas sat down on the edge of her bed, all the fight gone out of her. She'd been prepared for her own demise—she could accept that. But the others—no, they should not suffer for her disobedience.

Oh, please, Mother, no! "Combaron, listen to me. What I've done here is far more important than the feuding between our families. The future of our world may depend on what we do. The Khutani have told me so. This new kashallan bond isn't a sacrilege, but a sacred thing. The Khutani brought him here from the stars—he is *their* Dream-Chosen."

Combaron snorted with disgust. Sagas hurried on, not giving him time to speak. "You can do what you want with me—kill me if that pleases you. But don't turn your back on him! Don't go against the holy Ones' will, please, Combaron. I'm begging you. They will abandon us—the Khutani have sworn it!"

"Makers talking to you, men from the stars—you talk like a Begta. Lies, witch, all lies. You are trying to frighten me with your predictions of doom, but they are nothing but a defilement of the truth. The Khutani will not abandon us—how could they? And, where would they go, hmm?"

Combaron slapped her hard, knocking her backwards upon the bed. Hand still raised, he loomed over her, face a mask of rage. "I will hear no more of this, witch! The Khutani dwell in the pools—where they belong. We serve them, and they serve us. That is the way it has been, and always *will* be. The Bebech are dead! There is no host, nor will there ever be again!

"This mutant sorcerer, this monster, this desecration from the black pit—I want him, Sagas. Do you hear me? I want him!"

He reached down, grabbed her by her necklaces, and jerked her up to face him. "Where is this corrupting demon from the Ghostlands? Where, accursed witch? WHERE IS HE?"

When she refused to answer, Combaron slapped her again,.

"COMBARON!"

He whirled, letting the dazed Sagas fall back onto the bed.

In the doorway confronting him stood a very old Avairei Matri. Ima Nansa had been mistress at Sulas before Sagas, and now every ounce of power and authority inherent in that position, was once more in her voice and demeanor. "You forget yourself, Ata. What is the meaning of this?"

"Ima Nansa." For just a moment, anger contorted his features; then he controlled himself and bowed, "This blaspheming piece of corruption has been ordered to Riath, along with her Umwira wizard master. She will tell me where I can find him or—"

"Or nothing. You will not touch her again; do you hear me? You will obey custom, and allow *me* to deal with this. You, Ata, are not in charge here. If Sagas is to be relieved of her duties as Ima Matri by order of Her Holiness in Riath, then I am mistress here, till the High Matri sees fit to send another to take Sagas's place. Do you understand me, Ata, or do you choose to declare a feud with *my* clan as well as the Caltia?"

Combaron blinked, then reluctantly backed down. He gave her a mocking bow. "I would not presume to overstep my authority as Ata Leyas. But this priestess must go to Riath. And before she goes, she must tell me where to find her Umwira accomplice."

"If she is to go to Riath, then you may arrange it," Nansa said. "But as to her knowing how to find the Ghostland sorcerer—how could *she* know that? If he has the power you claim, he could be anywhere by now. With his magic, he might have changed his shape, or turned himself invisible. He could even have flown to Riath itself. How would this poor deluded priestess know anything about where such a creature would be?"

Combaron's eyes widened with this new revelation. "Now, Ata, I would suggest you and these hulking Warlinga of yours get out of here and let the Ima rest. It will be a long and tiring journey to the capital."

"I will go. As you say, I have work to do; I must find her demon tempter. But I don't want her to get away—the guards stay.

Nansa snorted. "Sagas is not going anywhere. I will not have these big, scaly lummoxes cluttering up my keep, getting in everybody's way and destroying the furniture.

"Besides, what good would *they* be against a demon's magics? If you truly have to have a guard posted outside this door, then get your own apprentices to do it. Their priestly training is better suited to the job. Don't you agree?"

He blinked, then nodded slowly. "Good—away you go then." Nansa glared at the Warlinga. "San Hanno, I'm sure you have duties elsewhere. I suggest you see to them, hmm?"

Hanno looked from the Ima Nansa to Combaron, his tail curled and uncurled with indecision. Receiving no sign from the Dingay, he bowed to the old woman and left, taking his two clansmen with him. Nansa held her ground, staring pointedly at the priest. Finally, he left, too, grumbling under his breath.

When the door closed behind them Nansa chuckled, shaking her head in disbelief. "Gullible, puffed up little slimeworm. Too bad nobody thought to drown him at birth." Turning to the woman curled up on the bed, she asked, "Are you all right? How badly did he hurt you?"

Sagas rolled over and sat up. Bringing a hand up to her face, she cautiously explored her swelling cheek. Her voice a bit shaky, she said, "I'm all right, thank you, Ima."

Nansa surveyed her critically for a moment, then nodded to herself. Yes, she was fine. Shaken up though; Sagas hadn't counted on Combaron's physical assault. By the Holy Ones, who would have? The man was dangerous, perhaps insane. All of Sulas would have to be very careful from now on.

Coming over to sit beside her on the bed, Nansa clicked her tongue in exasperation, then patted Sagas's hand. "I don't know if you are incredibly brave or incredibly stupid, Sagas, but you were always an intense one—regardless of the consequences."

Sagas sighed. "True enough, Ima, but it doesn't matter what happens to me. I knew my probable fate when I agreed to obey the Khutani. What concerns me most, is the Kashallan and the others who unwittingly helped me defy the Dingay."

Suddenly, she clutched at the old woman's hand, her eyes fierce with her desperation. "Oh, Nansa, Combaron must not find and kill him. Please, Nansa! I beg you, help him. So much depends on him. If he should be killed—"

"There, there, child, don't fret yourself so. Whatever happens now, it is out of your control. I will do what I can; so don't give up hope yet. Keep your faith and pray."

Chapter Twelve

T he Kashallan was tired, but couldn't relax. After Tani fed, the bondmates had been left to themselves while most of the Khutani adults and the Makers counseled with one another. Tani trusted their elders to solve their problem. Dunnagh, on the other hand, guessed he was doing enough fretting for both of them. He was worried; something must have happened. It had been too long since one of the Avairei came down to check on them.

Suddenly a loud thunking began on the rim of the Birthing Pool. An Avairei priestess, withered with age, was banging with her cane to catch his attention.

<<Who is that, Kasha?>> Tani's sleepy voice asked.

<<No one I recognize. She seems very old. Are you sure you don't have a memory of her, Shalla?>>

A note of exasperation colored Tani's mental voice.<<From my encoded memories, I probably *would* know her, if I was close enough to taste her, Kasha. But looking at her through our eyes, as I am, I have no idea who she is.>>

<<Well then, let's go find out who she is, and what she wants.>> Dunnagh began to swim towards her, but a sharp nip from his innards stopped him. <<Ouch! Tani, what did you do that for?>>

<<I think we should do as our Amla Gladdris said and stay here.>>

Now it was Dunnagh's turn to be exasperated. <<Tani, she's old. I may not be up to taking on a Warlinga right now, but I think I can handle *her* if she starts trouble. So stop worrying. She may have some information for the Elders. I want to know why Sagas and the Avairei we *do* know, haven't been down to check on us lately.>>

<<Oh, all right. I guess you have a point.>>

With powerful strokes, the Kashallan swam to where the old woman was waiting. She saw him coming, and quit banging her stick. Treading water near the rim of the pool, he looked up and smiled. "Ima?"

She folded her stick-like arms, rested them on her cane and leaned upon it, studying him. "Well, child, you certainly took your time! It's a long walk back here for one of my years. And I am more tired, after standing here, while you dithered about coming to me or not."

Instead of answering her, he climbed out of the pool, picked her up in his arms and carried her into the alcove. He gently sat her down on his bed, arranging his blanket and pillow for her comfort. Sitting down cross-legged in front of her, he smiled. "Do you feel better now, Ima? I apologize for my bad manners. You were right. We were 'dithering,' as you put it."

Nansa snorted. "At least you're honest about it. Do you know who I am, child?"

He shook his head. "No, I've never seen you before. I might be able to tell, if I could *taste* you." The Kashallan held up his swollen hands. "Unfortunately, I haven't grown the adaptations I need, to make that kind of assessment yet."

"There is no other way?"

"Yes, there is another way. But I would hurt you, Elder, and I wouldn't want to do that."

Nansa laughed. "I'm not as fragile as all that. Do what you need to—I'm curious."

"All right." He reached out, took one of her hands and raised it to his mouth. Nansa remained rock-steady as he bit down, then sucked out a small taste of her blood. He let her hand fall, and closed his eyes, savoring her taste and reading its wealth of coded information.

At last, he opened his eyes again and smiled, displaying sharp triangular teeth. "You are Nansa. You were Ima Matri here once. My kindred know you well. You also have an old injury to your right knee which is giving you trouble today." He sighed. "I would like to heal that for you, but I can't. I'm sorry. I'm still too young."

Nansa patted his hand to reassure him. She hadn't expected him to be like this, and was moved. No wonder Sagas was willing to die for him. What a strange mixture of the alien and Khutani he was.

"Don't concern yourself about it, child. I've lived with that knee giving me trouble for nigh on thirty years. I can cope with it a while longer. There are far more important things we need to worry about."

"What has happened?"

"Well, to start with, that fool of a Dingay brat is back."

"Combaron? Sagas warned me about him."

"Yes, and with good cause. He's placed her under arrest and is sending her off to the Capital for trial, as soon as Gormach of Tragar can come here to escort her."

"He won't have her. I'll—"

Nansa held up her hand, silencing him in mid-flow. "Hear me out, young one. It's not only Sagas who Combaron's got it into his head to take to Riath for execution. It's you as well. He's searching for you right now."

"If he wants me, why doesn't he come and try to take me? Doesn't he know where to find a kashallan bonded?"

"No, he doesn't, at least not yet. And thank the Great Mother he hasn't figured it out before now, or things might be worse than they are."

"But how could he not know? Where else would he look for a bonded pair than in the Birthing Pool?"

"Ah, that is the whole point. He doesn't know where to look, because he thinks you are not a kashallan, but Umwira wizards come down out of the North to destroy us."

Her words sent a shiver running down Dunnagh's spine. The monster on the fiery plain had thought him a mutant from the Ghostlands, too. Were these two unrelated events somehow related? Not likely. "He what? Is the man crazy?"

"Probably."

"This is incredible. How did he get such an amazing idea?"

"I'm sure I don't know. Something obviously went wrong with that one's breeding program. But all the Dingay are a strange lot—have been for some time now. The point is that he *will* eventually figure it out, and come looking for you here."

The Kashallan swore in Caldoni, then closed his eyes taking counsel with the two halves of himself. When he opened them again, he said, "I must consult my Elders of course, but it's clear to me that I will have to leave

Sulas—and soon. The Makers have designed a formula for me to drink on my journey, just in case this became necessary. But I cannot, and will not, go alone. The Chosen's kindred, Sagas, and anyone else who wishes to come with me must leave with us. For I promise you this, Ima, if I have to flee because of this Dingay threat, the Khutani will also leave and Sulas will die."

Nansa shivered, visibly shaken. "Then it is true what Sagas claims. The Khutani will abandon us?"

The Kashallan nodded. "If I am rejected by your people, then my Khutani kindred will reject you as well. It is that simple, and that final. I'm sorry, Ima."

"I see. But how will you do this? If you try to leave, Combaron will have you, and his pet Warlinga will kill you. But if you stay down here and try to hide, it is only a question of time before he finds you as well. And as for Sagas—I don't see how it can be done."

"There is no need for me to go up through the keep to leave Sulas. There is a way out from here. But in order for my plan to work I need your help."

Nansa stirred, her voice bright with excitement. "Ah, the hidden passage! I have read of it in some of the ancient texts, but its exact location has been lost to us."

He smiled. "Its location has not been lost to *us*, however. The entrance, in fact, is right in this room. So, get a message to the slave pens. My host's kinsman Nathan will take care of freeing Sagas, and planning our escape."

Nansa's mouth dropped open in surprise. "To the slave pens, Kashallan? But how can such helpless creatures be of any use to you now? I would think they would be more of a burden than an asset."

Dunnagh shook his head. "Like other Timornans we've encountered since coming to this world, Ima, you underestimate us. We lack the natural weapons of tooth and claw, true enough, but natural armament is only one solution to the problem of defense. The use of tools and technology is another.

"I, Dunnagh, was the equivalent of a Warlinga Hunt Leader before I came here. But not all my people are warriors. Among those at Sulas with me, are two trained in skills similar to what the Avairei learn."

Nansa gave him an incredulous look, unable to speak.

"I know it is hard for you to believe—having no experience of the universe outside this one small planet. But I am telling you the truth. And you surely know that a bonded pair would not lie to you."

"Yes, I do, but it is all so hard to believe, Kashallan."

Tani took over their speech and chuckled. "My Kasha thinks much the same—only about Timorna and her peoples."

"I see! All right, I will trust your judgment. Tell me what you need."

"I will need some large flasks for my formula, and Loti to carry them. We will also need food and other supplies for the rest who are going with me. All the equipment and people must be brought down here, if we are to leave through the hidden path. Is that possible?"

"You don't want much, do you, child?" she grumbled. He opened his mouth to speak, but she waved him to silence. "All right, I understand your reasoning and it is valid. It may take a little time, but I'll do what I can.

"Those two young apprentices of Temog's are still running around loose, and nobody will pay any attention to them. I'll get them to bring down the bottles and go out to the slave pens after dark and collect your kinsmen."

Chapter Thirteen

It had been a weird day, Nathan decided, when he lay down next to Tessa that night. Weasel-face had come back to Sulas early that morning, looking mad enough to chew nails. He stomped into the inner keep, with Hanno and a couple of the Warlinga trailing behind him. The Warlinga came back shortly afterwards. But for the rest of the day, there were unsettling noises coming out of the Avairei's inner sanctum.

It seemed like nothing he need be concerned about. On the other hand, that was where the other fool priests took Dunnagh. He couldn't help worrying about his friend's safety. After they finished work, Nathan tried to find out what was going on in the keep.

None of the humans knew any more than he did, nor did the Loti in the nearby pens. When he'd asked the Begta, all the little fur-balls could tell him was that the "bad Avairei," was searching for the Kashallan—whatever—or whoever that was.

Hoping to abandon his troubles for a time, he drew Tessa closer. Giving him a throaty laugh, she snuggled against him. She lifted up her face for his kisses, and ran her hands down his belly. She brushed the curly hairs of his crotch, and stroked the shaft of his sex. With a sigh, he gave himself over to the sensations she was invoking in his body with her exploring hands.

He had just shifted his position to lie over her, when the gate to their enclosure banged open. He froze. All his desire for intimacy dispelled in an instant when he saw who was entering their pen. Throwing aside their blanket, he rose into a fighter's crouch in front of his partner.

"Nathan, what's wrong?"

Without taking his eyes off the approaching group, he said under his breath, "Weasel-face just came in with some of his Warlinga."

Peering around his back, Tessa gasped. "It's that awful Combaron. Nathan, what could he want at this time of night?" She shivered, wrapping the discarded blanket about her shoulders.

Nathan snorted. "Well, whatever it is, it probably means trouble." He glanced back at her, feeling his earlier unease return. "Last time he singled us out for his 'attentions,' he wanted somebody to warm his bed. I have no intentions of sleeping alone tonight. So, stay out of sight as much as you can, Mo Cri."

As he rose Tessa touched his arm. "Be careful yourself! I don't want to sleep alone tonight, either." He patted her hand then moved forward to confront their unwanted visitors.

All the Lann Gheal men must have had the same thought as Nathan, because they immediately stood, forming a protective wall in front of their female comrades.

Combaron eyed the wall of mutant slaves blocking his way, his jaw tight. "Where is he?"

"Where is who?" Nathan asked.

"Your demon leader!"

"I've been called a lot of things before. Demon, that's a new one."

The Warlinga growled. Combaron focused on him, a dangerous gleam in his eyes. "Don't play games with me, mutant, or I will make you very sorry for your insolence. I want to know where the blue-eyed sorcerer that is your *true* leader is hiding. I want him and I want him now!"

"Sorcerer?" Nathan laughed, waving his hand in dismissal. "Oh, that sorcerer! He flew off on his magic carpet days ago—"

Before Nathan finished, a Warlinga uncoiled his tail and knocked him to the ground.

Nathan sprawled, the air exploding out of his lungs in a painful grunt. Eyeing the Warlingas' tails cautiously as he sat up, he sucked in great lungfuls of air, trying to catch his breath. "I don't know what you're talking about," he finally muttered.

Singey reached down a hand and helped Nathan to his feet. "Our leader is right. We really don't know what you are talking about, Ata."

Combaron snorted. "I don't believe you, any of you. Your mutant magic is strong, but I will defeat you all—I will find him." Combaron stepped closer to the two men. He smiled slyly, then whispered, so only they could hear him.

"If you tell me where he is, I can protect you from his wrath. With him out of the way, you won't have to worry. You could use your lesser skills to help me and my family with their plans."

Singey stepped back a pace. He drew himself up to his full height and looked down his aristocratic nose at the shorter man. Assuming an offended expression, he said in his most irritating patrician voice, "Really, Ata. We would have nothing to do with such superstitious nonsense. And, I, personally, find your accusation most insulting."

To Nathan's surprise, the priest dropped his eyes and looked away.

"If you are referring to our missing companion," Singey continued. "Some of *your* people took him into the keep days ago. The rest of us have neither seen, nor heard from, him since. And, furthermore, how could our leader be a sorcerer? That's preposterous."

Singey laughed. "If he was, do you think any of us would be in our present state? Hardly!" He favored all of the intruders with a look of haughty outrage, and folded his arms dramatically across his chest. "We've answered your question, so I suggest you leave! We will have plenty of work assigned to us tomorrow, and we need our rest."

Speechless, Combaron shook with frustration. He stared at them a moment longer, then spun on his heel and stormed out of their pen; his guards trailing silently after him.

Singey let out a long sigh. To no one in particular, he said, "I'm glad that's over!"

"You did well, Sir," Rhys said from somewhere behind him.

Singey glanced back over his shoulder. "Thank you—I hope it helped."

"I don't know if it helped, either, but thanks, Philip." Nathan murmured. He took in an experimental breath, letting it out slowly. "I sure wish I knew where Dunnagh was. I wonder what kind of a mess he's gotten himself into this time."

Tessa let out a strangled sound, somewhere between a laugh and a sob then sank heavily to the ground. Nathan crouched down beside her. "What's wrong, love? Are you hurt?"

She shook her head, unable to speak. The two men glanced helplessly at one another. Singey shrugged. Tessa laughed. When she got herself under control, she said, "You two really don't know what you just did, do you?"

"Tessa," Nathan said, "I'm really not in the mood for games. My side hurts like—"

"I am not playing games, Nathan," she snapped. "This is so incredible—I don't know what to think." Tessa looked from one puzzled face to the other. She shook her head then giggled nervously. "Philip, you told Ata Combaron that you didn't believe in magic, but how can you explain what just happened?"

"What, in your opinion *did* just happen, Tessa? I don't understand?"

Tessa growled in exasperation. "Oh, men, think! You told him yourselves—*yourselves*. Both of you, talked to that priest, in his own language. You never asked me to translate once."

Nathan sat down hard beside her. "Oh shit, she's right! But how?"

"I'm not sure how you did it," Tessa said. "When the elderly priest came to fix Marnez's shoulder, he tried to tell me something about having his Gods—the Khutani—take care of our language difficulties. Well, I guess they did." Unable to control herself any longer she burst out into nervous giggling again.

The porridge *had* tasted particularly vile the last few days. Could that have something to do with their new language ability? Nathan shook his head—*nah, that's crazy.*

LATER THAT NIGHT, AN unidentified sound awakened Nathan from an uneasy sleep. Without moving, he cracked open one eye and waited, listening. There it was again—a furtive rustling. Then, the sounds of a brief struggle and a muffled cry, quickly choked off. He swore under his breath, threw off the blanket and rose into a crouch. He glanced around, heart pounding, his senses straining to pick out detail in the dim light.

"Nath—"

Nathan put his hand over Tessa's mouth, then next to her ear, he whispered, "Quiet, love—something's wrong!" When he was sure she was awake enough to understand his warning, he straightened.

The noise from the Warlinga drinking party that had been keeping him awake earlier was all but ended. Damn, he wished he could see better; he still didn't know what roused him. Tessa was sitting up now—he could feel her trembling.

From outside the shelter a low voice whispered, "Hey, Nathan, you awake?"

"Yeah, Rhys, I'm awake. What's the problem? And it better be good—you're disturbing my beauty sleep."

A soft chuckle from the darkness, then, "Chang and me just caught a couple of visitors dropping by for a late-night chat."

"What is it with these Avairei? Twice in one night—don't they ever sleep?" he grumbled under his breath.

"What? I didn't catch that," Rhys said.

"Oh shit! Give them an appointment, and tell them to come back in the morning—"

"One of the boys says he's got a message for you, personal-like, Sir," Chang cut in. "He says it's from somebody named Kashallan, but as best I can figure he means Dunnagh, Sir."

Swearing under his breath, Nathan groped his way out of the shelter to where the armachda crouched. By now the rest of his people were awake, and coming over to see what was going on. Huddled between Rhys and Chang, Nathan saw two very frightened Avairei. He couldn't see them well in the dimness, but, from what he could tell, they did indeed appear to be children—elder teens perhaps. "All right, Rhys, Chang, start from the beginning and tell me what this is all about."

"I was coming back from the privy when I heard these two sneaking round outside our pen," Rhys said. "Chang was sleeping next to me—so I goes back and tells him. Next thing we know, they're inside, and heading our way—so we jump them." He sighed. "And it's a good thing they just falls to the ground when we rush them, otherwise... "

"Are they hurt?"

"A few bruises maybe, but mostly they're frightened."

Nathan breathed a sigh of relief. Thank the Gods for that. He didn't even want to contemplate trying to explain to their elders how two children playing a prank had been killed by a couple of berserk armachda. "So what's this about a message for me?"

"When we could get them to talk, they asked for you by name, sir," Rhys said. "But they wouldn't say no more."

Nathan crouched, and addressed the Avairei directly. "All right, lads, nobody's going to hurt you. You startled my men trying to sneak up on us like that. It could have got you killed, so don't ever do it again. But you're all right, and thank the gods for that. I'm Nathan; tell me your message, and who sent you."

The bravest of them said in a voice that was still a bit shaky, "Ima Nansa and the Kashallan sent us. They warned us not to let the Warlinga, or any of Ata Combaron's people see us. That's why we were sneaking in."

"That's the 'who,' now tell me the 'what.'"

"The Kashallan says he needs you, because of Ata Combaron. He must escape now, tonight. He wants you to come, and bring Ima Sagas, the Loti, and everyone—so we can go!"

Nathan was confused. This was like trying to put a jigsaw puzzle together with some of the key pieces missing. Where was Dunnagh, who was the Kashallan, and where were they supposed to escape to? Those were the questions he needed answered for starters.

"Let's back up a moment, lad, I'm still not sure who this message is supposed to be from. You said your Ima and the Kashallan, but kashallan is a word in your language I don't know, so tell me again."

"The Kashallan is your leader—or at least part of him is," the other boy chimed in.

Oh, yeah, thanks for sharing—now I'm even more confused than before.

"Sir? How do we know this isn't a trick just to see if we'd try to escape, so they'd have an excuse to get rid of a few of us?" Marnez said.

Good point. I wouldn't put something like that past Weasel-face. But the boy's next words changed his mind, and settled their course of action.

Taking up the narrative again, the first Avairei said, "The Dream-Chosen said, that I was to tell you, if you got stubborn—I was to say to you: 'Ta, shay, kairt, an, try, anish.'" He smiled. "Did I remember it correctly? The Chosen said it meant 'the time is right—now in your language.' Did you understand me?"

Oh, by the Gods, he did understand. That message was from Dunnagh all right. If the Caldoni language wasn't enough to convince him, there was that phrase "Dream-Chosen" coming up to trouble his mind again. No, there was no question now, this summons was definitely from Dunnagh. He'd gotten himself into some kind of trouble in there, and needed them to come get him out of it.

Rhys chuckled. "Well, that settles that, doesn't it, Sir? But I still don't understand what the Ce'awn wants us to do, exactly."

"All right, boys, you said the magic words—we believe you. If we are to escape tonight, tell me again what we are supposed to do. And tell it slowly, one thing at a time."

It took a while, but they finally got the information they needed to form a plan of operation. Nathan called for quiet and summarized the action. "I can't see any way around it; we will have to split up." He sighed, thinking of the last time they divided their force, and what a disastrous mistake that had been.

"We have two main objectives. One is to bring all the Loti who will come with us, and as many supplies as we can find, down to these pools under the keep, where the Ce'awn is. The second objective is to enter the main part of the keep, and rescue some of the Avairei who Dunnagh also wants to come with us. Everybody got that?" There were murmurs of agreement. "Questions?"

"We've talked about using the farm tools, but this would be a lot easier to pull off, if we had some real weapons, Sir," Marti said. "Without them, it will be damn near impossible, especially if we're discovered."

"Good point." Nathan turned to the priests. "What about weapons—knives, spears, anything? I know Dun—uh, this Kashallan of yours, would have told you what we would need. Didn't he say anything about weapons?"

"He did, San Nathan," one of the boys said. "The Kashallan said you would need them. We have a few small knives for you that we use in our rituals, but Avairei don't carry weapons—that is what Warlinga are for. The only fighting weapons here belong to them." He brightened. "But my

Ima did what she could—she sent the Warlinga some drugged beer—to celebrate Ata Combaron's coming victory—"

"Only the Ata doesn't know he sent it," the other interrupted. "Ima Nansa said it would make them sleep. That was the best she could do. We are sorry."

Nathan sighed.

"The farm tools are better than nothing," Taleish said.

"Good point," Nathan said. "The store shed isn't locked we can raid it on our way out."

"Near the kitchens is where the entrance down to the spring, for folk as big as the Loti is located," Rhys said. "I've gone down there with the Loti to collect water before. Is there a passage from the spring, where they let us slaves go, to the inner sanctum, where you priests work? Because I'm thinking we need to go to the pools proper, to meet our leader, correct?"

"Yes, that is where the Kashallan is. And, you're right; there is a passage. It's not used much anymore. The apprentices use it from time to time when we—" His friend jabbed him in the ribs with his elbow. "Uh—never mind. It will be a close fit for the Loti. But without tied-on packs, they can make it."

"Good, one of you lads will go with Rhys here, and show him the way. The other will come with me. Rhys, since you've been working down there, you'll head up the supply squad. Oglas, Marnez, Taleish, Tessa and Singey, you go with him. Chang, Marti, Moraga with me. We'll get the Avairei."

Nathan paused, listening. The Warlinga barracks was quiet. He stood and glanced towards the sentries by the gate. Blurred lumps lay sprawled upon the ground over there—snoring. Now was as good a time as any. "Rhys, you take your people and head out now. We'll give you a head start, then we'll go. Don't wait for us—get the supplies and go on to where the Ce'awn is. We'll be along when, and if, we can."

Hastily grabbing their few possessions, the first squad disappeared into the night. Nathan waited till he heard the Loti from the next pen leave with his men then motioned his own band to move out.

As they were slipping by the Begta's enclosure, a low voice called, "Hey, starmans."

They froze. *What now?* "What do you want?" Nathan murmured.

"Begta want to run away, too."

"How do you know we're running away?" Nathan said.

"I climbed on roof of shelter, and listened. First I listen starmans make funny noise on top of female—then I hear Avairei come with message. Begta go with starmans, eh?"

Marti made a strangled sound, stifling a laugh. Nathan swore. "No, you can't come, you little eavesdropper! Besides, why should we take you? You Begta got us into this mess in the first place!"

Silence...

Nathan was about to move on when the voice stopped him again. "I know where can get Warlinga's weapons. You take Begta, I show."

"Yeah, I do too—in their barracks, ha ha! No way, furball!"

"Nah, weapons not in barracks—can get easy, no Warlingas. I show."

"We better take them," Chang said. "We could use the arms—if he isn't lying and does know where to find them. Warlinga weapons would be better than shovels if we have to fight. They might also rouse the guard if we leave them behind."

"You're right." Addressing the voice, Nathan said, "All right, you can come—*provided* you remember that star man is boss man, and you listen to me, all right?"

"Begta will listen." Five dark, woolly bodies scrambled over the wall and crouched in the dust before him, awaiting his orders.

The young priest hissed. "We can't take Begta into the inner keep. My Ima will—"

"Your Ima will have to live with it," Nathan snapped, "because we can't leave them here!" The priest muttered something else, but Nathan ignored him. "Which one of you knows where the weapons are?"

"Me."

"What's your name?"

"Dado."

"Right, Dado, you come with me. The rest of you catch up to Rhys by the kitchens and help them gather supplies."

Dado led them to a small hut tucked up against the outer wall behind the Warlinga barracks. When the Avairei lit his lamp, they discovered a workshop where the lizardmen made and repaired their gear. Most of the weaponry scattered around on the workbenches were unfinished. But there were a few items that were useable amid the clutter. For raw materials, like balls of cordage, and bone blades without handles, the place was a gold mine.

"We can attach some of these blades to the farm tools." Chang snatched up a leather sack and the armachda quickly filled it with anything they thought might come in handy.

As they were about to leave, Nathan put a hand on the Begta's shoulder, turning the little man to face him. "If you knew about this place, why didn't you escape a long time ago?"

"Warlinga catch us—nowhere can run. Warlinga find, Warlinga kill poor Begta."

"Right. The Warlinga still might catch us, you know?"

The Begta shook his head vigorously. "No catch us. Kashallan will take us under the mountain. Warlinga will not find us, Warlinga will not catch us!"

Chapter Fourteen

The Kashallan crouched in the dimly lit chapel, facing the alcove's far wall. <<Let's see.>> He ran his hands over the rock's pitted surface. <<They said the trigger points would be somewhere about—ah, here.>> His fingers slipped into slight indentations in the stone. Or, at least some of them did. The trigger points to open the hidden passage were designed for a four-fingered, not a five-fingered hand.

<<Now if the hand buttons are *there*, then, just below it on the floor, should be the foot lever.>> He ran his hand downward till it reached the ground. Mindful of his still sensitive fingertips, he felt around in the dirt at his feet. <<Damn. Nothing.>>

<<It's been a long time, Kasha,>> the symbiont reminded him. <<Maybe it is buried. It has to be here.>>

<<You're right, Shalla.>> Getting to his feet, Dunnagh walked to the Altar, picked up a bowl, and returned to the site on the floor. Using the bowl as a primitive shovel, he scooped dirt out from around the rock's base.

Ah, there it was—a long, slim bar lever set into the stone near the base of the wall. It was going to be a bit tricky for someone of his proportions to open the portal. This mechanism had been designed for a far different creature.

The Elders had said he would have to step on the bar, while at the same time pressing the finger points. <<Tani, who was this set-up designed for?>>

<<I never thought to ask, but this is very old, so I would guess the Bebech.>>

Dunnagh grunted. <<They must have been strange looking creatures.>>

A hint of dry amusement in the mind voice: <<All things are relative, are they not, my five-fingered giant, Kasha?>>

Dunnagh chuckled. <<True enough, Shalla, I stand corrected. I'll just clear more of this dirt away to make sure the mechanism will move freely.>>

Turning his back to the entrance he concentrated on the task, and the need to be careful of his hands as he worked.

"Trying to dig your way out, demon?" a cool voice asked.

The Kashallan froze, Dunnagh mentally kicking himself for the lapse in alertness. He stood and turned to face the intruder. Combaron Dingay and three of his followers blocked the doorway. Dunnagh stepped forward, hiding what he had been doing with his shadow.

"How touching," the priest said. "Are you that afraid of me that you were trying to dig your way out? Or were you just planting a bed of saben mushrooms."

"What do you want, Combaron?"

"Why, you of course." The priest smiled in triumph. "I have caught your witch, do you know that?"

"I know it."

"And yet you have made no attempt to come for her." Combaron shook his head, clicking his tongue. "A pity, she is very loyal, you know. She refused to tell me anything—even when I, mmm, *pressed* her. But then, if you had come looking for her, I would have caught you, too."

The Kashallan returned the smile, displaying his own newly acquired sharp-pointed teeth. "Perhaps!" Then, becoming deadly serious, he said, "You play a dangerous game, Dingay. Do you even know, or care, how dangerous it is? Your people's very survival is at stake here—doesn't that worry you?"

Combaron waved a dismissive hand. "Please, wizard, don't try to scare me with empty threats. Your witch has already tried and failed."

"You really are that dense? You still believe I'm an Umwira wizard? I hope you're not planning on breeding. It would be a shame to burden another generation with such obviously inherited stupidity."

Combaron's eyes widened at the insult. "You'll pay for that," he hissed. Turning to his apprentices he said, "Take him!"

Stepping around their mentor, the priests advanced on the Kashallan, holding out protective charms in one hand, and binding cords in the other.

Dunnagh was so startled by the sheer ridiculousness of the attack, he froze—almost letting them take him. A warning nip from his inner companion finally jerked him out of his paralysis and into action. No matter how foolish this might appear to a combat-trained soldier, these fellows were serious. They meant to capture or possibly kill him. Neither prospect appealed to him. If they wanted him, they were going to have to fight—and fight hard for the privilege.

<<Just be mindful of our fingers; if you damage our growing tentacles—>>

Dunnagh had no more time to listen to the symbiont's warning. He leaped sidewise out of reach, as they rushed him. Landing in a fighter's crouch, he struck out with a well-aimed kick to the nearest man's middle. The Avairei let out a grunt of surprise and bent forward. Before the priest could fall, Dunnagh hit him again across the throat with the callused side of one hand. There was a satisfying crunch, then a strangled gurgling as the man slid to the dirt.

<<One down,>> Dunnagh counted grimly.

<<Ooo! That was interesting,>> Tani cried, pumping more adrenaline into its host's already flooded bloodstream.

The remaining two Avairei backed off. They'd been prepared for magic, and were shocked by his physical attack. At Combaron's urging, they laid aside their useless charms, and came at him again from different directions. Dunnagh feinted towards one priest then struck out with a kick that put the other temporarily out of the fight.

But he was slow on his recovery, giving his remaining opponent time to move in and slip a thong around his neck. The Kashallan staggered as the man jerked him off balance, tightening the noose.

Moving with the man's attack, to relieve the pressure on his windpipe, Dunnagh slammed up against the priest's chest. Bending at the knees so as to be at the proper height, he flung his head backward into his opponent's face. At the same time he ran his foot down the other's inner leg to stomp hard on the priest's foot.

The Avairei let out a cry of pain, momentarily loosening his hold enough for Dunnagh to twist sidewise and jam an elbow into the man's unprotected stomach. Dunnagh jerked free, then, swiveling round, he delivered several brutal kicks to the Avairei's chest and belly. The man collapsed, either unconscious or dead.

<<Still having fun, Tani?>> Dunnagh asked, rubbing his bruised neck.

Silence.

Dunnagh whirled to check on his third adversary. The priest was still winded. He hadn't recovered enough to pose much of a threat—yet. But Dunnagh wasn't about to back off and give the Avairei a chance to recover. Not when his freedom and survival were at stake. When the priest saw Dunnagh coming for him, he backed away, eyes wide and pleading. "I'm sorry, lad," Dunnagh told him, "I'd like to oblige you, but I can't afford to have you at my back. I'll be quick."

Backed against the wall, the priest stared, his breath coming in ragged gasps.

<<Be careful of our growing tentacles,>> Tani reminded the host.

Damn, he had almost forgotten. How was he going to do this?

"I'm sorry," the Kashallan repeated, then, pinning the Avairei's arms to his sides, he leaned forward and sank his sharp new teeth into the man's vulnerable neck. The Avairei spasmed and collapsed, falling against him.

Suddenly engulfed in a cascade of unfamiliar sensations, the Kashallan paid little attention to his victim's dying convulsions. The warm, rich taste of blood was in his mouth, flooding his awareness with a wealth of stimuli. For the young symbiont, the blood triggered encoded memories.

<<The Blood Gift, I remember—mm, yes-s....>>

The Kashallan moaned with pleasure, swallowing again and again—filling his mouth with the rich purple wine of the man's life blood. Dunnagh inwardly writhed, but continued to swallow, caught up in his bondmate's encoded need. The smells of copper and vanilla clogged his nostrils. The metallic, flavor of alien blood filled his mouth, his throat. The stimulus was overwhelming for them both, though in different ways.

Never having been allowed to receive the blood-laced Massa root mush, the Avairei habitually fed all young Khutani, Tani reveled in this new experience. And like any child offered a treat, it gorged shamelessly. Though quite young to be given such a rich feast, the symbiont's awakened desire for the Blood Gift was a normal part of Khutani maturation.

But for Dunnagh this vampiric glut triggered terrifying racial memories that for once overruled his bondmate's compulsion. Dunnagh didn't know if what he was feeling, was ecstasy or revulsion—and was afraid to find out. Teetering on the threshold of insanity, he mentally screamed for Tani to, <<STOP!>>

Tani finally became aware of its bondmate's distress, and reluctantly abandoned its feast. Relieved, yet still unnerved, Dunnagh took in a deep calming breath. The flood of images and sensations faded as Tani released its control of their shared body.

The Kashallan let the corpse slip from numb hands to the floor at his feet. He glanced around the chapel; he was still in danger. Where was Combaron?

Combaron was studying him from his position by the entrance. The Dingay smiled, bowing slightly. "Very impressive! But don't savor the *taste* of your victory just yet, demon."

He withdrew from his belt a small knife, its shiny surface marred by a dark, lethal stain. Combaron held it up to show him. "Is it yours, by chance? That would be most ironic—to know that you will die by your own blade, don't you agree?"

The Lann Gheal dagger and priest's words had a sobering effect—like being drenched with cold water. The danger he represented dispelled any lingering anxieties Dunnagh might have about his newly discovered vampirism.

Combaron stepped closer. The Kashallan moved back a step. "Ah," the silky voice purred. "I see you also recognize the little 'gift' I have prepared for you upon its tip. I am glad."

Yes, the Kashallan did know—or at least Tani did—and the symbiont was afraid.

<<Tani, what's wrong? Even with the knife, I can take him.>>

<<No Kasha! Don't even try to fight him. There is poison on the blade—one of the few poisons on Timorna that is fatal to the Khutani. A scratch with the blade and we will die—horribly. Oh, Kasha, what will we do?>>

Oh, Shit! What will we do indeed. <<Don't fret, Tani, I'll think of something.>> *I hope.*

Combaron smirked, and stepped a little closer, his eyes alight with malice. "What's a matter—not going to fight me? Afraid to risk a cut? There's no escape, you know. I will have you this time. Care to get down on your knees and beg me for mercy?"

Chapter Fifteen

The hours of Sagas's imprisonment seemed to crawl by. It was so hard not knowing what was going on out there—not knowing if He was safe. Nansa had told her about the escape plan, but secretly she doubted it could be done. Like her elder, Sagas too found it hard to believe that defenseless slaves could rescue them from this hopeless trap.

"Sit down, daughter, you're giving me a headache with all your pacing," the old woman grumbled. Nansa had been drowsing in Sagas's favorite chair, awaiting word from the rescue party. Now the old woman sat up straighter and reached for her forgotten tea. "You'll do nobody any good, least of all yourself, by carrying on like this."

With a sigh Sagas flopped down in a smaller visitor's chair across from her. She began instead, to twist the folds of her kilt between her hands. "I'm sorry, Nansa, but I can't help worrying. It's been so—"

I'm sure everything's all right, daughter. The apprentices had to wait until the Warlinga were good and drunk before delivering the Kashallan's message, that's all. Just be patient."

Sagas snorted. "Maybe. Oh, I'm sure you're right but I—"

Both women turned at the sound of a soft knock. Then a triumphant young face popped around the door, pushing it wide. Timma beamed at the two Imas, his eyes alight with excitement. "San Nathan says, you should come now—he says there isn't much time."

"And who is this San Nathan to be giving us orders, hmm?" Nansa said. "You show some respect, young Timma, or I'll yank your braidlets for you, I will."

Timma gulped, and looked down, chastened, but Sagas could see he was too excited to be cowed for long.

"Imas, please come." He glanced anxiously into the hallway. When he turned back to them, Sagas caught the gleam of budding hero worship in the young one's eyes.

"San Nathan is the Kashallan's Hunt Leader. He and some of his kin are here to rescue you, and escort you to the Kashallan. Please come, Imas, Ata Temog says he is worried because nobody knows where Ata Combaron has gone."

Sagas rose and crossed to her bedchamber. Picking up her bundle from just inside the door, she turned back to the old woman. "Nansa, come with us, please! The Holy Ones alone know what the Dingay will do when he finds out you've helped us."

"Sagas." Nansa snapped. "We've been over this before, and I'm tired of it. I'm too old to be running around the countryside. Besides, Combaron wouldn't dare hurt me, my family—"

"All right, what's the problem here?" a strange voice growled from the corridor. "Timma, I told you to tell them to hurry." Nathan propped a spear against the wall. He gave Timma a stern look then pushed past him into the room, Temog at his heels. Once inside, he folded his arms across his chest, and focused his scowl on the two women.

Ignoring Nathan, Sagas addressed Temog. "Ima Nansa won't come with us, because she thinks she'll be a burden." She touched her still-swollen cheek. "But if she stays, Combaron will kill her—I know it."

"Sagas is right, Ima you must come," Temog said. "You can't trust someone like Combaron to respect your family's position and neutrality—"

"What's a matter with you people? We have no time for this," Nathan cut in. Addressing Sagas directly, he said, "I was given my orders. I'm to bring you, and I will, if I have to tie you up and carry you, Ima." Nathan unfolded his arms and took a large ball of leather cordage from a pouch at his waist. He held it up, then stepped towards her.

She glared right back at him, and, folding her own arms across her thin chest, repeated through clenched teeth, "I'm not leaving Ima Nansa here for Combaron to kill her."

Nathan looked at Temog; the Ata nodded. He sighed, replaced the cordage in his pouch and picked up the old woman. "Sorry, Ima, you've been outvoted. You're coming." With no further ado he walked out, leaving a smirking Sagas to trail after him.

In the hall, Sagas gasped, catching sight of two broken bodies lying discarded against the wall. She shivered as a cold stab of foreboding pierced her heart.

Oh, Mother. Why did it have to come to this—Avairei against Avairei, each with our Warlinga to kill for us.

Moraga hurried forward to return Nathan his spear. "Give her to me, Patrol Leader; I'll carry the wee granny piggyback." With a nod, he shifted his burden to her broad back, and took his place near the head of the line.

From her new vantage point, Nansa saw a small, furry shape sneaking back into Sagas's room. "What's that thieving Begta doing in here?" She pointed at Dado's retreating back.

Nathan turned and saw the Begta disappearing around the doorframe. In two long strides he caught up to Dado. He grabbed a handful of woolly fur and hauled the Begta around to face him. "Oh no you don't, furball! No pretties. Later, remember? I told you I'd give you lots of pretties when we get back to the base." Nathan shook him. "Now you stay with us—or I'll tie you up and leave you for the Warlinga to eat, you little sneak, understand?"

"I-I understand—I be g-good. D-don't let Warlinga eat poor little Begta, eh?"

Nathan snorted. "Poor little Begta, my ass. You just behave or I'll eat you myself." He gave Dado a shove forward. "Get up there where I can keep an eye on you."

They hadn't gone much farther down the hall, when Sagas stopped and clutched at Temog's arm. "Temog, did I hear you say that nobody knows where Ata Combaron is?"

"Yes, why?"

"Where's Pela?"

"I don't know, Sagas. I've been confined to my rooms like you." He glanced around the empty corridor.

Sagas glanced around wild eyed. "He was after her once before, if he—I have to find her." Without waiting for Temog's reply Sagas headed down a side corridor.

She only got a few paces before Nathan caught up to her and planted his bulk in her path. "And, just where do you think you're going now, Ima?"

"I have to find my apprentice, Pela."

Nathan shook his head, cutting her off. "What is a matter with you? This isn't a game we're playing here," he growled in an angry whisper. "You could get us all killed with this nonsense—come on." He made a grab for her arm, but she jerked it away and stepped out of reach.

"I'm not going anywhere without Pela," she hissed. "I've done my duty to the sacred Khutani—it doesn't matter what Combaron does to me now, but Pela is important. We have to find her!"

Nathan cursed and reached for his cordage. "Ima, we don't have time for this."

"Sagas, listen to the Kashallan's hunt leader and stop wasting time," Nansa said. Sensing trouble the others had gathered around them, while they argued.

"I won't go without Pela," she repeated stubbornly.

"Pela's in the chapel with the rest of the Avairei coming with us, daughter, so stop arguing with him and hurry."

They were almost to the chapel that lay nearest to the pool's entrance, when Chang, who had accompanied Timma in the point position, motioned for them to stop. Gliding back to Nathan, he mouthed, "We got company coming!"

"Who?"

"One of the Warlinga—the overseer Hanno, maybe. He's staggering a bit, but still sober enough to be dangerous. He's looking for someone or something."

"He's looking for Combaron, most like," Nansa said from Moraga's back. "Probably figured out that the beer I sent them was drugged and knows it didn't come from the Dingay."

Startled, Nathan glanced over Moraga's shoulder at Nansa; he'd forgotten all about the old granny. He rubbed his hand across his face. He didn't like it, but it looked like they had no other choice. "We'll have to kill him, no help for it."

"How?" Nansa asked.

Nathan looked irritated. Ignoring the old priestess, he addressed his squad, "We'll only have one chance, if we're lucky. So, the best way may be to have somebody distract him while the rest of us jump him. Yes, that's the only way it might work."

"I'll do the distracting; you take care of the rest," Nansa chimed in.

"What? NO absolutely not!"

Nansa slid down off Moraga's back and came around to face him. She shook her finger under his nose and said in a whisper. "Now you listen to me. This is *my* keep. Hanno knows he's not supposed to be wandering around here in the middle of the night, or at any time for that matter. He won't be suspicious if *I* confront him, because he would expect that. I am the only logical choice. If he sees any of *you*, he will be on the alert."

"She has a point," Moraga said.

Yes, damn her, she did. "All right, you're hired, you got the job. But when things start getting nasty, you get back out of the way, understand?"

Nansa looked down her nose at him, offended. "Of course I understand. I'm no Warlinga—that's *your* job!"

Nathan grunted, then motioned for his people to take their places. Holding Moraga back for a moment, he murmured, "Stay with the civilians. If this gets out of hand, get them down to those pools as fast as you can." She nodded solemnly.

"And keep your eye on that little furball," he added. "I don't want him running off to find pretties again, I got enough to worry about."

HANNO WOVE HIS WAY unsteadily down the corridor. By the Great Hunt Leader, where was Ata Combaron? The demon had worked his evil magic on his kinsmen. He had tried his tricks on Hanno himself, but failed. Hanno was too strong. Yes, he was much stronger than the Evil One thought. He would show him. He would take his revenge and then—

But where was that damned priest? He must warn him—get help. Probably off with a woman somewhere, indulging himself, the perverted son of a Begta. Damn, where in this maze could the fool be?

"San Hanno! What are you doing in here at this time of night?"

Hanno froze. Peering into the gloom ahead, he tried to focus on the shadowed figure standing about halfway down the corridor. *It's the old Ima. Damn my luck, what's she doing out of bed, at this time of night? Where's Combaron—I don't want to explain this to her!*

Coming closer, he swayed, and put a hand against the wall to steady himself. Blinking down at her, he struggled to get his tongue around the words he wanted to say. "I need t' fin—"

Suddenly, a strong pair of hands looped a leather thong around his throat, and jerked it tight. Hanno bucked, clawing at the thong. As the cord jerked tighter, he felt the sharp bite of two spear-points plunging deep into his flesh. Hanno convulsed, trying to throw off his unknown attackers.

The points of their blades bit deeper, forcing him down to the floor. As his blood and his life slipped out of him, he looked up, and was not surprised to see one of the mutant slaves bending over him. As the blackness closed about him forever, he thought, *Curse you, Combaron, the sorcerer has tricked you and won after all.*

"THEIR KILL WAS BRUTALLY efficient. The Kashallan wasn't exaggerating about his kinsmen's abilities." Nansa glanced at Sagas, staring wide eyed at Hanno's spasming corpse. "Rather frightening to contemplate, isn't it?"

Sagas jerked her head around. "What?"

The old priestess grunted as if Sagas had agreed with her. "Yes, very frightening. We wouldn't listen to them, so now the Khutani have chosen to ally themselves with this alien warrior race. I wonder what that will mean for the Avairei in the future."

Chapter Sixteen

The moment they entered the main cavern, Sagas put her hands to her head and cried out in horror. The sound—if sound could describe what they were experiencing, was more felt than heard. It was an eerie, high-pitched screaming that was barely within audible range. It vibrated through their bones and set their nerves to crawling with its urgency.

"What is that?" Nathan demanded, rubbing his ears.

What, indeed? In all her life Sagas had never experienced such a thing. She glanced at the old priestess. Nansa held up her palms—she didn't know either.

Sagas closed her eyes, trying to focus in on its meaning. She heard in the sound frustration, anger, and overpowering fear. "Combaron!" she screamed. "The Dingay has found him." Dropping her bag, she raced along the walkways toward the Birthing Pool.

Nathan gaped. "Follow her, warrior! Your leader is in great danger," Nansa shouted.

Fear goading her, Sagas flew down the walkways. She could hear someone following, but dared not wait. The urgency conveyed to her from the Khutani, blotted out all other thought.

When Sagas burst into the little chapel by the Birthing Pool, time seemed to stand still for her. She saw the Kashallan backed up against the far wall. Combaron had his back to her, a darkly stained knife in his raised hand. By the Holy Ones, she knew what was on that blade!

Without giving herself time to think, she snatched up a stone flask from the altar, and slammed it down as hard as she could on the back of the Dingay priest's head.

Combaron crumpled to the stone floor without a sound, the knife flying straight towards the Kashallan. He saw it coming and leapt sideways to avoid the deadly blade.

Sagas let the bottle drop from her shaking hand, staring down in amazement at what she had just done. Finally, remembering the reason for such a desperate act, she looked around frantically for the Kashallan. He was leaning against the wall nearby, taking several deep breaths. Sagas hurried to him. "Are you all right, Holy One? Did that knife touch you?"

"No. I don't think so." She swayed with relief, feeling suddenly dizzy with the aftershock. He pulled her into his strong arms, hugging her to his chest. "Thank you," he said, laying his cheek against her bowed head. "I thought he would kill me for sure."

At that moment Nathan burst in out of breath. Dunnagh looked up. "You're late, Mo Hara."

Nathan's eyes darted around the alcove. Noticing the four crumpled bodies, he grinned crookedly at Dunnagh. "Yeah, well, I didn't want to spoil all your fun." Then he sobered. "You all right?"

"Yeah."

"Good. You stupid ass, I guess you got yourself into trouble, doing something heroic and stupid again, right?"

Dunnagh laughed. "It's good to see you too, Nathan."

Nathan blinked rapidly a few times then looked away. "Yeah." Spying Combaron's knife, he stooped to pick it up. "Don't touch it!" Dunnagh warned. "The blade's been poisoned."

Disentangling himself from Sagas, the Kashallan picked the knife up by its hilt, and stuck the blade into the green flame of the lamp on the altar. The poison hissed and flared a bright orange. He held it a while longer in the heat, then drew it out, cleansed. Now the blade was entirely silver once again. Dunnagh held it out to his friend. "Keep it if you want. It's safe now."

Nathan took the offered blade; puzzled. "Thanks. How did you know—"

"Ce'awn, Nathan!" Oglas hurried in, breathing hard. "Rhys says to tell you that he's got the supplies and everyone's by the main entrance. If it's safe he wants to move them out. A cook's helper discovered us just as we were finishing up. The lass ran to give the alarm, before we could stop her. Rhys says we may not have much time!"

Nathan looked at Sagas, but it was Dunnagh who answered. "The entrance to the hidden passage is in here, Oglas. Tell Rhys to start sending the people across the causeway. I'll have the portal opened by the time they arrive."

"Yes, Sir."

Studying the wall carefully to get his bearings, the Kashallan crouched down and fitted his hand awkwardly into the indentations in the rock. He pressed. Blinding pain shot up his arm. Gritting his teeth, Dunnagh ignored the discomfort, and pushed harder.

The pain struck him a hammer blow that rocked him back onto his heels. <<Stop! Oh, please, Kasha, stop. You're damaging our growing tentacles! PLEASE DON'T!>> Tani screamed into Dunnagh's mind.

Dunnagh swore. <<Tani, I know it hurts, but we have to get this damned thing open!>>

"Kashallan, what's wrong?" Her expression anxious, Sagas crouched beside him.

"It's my fingers—the adaptations aren't completed yet. They're too sensitive. I can't press hard enough on the finger points to get the portal open." He looked down with disgust at the offending digits.

She pushed him aside. "Let me do it. My hand will fit better anyway. Just show me where to press, and when."

She was right; her hand did fit better into the shallow cavities than his did. Standing sideways to the wall, he placed his heel firmly against the floor mechanism. Motioning for her to push inward on the hidden releases, he flung his considerable bulk down hard against the lever under his foot.

There was a grinding sound deep within the stone, and a section of the wall slid aside, revealing a black passage beyond.

The Kashallan pushed himself away from the wall and stretched, trying to unknot the tightness in his back and shoulders. The first of their companions were starting to arrive. "Get them inside as quickly as you can," he told Nathan.

Earlier that day, after Temog's apprentices had brought the empty leather containers to him, the Kashallan had given them to the Khutani to fill with his new formula. Then, he'd left them stacked in their net carrying sacks in the corner of the alcove.

Speaking quietly to Sagas, he pointed to the nets. "Please make sure those come with us, or I'm going to be very hungry on this little journey.

Now I must go to my kindred one last time, and let them know I'm not hurt."

Nathan stared at Dunnagh's retreating back. "Dunnagh? By Our Ancestors, where are you going now?"

As if speaking to an unruly child, Sagas drew herself up to her full height and said in a stern voice, "The Kashallan has given you your orders, Hunt Leader. I suggest you comply."

Nathan blinked. "Right." When she continued to glare, he bowed, giving her a bemused look. "Well, at least I know now for sure, who this Kashallan is," he muttered as he followed Marti and a group of natives into the passage.

"AND NOW WHERE ARE YOU going, hunt leader," Sagas murmured, when she saw him emerge out of the tunnel once more.

Startled, Nathan stopped and peered into the gloom. He hadn't noticed the bossy priestess standing in the shadows by the portal. "I'm going to find Dun—the Kashallan."

Sagas stepped into the light and folded her furred arms across her chest, blocking his way. "The Holy One will come, when he is ready. He communes with the Sacred Khutani now and may not be disturbed."

Without bothering to answer, he brushed past her and stepped into the chapel. When she opened her mouth in protest, he held up his hand to stop further argument.

"Look, you may not want me to bother your precious 'Holy One.' But everyone is inside now—and we have to get going. Do you want him to be captured? Can't you hear the searchers coming?"

Far off they could hear the sounds of men and women calling to one another. "If they're this close; it won't take them long to discover us."

She lowered her eyes, and mumbled, "Yes, you are right."

"Damned right, I am." Nathan said. Looking around, he saw no evidence of Dunnagh. Damn him, this was no time for more of his crazy heroics. "Where is he; do you know?"

"At the Birthing Pool."

"Where?"

"The pool lies just outside this chamber. I'll get him, if you think it's—"

Before she could stop him, Nathan stepped out of the chapel. "I'll get him, Ima. You go join the others. Ima Nansa says she needs you."

Nathan didn't know if the old woman needed Sagas, but *he* sure didn't need her hanging around, telling him what to do. It was bad enough trying to keep track of Dunnagh, he didn't have time to babysit the haughty priestess, too.

Now where did she say Dunnagh had gone? Oh, there he was, bending over that bubbling pool. "Hey! Dunnagh, they're coming. We have to get out of here!" Nathan repeated his warning, but the figure didn't answer. He remained still bent over the water.

"Dunnagh?" Nathan came a little closer, trying to see more clearly through the mist rising off the pool's surface.

Suddenly, he realized that Dunnagh's entire upper body was submerged in the water. "Oh, Gods, the poison!" Maybe he had been cut and hadn't felt it. Nathan raced across to the prone figure. Grabbing a handful of Dunnagh's red braids, he jerked his friend's head out of the pool.

What he saw then, made him step back and let go his hold, speechless with shock. Several gray eel-like creatures were clinging to Dunnagh's arms and shoulders. One of the hideous things even had a coil of itself curled around his neck. The creature had molded its mouth to Dunnagh's, and he was swallowing repeatedly. A dark liquid trickled out of the corners of his mouth and down onto his chin.

Nathan shuddered with revulsion. As he stared, paralyzed, a massive creature loomed out of the depths, heading straight for them. "Dunnagh, look out!" Nathan reached for his friend again. The smaller, slithering beasts released their hold on Dunnagh and dropped back into the foaming liquid. Dunnagh slapped Nathan's hand away, wiped his mouth hastily and stood. For just a moment, fierce, alien eyes stared at Nathan from out of Dunnagh's well-loved face.

Nathan blinked, but when he looked again, it was the old familiar Dunnagh who warily watched him. "Dunnagh?" he said, "—uh, we have to go. Everybody's in the passage and—"

Suddenly, a shout rang out from further down the causeway. Dunnagh looked into the pool one last time. The great eel-like monster still hovered just below the surface. He held out his hands to it, tears glistening in his eyes. Another, nearer shout, jerked Dunnagh's head around, and then they were sprinting for the alcove.

When they reached the stone portal, Dunnagh pushed Nathan through the opening and slammed his heel down hard on the floor mechanism. He dived for the doorway as the stone began to grind its way shut behind them.

Chapter Seventeen

When the door closed, the darkness enveloped Nathan and Dunnagh like a shroud. No light at all penetrated the gloom. Nathan sank to the floor and lay on his side, panting. The ponderous weight of the mountain seemed to press down upon him, robbing him of hope and breath. "If somebody opens that door right now we'll be in for it," he said into the gloom, but received no reply.

Nathan listened, searching for a warning of danger in the blackness. Were they safe now? He heard nothing at all from the other side of the stone. Its massive bulk seemed to be an impenetrable barrier. On this side of the portal, a tiny waterfall splashed somewhere in the darkness ahead.

Closer to hand, he heard Dunnagh's ragged breathing. Nathan froze—was he weeping? He groped searching, at last touching living flesh. "Dunnagh?" No answer. Nathan moved closer. Hands taking the place of useless vision, he touched Dunnagh's shoulder.

The man was trembling, trying to hold back deep, gut-wrenching sobs. *What's wrong with him? Gods, what have those crazy priests done to him?* He pulled Dunnagh against him, his lips brushing the bent head pressed to his chest. Nathan held him tight, offering the comfort of his living warmth. "Are you all right? Are you hurt?"

Dunnagh clung to Nathan for a moment longer, then eased out of his embrace and sat up. "I'm all right, Nathan—and I'm not hurt."

"What's wrong then—and why are you crying?"

"Nothing—I-I'll tell you later—right now we need to get out of here." Raising his voice, Dunnagh shouted, "Rhys! Bring a lamp back here; we can't see a thing." Dunnagh stood up, groped for Nathan's hand, and pulled him up beside him.

Ahead in the passage a glimmer of green light, cast grotesque shadows on the rock walls. "What took you so long?" Nathan grumbled as Rhys came up to them. He wanted the evidence of his eyes, before he'd believe Dunnagh was all right.

"Sorry, Sir, there's a large open cavern just up ahead. We've been trying to take an inventory, and redistribute the loads equally among us," Rhys said.

"Good idea," Dunnagh said. He slapped Nathan on the back with a feigned heartiness. "Come on, Mo Hara, stop worrying; let's go see who and what we have."

Rhys started down the passage, then hesitated. "Uh, Ce'awn, any chance we'll be followed?"

"A good question, Rhys," Dunnagh said. "I believe Sagas or the old Ima said something to me about Gormach coming to fetch us. It isn't likely he'll find us in these caverns, but we'll keep an eye out just the same."

In the flickering lamplight, Nathan thought he saw Dunnagh's expression harden. Then as the light passed on, he heard Dunnagh mutter, "The Butcher—I have a debt to settle with that one. We'll meet again—I know it. But not now, I'm not ready, please not yet..."

Continuing his conversation with Rhys in the next moment, Dunnagh said, "I doubt very much if anyone left in Sulas even knows of this passage's existence. So they won't be looking for the trigger-points to open the portal. They probably think we vanished by magic—judging by what that fool Combaron believed. I expect we're safe from the keep's Warlinga until we surface again. But there may be other creatures wandering these old pathways that we will want to avoid if possible; so we'll have to stay alert."

Rhys murmured his agreement, accepting Dunnagh's information without comment.

Catching up to Dunnagh, Nathan muttered, "How do you know more about this place than those crazy Avairei? Dunnagh, you've never been here before! What's going on?"

Dunnagh pretended not to hear him and kept on walking. Nathan grumbled a curse and hurried to catch up before they left him in the dark.

Epilogue

After they'd taken a couple more turns in the tunnel, the cave widened out into a large, high-ceilinged grotto. Coarse gray sand crunched under foot, and from somewhere in the gloom came the sound of water brushing against a murky shoreline.

The exiles were huddled together waiting for him. Dunnagh took the lantern from his subordinate and walked among them. *My people*, he suddenly realized. Human and Timornan—that is how he must think of them now. They had given up so much for his sake. By their agreement to follow him into exile and possible death, they aligned themselves with him forever, accepting his outlawry for their own.

When he saw Ima Nansa among them, the Kashallan took her hand and kissed it. "I am glad to see you. I was worried you would be stubborn and choose not to come with Sagas."

"Choose!" the old woman snorted. "As if I had any *choice* in the matter. Humph. That big Hunt Leader of yours picked me up and carried me away. Against my will, I might add."

The Kashallan laughed. "But not against my will, dear Ima, not against mine."

She folded her skinny arms across her narrow chest, and sniffed. "All right, I'm here, child, now just what do you plan to do with me, hmm? I'm too old to be walking around these caves in the cold and the dark."

"Now, Old One, don't fret. I know you're worried about becoming a burden, but you won't be, I assure you." He put an arm around her shoulder, drawing her forward. "You'll travel the same way I plan to travel, and though it will not be as restful as a litter, it's the best I have to offer under the circumstances." Looking over her head, he called out, "Tessa, will you find your friend Cati, please."

A short time later Tessa, hand in hand with the Loti, returned. "I'd like you to meet someone, Tessa. This is Ima Nansa. She was Ima Matri at Sulas before Ima Sagas. She will need some assistance while we travel, and I think you two might enjoy each other's company."

Returning his attention to Nansa, he said, "Do you remember me telling you that among my Chosen's kindred there were those trained like the Avairei? Tessa is such a one. She knows little of Timorna, unfortunately. I would be grateful if you would begin teaching her as we travel."

"Yes, Kashallan, I will do that gladly." Nansa held out her hands. Tessa took them and smiled. "It's an honor to meet you, Ima."

"Good." Then, inquiring of the Loti, "Will you carry them for me, Timornshaya?"

At the ancient form of address to her kind, meaning "caretaker of the land," Cati's eyes widened. "Loti haven't been given that term of respect in living memory. This, more than anything, proves the truth of the rumors that filtered down to us." Eyes shining, she bowed. "Your will, Child of the Pools."

The Kashallan gave her a formal bow in return. He stepped to her side and began fumbling with the packs across her broad back. After a futile try to untie them he gave up. The pain once more prevented him from doing even the simplest manual tasks. <<Damn it, Tani, how long is this going to last?>>

<<Stop complaining, Kasha. We have left the pools—I don't know,>> the symbiont said.

Dunnagh tasted the symbiont's frustration with him, but he also sensed his bondmate's fear and immediately apologized. <<I'm sorry, Shalla, that wasn't fair of me. I know you're doing your best. It's just so—maddening!>>

<<And do you think it's not frustrating for me, too?>>

<<Right!>> With a sigh, he dropped his useless hands to his side, looked around, and caught Nathan's eye. "Nathan, will you give me a hand with this?"

Giving his friend a worried look, Nathan untied the packs, then laid down a folded blanket across Cati's back as a makeshift saddle. He helped

Tessa take her accustomed seat, and with a wicked gleam in his eye, Nathan lifted the old priestess to sit sidesaddle in front of her.

Nansa let out a startled squawk and clutched the Loti's shaggy pelt. Tessa murmured something soothing and tucked the old woman inside her blanket.

Dunnagh looked around at the shocked Avairei faces and laughed, enjoying their surprise as much as Nathan was enjoying it. 'I'm amazed that in all your reclaimed time upon this world, you Avairei never thought of this means of travel.

"On the Chosen's home world there are animals that are similar in shape to the Loti. They are called horses, and people ride them in this manner all the time."

Nansa gave a loud snort, but made no further protest. Secretly, the Kashallan thought she was excited and pleased, but didn't want to let anyone know.

The Kashallan was turning away, when he caught sight of five little men, crouching uncertainly at the edge of the light. Offering up a silent prayer of thanks to every Caldoni and Timornan god he could think of, he hurried over to them. Giving the Begta a salute of respect, he crouched in front of them. "I'm glad you have come with us, Begtanshay. I may have need of your counsel soon."

Shyly, they gathered around him. "Do you know where we are?"

Dado nodded. "We by River Magre."

"Yes, we are, good! And do your people still travel these pathways?"

Dado shook his head. "No."

"Why?" the Kashallan asked, suddenly worried. Dado shrugged. "Is there danger here?" Another shrug. "Could you help me find the way? My kindred only remember the river path."

Dado bobbed his head. "We will help."

Breathing a sigh of relief, the Kashallan patted him on the back and stood. "Good."

Stepping away from the Timornans, he motioned for Singey and the armachda to follow him down the beach. When they were far enough away to not be overheard, he said, "I know everyone's tired. It's been a long night for all of us; but, just to be safe, I want to keep going.

"If we follow the river here for a while, we should come to some old ruins. Keep a lookout for them. We can camp there and rest. When we're rested and refreshed; we'll have a council and decide what's our best course of action."

Dunnagh then fixed Nathan with his give-me-no-argument stare. "You're in charge of the patrol from now on. I have a responsibility to all Timornans now, not just the humans among us. I'm sorry; I can't take time to explain right now, but things are different since I left you in the slave pen. I have agreed to certain... 'commitments.' I have been bound by my warrior's oath to serve this world and its peoples."

Including the rest of them in his next comment, he said, "Someday you will all have to decide for yourselves where your allegiance lies. But for now we must all work together to get to a place of safety. Agreed?"

A shocked and bewildered silence followed Dunnagh's revelation. Finally, there were nervous murmurs of assent. "Thank you," he said, voice quivering with emotion. "This isn't easy for me, and I appreciate your support."

About to move on, he paused, a new thought coming to mind. "Nathan, you should include the Begta in your scouting and sentry patrols from now on."

"What?" Nathan exploded. "I can't do that! They'll probably run off after a *pretty* the first time I send them out to scout, and then where will we be?"

"No, they won't. They have as much at stake in this as the rest of us. And they're smart enough to know that they're safer traveling with us than wandering off by themselves. For now, at least, you can trust them to do what you tell them." He chuckled. "Don't forget, they are excellent hunters and trackers. They caught *us*, didn't they?"

"Yeah, I remember, and that doesn't make me sleep any easier," Nathan grumbled. Then, he temporized. "All right, all right. Don't look at me like that. I'll do it. Just don't expect me to be happy about it."

"I wouldn't dream of it," Dunnagh said, trying not to smile. "All right, let's get going—the quicker we find those ruins, the quicker we rest."

The End
This story is continued in Book Two: *The Hunted Kashallan*

Additional information for the Tales of the Kashallans series

Note to the reader: it is my hope that by reading the text of these fantasy books, the alien words peppering the writing are clear on their own. But for those readers who enjoy such things, and those who may get confused from time to time by the many foreign words from the various races and cultures on my imagined world Timorna, I offer the following notes to aid with clarity.

Best wishes and happy reading!

Celu Amberstone

Pronunciations of unfamiliar words:

Consonants
The sound [ch or kh] represents the ck in the word lock [lahkh].
Other consonants are pronounced like in English.
An apostrophe in a word represents a glottal stop.
Vowels
A – like father AI – like in ice AY – like in way
E – like in ate EI – like in island
I – like in see
O - like in low
U – like in too
Y – like in eat
H – when next to a vowel shortens and softens the vowel sound

Timornan words (general)

Timorna [tim-MOR-na] – The name of the uncharted planet where this story takes place.

The Great Destruction – A nuclear holocaust that almost destroyed life on Timorna, thousands of years ago.

The Burning Times – A time when the radioactivity was at its highest, just after the destruction.

Sorins [SOR-inz] – A weather condition in which the wind blows straight out of the north, picking up radioactive dust and other harmful substances as it heads south. During the Sorin seasons all life must seek shelter, or go dormant, to survive.

KHUTANI [KOO-TAH-NEE] – The ancient eel-like symbiotic race living on Timorna in its deep undergrownd waterways, who were responsible for storing the genetic patterns and keeping life alive during the Great Destruction and the Burning Times that followed.

Amla [AHM-la] – The term used by the Khutani and kashallans to refer to a parent.

Amsi [AHM-see] – A Khutani term used to address a peer of its kindred.

K'amsi [k'AHM-see] – A Khutani term of respect for an elder of that race.

Sh'amsi [sh'-AHM-see] – A Khutani term used to address a younger sibling.

kashallan [kah-SHAH-lan] – A host-symbiont bond. A partnership between two intelligent beings sworn to serve as guardians and healers of the planet Timorna.

Kasha [KAH-shuh] – The intimate name a symbiont in a kashallan pair uses for its host.

Shalla [SHAH-luh] – The intimate name a kashallan host uses for his symbiont.

The Kashallan – This term refers to a particular pairing, that of the human, Dunnagh Kai, and Tani, the Khutani symbiont. They are the first bonded pair in over seven hundred years.

Bebech [BEH-bech] – A native race that served as hosts of the Khutani, who were killed off by plague.

kavay [kah-VAY] – A blue substance created by the Khutani that when introduced into a living organism makes its survival possible on Timorna.

kavay alignment – The process by which the body is metabolically changed at such a deep level that, once alignment occurs, a constant supply of kavay must remain in the diet, or death will occur.

Sweh'an [SWAY'-ahn] – Another type of host-symbiont bond, this time between a mortal host and a spirit being from another dimension that will use its powers to aid a host, in exchange for possession of the host body at agreed times, so that it can experience a physical reality.

H'an [h'-AHN] – The host for a Sweh'an spirit.

Swe'a'sa [SWAY'-ah'-sah] – The intimate name the host uses to address her Sweh'an spirit companion.

H'an'si [h'-AHN'-see] – The name the Sweh'an spirit uses to address its host.

Cha'Han [CHA'hahn] – The Avairei priest who is bound to the Sweh'an bonded host as her companion.

Ba'etchat'seh [bah'-AYCHAHT'sah] – The Timornan version of a padded cell, used to discipline the Sweh'an when its behavior while taking its pleasures becomes too troublesome.

Wa'chassey'ul [wa'-CHSAY'-ool] – A Warlinga bound by magic to the will of the Sweh'an as both lover and mortal guardian.

AVAIREI [AH-VYE-RAY] – One of the four intelligent species bred by the Khutani. A furry, bipedal race with cat-like features and a long mane.

They are the priests, scholars and healers of their society. Their function is also to care for the Khutani in their underground pools, and to distribute the medicines the Khutani make for the creatures they introduced to their world after the Great Wars nearly destroyed all life on Timorna.

Ata [AH-tuh] – (Father) A term used when addressing a male Avairei.

Ima [EE-muh] – (Mother) A term used when addressing a female Avairei priestess.

Ima Matri [EE-muh MAH-tree] – The priestess who is head of a Avairei keep like Sulas.

High Matri – The head, and ruler over, all of the Avairei family clans.

Ata Leyas [AH-tuh LAY-ahss] – (Healing Father) The male Avairei who is second in command of the religious hierarchy at a keep.

WARLINGA [WOR-LING-ga] – Another of the intelligent species bred by the Khutani. Large two-legged lizardmen naturally endowed with teeth claws and long muscular tails. Their function is to be warriors and hunters. They were bred especially to protect the Khutani-held southern lands from the Umwira, the mutated remnants of the original people who caused the Great Wars.

Chi'awari'ga [CHI'-ah-WAHR-ee'-gah] – An ancient Warlinga ceremony of single combat to settle a feud or other dispute.

Accavett [ah-cah-VET] – The women's quarters in a Warlinga keep.

Sa [sah] – A title of respect for female Warlinga.

San [sahn] – A title of respect for male Warlinga. The terms Sa and San are also used for humans as well because many of them are warriors, too.

LOTI [LOW-TEE] – A third intelligent species. They resemble centaurs with long, shaggy fur. Their function is to farm and care for the land of Timorna. They are also artisans, weavers and craftsmen.

Timornshaya [tim-morn-SHY-uh] – A term of respect offered to the Loti people.

BEGTA [BEKH-TA] – THE last of the four intelligent species created by the Khutani. Small, woolly-furred simian-like people with long arms. They live in the wilder regions of the south. The Begta are an outcast people, hunters and gatherers, who are notorious thieves. They are despised by most other Timornans, and often hunted for food, or sold as slaves.

Domail [dough-MAIL] – A Begta victory dance.

Begtanshay [BEKH-tahn-shay] – A term of respect given to the Begta people by the Khutani and the kashallans in earlier times.

UMWIRA [OOM-WEER-UH] – This is a name given to the mutated descendants of the planet's original intelligent inhabitants by their enemies. Also known as the Ghostlanders, they are the people who were responsible for the Great Destruction. They are the sworn enemies of the Khutani and wish to destroy all that the Khutani have created, so they can reclaim the more favored lands in the South.

Clans of the Western Umwira – The Western Clans are related to the Ghostlanders and descended from the original inhabitants of Timorna; being exposed to the poisons of the north and west where they live, they have mutated and interbred with slaves taken from the Khutani-held lands, so that they don't resemble the peoples before the wars.

The seven clans are: Blue Stone, Sand Mountain, Bitter Water, Red Wind, Rock Salt, Green Clay, Twisted Grass.

Plants and Animals on Timorna

Taba worm [TAH-buh] – A long, thin worm that lives among the liru reeds, in both the Swamp and the Broken Lands. Eaten by the Begta. The appearance of a bowl of taba worms is rather like blue spaghetti.

gumati [goo-MAH-tee] – A frog-like creature with four hopping legs, living in the Swamp. Eaten by the Begta.

budasen [BOO-dah-sen] – A stork-like creature with long neck and legs. It has big paddle feet for running across the surface of grassy ponds. Not a bird; it has scales, and can't fly.

pomong [puh-MAHNG] – A lizard-like predator with a long, sharp tail. It preys on the budasen.

snayga [SNAY-guh] – A small predator that swims in large schools. Eating habits like the piranha of old Earth.

vistri [VIST-tree] – A six-legged scaly predator about the size of a large dog, and like dogs hunt in packs. Very dangerous.

winglah [wing-LAH] – Any large creature of the western lands that has through the generations mutated into a dangerous monster because of exposure to the Sorins.

obeylem [oh-BAY-lem] – A large plant-eating creature, living in the Swamp. It has six limbs (four long legs for walking, two short arms for grabbing food), also a long tail and neck. Hunted for their meat.

bolacht [BAh-lach] – A herd beast introduced by the Khutani to meet the needs of the Speir'dina. Provides meat milk wool and can be ridden as well.

madag [MA-dag] – Timorna's answer to a herd dog. Looks something like a small armored dinosaur. Can fight vistri, but gentle with humans and other Khutani-bred races

shri moss [shree] – A short yellow moss, growing everywhere as ground cover.

liru reeds [LEER-roo] – A tall, brown bamboo-like plant growing in the canyons of the Broken Lands and parts of the Swamp.

kavalpa trees [kah-VAHL-puh] – Tall, black trees like weeping willows that usually grow up around a spring or other water source. When their long branches touch the ground, they root themselves, thus forming, over time, large thickets that give shelter to many of Timorna's inhabitants.

masa root [MAHS-suh] – A plant with a large edible root, eaten by most Timornans. Cultivated by the Loti.

lamra [LAM-ruh] – A corn-like grain developed from the liru reeds. A staple food in the diet. Cultivated by the Loti.

dahalli [Da-hal-lee] – A thorny shrub that can grow quite tall with purple broad leaves and bright orange berries that are sweet.

clamisa – A mutated form of masa root growing across the Shallow Sea in the West. A staple of the western Clans

oko – A small armored predator in the western lands it looks something like an armadillo. Thought to be sly by the Western Clans.

dhuura – A sea creature found in the Shallow Sea. It also is a food staple for the Clans of the coast.

leongon – An armored shark-like predator in the Sea.

nagril – A nearly transparent jelly/shrimp-like creature that feeds much of the sea life on Timorna.

cobura – A furred sea animal.

aluutae – A reed/grass-like plant growing in the West used for basket making.

Land features

Ghostlands – This is a wide peninsula of barren land that connects the Favored Southern land with the blackened and radio-active northern continent. Living mostly underground this is the land where a cabal of techno-wizards has control of what is left of the old technology. They also have tremendous Psy powers which they have gained through exposing themselves to mutations sought in the poisoned places in their land.

Broken Lands – A region of canyons and mesas where some of the Begta bands live, and where the humans set up their base.

Yeyen Banai [YAY-yen ban-EYE] – A large valley surrounded by a high rim of mountains. This is where most of Timorna's Khutani-bred population lives.

Rim Wall – The mountains encircling the Yeyen Banai.

Jeban Pass [JAY-bun] – The main route from the Broken Lands through the Rim Wall to the shelter of the Yeyen Banai Valley beyond.

The Great Swamp – A low-lying stretch of land to the south of the Broken Lands. Very dangerous to travel, since it is pockmarked with poisonous pools, and subject to constant earthquakes.

Lake Ticca – A large lake at the edge of the Great Swamp, out of which the Shaden river flows. In its center is the island fortress of Ticca keep.

Shaden Falls [SHAY-den] – The portage around this waterfall is the main southern route from the Swamp through the Rim Wall to the Yeyen Banai Balley.

The Shallow Sea – The straight between the land of the Western Clans of the Umwira and the northwestern edge of the Swamp.

Timornan Keeps and Fortresses

A vairei keeps:
   Riath [REE-ahth] – the capital
Sulas [SOO-luss]
Ticca [tee-KAH]
Shaden [SHAY-den]
Ha'limra [ha'-LEEM-rah]
Warlinga fortresses:
Tragar [TRAh-gar]
Meh'gach [MAY'-gakh]

Caldoni words adopted into the Timornan language

Speir'dina [SPEER'-din-uh] – The term chosen by the humans to refer to themselves after they accepted that they had become a part of Timornan society. Literally it means sky people.

Teh'lach [TAY'-lahkh] – A pseudo-family group among the followers of the Kashallan, containing members of several different species.

Speir'van [SPEER'-vahn] – Literally, "sky-woman." Used by the Speir'dina as a term of respect for a high-ranking human woman, such as Sairsa the first kashallan's human wife.

Other Caldoni words and phrases

Caldon [KAHL-don] – The world where Dunnagh and many of the Lann Gheal armachda are from.

Cumarsaid [KOO-mar-sayd] – A trance-like state in which the practitioner opens his awareness to communicate psychically with other life. This discipline was practiced as part of the ancient Caldoni warriors' training and is still taught today.

Lann Gheal – A term meaning "Bright Blade," it refers to a mercenary organization formed on Caldon. Their purpose is to keep alive many of the ancient warrior traditions of their race. They are not for sale to the highest bidder in a conflict, and will only fight for what they believe to be right.

armachd (plural: armachda) [ar-MAKHT, ar-MAKHT-uh] – Warrior.

Geish (plural: Gessa) [gaysh, GAY-suh] – A charge or compulsion laid upon someone that binds them to do a certain thing. A Geish is usually of divine origin, but also can be laid by one person on another.

Fir Gall [feer gahl] – A foreigner.

mo – This word means "my," but when used with other words often changes the sound at the beginning of the next word.

Cara [KAH-ruh] – Friend. mo hara [moh HAH-ruh] – My friend—my love. Mo hri [moh hree] – My heart. Mo gra [moh grah] – My love.

Ce'awn [kay'-OUN] – A chieftain. mo he'awn [moh hay'-OUN] – My chieftain.

Ceartachd [Keer-takht] – A word meaning the "rightness" of a thing.

Ca'companachta [kah'-kom-pah-NAKH-tah] – Literally meaning "battle companions," it is a relationship of lovers who also fight together.

Bacach [BAH-kakh] – An unlikable person, an evil man.

Amadan [AH-muh-dahn] – Idiot; can be used affectionately or as an insult.

Dina [DEE-nuh] – People.

kina [KEE-nuh] – Kin or kindred.

le'ayn [lay'-AIN] – Twin. Literally, "half of one."

shenahi [SHEN-ah-hee] – Ancient Caldoni storyteller or bard.

Pibroch [pee-BRAHKH] – A musical instrument like a bagpipe.

Faltia, cuj milla faltia [FAHL-tee-uh, coodge MEE-luh FAHL-tee-uh] – Welcome, a hundred thousand welcomes.

go ra my get [GOR-rah-MY-uh-get] – Thank you.

Ru'a [ROO'-ah] – "The red." It refers to a person with red hair; for example, Dunnagh Ru'a (Red-haired Dunnagh.)

colcannon [kohl-CAN-nun] – A native Caldoni dish made with potatoes, cabbage, and onions.

Also by Celu Amberstone

Renewal
The Prophecy of Manu
Teoni's Giveaway

Rituals
Blessings of the Blood: A Book of Menstrual Lore and Rituals for Women
Deepening the Power: Community Ritual and Sacred Theatre

Tales of the Kashallans
The Dream-Chosen
The Hunted Kashallan
The Outlawed Bond
Uncertain Refuge
Prey of the Umwira
Blood Magic's Snare

Standalone
Refugees and Other Stories

About the Author

Celu is of mixed Cherokee and Scots-Irish ancestry. Celu Amberstone was one of the few young people in her family to take an interest in learning Traditional Native crafts and medicine ways. This interest made several of the older members of her family very happy while annoying others.

Legally blind since birth, she has defied her limitations and spent much of her life avoiding cities. Moving to Canada after falling in love with a Métis-Cree man from Manitoba, she has lived in the rain forests of the west coast, a tepee in the desert and a small village in Canada's arctic. Along the way she also managed to acquire a BA in cultural anthropology and an MA in health education. Celu loves telling stories and reading. She lives in Victoria British Columbia near her grown children and grandchildren.

About the Publisher

Kashallan Press is an independent publisher releasing books by author Celu Amberstone. Among her books are critically-acclaimed works now re-released by Kashallan Press, and new works showcasing her talents in writing both fiction and non-fiction.

www.ingramcontent.com/pod-product-compliance
Lightning Source LLC
Chambersburg PA
CBHW030352030726
47497CB00002B/304

* 9 7 8 1 7 7 7 5 3 7 9 3 7 *